Also by J. N. Williamson

Novels

The Ritual *1979*
The Houngan *1980*
  (1984, reprinted as Profits)
The Tulpa *1981*
Premonition *1981*
Horror House *1981*
Queen of Hell *1981*
Death-Coach *1981*
Ghost Mansion *1981*
The Banished *1981*
Death-Angel *1981*
The Evil One *1982*
Horror Mansion *1982*
Playmates *1982*
Brotherkind *1982*
Death-School *1982*
Death-Doctor *1982*
The Dentist *1983*

Babel's Children *1984*
Ghost *1984*
The Offspring *1984*
The Longest Night *1985*
Wards of Armageddon *1986*
  (with John Maclay)
Evil Offspring *1987*
Noonspell *1987*
Dead to the World *1988*
The Black School *1989*
Shadows of Death *1989*
Hell Storm *1990*
The Night Seasons *1991*
Monastery *1992*
Wardogs *1992*
Don't Take Away the Light
  (work in progress)

As Julian Shock

Extraterrestrial *1982*

Novellas

Hour *1983*

Flags! *1984*

Collections

Anomalies *1983*

Nevermore! *1984*

The Naked Flesh of Feeling *1991*
(Untitled; in press, scheduled 1992)

Editor

Masques *1984*
Masques II *1987*
How to Write Tales of Horror,
  Fantasy and Science Fiction *1987*
The Best of Masques *1988*
Masques III *1989*
Masques IV *1991*

Nonfiction (Humor)

The *New* Devil's Dictionary (Creepy Clichés and Sinister Synonyms) *1985*

Sherlockiana (Editor)

Illustrious Client's Case-Book *1946* (Foreword by Vincent Starrett)
Illustrious Client's Second Case-Book *1949* (Introduction by Ellery Queen)
Illustrious Client's Third Case-Book *1953* (Introduction by Christopher Morley)

Critical Work (Juvenilia)

A Critical History and Analysis of the "Whodunit" *1950*

Masques IV

All-New Works of Horror & the Supernatural

Edited by J.N. Williamson

MACLAY & ASSOCIATES
Baltimore / 1991

Maclay & Associates, Inc., P.O. Box 16253, Baltimore, MD 21210.

Contents

Introduction

("There were much glare and glitter and piquancy and phantasm....There were much of the beautiful, much of the wanton, much of the *bizarre*, something of the terrible, and not a little of that which might have excited disgust....The masquerade license of the night was nearly unlimited..."
—*The Masques of the Red Death* by Edgar Allan Poe.)

Eight years ago when Maclay & Associates Inc. and I agreed to create *Masques,* horror fiction was said to be in decline. In that category Stephen King's novels were the only ones regularly making hardcover best seller lists. I'd published a dozen novels by then but had recently learned one of my publishers was giving up the ghost (it was reincarnated later), a second was being subsumed (moving from Chicago to New York, and oblivion), and a third was reaching the decision that they could live without me. (As they did for six years before offering me a four-novel contract.) It appeared a dreadful time for a Baltimore-based local publisher to seek a national marketplace with an anthology of horror/supernatural fiction — even if Edgar Allan Poe *did* have not one but two gravesites in the marvelously Gothic cemetery John Maclay showed me.

That first *Masques* was notably well-reviewed, and nominated for a major award; several of its stories drew raves, and more honors.

Seven years to the month since I wrote the introduction to this series' progenitor, the fiction of fright is once more said to be slumping — yet the fourth book of *Masques* is being published in hardcover, in a boxed, signed, and numbered edition, and in trade paperback form. And Stephen King's novels have been joined on the best seller lists by those of Dean R. Koontz, Anne Rice, Thomas Harris, and occasionally one or two other novelists who may eschew the horror category but certainly imbue many of their suspenseful works with the moods or principles of horror.

Who says it isn't a viable category?

Being less flippant about it, how many novels of other categories — even true crime books — sell with gusto and deeply involve their readers by employing the ideas, surprises, violence, and atmosphere of horror fiction? (And how many honest horror novels might continue to sell as briskly as ever if they were in disguise?) In what painstakingly explicated but understandable way do books about "the mob" or serial murders—"real life" ghostbusters and haunted houses—movie tie-in novels or collections linked to super heroes (or villains), comic book detectives or monsters or ventures into sword and sorcery fantasy—differ in terms of the elicitation of chills or revulsion, inquiry into evil-doing and warped minds, astonishment in the face of revelation, unusual perceptions of reality, tension, wonder, sheer *scariness?*

At least as importantly. . .why does anyone think they are superior?

There are, of course, some answers. Please don't reply "believability." Nor subtlety. Nor credibility gained by uncertainty of story line since the bad guys in "real" books have generally been captured or else the writer couldn't do a drawn-out profile of them, and the dead victims are going to remain dead however greatly we may empathize with them. Nor, least of all, should you reply "literary quality." A few of the non-fiction writers in true crime and some screenwriters are quite talented but the majority make the horror writers who faded from sight during previous "soft" stages seem like literary giants. (And Jess Cagle and Ty Barr, writing in *Entertainment Weekly,* defined "screenwriter" this way: "In Los Angeles, anything with opposable thumbs.")

A question that is probably better—because it can be answered without bringing a lot of unhappiness to other people—is this: Why has *Masques* endured and arrived at a fourth volume when many anthology series, writers, editors, lines of horror, and publishing houses have so thoroughly relinquished their ghosts that reincarnating them would definitely require divine intervention?

An answer: Some very good publishers, specialty houses among them, learn how to pinpoint and, yes, specialize for their audiences. They're not in the position of needing to make a national best seller list for various reasons including the fact that they *cannot* advance huge sums of money to anyone or invest big dollars in advertising, and they *cannot* take many chances on dubious ideas (or writing hopefuls). If they did, they would be in the same position as larger publishers who must then count on other categories picking up the slack. Most of the time, specialty publishers simply *don't* publish "other categories"; instead, they focus on a couple—or a couple of authors or editors with whom they can get along pleasantly—and wind up doing (more times than not) two remarkable things: Publishing a handsome book on which they have lavished personal attention and care, and marketing the product in a manner that by any measurement *except* leading best seller lists exceeds the capability and inclinations of a diverse and high risk-assuming larger publishing house.

It may well be the way the majority of books is published in the future with the exceptions of educational books, those by authors with an international reputation, and throw-away books of revelation (or exhibitionism!) by or about this week's celebrities.

Other answers: Upwards of seventy-five writers have now been included in the quartet of *Masques* books, forty-two—till now—one time each. The line preceding those sentences of Poe's at the beginning of this introduction reads, "...It was his own guiding taste which had given character to the masqueraders." Although such writers as Rex Miller, Ray Russell, Ramsey Campbell, Bob Bloch, Ardath Mayhar, Graham Masterton, Chet Williamson, Jim Kisner, Joe Lansdale, Jessica Salmonson, Gahan Wilson, and Tom Monteleone haven't needed me or anybody else to give them character, I will accept the responsibility for believing that three principal ingredients should go into the making of *Masques:* Front to back originality. The interchange, from volume to volume, of established writers, rather than the easier method of drawing from a "stable" of friends. And carefully selected newcomers (meaning both people with one book or a few commercially-published tales to their credit, and those who were either completely unpublished in fiction or making their debuts in hardcover books—of whom four are present here in *M IV*).

Standard publishing houses often wince if anthologies they're contracted to do don't include work by King, Ray Bradbury, Miller, Campbell, the Wilsons Gahan or F. Paul, Bloch, Masterton, Charlie Grant, Chet, Ed Gorman, Dennis Etchison, Gary Brandner, Rick McCammon, Kathryn Ptacek, or Dan Simmons. All have attended these *Masques,* and more than 25% of the yarns or poetry appearing in the first three books of the series were nominated for or won awards, collected by individual authors, or reprinted in annual "bests of."

But these anthos have also introduced, one way or the other (and among others), Kisner, Alan Rodgers, Katherine Ramsland, Stanley Wiater, Gary Braunbeck, G. Wayne Miller and Joseph A. Citro. In a supposedly near-finite field of fiction writers, ten *Masques* "I", *II* or *III* contributors went on to publish their own books for the first time. Overall, ten percent of the anthology's wordworkers have been newcomers.

Originality; fresh imagination. According to the results of a recent survey conducted by Kathryn Cramer ("The Horror Field Now," Part 1) in *The New York Review of Science Fiction* (May '91), those qualities rank as the third most important in good horror fiction. Utilizing the sixty-seven responses filled in after she passed out one hundred questionnaires at World Fantasy Convention in November of '90, Dr. Cramer found effective characterization mentioned first, the rather ambiguous "good writing" in second place.

It's the hope all of us share that every piece of writing we read the rest of our lives will be well-written, of course. Interesting, credible characterization is one of the hardest things to accomplish in the short fictional form and certainly ranks with the basic idea for a story in motivating the horror writer, I think. Readers of the first *Masques* will readily recall McCammon's gaunt, skinny, fatigue-clad Price — "Charlie's in the light" — in "Nightcrawlers"; F. Paul Wilson's "Soft" protagonist with his "limp and useless muscles squishing"; Dennis Hamilton's massive Nuñez ("the monstrous groaning of the staircase") in "The Alteration." *Masques II* included King's "Popsy" ("stroking the boy's hair gently, with great love"); Bill Nolan's memorable junkyard owner, Latting ("You got *severe* internals"); Lansdale's perfectly envisioned feline ("Cat hangs claw in Dog's eye" in Joe's "Dog, Cat, and Baby"); and Tom Sullivan's "The Man Who Drowned Puppies" (MacIver: "You could not allow fallowness or death or the smell of death to collect in the villages").

And in *Masques III,* remember these jewels of characterization? "He was not an ignorant man and in some ways he was extremely intelligent. . . . He was grossly abnormal" (Rex Miller); "His voice was windy-sounding, like air through a straw" (Citro); "And you know, I think I could be a coal miner, bent over in those endless, low tunnels, without any fear" (John Maclay); "And then, as always, it was happening. But not to me. Never, to me" (Diane Taylor); "The wind almost knocked her off-balance — but she held firm, knowing something about feelings and night, love and tears: all of them could only be judged by what they drew from suffering" (Braunbeck); and "Kevin O'Toole was almost my age, but sometimes it seemed that he was five years older and five years younger than I at the same time. He read a lot" (Simmons).

In Dr. Cramer's survey, she asked participants to specify the leading influences on their ideas about horror, and short fiction was mentioned first, horror novels second, anthologies third. To my unscientific mind, that amounts to replying that horror stories in anthologies are the respondents' primary influence—at least since the demise of *Night Cry* and *Twilight Zone* magazines and before the emergence of *Pulphouse* and *Pulphouse Weekly*.

You see, it's difficult for me to imagine—because of their striking originality; their ideas—the tales in *Masques IV* by Chet Williamson, Kisner, Rex Miller, Dan Simmons, Lois Tilton, Rick Hautala and Gahan Wilson being published anywhere today except in an anthology or individual collection. Those writers have things to say that might be far too strongly expressed for most newsstand publications. I also think that the development of character exemplified here by Ed Gorman, Mort Castle, Maclay, newcomer David Connolly, Ptacek, Bruce Boston, Tilton, and Darrell Schweitzer—and the poetic insights of t. Winter-Damon and Denise Dumars—required either the freedom of a small press magazine or a permanent book. Editors and publishers say they want a lot of things; acceptance of the unique and creative, sometimes outrageous yarns of some of the authors I already cited plus that of Cameron Nolan, Ray Russell, John Coyne, Kris Rusch, Paul Wilson, Brian McNaughton, Gary Brandner, and Graham Masterton is (or could have been) something else.

Which sums up the singular usefulness of the commercially-detested anthology: Writers and readers alike who truly want to peer briefly down the labyrinthine corridors of the human mind, heart and soul have rather little choice except to look for top-flight horror anthologies.

And probably those books won't be published by the giant houses. "We don't do well with them" is the standard answer to an agent or editor with the proposal for a new antho. "We just contracted the one we're doing this season." They give the impression that such books are almost never published—but that simply isn't the case. Since *Masques* the First came out in '84, short fiction of mine—though my name does not start with "K" as do, say, Koontz, King, T. E. D. Klein, and Jim Kisner—has been chosen for thirty-four anthologies, roughly five per year. Things clearly aren't quite how they might appear—especially when I can recall without strain a dozen or more anthos during the same period to which I *wasn't* invited!

It is also supposedly the case that "new horror"/"Splatterpunk" fiction has supplanted "traditional" or "quiet" horror. There have even been suggestions that publishers now prefer vampire tales specifically, or yarns about serial killers, possibly to the exclusion of other forms of horror. Not so. My most recent novel sales are about a supernatural region of Arizona, a quest that leads to Hell, an alcoholic who must stop the spread of killing fungi at the county jail, a family trapped by winter in a converted monastery, middle-aged men kidnaped by time-displaced soldiers and forced to undergo basic training, and my boyhood. Not a vampire or serial killer in the lot (though I have such a book in mind).

Nor was my choice of stories for *M IV* made with the urgent hope of meeting some arbitrary, shifting mood or fad. Magazine editors may on occasion need to bow to trend, but books should be written or gathered in the hope they will be read and reread for years to come.

Yet it isn't impossible, now that the selection process is over again, to categorize what you're about to read. You'll find *one* vampire yarn, though I won't tell you which one, half a dozen all-in-your-head tales, three it-should-have-been-a-love stories, one curse, three futuristic, about four tied to past events; you'll read three anthropomorphic yarns (and possibly two anthropocentric), four tales of vengeance (give or take), at least three about child abuse, one as up-to-date as the most recent war (involving *us*), two ghost stories, a reversion-to-beasts epic, and—depending on how you want to look at them— five or six inhuman monster yarns. (I like them a lot as a rule.)

For the timid soul leafing through such a book as this for the first time, I can report that only four or five of these tales show human beings dying "on camera," so to speak—though people are *about* to perish in approximately seven others. According to the rule that, in good fiction, main characters are drastically changed by the end of the work, *Masques IV* is definitely on safe ground. They change so eighteen times herein, and the total would be higher if there weren't three stories without human protagonists!

There are no serial killers unless you'd like to count the vampire.

A more traditional breakdown (in three parts!): *Horror:* 36%; *supernatural:* 27%; *both:* another 36% (roughly). 58% are "mainstream" horror (or supernatural) tales, 23% are overt and maybe representative of that "new horror" classification, and 9% seemed like line-straddlers to me.

The third grouping was intriguing, I thought: 36% of this book's fiction writers crafted fiction I think of as light or downright amusing. That's probably a much higher percentage than there was in the previous *Masques,* but I'm growing tired of using my pocket calculator.

The bottom line to all this—actually, from about the halfway mark of this formal introduction on—is that I enormously enjoyed the stories and poems you're about to read, I believe they exhibit no conceivable sign of a slump in the very busy genre identified by the secondary name of this anthology series, and nearly everyone I've asked to the *Masques* so far has had—well, a ball.

Now, though, the most important guest has arrived. The person wears no "corpse-like mask" and isn't shrouded "in the habiliments of the grave." The "throng of the revellers" does wait, however, for the guest's "strong shudder," because it is *you.*

Let the masque begin!

J. N. Williamson
May and June 1991

Acknowledgments

For many reasons, the anthology *Masques* would not have become a series without the unique contributions of my wife, Mary; John Maclay and Joyce Maclay, Maclay & Associates; the late Milton L. Hillman, who generously gave us the title; Ray Bradbury, Stephen King, and Dean R. Koontz; D. W. and Diane Taylor; and Mort Castle.

Ongoing thanks for help with the earlier volumes or for *Masques IV* specifically must be expressed to the following people, publications, or organizations:

Paul Dale and Gretta M. Anderson, *2AM;* Bastei-Lubbe; Robert Bloch; Tyson Blue; British Fantasy Society; Ginjer Buchanan, Berkley Books; the *Chicago Star;* Rich Chizmar, *Cemetery Dance* magazine; agents Don Congdon, Michael Congdon; Ellen Datlow, Teri Windling, James Frenkel, *The Year's Best Fantasy & Horror;* designer Glen M. Edelstein; Ediciones Martínez Rocá; Peter Enfantino, *The Scream Factory;* Delores J. Everts; *Fantasy Mongers;* Futura Publications; Garden Editoriale; David Hinchberger, The Overlook Connection; jacket designer Raquel Jaramillo; Kathleen Jurgens, *Thin Ice;* Rick Kleffel, *Midnight Graffiti;* David Kuehls, *Fangoria;* agent Norman Kurz; Allen Koszowski; *Library Journal; Locus;* Barbara Lowenstein; agent Uwe Luserke; agent Kay McCauley; agent Kirby McCauley; Harry O. Morris; Stanley Mossman; *Mystery Scene; OtherRealms;* agent Lori Perkins; *Publishers Weekly;* Katherine Ramsland; *Richmond (Va.) Times-Dispatch;* Robson Books; *Rocky Mountain News; San Francisco Chronicle;* Stuart Schiff, *Whispers; Science Fiction Chronicle;* Dean Wesley Smith, Pulphouse; Lin Stein; Peter Straub; *True Review;* Gordon Van Gelder, St. Martin's Press; Ruben Villegas; Stanley and Iris Wiater; Robert and Phyllis Weinberg; Ron

Wolfe; and World Fantasy Award committees.

Masques IV is dedicated to the delightful memory of the clever and highly original writer, James Cardwell — also known as "Adobe James." One of his final short stories, "The Spelling Bee," was a highlight in the editor's work on the third *Masques,* and getting to know Jim in his last years — a bit — was a highlight of my life. Find him; publish him; read him. The reward you'll get will be your pleasure.

The Pack

Chet Williamson

One decade has passed since Chet Williamson sold his second story to *Rod Serling's Twilight Zone,* and it's difficult to imagine a career that has (among those of us who don't mind being called horror writers) grown more impressively in terms of versatility, intelligent distribution of one's time and talent, and popularity among readers and other writers. Except for the Pennsylvania native's literate style, it's also hard for the handful of his readers who have not committed his name to memory to comprehend that the same author is the creator of *Dreamthorp, McKain's Dilemma,* and *Reign* (three of his novels, the last of which made the Horror Writers of America final ballot), "The Confession of St. James" (in *Night Visions 7*), "From the Papers of Helmut Hecher" *(Lovecraft's Legacy),* and his tales in *Playboy* and *The New Yorker.*

But, he is. Because, in a phrase, the word "Biedermeier" (artistically or intellectually uninspired) is the antithesis of Chet's work. He told interviewer Stanley Wiater in *Dark Dreamers* that he doesn't fit any school of horror fiction and added, "You can write about *anything* if you write well."

Nominated for the Edgar, the World Fantasy Award and, prior to *Reign,* the H.W.A. Bram Stoker, Chet Williamson does. So read "The Pack" and, when you've finished, you may just want to go back and read it for the truths as well as the gross-outs. They're there in all his writing.

They didn't remember rising. They were just dead one minute, up and around the next. Those whose noses were crushed were the lucky ones. They couldn't smell the others, and they couldn't smell themselves. That was the worst of it for those whose noses were still working.

Rusty's nose worked just fine, and the stench annoyed him. He didn't know if he'd ever be able to get it out of his nostrils, ever be able to scent game again. The leader ought to be able to scent the pack's prey. And he was the leader, there was no doubt of that. He was the biggest, for one thing. A mutt, to be sure, but there was a lot of German shepherd in him, and his thin, taut frame indicated that either a Great Dane or a Doberman had participated in a train pulled on his mother or grandmothers. He was also in the best condition of the motley crew gathered around him, which wasn't saying a whole hell of a lot.

Jesus, Rusty thought, they looked like shit. Fluffy in particular, one of the few he knew. He had humped her damn near every time she'd been in heat, but had never connected well enough to impregnate her. She was a mutt too, a small, yellow, long-haired bitch who had always carried her tail up and waving, as if to advertise the availability of her hindquarters. Now that tail was matted and askew, the hindquarters grotesquely large and swollen by the compression of her stomach where the 4 × 4 had mashed her. Her rear had had no choice but to split apart, and what Rusty remembered as tight and hot organs had given whelp to strands of dirt-caked gut on which she sat, resting her unbroken forepaws on a thick loop of her intestine.

Rowdy was the only other he knew, an old, old dog who had been dead a long, long time. He'd been run over many times, left to be simmered by hot summer rains and fried in the skillet of high noon asphalt. He lay on the grass more like a well-used welcome mat than a dog. It seemed that only the hemisphere of his skull had not been flattened, and dry, puckered little things that Rusty figured were eyes watched him from that mass of fur and splintered bone, and waited for him to offer a plan.

For a plan was what was needed. There had to be a purpose in what had happened, in what had drawn them all here together.

A plan. Rusty shivered at the thought. And then he shivered again at the thought of *thought*. His mental processes seemed so complex now, and he could tell that those of the others were similar. There had been such *simplicity* before the awakening — looks and growls and barks and motions that indicated all the necessities of canine existence:

Play!
Eat!
Shit!
Roll in it!
Fuck!

But now there was far more than could be communicated by *You smell my asshole, I'll smell yours.* Now there was memory and subtlety and, at long last, understanding of everything Rusty had seen and heard while he lived with the people who had called themselves his family. He knew what family was now, understood it. Males who fucked, bitches who whelped, them and the pups living together, enslaving the dogs, making them trade their freedom for food from cans (vomitous horsemeat shaped like a fat cylinder, the rings of the lid impressed upon the first bite), making them give up the heritage of the pack for a stroke once or twice a day, a walk on the end of a leash, an occasional flight of liberty when a bitch in heat might be fucked, a pile of dung might be rolled in, a wounded rabbit tormented and eventually killed.

And what response from the humans when these joys were over? A newspaper on the nose, the end of a leash across the hindquarters, stinging the anus, burning the balls. Torture, pure and simple. And then at last, after a lifetime of cowering and cringing and tail-wagging and licking the hand of the goddamned male and his bitch and their pups, after *years* of that, when the only thing you want to do is lie and rest, then the final visit to the Great Devil in his white coat, the spurt of the needle, the ultimate injection, oh yes, he knew, he'd lain by the fireplace many times while the "family" watched that show on the television (television — Christ, he even knew its name now! And *Christ,* he could even curse like the humans had!). He had seen the actor pretend to be the vet and kill the dogs with sorrow on his pasty, blotchy face, and Rusty's "family" had watched too, snuffling, the bitch wiping away tears and the male blinking, pretending his own tears weren't there, when all the time they knew that when Rusty got old and tired, they'd take him to the *real* Great Devil as soon as he sneezed, or puked on the carpet, or shit in the house.

And if not the Great Devil, then dogs died as Rusty and all who now surrounded him had died — crushed, battered, squashed, splattered by the cars, the trucks, the great, stupid machines that carried the humans everywhere because their legs were so weak, so slow.

"Did they ever try to stop?" Rusty clearly wondered, and the thoughts were like words to the others. They heard, and thought, and he heard in return.

"Stop?" The word came from Rowdy, and in Rusty's mind it was festooned with ornaments of flayed fur. It sounded like Rowdy looked. "They *tried* to hit me. And they did. Too old to get out of the way. Just crossing the road. Just wanted to get to the cool of the oak trees and take a good long piss against them. Took me down. One great flash of yellow fire, and that was all. Next thing I remember, I'm crawling here, moving like a rug, dragging myself along like nothing's ever moved before, like nothing should be *able* to move. And why? There's got to be a reason why. I'm older than you, seen more, heard more, maybe now I understand more. But I don't understand why. There's got to be a reason."

"There's a reason," said a young but twisted thought, and the pack turned what was left of their heads and looked with what was left of their eyes at another dog. Sparks was the name his "family" had given him. He had enough eyes to serve all of them. They had been pushed from their sockets by whatever vehicle had struck him. One looked one direction, one the other, so that his ovoid gaze seemed all-encompassing. "There's a *good* reason. To devour what devoured us. To eat what ate us away."

The thought struck a flame in Rusty, and he licked his chops with a caked tongue. "The family," he thought. "Humans."

The compressed muscles of Sparks's haunches pulsed in a futile effort to wag his tail. "Humans."

Rusty looked around the ring of broken creatures. Dry, parchment tongues panted in agreement, those tails wagged that could, heads nodded, even one that dangled from a thick strand of neck muscle that was barely visible beneath the sheep dog's shaggy hair. "It must be," Rusty thought. "Why otherwise would we have been given life once more, given knowledge, understanding, the complexity of thought necessary to finally realize the perfidy of our persecutors?"

"There may be no reason like that," stated a broken-faced dachshund, its jaw and snout poking at right angles to each other. "It may rather be a situation akin to the kind of entertainment that the 'families' watch on the television — radiation, chemicals, nitrates from manure on the farms oozing out of the soil and into. . . the soul. There may be no purpose at all, merely a random chain of events."

"I for one," thought Sparks, "do not believe in a purposeless cosmos."

"You believe in God then?" inquired the dachshund.

"I believe in *Dog*." Sparks grinned, and Rusty thought the effect was hideous.

"Fuck your palindromes, and fuck your philosophy," mentally growled a junkyard dog whose middle resembled a veterinarian's anatomical chart. "All I know is that I'm back and I'm pissed and though I don't have much of a stomach to digest it with, I want to tear out some human guts, and get a little back."

"I did not say," clarified the dachshund, "that I did *not* want that as well. I simply feel there may be no moral or theological justification of such acts. But whether there are or are not, I'd like to rip some humans myself. 'Wiener,' they called me. 'Little Wiener.' And that was only the first of many injuries, both mental and physical."

"Whatever the reason," thought Rusty, "we have all returned, and we all have the same basic drive—as Sparks so eloquently put it, to devour what devoured us. We are a pack, and together we can triumph."

Fluffy resettled her forepaws on her filthy bowels. "They may come after us, try to kill us."

"We're already dead, bitch," thought Sparks. "If we're moving around in *this* condition, bullets aren't going to be too effective, do you think?"

"But in this condition," she replied, "do you think we'll be able to pull down humans? I mean, look at Rowdy."

"It's true," Rowdy thought, "I'm not as spry as I used to be. But I do have means of locomotion, albeit slow. If the more active of you can bring our prey down, I can still participate in the final rending. Pieces of teeth remain in here, sharp, capable of cutting." And a mass of compressed fur rose up so that Rusty and the others could see smooth bits of yellow beneath. Rusty's newfound imagination could not, however, conceive of those pitiful bits of enamel abrading human flesh, if, indeed, they were still attached to what remained of Rowdy's jaw. Still, Rowdy was one of the pack.

This last thought he communicated to the others, and they agreed that the stronger would pull down the prey, but not finish it until all were there to share in the death and the eating.

"Can we eat?" wondered a desiccated terrier.

"We can try," Rusty thought. "Perhaps it will pass through us, perhaps it will be only symbolic. But still, this should be the law of the pack—to devour what devoured us."

Rusty lifted his head and tried to catch the sound of traffic to determine the whereabouts of a road. To scent gasoline or exhaust would have been impossible with the stench of carrion in his nose. Finally, from far away he heard the sound of an engine. "Come. Let's hunt."

The pack began to move in the direction of the road, but quickly learned that they would make dreadful time if they waited for Rowdy. So Rusty and Sparks got on either side of the irregular disc of leather and fur, dug their fangs into the mass, and hauled their companion along. The dog had been dead so long that Rusty tasted only the ghost of vileness. Once or twice Rowdy's matted hair got caught on roots and in branches, but the old dog writhed and twisted while the young ones tugged, until they reached a state game trail.

On the way, Rusty's eyes (still sharp, despite yellowing of the white and minor leaking of the vitreous fluid) discerned a rabbit standing in darkness next to a stump. Although his first reaction was to immediately drop Rowdy's fur pie and race after the creature, something made him hesitate. He thought at first that it might be increased intelligence, that the mental maturity he and his cohorts had achieved had shown him the futility of chasing rodents. But as the stump and the creature that stood next to it retreated in his peripheral vision, he realized that there had been something dreadfully *wrong* with the rabbit, if rabbit it was. It had seemed terribly thin, reduced in girth beyond the effects of emaciation. He had seen rabbits like that before, but where?...

He nearly damned himself for being so obtuse. Roadkill. Of course. He had seen rabbits that had been hit right across the torso by cars, their spines splintered, their innards smashed into one another so that their heads and hind legs looked perfectly natural, but what lay in between could have been slipped under a door. It was just like the dried up terrier's guts, the terrier who, like all of them, had been born again into this world.

And if a terrier, why not a rabbit? Why not cats, for Christ's sake? And turtles? And deer and squirrels and mice? Rusty had always liked to chase animals smaller than himself, though he hardly ever caught them. But he did not think he would like to chase the rabbit he had seen, and he wondered what its own prey might be.

The thoughts were blotted out by the sound of an engine idling, and Rusty saw a wooden bar ahead, the gate that kept vehicles out of the game trail. A car was next to that gate, perhaps fifty yards back from the main road, in the small parking area bounded by trees. Through the open windows of the car he could hear strains of that abysmal music that still drove spikes into his sensitive ears.

The pack crept closer to the car on splintered limbs, some of them trailing strands of gut like bridal trains behind them. Rusty heard voices now, one pleading, one protesting, and then the engine went dead, the music stopped. The pack froze in an instant, and the only sound was the soft clack of the dachshund's misaligned jaw as he excitedly tried to moisten his tongue.

Rusty and Sparks opened their own jaws then, letting Rowdy's ragged edges flop quietly to the earth, and looked at each other. Sparks's dueling eyes were wild with anticipation of the kill, and his legs trembled. The other dogs were ready too, their tongues hanging from their mouths like dry leaves.

"Wait," thought Rusty. The pack looked at him curiously and, he felt, angrily, as if frustrated at being heeled. But he was the leader, and the leader had a plan. "Let's get them out. Out in the open."

The pack pictured it in their minds and found it good. After a moment of plotting, Fluffy dragged herself to where the bitch inside could see her, while the others went to the front and back of the car. Lying on her mass of gut, she began to whimper, softly and pitifully.

"Ben..." came the bitch's voice. "Ben, there's something out there..."

"Come on, it's just an animal or something. Forget it."

"No, it's...a *dog*."

Fluffy increased the volume now. It sounded, Rusty thought, like when she'd been mated a few times and was begging for more, and he gave a dog smile in the darkness.

"Oh, it *is*, it's a little yellow dog, and it looks hurt, the poor thing." The door opened, the bitch got out and knelt next to Fluffy, who was trying her damnedest not to let a loop of intestine pop out from between her forelegs. "Oh, Ben, come quick..."

Come quick, Ben, Rusty thought to himself.

Ben came quick, heaving a sigh of annoyance and frustration, opening the door, stepping out, and Rusty the first, around the side of the car, battering into the male snout first, burying his fangs in the midsection, through the shirt, the soft, yielding skin, into the guts, like the guts the humans so gaily and thoughtlessly scattered on their moonlit roads, the guts of the pack. And now others were on the male, and from the passenger side Rusty heard the squeal of the bitch as Fluffy and the junkyard dog, the terrier and the dachshund brought her down.

Rusty buried his snout in the male's viscera, bit and bit again, tasted the chunks his sharp teeth detached, spit, shook them out, bit again, ripped more soft gut, heedless of the fists of the man raining down on his back, on his skull already broken, fists driving shards of white bone deeper into his brain, his brain that thought more clearly than it ever had before. He felt the others beside him, ripping, snarling, taking the man to pieces more surely than tires and metal underbodies had rended those of the pack, pressing them down into the asphalt, making them one with the road, and Rusty thought of Rowdy, then thought, *"Stop!"*

They did. It was as though they shared a mind, shared a will, and their bloodied snouts, bent jaws, dripping teeth came up from both the male and the bitch.

"The bitch?" Rusty thought, and Fluffy's thought came back to him, "Dead."

He looked down at the male. The chest was still rising and falling, though the stomach was torn wide open, the bowels flopping over the edge of the bloody pool. Rusty looked at Sparks, who was chewing vigorously on a dripping piece of meat. "Rowdy."

Sparks nodded, spat the chunk away, and padded toward the matted pile of dog. Together he and Rusty dragged what was left of Rowdy over to the male, and set the old dog down so that the edge of Rowdy touched the male's forehead. Rowdy pulled himself over the male's face by short jerks, unseen pieces of claw dragging the mat up and over until the male's panting face was hidden. Then the mass quivered, shook, and Rusty saw the dome of Rowdy's skull move up and down, up and down, until the dog's hair turned red with the blood it soaked up. When Rowdy finally slid off, the male's face was stripped of all its skin, and most of its muscle. The chest no longer rose and fell.

"Rowdy has fed. Now devour what you will," thought Rusty, and sank his fangs into the male's windpipe, feeling the blood, still warm, burst into his mouth, run down his chin.

The dachshund ripped with crooked jaws at the front of the male's pants, tearing away the fabric with difficulty, and finally gnawing at the shriveled pouch of flesh until it came off, and he chewed with satisfaction. "Family took mine long ago," he thought gleefully, and Rusty laughed, then stopped, feeling pity for the dachshund.

He sat up, felt the warm blood running down his jaw, watched the dogs greedily burrowing into the body of the male, then went to the other side of the car. Fluffy was chewing happily on the bitch's thigh, and the junkyard dog was gobbling pieces of gut. He stopped, stretched, and rolled over in the puddle of blood so that Rusty could see the pieces of bitch flesh pressing against the lining of the dog's exposed stomach. Then Rusty looked at the nearly decapitated sheep dog. The jaws of the dog's head, hanging from a strand of muscle and skin, laboriously worked at tearing away a hunk of the human bitch's bowels, but when the dog swallowed it, the meat merely crawled through its severed esophagus and dropped onto the dirt. The sheep dog turned, angled itself so that the jaws could grasp the morsel again, the throat could swallow again. But the esophagus excreted again, and the dog picked it up, swallowed, over and over.

Rusty, saddened nearly beyond the capacity of a dog to feel sorrow, turned away, walked to the front of the car, listened to the feast, of dead meat filling dead meat.

Days passed, and the dogs continued to hunt. Fewer cars drove through the woods now, but the pack had learned new ways to take their prey. The cars had to pass through several hollows, and Rusty and Sparks, the two most vigorous of the pack, would stand on the rocks at a level just above the car windows. Then, when a vehicle passed, they would leap through the windows into the car, and savage the humans within. The cars crashed, the humans (if they had not already been killed by the dogs) injured or made insensible, and the pack fed. If the windows were rolled up, it made no difference, for the skulls of the dogs, already broken, shattered the glass, allowing entrance.

Then, one night, a car filled with policemen parked by the side of the road near the rocks. The pack killed them all. Their bullets went through the dogs, spitting away only small pieces of meat the dogs could do without. The blast from a shotgun, however, did shear off Sparks's left front foreleg, which, after the slaughter, they retrieved and reattached. It was a bit tricky. Rusty held the leg in his jaws while Sparks pushed his stump against it. Somehow the crevices wedged together firmly enough so that the limb remained in place, though Sparks used it as little as possible, and it became more of a liability to locomotion than an aid.

Three days after the devouring of the policemen, more humans came to the edge of the woods. They were armed with shotguns, and had dogs on leashes. But the living dogs refused to go among the trees, and sat and howled and cowered, until the humans, cursing and scowling, put the dogs back into their trucks and cars and drove away, glancing out their windows in discomfort. Though the pack's nostrils were caked with decay, they could still scent the humans' fear on the wind, and they laughed.

And continued to laugh and hunt and prey until the day Sparks disappeared. Or rather, until most of him disappeared. The left foreleg remained, the limb that had become not so much a part of him as a prized possession, like a shit-caked rag or a rotting rabbit carcass would have been when the pack lived.

The pack remained together most of the time, but, as dogs will, they would go off by themselves from time to time, or in a pair or a trio. One night Sparks went off alone, just for a trot, to make the motions of pissing against a tree to mark territory (though none of them were any longer capable of producing urine. If they drank, it merely flowed through and out of them, so the pissing motion was now more symbolic than ever). The longest any of the dogs had ever been gone before was an hour at a time, so when nearly the entire night passed without his reappearance, the pack began to worry, and went to look for him.

They found only the pitiful left foreleg, in which no life remained. That, and some fragments of bone that appeared to have been shattered by remarkably strong teeth. There was no blood on the ground (Sparks and the other dogs had emptied their blood on the roads long before), but the brush was torn up as though there had been a tremendous struggle, and broken branches showed where a large body, no doubt the same creature that had devoured Sparks, had crashed through it.

The pack was silent, keeping its individual thoughts to its separate selves. The dogs poked about with dead noses, trying to catch a scent, something that would tell them what it was that had cut out a member of their pack. For a moment, Rusty thought he caught a trace of something familiar, something large and gross and dimly remembered, but then it was gone, and would not come again, and he was unable to recall it strongly enough to claim the memory he was sure was there.

By the time they gave up, it was morning, and they crept, crawled, and slid silently back to the lair they had found in the shelter of two fallen trees. They lay there on the thick carpet of dead pine needles and leaves, lay and rested, though none of them was capable of sleep.

"Was it a monster?" the dachshund thought, and Rusty knew the query was directed to him alone.

"I don't know," Rusty replied. "I thought *we* were the monsters, and now. . ."

"Another pack?"

"No. You saw how high the branches were broken. Not a dog. Or dogs."

The dachshund grinned lopsidedly. "God then."

"And not God."

"What would you call something that can devour one of us? Give us long enough and we'll be gods to men — or demons. They'll come to fear us and avoid us. They'll make these woods forbidden — sacred, if you will." The dachshund gave a thoughtful whine. "Funny how things come around. Men were gods to us. They crushed us, devoured us, and now we devour them. What were *we* Gods to, Rusty? What did *we* devour?" He thought silently for a moment. Rusty concentrated on a solution, remembering that he was the leader. "Could it have been man?" the dachshund asked.

"There were no gunshots. And men would not have devoured Sparks. Not in that way."

Rusty, unable to come up with an answer, brooded, and was still brooding when night fell again. It had begun to rain, but none of the dogs were bothered by it. The drops merely matted their fur a little more, beaded on their exposed viscera, pooled in the hollow pouches of their rotted flesh, so that every now and then they would have to twist one way or the other to let the malodorous water run out onto the forest floor.

Rusty mentally inquired if the others were ready to hunt, but he felt only mild interest in return. Their last few nights of hunting had been unsuccessful. Humans hardly dared to travel the road anymore, and when they did they drove so fast that Rusty and Sparks found it difficult to leap at the windows. Indeed, on the last attempt, while Sparks was still alive, Rusty had landed on the car's trunk and slid right off, while Sparks had missed the vehicle completely.

Something else interested the pack tonight. Fluffy, the only female among them, had somehow gone into something that passed for estrous, despite the mutilation of her sexual organs. She dragged her posterior along the ground, whining and moaning, her vegetation-coated insides roiling behind her like thick, drunken serpents. The males crowded around her, sniffing futilely, but recalling the scent, and what remained of their penises left their sheaths reluctantly, as if sheer will rather than blood engorged them, making them a sickly yellow rather than the thrilling pink of former matings.

Rusty ignored them. His equipment would have functioned better than any, but he wasn't in the mood, and wondered how the others could be. He felt no sexual stirring whatsoever, and suspected that the pack was planning to rut (or attempt to rut — what could they really *do* with that conglomeration of bowels and fissures that used to be Fluffy's slit?) more for the sake of nostalgia than out of any real lust.

For a while he sat there, watching the others follow the bitch through the woods. Soon they were out of sight, and he sighed for the lost times that would not come again, and thought about taking the pack elsewhere, away from the woods where prey no longer came, perhaps into the cities, from which humans could not flee. The dogs could hide there almost as easily as in the woods, and the supply of prey would never run low.

Rusty trotted back to the shelter, crawled in, and lay down, his head on his forepaws. He could hear them now, and guessed that they were a half mile or more away. He heard the feigned yaps of anger as the males fought for dominance, then Fluffy's rather unconvincing yowl as something Rusty didn't care to think about was penetrated, then a long period of silence, during which, he surmised, a mere charade was performed for old time's sake.

Screams shattered the silence — authentic, sincere cries, yelps, growls that Rusty took at first to be the vocal outbursts of passion, and, upon hearing them, forgotten lust launched itself in his haunches, engorged his rod with memory alone, pressing it from its sheath. Aroused, he stood, drinking in what he took to be the sounds of hot, wet sex, until he realized that such could not take place in cold, dry bodies.

The screams were screams of pain, of terror.

But what could terrorize the dead?

Rusty launched himself toward the sound. He was supposed to have been the leader, and he cursed himself for not going with them, as he thought of what it could have been that had taken Sparks. He pushed himself through the brush, taking the most direct route to the sounds of his shrieking pack. There was no moon, and the darkness was thick and blinding. Several times he battered his already crushed forehead against the trunks of trees, but it had no more effect on him than if he had been wearing a helmet. He simply righted himself, aimed himself in the direction of the sounds, and charged once more, bouncing, ricocheting off oaks, maples, pines, until he broke through a final thicket whose thorns and brambles tore at his scraggly coat like sharp wires, one of them piercing his eye and holding him captive until he wrenched himself away from it, ripping the eyeball, leaving half of it hanging on the thorn, and entered a small clearing.

With his one remaining eye, Rusty saw the carnage that had been his pack. He saw Fluffy's head lying on the leaves, the jaw flapping up and down, trying to drag it toward the mud-yellow body from which great chunks of dead meat had been chewed away; saw the junkyard dog, his middle bitten through so that only a rod of spine connected the two halves, trying to push himself to his feet like a broken bridge in a windstorm; saw the dachshund's short legs swinging at something that towered above it, a deeper darkness against the dark of night, and that darkness detaching itself, falling toward the dog and entrapping his pointed head in blackness. There was a thick crunch, and the dachshund's head vanished in a cacophony of splitting bones and tearing gristle. The legs of the headless body continued to jerk, but with no sense of balance, no eyes to guide it, no ears to hear, it could do no more than wait to join its cicerone in the maw that had stolen it. With the next bite it was divided once more, then, with the last, was reunited with its other pieces.

Whether it continued to live in the stomach of its devourer was a possibility that occurred only dimly to Rusty. Such metaphysical thoughts on the afterlife of the afterlife were far from his mind now. The destruction of his fellows had maddened him, returned him to that state of canine savagery to which rational thought was a stranger, and he thrust himself at the greater darkness over the bits and pieces of the pack. Something sharp-edged and brutal battered him, hurling him to the side and against a tree whose trunk cracked his spine. Then that something pressed against his chest like God's hammer, pinning him to the ground, and Rusty heard a snort, but saw no breath steam from the creature's nostrils. It was as dead as Rusty, but not as dead as the pack.

The horse's head came down, buried itself in Rusty's guts, and chewed. Its teeth and jaws were strong, even stronger than the musky, tinny taste of its fellows' canned flesh that Rusty had wolfed down a thousand times. And as Rusty watched himself entering the horse's dead mouth bite by bite, he wondered with his recently-found imagination what would devour the horse? Then his head was taken, the brain smashed, swallowed, and the thoughts ceased.

Grain? thought Rowdy, continuing Rusty's thought. Dead oats? Dead apples come alive again? And what would they do? Bounce up the road on which they fell and were run over? Fruit roadkill? But how could they bounce if they were squashed? And how could oats devour, or hay destroy, or clover hate? But hell, there'd be *something.*

Rowdy shook the half dome of his skull. The thoughts were too much for him, and he lay still while the horse finished its meal, going from chunk to chunk, its grinding teeth preparing the flesh for its ruminant stomach, unused to meat and bone. The feast would kill it, Rowdy thought, if it weren't already dead.

It came up to Rowdy, and he saw the great rift in its once proud neck where the car or truck must have struck it and killed it. It sniffed at Rowdy for a moment, but Rowdy remained still. It was easy for a dead thing to pretend to be dead.

The horse moved on then, and Rowdy waited until it was gone, then examined the small remnants the beast had left. Nope. They twitched and moved, but they weren't worth a bitch's spit. He'd have to find another pack, and he would. He moved slowly, but he had time. Yep, time was all he had. What kind of creature, dead or alive, would bother a ratty old hunk of kitchen carpet like him?

He had scarcely traveled ten yards when he felt the first flea bite him. And him without a leg to scratch with.

"Fool: it is you who are the pursued, the marked down quarry, the destined prey."

— George Bernard Shaw, *Man and Superman*

Children

Kristine Kathryn Rusch

.

Something quite special has been happening in Oregon these past few years. I'm not referring to the Pulphouse publishing empire, but one of the primary reasons for its success, the versatile editor who has recently added to her backbreaking schedule a similar post with *Magazine of Fantasy and Science Fiction.*

But I'm not referring to Kris Rusch's genius as an editor, either. I'm talking about the emergence of an author of universally-praised short fiction ("Skin Deep," "Fast Cars," "Fugue," "Trains," and "Sing") — appearing in *Asimov's, Alfred Hitchcock's,* plus *The Year's Best Science Fiction* ('89) and *The World's Best Science Fiction* (also '89) — and of two, splendid novels from NAL — *The White Mists of Power,* and *Afterimage* (with talented Kevin Anderson) — all in the past few years!

Here's a story your editor received too late for inclusion in *Masques III* or it certainly would have been there. It's present now because she allowed me to hold onto it for more than a year, and because I believe it's one of the 12 to 15 best-imagined and truly disturbing stories this series has published. Yes, Kris Rusch is a fine editor; see the 1990 *Science Fiction Writers of America Handbook,* edited with Dean Wesley Smith, as an example. Yet she is at least as gifted and thoughtful a writer. See for yourself in..."Children."

Bear Trap Lake
June 17, 1987

McIntyre leaned forward as he pushed his paddle in the water. The muscles in his arms ached. He didn't know how much longer he could keep rowing the canoe.

He shot a quick glance over his shoulder. The swimmer still hounded him. The whole afternoon had the feel of a nightmare; the growing panic, the illogical but certain knowledge that the thing which pursued him was evil, and the utter, ruthless determination of the swimmer. The swimmer had grabbed McIntyre's canoe twice, and only luck and a good sense of balance had kept him from capsizing.

Splashes echoed behind him, and he braced himself for another hit. But nothing happened. The swimmer glided up beside him and McIntyre screamed. He yanked his paddle out of the water and swung it like a sword. The paddle slapped against the swimmer's skull, slicing through the skin. McIntyre leaned over the side of his canoe, and watched the bloody bubbles rise as the child sank beneath the waters.

Madison, Wisconsin
May 4, 1969

Shouts and the tinkle of breaking glass woke him. He lay for a moment on the stained mattress, his legs trapped under Patty's, listening, before he realized that another riot was going on. He tried to remember if he knew of any action that day, but he thought of nothing.

Patty sat up and pushed her hair out of her face with one hand. "What's that?"

McIntyre shook his head.

Downstairs a door banged and Jason screamed, "Piiigs!"

McIntyre heard footsteps on the stairs and suddenly the bedroom door swung open. Patty grabbed for her dress. Jason looked in.

"Hey, man," McIntyre said as he reached for a sheet to cover his nakedness. Something crashed beneath the window.

Jason didn't even notice. His thin face was flushed. "You gotta see this," he said. "It started on State Street, but they brought it down here."

"What happened?" Patty asked. She had pulled her dress on. It pooled around her legs, but her buttocks were still visible. McIntyre felt her growing excitement.

"I don't know, but it's a mess. You gotta see it." Jason ran down the hall to the other rooms, flinging the doors open so hard that they banged against the wall.

Patty stood up and McIntyre handed her a pair of underwear. He slipped into some cutoffs and shoved his feet into his sandals. Patty had already started for the door.

"Wait," he said, and closed the windows. Immediately the shouting became muffled. "Last time they used gas. We want to sleep here tonight."

She nodded. He took her hand and together they ran down the worn stairs and out the front door. On the sagging porch, they stopped. Kids filled the street, screaming, yelling, some holding rocks, others with the tattered remains of signs. Cops were using nightsticks to move the crowd forward.

McIntyre took a step back. He didn't want to be part of that scene; it looked too dangerous to him. But Patty loved danger. She pulled him forward and rather than lose her, he followed her into the street.

The air was thick with the smell of sweat and fear. McIntyre coughed and brought an arm up to his face. Somehow Patty's hand slipped through his and he watched her run to the other curb. She was yelling something or maybe she was screaming. He tried to reach her — after what he had done two days before, he was scared to let her do anything alone — but he kept colliding with other bodies that pushed him forward in a wave. A woman brushed past him. She was moaning and blood was running from her left ear. Patty stood at the fringes of the crowd. As she waved her arms above her head, the motion hiked her dress up to show the edges of the underwear he had given her a few moments before. Then he lost sight of her. He finally made it to the curb as Patty crumpled onto the grass.

By the time McIntyre reached her, blood covered her face. He touched the sticky wetness. "Patty?" he said, but couldn't hear himself over the noise.

A car window shattered beside them. He thought he saw her eyelids flicker, although he wasn't sure. But he did know the exact moment she died. One moment, she was in her body, regulating its breathing, making its heart pump, and the next minute, she had left. And that was when he started to scream.

Bear Trap Lake
June 17, 1987

He pulled the canoe up onto the shore and winced as the aluminum scraped the sand. Then he grabbed the rope, made sure it was firmly tied to the bow and tied the other end to an oak. He staggered across the sand and collapsed on the grass. The rich smell of the land filled his nostrils.

"Dad?"

The shout came from the cabin. McIntyre didn't move. He was

too tired. His limbs hurt and the skin on his back was beginning to throb. He must have gotten too much sun.

"Dad?"

The call was closer. Sean knelt down beside him.

"I thought that was you. You okay?"

"I'd like a beer." McIntyre's voice scraped sandlike against his throat.

"Okay, you got it. Looks like you need some lotion too."

"Yeah." McIntyre breathed the word and the blades of grass in front of his face moved. He rested, almost dozing, as images of the afternoon ran through his mind.

He had decided to take a leisurely trip around the lake. Bear Trap was small, with five cabins and lots of open water. On weekdays, he and Sean were the only ones there. Seeing the swimmer dive in at the public landing had surprised him. It hadn't been until he had realized that it was one of the children paddling at him that he had grown frightened.

Cold, wet goo spurted on his back and McIntyre jumped.

"Sorry," Sean said as he rubbed the lotion in. "You really got fried. Why didn't you come in sooner?"

McIntyre shrugged. He imagined himself trying to explain what had happened to his son: Well, Sean, I had to kill a kid before I could get off that lake. But don't worry about it. I've killed kids before.

The lotion soaked into his back, easing the burn and stinging at the same time.

"I got you the beer, too."

McIntyre pulled himself up. He was going to be sore for days. Sean handed him the beer and McIntyre poured it into his mouth, not caring that some ran over his lips and dribbled off his chin. The icy coldness made his throat ache. After he finished half the can, he stopped, wiped his face with the back of his hand and took a deep breath.

Sean smiled. He had his mother's smile, crooked, whimsical, and fey. Sometimes, McIntyre felt that he touched her through their son.

"Help me inside," he said to shake that lonely thought.

Sean pulled him up, and together they walked to the cabin they had finished building the summer before.

Highway 53
April 2, 1983

The extension course had gone well. Even after two sessions, McIntyre still didn't believe the enthusiasm that a group from Solon

Springs, Wisconsin, showed in learning how to trace their family histories. He remembered that excitement from tracing his own history, but he had thought that was due to the peculiarity of his family background.

He steered the car carefully onto the highway. The road was thick with early April ice and slush. As he headed into the darkness, he felt a presence. He flicked on the brights and searched for deer in the trees.

Something thudded against the passenger side and he looked sharply. A packed wad of snow slid down the window. It had probably fallen from one of the branches above. The Oldsmobile swerved slightly and he righted it when a body slammed into the windshield.

McIntyre drew his breath in sharply and pumped the brakes. Then he looked up and found himself face to face with one of the children.

Children had been his grandfather's word, but it only described their general shape and form. The eyes were hollow, dark, lacking whites, but reflecting light like a cat's. The creature pressed its face against the window and McIntyre could see its gray skin. Its hands were splayed, the long fingernails tapping like claws against the glass.

The car swerved again, but this time McIntyre couldn't see. The back end fishtailed on the ice. McIntyre struggled to straighten it. The creature seemed to be laughing. It slid its hands up to the top of the windshield, stretched its body along the glass and pulled, McIntyre stared for a moment at its shrunken penis, and the long, lean bones sliding into its pelvic girdle. He had learned over the years just how strong these things were. It would break in. And then it would kill him.

He made himself look away from the creature and out the windshield. The car was heading straight for the trees. He tried to turn the wheels, but they slipped on the slush. He had promised himself when Carol had died in January that he would let the next child go. But he couldn't. He pulled his foot off of the brake and stepped on the gas. The car lurched forward, slipping in the muck and finally slamming into an old pine. The creature flew back in a crunch of metal and glass, and hit its head on the tree trunk.

McIntyre shut off the ignition and shakily let himself out of the car. The front end was damaged beyond repair, but he seemed unharmed. He stepped around the wreckage and looked down. The body was twisted between the tree and the car. Bone shards and bits of brain tissue hung from the flayed skin at the back of its skull. He leaned against the passenger door to catch his breath before taking the shovel out of the trunk. He tried to ignore the blood that slowly stained the snow red.

Bear Trap Lake
June 17, 1987

Sean cooked dinner that night. McIntyre had a thudding headache and his back burned so badly that he couldn't lean against a chair. He sat on a stool and watched his son throw strips of chicken breast into the wok.

"The weirdest thing happened to me today," Sean said. He scraped the utensils against the pan as he stir-fried the meat. "Just after you went out canoeing."

McIntyre rubbed his hand against the back of his neck. The smell of cooking chicken made his stomach growl. "Oh?"

"Yeah. I had made myself some ice tea and I was heading out to the hammock when this thing ran through the kitchen."

McIntyre looked at his son. Sean kept his face averted as he added onions, bamboo shoots, water chestnuts and snow peas to the wok. "Then what?" McIntyre said.

"It was little, you know. And at first I thought it was a naked child. But it didn't look like a child." Sean laughed nervously. He shot a glance at his father. "I really did see this."

"I know," McIntyre said. "Tell me what happened."

"Nothing really. It just looked at me and then it scampered out through the living room door. By the time I got there, it was gone." Sean poured sauce over the entire mixture and stirred it. "Weird, huh?"

McIntyre didn't say anything. The first time he had seen one of the creatures had been on the day his father had died. McIntyre had been sixteen, like Sean.

"Dad?" Sean stopped stirring.

"I don't know what it is, Seanie. But if it's any consolation, I saw it too."

Sean grabbed a potholder and spooned the contents of the wok into a bowl. He placed rice in another bowl and brought them both to the table. "It scared me, Dad."

"It should." McIntyre grabbed a bowl and put food onto his plate. "They're dangerous."

* * *

Madison, Wisconsin
August 18, 1971

Books, papers, dirty dishes and empty Coke cans covered the kitchen table. McIntyre was lost in a physics problem, deep within the spiral of numbers, all interconnected and beautiful, when Sharon set the baby in his lap.

Seanie drooled on the page. McIntyre looked up. Sharon smiled in a way that always made him smile back.

"I just realized I have to do a textural analysis of Elizabeth Barrett Browning's work, too. I didn't read the last question on the take-home."

McIntyre wiped the baby's spit off the paper and then rubbed Seanie's mouth. "And you don't have the poems."

"Not a one."

He sighed. He wouldn't be able to concentrate on his physics again until after Sean went to sleep. "I suppose it can't wait until tomorrow."

"Oh, it could," she said. "But I'd flunk. The test is due at my 7:50."

"Who's going with you?"

"You worry too much."

"Who?"

"I'll stop at my sister's on the way."

"All right." He set his physics book on top of the page he had been working on. "But you owe me."

She shrugged, then bent down and kissed him. Her skin smelled like sunshine and perfume. She ran her hand on the baby's bald head, then grabbed a notebook off the table and let herself out the back door. As the screen banged shut, she turned around and waved. He watched her walk through the trees lining Vilas Park.

When McIntyre no longer saw her blonde hair flowing out behind her, he pulled a book on Celtic mythology out from under a stack of papers. He cradled the baby in one arm and thumbed through the copy, searching for a familiar child-like form. The book said that the children were rare, that they haunted families for generations because of simple things, mistakes long gone. McIntyre hoped that the book had the secret to ending the curse. But then Seanie choked, coughed and started to wail. McIntyre placed the book back in its hiding place.

The baby continued to cry for most of the evening, until McIntyre cuddled with him on the living room floor in front of the television.

The shrill ring of the phone woke McIntyre up. The tv was broadcasting static. Sean was asleep on his back. The grey light of dawn filtered in through the uncurtained windows. McIntyre wondered where Sharon was. He grabbed the screaming phone and rubbed the sleep out of his eyes.

"Yes?"

"Is this Sharon Blason's residence?"

"Yeah " McIntyre came fully awake. The voice sounded official.

"This is the Madison Police Department. Are you her husband?"

"Sort of."

"We have a situation down at Camp Randall. A squad will be at your home shortly to pick you up."

McIntyre felt cold. The demonstrations had slowed down. And Sharon hadn't been involved with the movement anyway. "What kind of situation?"

"It's better that the officers tell you in person, Mr. Blason. "

"What kind of situation?" The panic in his voice woke up the baby. Seanie whimpered.

"I'm sorry, sir. But your wife is dead. The squad will take you down to the morgue to identify her body."

"No," McIntyre said. He watched Sean grab the edge of a blanket and fall back into sleep. "I want to see her now."

"Mr. Blason, it's not a good —"

"I don't care." He set the receiver down, got up and washed his face in the kitchen sink. Then he called Mike, his upstairs neighbor, and asked him to come down and watch Sean. Mike arrived at the same time the squad car did.

McIntyre didn't remember getting into the squad or driving the short distance to the stadium. But he did remember watching the iron gates rise in front of him, and passing the two obscure Civil War soldiers decorating the archway. He hadn't known that Sharon crossed behind the stadium on her way home. If he had known that he would have insisted on walking with her. He explained that to the officers, over and over. They said nothing as they led him to her.

She lay beneath one of the tall old trees decorating the path. Her shoes were missing and her dress was ripped. Her long blonde hair was tangled and black with matted blood.

"It's Sharon," he said calmly enough. He had seen death before. He was getting used to it.

But that afternoon, when Seanie had smiled his first real smile, sweet, whimsical and fey, McIntyre had started to cry.

*   *   *

Bear Trap Lake
June 17, 1987

"Dad?"

Sean's whisper echoed across the darkness. In the silence between his question and McIntyre's answer, something fell in the kitchen.

"What?"

"Hear that?"

McIntyre sat up in bed. The moonlight outlined Sean standing in front of the window. The house was quiet. The woods were quiet. All McIntyre heard were the waves lapping against the shore. "No."

"There's something downstairs."

"It's probably a raccoon."

"Yeah, probably."

McIntyre lay back down, wishing Sean would leave so that he could investigate. Below them, a chair scraped across the linoleum.

"Whatever it is," Sean whispered. "It sure wants to get caught."

McIntyre frowned and rolled out of bed. He padded barefoot across the hall and grabbed the hunting rifle. The gun wasn't loaded, but no one had to know that. It was big enough to scare a person, and his presence was enough to frighten a raccoon. He didn't want to think about the possibility of the noise being anything else.

He started down the spiral staircase. Sean was right behind him. "No," McIntyre whispered. "I'm going alone."

"No, you're not," Sean said. He followed his father down the iron stairs and into the kitchen. Nothing moved in the darkness. McIntyre flicked on the light.

The screen door stood open and the garbage pail had been tipped over. Garbage covered the floor. McIntyre relaxed. "We've got to find a better way to store that shit."

He turned toward Sean. His son was staring at the refrigerator. There was a tiny, bloody handprint on the freezer door.

Elmira, Wisconsin
October 20, 1976

"I wonder which one of us it's come for," McIntyre's grandfather said. He stuck a finger in the footprint. "Blood's still wet."

McIntyre started up the porch steps. Grandfather grabbed his arm. "Don't tell me you haven't seen 'em, Davie. They come after a McIntyre has his first woman and they stay with him until he dies."

McIntyre wrenched his arm free. The children he had seen over the years — and killed — had been nightmares. Figures of his imagination taking form in the daylight.

"Running from me won't help either of us, Davie. They may kill our lovers, but it's the McIntyres they want."

McIntyre turned. His grandfather stood beside the bloody footprint. The old man's eyes still twinkled with intelligence.

"What do they want us for?" McIntyre whispered.

"I never took the time to ask one of them." The old man pulled himself up the porch steps. "But they've been there ever since I slept with Tina Wood sixty years ago. And I know your daddy started seeing 'em after he started seeing your ma. And I don't know about you. You kept it real quiet and if you hadn'ta run right now, I would have guessed you hadn'ta seen 'em at all."

"What are they?"

His grandfather shrugged. "Children. I think they're just children."

"It makes no sense."

"Maybe not. But they follow rules, Davie. They hunt alone. If you kill one of theirs, they kill one of yours. If you don't kill them, they kill you. Either way, you don't win."

McIntyre frowned. "You ever tried letting them be?"

"No." The old man took a deep breath. "But I think your daddy did."

The thought made McIntyre ache. He opened the door and let himself inside. His grandfather's house smelled like leather and old books.

"Davie," his grandfather said. "We got a better chance together than we do by ourselves."

"I'll be right back," McIntyre said. He ran toward his grandfather's bedroom, opened the closet and pulled out the old deer rifle. He had to dig for the bullets. He loaded the gun and then ran back for the porch. When he reached the dining room, he heard a scream and a thud. Gingerly he opened the door. His grandfather's heels rested on the top step. His grandfather's head lay in a pool of blood on the concrete sidewalk.

Bear Trap Lake
June 17, 1987

"You know what these things are, don't you, Dad?"

McIntyre didn't answer. He grabbed Sean's elbow to keep them together. "We're going to go back upstairs and get the bullets," McIntyre said. "This time we're going to do it right."

"Dad?"

Metal clanged in the utility room. Suddenly McIntyre knew where the creature was. Sean yanked his arm free and ran in the direction of the noise. Then the lights went out.

"Sean?" McIntyre's voice sounded hollow in the quiet room. He heard a rustle off to his left.

"It's okay, Dad. I'm coming back toward you. Just stay still, okay?"

"All right, Sean."

McIntyre was holding his breath. As his eyes adjusted to the darkness, he could see Sean make his way across the kitchen floor. Behind the boy, a shadow moved. McIntyre opened his mouth to shout a warning, but Sean screamed first. McIntyre started toward his son, thinking that they couldn't kill Seanie. It wasn't fair that they killed Seanie. McIntyre couldn't have protected himself from them this long only to have them kill his son.

Something leaped onto McIntyre's back. Sharp claws digging into his sunburn made him cry out. He whirled, trying to shake the thing off of him, catching its slightly musty odor every time he moved. He slammed into the counter and the creature let go. McIntyre turned and the creature reached for his face, its claws narrowly missing his eyes. McIntyre grabbed the creature's arms, squeezing them until he felt bones snap. The creature screamed, and McIntyre dropped it. It landed heavily on the floor and then ran out into the darkness.

"Sean?" McIntyre called.

He saw his son in the moonlight, lying in the same position they had found his mother in.

"Seanie?"

McIntyre knelt beside Sean and touched his face. McIntyre's fingers came away sticky with blood. Goddammit, he thought. He had let that one go free, and Seanie was still dead.

Fond du Lac, Wisconsin
February 26, 1966

McIntyre's father knelt beside the crumpled body. McIntyre stood beside him.

"I can only tell you this once, Davie," his father said. "You see one of these, you leave it alone. You don't touch it. After tonight, the score will be even. And if one comes after you, you let it. You may not save yourself, but you'll save a lot of others. You understand me, David?"

McIntyre looked at his father's face. The older man was serious. "Yeah, Dad," McIntyre said. "I understand."

His dad went to the shed to get a shovel so that they could dispose of the creature. McIntyre knelt beside the tiny body and noted how the skin along the back of its head flapped open, how the bones splintered and mixed with its grey brain tissue, how its blood melted the snow. He memorized the details because he knew he would never see anything like it again.

Sea Gulls

Gahan Wilson

When I last saw Gahan Wilson, the great cartoonist was displaying a sign with my name and I was holding one bearing his, for the photographer. We were in Columbus, Ohio, where a poster ("Mindkind") for which Wilson had provided the illustration and I the text was being offered. Of course, his reasons for being there included the chance he had to return to Thurber House. Fast growing Columbus was home to the nonpareil writer and cartoonist James Thurber, an idol of Gahan's and, I might add, mine. (It was Jim who reminded us all, "You can't very well be the king of the beasts if there aren't any.")

While in Columbus, the Jim Kisners and Williamsons introduced the creator of *Twilight Zone*'s film column to a chocolatey concoction called a "Frostee." Gahan liked it, thereby making it unlikely that he's exactly what old Jim called a "smugbottle": a man who boasts of his knowledge of wines (also Thurberized as a "fuss-grape"), this story notwithstanding.

A real delight of the first *Masques* was "The Substitute" and here, in his return to this series, is another new Gahan Wilson treat that goes down as easily as if it were made of the smoothest custard. It's so cunningly illustrative one's imagination easily visualizes the artist's own drawings — in particular near the end of "Sea Gulls" when I imagined I *was* looking at a perfect panel of Gahan's.

You may wish to keep in mind another Thurber quotation when you've devoured this deft delectation: "Never be mean to a tiger's wife, especially if you're the tiger."

I have been sitting here, throughout this entire morning, watching the gulls watching me. They come, a small group at a time, carefully unnoticeable, and squat on various branches of a large tree opposite the hotel veranda. When each shift of them have gaped their fill of me, they fly away and their places are taken at once by others of their disgusting species.

Outside of their orderly coming and going, the deportment of these feathered spectators of my discomfort has been calculatedly devoid of anything which might excite the attention of anyone lacking my particular and special knowledge of their loathsome kind. Their demeanor has been more than ordinarily ordinary. They are on their best behavior, now they have sealed my doom.

I stumbled on their true nature, and I curse the day I did, by a complete fluke. It was, ironically, Geraldine herself who called my attention to that little army of them on the beach.

We had been sitting side by side on a large, sun-warmed rock, I in a precise but somewhat Redonesque pose, Geraldine in her usual, space-occupying, sprawl. I was deep in a poetic revery, reflecting on the almost alchemical transition of sand to water to sky while Geraldine, my wife, was absorbed in completely finishing off the sumptuous but rather over-large picnic the hotel staff had prepared for our outing, when she abruptly straightened, a half consumed jar of *paté* clutched forgotten in her greasy fingers, and suddenly emitted that barking coo of hers which has never failed to simultaneously startle and annoy me throughout all the years of our marriage.

"Hughie, look!" she cried. "The gulls are marching!"

"What do you mean, 'marching'?" I asked, doing what I could to conceal my annoyance.

"I mean they're marching, Hughie," she said. "I mean they *are* marching!"

I looked where she pointed, the *paté* jar still in her hand, and a vague complaint died unspoken on my lips as I observed that Geraldine had been scrupulously correct in her announcement. The gulls were, indeed, marching.

Their formation was about ten files wide and some forty ranks deep, and it was well held, with no raggedness about the edges. A line of five or so officer gulls marched at the army's head, and one solitary gull, I assumed their general, marched ahead of them.

The gull general was considerably larger than the other birds, and he had an imposing, eagle-like bearing to him. His army was obviously well drilled, for all the gulls marched in perfect step on their orange claws, and seemed capable of neatly executing endless elaborate maneuvers.

Geraldine and I watched, fascinated, for as long as ten minutes, observing the creatures wheeling about, splitting and rejoining, and carrying out whole routines of complicated, weaving patterns. The display was so astoundingly absorbing that it took me quite some time to realize the fantastic impropriety of the whole proceeding, but at last it dawned on me.

"This will never do," I observed in a firm, quiet tone, and carefully placing my cigar on the edge of the rock, I selected a large, smooth stone and hefted it in my hand.

"Hughie!" Geraldine cried, observing the rock and the look of grim determination on my face. "What are you planning to do?"

"We must discourage this sort of thing the instant we see it," I said. "We must nip it in the bud."

I shot the stone into their midst and they scattered, squawking in a highly satisfactory fashion. I threw another stone, this one rather pointy, and had the pleasure of striking the general smartly on his rear. I turned to Geraldine, expecting words of praise, but of course I should have known better.

"You should not hurt dumb animals," she said, regarding me gently but mournfully as a mother might regard a backward child. "Look, you have made that big one limp!"

"Gulls are birds, not animals," I pointed out. "And their behavior was far from dumb. It was, if you ask me, altogether too smart."

My cigar had gone out so I lit another one, using the gold lighter she had given me a day or so before, and I was so piqued at her that I was tempted to ostentatiously throw it away as casually as I would a match, but she would only have forgiven me with a little sigh and bought me another. I would only be like an infant knocking objects off the tray of his high chair, its bowls and cups replaced with loving care. I had learned, through the years, that there really was no way to get one's rage through to Geraldine.

That night, as we were having dinner on the terrace of the hotel, Geraldine stared out into the darkness and once again drew my attention to an odd action on the part of the gulls. This time her tiny little bark caught me with a spoonful of *consommé* halfway to my lips, and when I started at the sudden sound, a shimmering blob of the stuff tumbled back into the bowl with a tiny plop.

"The gulls, Hughie," she said, in a loud, dramatic whisper as she reached out and tightly clutched my arm. "See how they are staring at you!"

I frowned at her.

"Gulls?" I said. "It's night, my dear. One doesn't see gulls at night. They go somewhere."

But then I peered where she had pointed, and I saw that once again she was right. There, in the branches of the tree which I have mentioned before, were in view perhaps as many as thirty gulls staring at us, or more precisely at me, with their cold, beady little eyes.

"There must be hundreds of them!" she whispered. "They're everywhere!"

Again she was quite correct. The creatures were not only in the tree, they were perched on railings, stone vases, the heads of statues, and all the various other *accoutrements* with which a first-class, traditional French seaboard hotel is wont to litter its premises. They were all, to the last gull among them, staring steadily and unblinkingly at me.

"Do you think," I whispered very quietly to Geraldine, "that anyone else has noticed?"

"I don't believe so," she said, and turned to openly study the people sitting at neighboring tables. "Should we ask them if they have?"

"For God's sake, no!" I said, in a harsh whisper. "What do you think it looks like—being singled out by crowds of gulls to be stared at? How do you think it makes me *feel?*"

"Of course, Hughie," she said, loosing her hold on my arm and patting my hand. "Don't you worry, dearest. We shall just pretend it isn't happening."

Halfway through the wretched dinner the gulls flew off for mysterious reasons of their own, and when it was through I made my excuses and left my wife to attend to herself while I took a thoughtful little stroll.

I had some time ago sketched out the broad design of what I intended to do during our visit to this hotel; had, indeed, begun to plan it the very day Geraldine suggested we come here to celebrate our wedding anniversary, because it had dawned on me even as she spoke, fatally and completely and quite irreversibly, that we had already celebrated far too many anniversaries and that this one should definitely be our last.

But now it was time to put in the fine details, the small, delicate strokes which would spell the difference between disaster and success. Eliminating Geraldine would serve very little purpose if I did not survive the act to enjoy her money afterwards.

I wandered down to the canopied pier where I knew the hotel moored several, brightly-painted little rowboats, and even a couple of dwarfish sailboats, for the use of their guests. I knew full well that the sailboats would strike Geraldine as being far too adventurous, so I concentrated on examining the rowboats.

I was pleasantly surprised to discover that they were even more unseaworthy than I'd dared to hope. I quietly tested them, one after the other, and found that the boat at the end of the pier, a jaunty little thing with a puce hull and a bright gold stripe running around its sides, was especially dangerous. I felt absolutely confident the police would have no trouble at all in convincing themselves that any drowning fatality associated with this highly tippy boat had been the result of a tragic accident.

Just to make sure — I have been accused of being something of a perfectionist — I climbed into the tiny craft, pretended I was rowing, and then suddenly made a move to one side. The boat came so close to capsizing that I had considerable difficulty avoiding unexpectedly tumbling out of it then and there! I exited the craft carefully, with even more respect for its deadliness, and started walking up the path leading back to the hotel, whistling a little snatch of a Chopin mazurka softly to myself as I went.

The path took a turn by a kind of miniature cliff which concealed it from almost all points of view and when I reached this point the mazurka died on my lips as I saw that the ground before me was lumpy and grayish in the moonlight as though it was infested with some sort of disgusting mold, but then I peered closer and saw that the place was horribly carpeted with the softly stirring bodies of countless sea gulls.

They were crowded together, so tightly packed that there was absolutely no space between them, and every one of them was glaring up at me. The menace emanating from their hundreds of tiny eyes was, at the same time, both ridiculous and totally terrifying. It was also positively sickening, and for a brief, absolutely ghastly moment I was afraid that I would faint and fall and be suffocated in the soft, feathery sea of them.

However, I took several very deep breaths and managed to still the pounding in my ears and to steady myself. With great casualness, very slowly and deliberately, I reached into my breast pocket and withdrew a cigar. I lit the cigar and blew a contemptuous puff of smoke at the enormous crowd of gulls at my feet.

"You have exceeded your position in life," I told them, speaking softly and calmly. "You have overstepped your natural authority. But I am on to you."

I drew on the cigar carefully, increasing its ash, and when I'd produced a good half inch, I tapped the cigar so that the ash fell directly and humiliatingly on the top of the head of the remarkably large gull standing directly in front of me. Of course I had recognized him as the general. He did not stir nor blink, nor did any of the others. They continued to glare up at me.

"Whereas you are merely birds," I continued, "and scavenger birds at that, *I* am a human being. I am not only smarter than you are, I am stronger. If you attack me, I will simply shield my eyes with my arm and walk away, and soon other humans will see me and come to my aid."

I took another long pull at my cigar and looked away from them, as if bored.

"I guarantee you," I went on, "that I will not panic. I will survive, merely scratched, to see that you, and a great number of your kin, pay dearly for attacking your betters. Pay painfully. Pay with your lives."

I paused a little in order that my words might sink into their reptilian little heads, and then I began to walk casually along the clearing path, gazing upwards and smoking dreamily as I did so. I did not even watch to see how they slunk, in cowed confusion, out of my way.

The next morning, during breakfast, while I was having my second coffee and Geraldine her second herbal tea, I proposed brightly that we take a short row in the cove. I approached the whole thing in a very airy, casual fashion, but made it clear I would be saddened and a little hurt if she did not accept my whimsical invitation. Naturally I knew the whole idea would strike her as childish and that she would do it only to indulge me. She, herself, would never dream of instigating anything childish, of course. That, in our marriage, was understood to be my function.

To my relief — one never knew with Geraldine — never — she accepted with almost no perceptible hesitation. She even suggested we do it without further ado, seeing as how the sun was bright and the waters of the cove presently smooth and placid. We rose from the table and went directly to the gaily beflagged pier.

We were the first arrivals for water sports that morning and the little puce boat with its gold stripe bobbed fetchingly as it waited for us in the water. In a rather neat piece of seamanship, I managed to get both Geraldine and myself aboard it without her realizing how tiltable a craft it was. Smiling and chatting about how extremely pleasant everything was, I rowed us to an isolated part of the cove behind a rise of the shore which put us out of sight of our fellow vacationers.

Once I had reached this point I let go of the oars, took firm hold of the sides of the boat, and gave it the tipping motion I had practiced with such great success the night before. I was highly discomfited to discover that the little craft had somehow achieved a new seaworthiness.

"Hughie," she asked, "what on earth are you trying to do?"

I looked up at her, perhaps just a little wild-eyed, and suddenly realized that it must be Geraldine's considerable bulk which was stabilizing the boat. I would have to exert a good deal more effort if I was to upset it successfully. I began to shake the boat again, this time with markedly increased determination. I was uncomfortably aware that I had begun to sweat noticeably and that damp blotches were beginning to spread from the armpits of my striped blazer.

"Hughie," she said, a vague alarm starting to dawn in her eyes, "whatever you are doing, you must stop it now!"

I glared at her and began to shake the boat with a new energy verging on desperation.

"I've asked you not to call me Hughie," I told her through clenched teeth. "For *years* I've asked you not to call me Hughie!"

She frowned at me, just a little uncertainly, and had opened her mouth to say something further when, with a gratifyingly smooth, swooping motion, the little golden boat finally tilted over.

For a moment all was blue confusion and bubbles, but then my head broke water and I saw the boat bobbing upside down on the sparkling surface of the cove a yard or two away from me. There was no sign whatsoever of Geraldine so I ducked my head down under the water, peered this way and that, and was pleased to observe a dim, sinking flurry of skirts and kicking feet speedily disappearing into the darker blues far below the bright and cheery green hues flickering just under the surface.

I swam up to the little inverted craft, took hold of it, surveyed the coastline to see if it was empty of witnesses, and saw that this was, indeed, the case. Several gulls were circling overhead, but when I glared up at them and shook my fist in their direction, they flew away with an almost furtive air. I cried for help once or twice for effect, then pushed off from the side of the boat and swam for the shore where I staggered, gasping, up onto the hotel grounds into the view of my astonished fellow guests.

At first the investigation proceeded almost exactly along the lines I had envisioned it would. The general reaction toward me was, of course, one of great pity and everyone, the police included, treated me quite gently. It never appeared to occur to anyone that the business was anything other than a tragic accident.

But then things began to take an increasingly odd turning as the authorities, after a highly confident commencement, found themselves unable to locate Geraldine's cadaver, and by the time I was judged able to sit warmly wrapped on the veranda and overlook their activities, they had become seriously discouraged.

I watched them as they carefully and conscientiously trailed their hooks and nets up and down the cove and in the waters beyond, observing their scuba divers bob and sink repeatedly to no effect, and seeing them all grow increasingly philosophical as Geraldine's large body continued to evade them. There was more and more talk of riptides and rapid ocean currents and prior total vanishments.

Towards the end of this period I was on the veranda consuming a particularly subtle *crêpes fruits de mer,* and rather regretting it had almost come to an end, when the chain of events began which have led to my present distasteful predicament.

Startled by a sudden flurry of noise, I looked up to see a large bird perched on the railing which I had no difficulty in recognizing as the general of the gulls. As I gaped at the creature, he hopped from his perch over to my table, gave me a fierce glare, dropped something which landed with a clink upon my plate, and then flew away emitting maniacal, gullish bursts of laughter.

When I saw what the disgusting beast had dropped amidst the remains of my *crêpes* my appetite departed completely and has not, to be frank, ever been quite the same since. I recognized the object instantly for what it was — the wedding ring I had given my late wife — but to be absolutely sure, I rubbed the ring's interior clear of sauce with my napkin and read what she had caused to be engraved there years ago: "Geraldine and Hughie, forever!"

I carefully wiped the remaining sauce from the ring, and deposited it in the pocket of my jacket. I heard another burst of crazed, avian laughter and, looking up, observed the general of the gulls leering at me from a far railing of the veranda. I determinedly returned to my *crêpes* and made a great show of appearing to enjoy the remainder of my dinner, even to the extent of having an extra *café filtre* after dessert. I then strolled in a languid fashion down to the beach for a little constitutional before retiring.

It was a quiet, clear night. The Mediterranean was smooth and silvery under the full moon, and its waves rolled softly and almost soundlessly into the sand. I gazed up at the sky, checking it for birds, and when I was absolutely sure there were none to be seen, I threw the ring out over the water with all the strength I could muster.

Imagine my astonishment when with a great rush of air the general of the gulls soared out over my shoulder from behind me and, executing what I must admit was a remarkably skillful and accurate dive, reached out with his orange claws and plucked the ring from the air inches above the surface of the water. Emitting a final, lunatic laugh of triumph, he flew up into the moonlight and out of sight.

That night I was awakened from a very troubled sleep by a sound extremely difficult to describe. It was a soft, steady, rhythmic patting, and put me so much in mind of a demented audience enthusiastically applauding with heavily-mittened hands that as I pushed back my covers and lurched to my feet in the darkness of my room, my still half-dreaming mind produced such a vivid vision of a madly-clapping throng in some asylum auditorium that I could observe, with remarkable clarity, the various desperate grimaces on the faces of the nearer inmates.

I groped my way to the curtains, since the sound seemed to emanate from that direction, and when I pulled them aside and looked out the window a muffled shriek tore itself from my lips and I staggered back and almost fell to the carpet for I had suddenly given myself all too clear a view of the source of that weird, nocturnal racket.

There, hanging in the air in the moonlight directly outside my window, was the large, sagging body of my wife, Geraldine. She looked huge, positively enormous, like some kind of horrible balloon. Water poured copiously in silvery fountains from her white lace dress and her bulging eyes, also entirely white, gaped out like prisoners staring through the dark, lank strands of hair which hung down in glistening bars across her dripping, bloated face.

The sound I had heard was being made by the wings of the hundreds of gulls who were holding Geraldine aloft by means of their claws and beaks which they had sunk deeply into her skin and dress, both of which seemed to be stretching dangerously near to the ripping point. She was surrounded by a nimbus of the awful creatures, each one flapping its wings in perfect rhythm with its neighbors in a miracle of cooperative effort.

Sitting on her head, his claws digging almost covetously into her brow, was the gull general. He watched me staring at him and at the tableau he had wrought with obvious satisfaction for a long moment, and then he must have given some command for the gulls began to move in unison and the lolling, pale bulk of Geraldine swayed backwards from the window and then, lifted by the beating of gleaming, multitudinous wings, it wafted upward and inland, over the dark tiles of the roof of the hotel and out of my line of vision.

I had breakfast brought up to my room the next morning for I anticipated, quite correctly as it turned out, a potentially awkward visit from the police and preferred it to take place in reasonably private surroundings.

I had barely finished my first cup of coffee and half a *brioche* when they arrived, shuffling into my room with an air of obvious uncertainty, the inspector looking at me with the downward, shifting gaze which authority tends to adopt when it is not quite sure it is authority.

It seemed that a local farmer hunting just after dawn for a strayed cow had come across the body of Geraldine. It had been tucked into a small culvert on his property and been rather ineffectually covered with branches and leaves and little clods of earth. One particularly unpleasant feature about the corpse was that it had been brutally stripped of the jewelry which Geraldine had been seen to be wearing that morning. Her fingers and wrists and neck had been deeply scratched by the thief or thieves which had clawed her gold from her; the lobes of both her ears had been cruelly torn.

The police could not have been more courteous with me. Their community's main source of income originates from well-to-do vacationers, and the arrest and possible execution of one of them — myself, for instance — because of murder would be bound to produce all sorts of unfortunate and discouraging publicity. They were vastly relieved at the taking of Geraldine's baubles since it suggested not only the sort of common robber they could easily understand and pursue enthusiastically, it gave their imagined culprit a clear motive for spiriting the body away from the water and later trying to hide it.

Taking my cue from them, I confessed myself astonished and saddened to learn that my wife's drowned corpse had been so grossly violated and wished them luck in apprehending the villain responsible as soon as possible. The lot of us, from differing motives, were considerably pleased to have the affair resolved so amicably, and after shaking hands all around and giving them permission to look over my suite — an action understood by us all to be a mere formality — I took my leave of them and assumed my present situation on the veranda.

Just now I've noticed that in the midst of the latest shift of gulls taking their places to observe me from the overlooking tree is the general himself, and since I gather that signifies that something of considerably import is about to transpire, I've cast a sidewise glance at the doors opening out onto the terrace from the hotel's lobby.

Sure enough, I see the approaching police, all of them wearing expressions of unhappiness and great regret. Worse, I see the unmistakable glint of gold in the inspector's cupped hands. The gulls obviously paid another, quieter, visit to my rooms last night in order to leave my dead wife's pretty things behind in some craftily-selected hiding place. Perhaps the general did it personally. It would be like him.

Now I have risen, a *demitasse* held lightly in one hand, and strolled slowly over to the railing of the veranda. There is a considerable drop to the rocks below and if I tumble directly from here to there it will surely put an quick and effective end to a very rapidly developing unpleasant situation so far as I am concerned.

I have stepped up onto the railing which is a very solid structure built wide enough to hold trays of nightcaps or *canapés* and any number of leaning lovers' elbows. The police are calling out to me in rather frantic tones and I hear the soles of their large shoes scuffling and scraping on the stones of the veranda as they rush desperately in my direction.

My eyes and the general's are firmly locked as I step out into space. He lifts his wings and, with an easy beat or two, he rises from his branch.

Our paths cross in midair.

He can fly, but I can only fall.

The Coming of Night,
The Passing of Day

Ed Gorman

The coming of Ed Gorman to the horror and mystery scene has been like the passage of the swiftest kind of day: Sunny and pleasant from the moment one rises through the busiest, most interesting of hours. One moment, it seems, Gorman was just another solid new mystery hand who turned out horror novels on the side, usually bylined Daniel Ransom. The next instant he was the author of *Nightmare Child* and *The Forsaken* (as Ransom), *The Autumn Dead, A Cry of Shadows,* and *Night Kills,* co-editor of the *Stalkers, Dark Crimes* and *Black Lizard* anthologies (under his own name) — not to forget the vastly enjoyable *Mystery Scene* magazine.

Not that it seemed fast to Gorman, who is a lot like his rising career: Pleasantly sunny, interesting and productive, versatile enough to create praised short fiction such as "Drifter" in *Masques III* and western romps *(Death Ground; Blood Game)*. He and his writer wife Carol (*Chelsea* is one of her Young Adult novels staying in print) comprise the first couple I've known in a while to make me think of them as, precisely, "swell folks." Perhaps it's because Ed's unpretentious enough to speak of his limitations ("in longer books. . . I get too concerned about the language and not enough about the plot"), or because he is one who grew up in "violent circumstances" and has had "to fight for dignity and respect."

The quotes come from an interview with this fine writer in *Cemetery Dance* (Summer 1990) where he also discussed the darkly serious nature of some of his later work. The same very personal, bittersweet element that we admire in Ed Gorman so much is what will make his new story, written just for *Masques IV,* stick in most readers' minds.

Penny knew Mr. Rigler's schedule pretty well. After all, Mr. Rigler's eleven-year-old daughter Louise happened to be Penny's best friend.

So Penny knew just when to do it, just when to walk down the alley, just when to climb the slanting covered stairs that led up to the rear apartment, just when to find Mr. Rigler in the wide, sagging double bed where he slept off the hangovers he inflicted on himself after working the night shift at Raylon Manufacturing.

Penny—dressed in a white blouse and jeans and a pair of Keds (Mom always saying "Jesus Christ, kid, you think I'm made outta fucking money?" whenever Penny brought up the subject of Reeboks)—Penny moved through the noonday heat, pretty and shy as one of the soft blue butterflies she liked to lie on the grass sometimes and watch.

On her back was the red nylon pack she carried to school every day. Inside it smelled of the baloney sandwiches and Ho-Hos Mom always packed for her lunch.

She turned off the gravel alley and into the small junkyard of rusting cars that belonged to Mr. Rigler. He was always promising his wife and daughter that he was going to clean up the back yard someday— "Get ridda them eyesores once and for all"—but that was sort of like his promise that he was someday going to stop beating his wife and daughter, too. He hadn't kept that promise, either.

A week ago Mr. Rigler had broken Louise's arm in three places. He'd first hit her in the mouth with his fist and then shoved her over an ottoman. She'd tripped and smashed the arm. Mr. Rigler was pretty drunk, of course. There was so much shouting and yelling that half the block ran into the alley to see what was going on and then two cop cars came screaming down the street and the cops jumped out and they pushed Mr. Rigler around pretty hard, even though he was so drunk he could hardly stand up; and then Mrs. Rigler (who'd been screaming for them to arrest him) started crying and saying how it was all an accident, and the cops looked real frustrated and mad and said you mean you aren't going to press charges, and Mrs. Rigler kept crying and holding on to her husband like he was some kind of prize she didn't want to lose and saying no, she wouldn't press charges because it was all an accident and if those fuckin' cops knew what was good for them they'd get off her fuckin' property and right now. So the cops had left and Mrs. Rigler had taken Louise to the emergency ward.

Next day, Louise came over and showed Penny her cast and talked about how weird it felt to have something like this on your arm and how much her arm hurt and how she'd had to get five different X-rays and how cute the young doctor was. Then she'd started crying, the way she usually did after her father had beaten her or her mother, started sobbing, and Penny had taken her in her arms and held her and said over and over that sonofabitch that sonofabitch, and then Louise had said Why couldn't something happen to *her* father the way it had to Mr. Menetti, who used to beat his wife and child just the same way. But then one day they found Mr. Menetti burned char black in his bed. Seems he'd been drunk and smoking and had dropped his cigarette and the whole bed had gone up in flames.

Fortunately, the afternoon with Louise had gotten a little better. They both liked to smoke cigarettes so Penny got out the Winston Lights she stole one-at-a-time from her mother and they sat in front of the TV and watched MTV and drank Pepsi and told kind of semi-dirty jokes and laughed and gossiped about boys at school and generally had a good time until Bob came home.

Bob was Mom's newest boyfriend. He'd lived with them for a year now. He was a used car salesman, one of the few men on the block to wear a necktie to work, which Mom thought was real cool for some reason. He had black wavy hair and very white teeth and you could tell by the way he looked at you that he really thought he was pretty hot stuff. On all his sport coats you could see a fine white powder of dust from walking around the car lot all day.

Penny hated Bob but Mom loved him. After she'd been dumped by her last boyfriend, Mom had tried to kill herself with tranquilizers. She'd ended up getting her stomach pumped and staying in a mental hospital for three weeks while Penny lived with her aunt. Mom hadn't really snapped out of it for a whole year, till she met Bob. Now Mom was her old self again. "Oh, hon, if Bob'd ever leave me, I just don't know what I'd do," Mom would always say after she and Bob had had a fight. And Penny would get scared. Maybe next time Mom actually would kill herself.

She thought of all these things in an instant as she watched Bob's slow, sly smile.

Now, he stood there staring down at Penny so long that Louise finally got up and said it was time she git and so she got, and Bob said then, "Your Mom's not gonna be home for another couple hours."

But Penny didn't want to think about Bob now. She wanted to think about Mr. Rigler. The way she'd thought about Mr. Menetti before him and Mr. Stufflebeam before him (Mr. Stufflebeam was another who frequently used his fists on his family).

She went up the rear stairs quickly.

The covered porch smelled of heat and spaghetti from last night.

From the downstairs apartment came the sounds of dorky country music and a little baby crying. In this kind of heat, babies usually cried.

At the screen door, Penny knocked once and then listened very carefully. She didn't hear anybody talking or moving around. Louise, she knew, was across the city at a movie with her cousin. Mrs. Rigler was at the restaurant where she was a short-order cook.

And Mr. Rigler was sleeping off his drunk. He'd get up at two, shave, shower, fix himself something to eat, and then head for the factory in an old Ford that was nearly as junky as those dying beasts he kept in the backyard.

"Mr. Rigler?" she called.

She could hear a window air-conditioner roaring and rattling in the distance. But nothing else.

"Mr. Rigler?"

She waited a full two minutes and then went inside.

The apartment smelled of cigarettes and beer and spaghetti. Dirty dishes packed the sink. Without both arms, Louise could hardly do housework.

Penny went through the kitchen into the living room where aged overstuffed furniture was all covered with decorator sheets so they'd look newer.

The bedrooms and the bathroom were down a hall.

She was halfway down the hall when she picked up his snoring. He was really out.

When she reached the door, she peeked in and saw him on the bed. He wore a sleeveless T-shirt. You could see his huge hairy belly riding up and down beneath it as he breathed. His face was dark with stubble. The panther tattoo on his fleshy right arm looked as faded as the flesh itself. He smelled of beer and onions and cigarettes and farts. Penny's stomach grabbed momentarily.

She stood watching him. Just watching him. She wasn't even sure why.

She thought of Louise's arm. The way it must hurt. She thought about the time Louise's Mom had gotten her collarbone broken. And the time he'd given her not one but two black eyes.

He was the same kind of man Mr. Menetti had been. The same kind of man Mr. Stufflebeam had been.

"You sonofabitch," she said to the man who lay there in the silence of the bedroom. "You fucking sonofabitch."

Then she got to work.

* * *

Penny was back in her apartment watching a *Happy Days* rerun —
she dreamed of a world as nice as the one Richie Cunningham lived
in — when she heard the fire truck rumbling down the brick street,
siren singing.

They'd hurry in there with their axes and their hoses, but it would
be too late. Just as it had been too late with Mr. Menetti and Mr.
Stufflebeam. "Asphyxiation" was the word that had been in all the
newspaper articles.

After a time, she went out on the fire escape and looked across
five back yards to where the two red fire trucks filled the alley. Maybe
as many as forty or fifty neighbors had come out to watch.

The ambulance came next, a big white box, two attendants rushing
over to the back stairs.

After more time, Penny went in and opened a Pepsi and turned
on MTV. She really liked the new Whitney Houston video. She hoped
they'd play that before three o'clock, which was when she had to be
out of the apartment. Before Bob got home.

At two-thirty, she was in the bedroom, tugging on a fresh Madonna
T-shirt, when she heard the front door open and shut.

It could have been Mom but she knew better.

She knew damned well who it was.

By the time she was finished pulling on the T-shirt, he was leaning
in the doorway, a smirk on his mouth and a cigarette in his hand.

"Hey, babe, how's it goin'?"

"I'm on my way out."

"Oh, yeah? To where?"

"The park."

"Your Mom don't like for you to go to the park."

"Yeah," Penny said, staring right at Bob and knowing he'd get her
meaning. "She's afraid a child molester will get me."

He was still smiling, even when he took two quick steps across the
room to her, even when he slapped her hard across the mouth.

"That crack about the child molester s'posed to be funny, you little
bitch?"

She fought her tears. She didn't ever want him to see her cry. Ever.

"Huh? That s'posed to be funny?"

She didn't want to say anything, either, but she hated him too much
and words were her only weapon. "I could tell her. I could tell her
what you been doin' to me in the bathroom."

At first, Bob visibly paled. This was the first time she'd ever
threatened him this way. And there was great satisfaction in watching

him lose his self-confidence and look scared.

But he quickly recovered himself. She could see cunning now in his stupid blue gaze; he was Bob the used car salesman once again.

"You know what she'd do if you told her about us?"

"She'd throw you out," Penny said. "That's what she'd do."

"Yeah. Yeah, she probably would. But you know what she'd do then?"

He drew a long, white finger slowly across his throat. "She'd kill herself. 'Cause I'm the only hope she's got. The only god-damned hope she's got in the whole wide world. She's never had no other man stay with her as long as I have, not even your old man, that sorry sonofabitch."

She started to say something but he held up his hand for silence.

"I'm goin' in the bathroom and I want you in there in five minutes."

"No."

He stared at her. "Five minutes, you understand me, you little bitch?"

She shook her head.

He grinned. He was the old Bob again. "Five minutes, babe. Then I'll take you out to the mall and buy you a new blouse. How'd that be?"

She had the satisfaction of watching him panic again.

She'd taken three steps back to the nightstand and picked up the phone.

She didn't threaten, this time. She simply dialed her Mom's work number, and before he could slap the phone from her hand, she said, "This is Penny Baker. I'd like to speak to my mom please. Thank you."

"You little bitch —"

"Hi, Mom."

She almost laughed. Bob nearly looked funny. He'd totally lost it. Was starting to pace back and forth, running a trembling hand through his hair.

"Hi, honey, everything all right?"

"I just wanted to talk to you, Mom."

"Hon, I'm kinda busy right now. Is it real important?"

"It's about Bob."

He made a big fist and shook it at her.

"Bob?" Mom said. "What about him, hon?"

"Just that —"

But Mom didn't wait. "Nothin' happened to him, did it?"

"No, Mom, I —"

"Oh, God, hon, I have nightmares all the time about somethin' happening to him. Getting hit by a car in a crosswalk or gettin' mugged somewhere or—"

Penny heard the need then, heard it more clearly than ever before, the childlike need her mother felt for Bob. Bob hadn't been exaggerating when he'd said that her mother would kill herself if he left.

"You gonna tell me, hon?" Mom said, still sounding crazy with fear.

"Tell you?"

"Why you called, hon? Jesus, Pen, this is scaring the shit out of me."

"I just called to—"

"—yes?—"

"Tell you that Bob—"

And now Bob moved closer. She could smell his sweat and his aftershave. And in his eyes now she could see pleading; *oh, please, Penny, don't tell her; please don't tell her.*

"Tell me what, hon? Jesus, please just *say* it."

"That Bob's going to take me to the mall."

And then Mom started laughing. "God, hon, that's what you wanted to tell me?"

Bob knew enough not to approach her. He just stood there a few feet from her and held his hands up to God as if in supplication and gratitude.

"That's all you wanted to tell me?"

"Yes," Penny said. "That's all I wanted to tell you."

A few minutes later, Bob was in the bathroom. The water running and the medicine cabinet closing. He liked to get himself all cleaned up for her down there, he always said.

Penny lay on the bed. She listened to a distant lawn mower on the summer afternoon.

The water in the bathroom stopped running.

After a time the door opened and he said, "You can come in here now."

She didn't get up. Not at first.

She lay there for a time and thought of Mr. Rigler and Mr. Menetti and Mr. Stufflebeam.

The smoke and the fire and the too-late screams.

She saw Bob lying on such a bed now. And heard his own too-late screams.

"You don't want to keep the old Bob waitin' now, do you, babe?" he called again.

Oh, yes, someday it would happen; somehow. Bob on the bed with his too-late screams.

And then she got up and went into the bathroom.

Please Don't Hurt Me

F. Paul Wilson

Because of my admiration for *The Keep,* there was no writer I wanted more to be a part of the initial *Masques* than F. Paul Wilson. About his novel, in the enjoyable *Horror: 100 Best Books* (London, 1988), I wrote: "It's difficult. . . to imagine anything essential to the genre's form which was omitted," and expressed the opinion that *The Keep* could be an exemplar for hopeful novelists in "any modern genre (including the mainstream — which could *use* an infusion of originality, plot, suspense and so forth)."

So I was immensely pleased when Paul wrote "Soft" for *Masques* and when (in '89) he and Tom Doherty titled the practicing physician's first story collection *Soft and Others.* (Dr. Wilson's second collection, *Ad Statum Perspicuum* — "toward invisibility" — was the October '90 Author's Choice from Pulphouse, by the bye.)

Five writers from the inaugural *Masques* antho are again in attendance, and two — each gentleman answering to the name Wilson (Gahan is the other) — return, herein, for the first time.

F. Paul hasn't been idle since 1984. In addition to writing novels called *The Tomb, The Touch, Reborn,* and *Black Wind* — Dean Koontz called the latter "a stunner" — he has edited the second Horror Writers of America anthology. The burden of producing it has taken Wilson out of, into, again out of, and back into *Masques IV—*

With a possibly tongue-in-cheek, all-dialogue story that seemed to me so much an all-unknowing logical continuation of the young life sensitively delineated by Ed Gorman that I could not resist placing the tales back-to-back. Perhaps you'll conclude there's a happy ending, of sorts, to each fine story.

"Real nice place you've got here."

"It's a dump. You can say it — it's okay. Sure you don't want a beer or something?"

"Honey, all I want is you. C'mon and sit next to me. Right over here on the couch."

"Okay. But you won't hurt me, will you?"

"Now, honey — Tammy's your name, isn't it?"

"Tammy Johnson. I told you that at least three times in the bar."

"That's right. Tammy. I don't remember things too good after I've had a few."

"I've had a few too and I remember your name. Bob. Right?"

"Right, right. Bob. But now why would someone want to hurt a sweet young thing like you, Tammy? I told you back there in the bar you look just like that actress with the funny name. The one in *Ghost*."

"Whoopi Goldberg."

"Oh, I swear, you're a funny one. Funny and beautiful. No, the other one."

"Demi Moore."

"Yeah. Demi Moore. Why would I want to hurt someone who looks like Demi Moore? Especially after you were nice enough to invite me back to your place."

"I don't know why. I never know why. But it just seems that men always wind up hurting me."

"Not me, Tammy. No way. That's not my style at all. I'm a lover, not a fighter."

"How come you're a sailor, then? Didn't you tell me you were in that Gulf War?"

"That's just the way things worked out. But don't let the uniform scare you. I'm really a lover at heart."

"Do you love me?"

"If you'll let me."

"My father used to say he loved me."

"Oh, I don't think I'm talking about that kinda love."

"Good. Because I didn't like that. He'd say he loved me and then he'd hurt me."

"Sometimes a kid needs a whack once in a while. I know my pop loved me, but every once in a while I'd get too far out of line, like a nail that starts working itself loose from a fence post, and then he'd have to come along every so often and whack me back into place. I don't think I'm any the worse for it."

"Ain't talking about getting 'whacked,' sailor man. If I'd wanted to talk about getting 'whacked' I woulda said so. I'm talking 'bout getting *hurt*. My daddy hurt me lotsa times. And he did it for a long, long time."

"Yeah? Like what did he do to hurt you?"

"Things. And he was all the time making me do things."

"What sort of things?"

"Just...things. Doin' things to him. Things to make him feel good. Then he'd do things to me that he said would make me feel good but they never did. They made me feel crummy and rotten and dirty."

"Oh. Well, uh, didn't you tell your mom?"

"Sure I did. Plenty of times. But she never believed me. She always told me to stop talking dirty and then *she'd* whack me and wash my mouth out with soap."

"That's terrible. You poor thing. Here. Snuggle up against me now. How's that?"

"Fine, I guess, but what was worse, my momma'd tell Daddy and then he'd get mad and *really* hurt me. Sometimes it got so bad I thought about killing myself. But I didn't."

"I can see that. And I'm sure glad you didn't. What a waste that would've been."

"Anyway, I don't want to talk about Daddy. He's gone and I don't hardly think about him anymore."

"Ran off?"

"No. He's dead. And good riddance. He had an accident on our farm, oh, some seven years ago. Back when I was twelve or so."

"That's too bad...I think."

"People said it was the strangest thing. This big old tractor tire he had stored up in the barn for years just rolled out of the loft and landed right on his head. Broke his neck in three places."

"Imagine that. Talk about being in the wrong place at the wrong time."

"Yeah. My momma thought somebody musta pushed it, but I remember hearing the insurance man saying how there's so many accidents on farms. Bad accidents. Anyway, Daddy lived for a few weeks in the hospital, then he died."

"How about that. But about you and me. Why don't we—?"

"Nobody could explain it. The machine that was breathing for him somehow got shut off. The plug just worked its way out of the wall all by itself. I saw him when he was just fresh dead—first one in the room, in fact."

"That sounds pretty scary."

"It was. Here, let me unzip this. Yeah, his face was purple-blue and his eyes were all red and bulgy from trying to suck wind. My momma was sad for awhile, but she got over it. Do you like it when I do you like this?"

"Oh, honey, that feels good."

"That's what Daddy used to say. Ooh, look how big and hard you got. My momma's Joe used to get big and hard like this."

"Joe?"

"Yeah. Pretty soon after Daddy died my momma made friends with this man named Joe and after a time they started living together. Like I said, I was twelve or so at the time and Joe used to make me do this to him. And then he'd hurt me with it."

"I'm sorry to hear that. Don't stop."

"I won't. Yours is a pretty one. Not like Joe's. His was crooked. Maybe that's why his hurt me even more than Daddy's."

"How'd you finally get away from him?"

"Oh, I didn't. He got hurt."

"Really? Another farm accident?"

"Nah. We weren't even on the farm no more. We was livin' in this dumpy old house up Lottery Canyon way. My momma still worked but all Joe did was fiddle on this big old Cadillac of his — you know, the kind with the fins?"

"Yeah. A fifty-nine."

"Whatever. He was always fiddlin' with it. And he always made me help him — you know, stand around and watch what he was doin' and hand him tools and stuff when he asked for them. He taught me a lot about cars, but if I didn't do everything just right, he'd hurt me."

"And I'll bet you hardly ever did everything 'just right'."

"Nope. Never. Not even once. How on earth did you know?"

"Lucky guess. What finally happened to him?"

"Those old brakes on that old Caddy just up and failed on him one night when he was making one of his trips down the canyon road to the liquor store. Went off the edge and dropped about a hundred feet."

"Killed?"

"Yeah, but not right away. He got tossed from the car and then the car rolled over on him. Broke his legs in about thirty places. Took awhile before anybody even realized he was missin' and took almost an hour for the rescue squad to get to him. And they say he was screamin' like a stuck pig the whole time."

"Oh."

"Something wrong?"

"Uh, no. Not really. I guess he deserved it."

"Damn right, he did. Never made it to the hospital though. Went into shock when they rolled the car off him and he saw what was left of his legs. Died in the ambulance. But here...let me do this to you. *Hmmmmmmmm.* You like that?"

"Oh, God."

"Does that mean yes?"

"You'd better believe that means yes!"

"My boyfriend used to love this."

"Boyfriend? Hey, now wait a minute—"

"Don't get all uptight now. You just lie back there and relax. My *ex*-boyfriend. *Very* ex."

"He'd better be. I'm not falling for any kind of scam here."

"Scam? What do you mean?"

"You know—you and me get started here and your boyfriend busts in and rips me off."

"Tommy Lee? Bust in here? Oh, hey, I don't mean to laugh, but Tommy Lee Hampton will not be bustin' in here or anywheres else."

"Don't tell me he's dead too."

"No-no. Tommy Lee's still alive. Still lives right here in town, as a matter of fact. But I betcha he wishes he didn't. And I betcha he wishes he'd been nicer to me."

"I'll be nice to you."

"I hope so. Tommy and Tammy—seemed like we was made for each other, don't it? Sometimes Tommy Lee was real nice to me. A *lot* of times he was real nice to me. But only when I was doin' what he wanted me to do. Like this...like what I'm doin' to you now. He taught me this and he wanted me to do it to him all the time."

"I can see why."

"Yeah, but he'd want me to do him in public. Or do other things. Like when we'd be driving along in the car he'd want me to—here, I'll show you..."

"Oh...my...*God!*"

"That's what he'd always say. But he'd want me to do it while we were drivin' beside one of those big trucks so the driver could see us. Or alongside a Greyhound bus. Or at a stop light. Or in an elevator—I mean, who knew when it was going to stop and who'd be standing there when the doors open? I'm a real lovable girl, y'know? But I'm not *that* kind of a girl. Not ay-tall."

"He sounds like a sicko."

"I think he was. Because if I wouldn't do it when he wanted me to, he'd get mad and then he'd get drunk, and then he'd hurt me."

"Not another one."

"Yeah. Can you believe it? I swear I got the absolute worst luck. He was into drugs too. Always snorting something or popping one pill or another, always trying to get me to do drugs with him. I mean, I drink some, as you know —"

"Yeah, you sure can put those margaritas away."

"I like the salt, but drugs is just something I'm not into. And he'd get mad at me for sayin' no — called me Nancy Reagan, can you believe it? — and hurt me something terrible."

"Well, at least you dumped him."

"Actually, he sort of dumped himself."

"Found himself someone else, huh?"

"Not exactly. He took some ludes and got real drunk one night and fell asleep in bed with a cigarette. He was so drunk and downered he got burned over most of his body before he finally woke up."

"Jesus!"

"Jesus didn't have nothin' to do with it — except maybe with him survivin'. Third degree burns over ninety per cent of Tommy Lee's body, the doctors at the burn center said. They say it's a miracle he's still alive. If you can call what he's doing livin'."

"But what — ?"

"Oh, there ain't much left to him. He's like a livin' lump of scar tissue. Looks like he melted. Can't walk no more. Can barely talk. Can't move but two or three fingers on his left hand, and them just a teensie-weensie bit. Some folks that knew him say it serves him right. And that's just what I say. In fact I do say it — right to his face — a couple of times a week when I visit him at the nursing home."

"You. . .visit him?"

"Sure. He can't feed himself and the nurses there are glad for any help they can get. So I come every so often and spoon feed him. Oh, does he hate it!"

"I'll bet he does, especially after the way he treated you."

"Oh, that's not it. I make *sure* he hates it. You see, I put things in his food and make him eat it. Just yesterday I stuck a live cockroach into a big spoonful of his mashed potatoes. Forced it into his mouth and made him chew. Crunch-crunch, wiggle-wiggle, crunch-crunch. You should have seen the tears — just like a big baby. And then I —

"Hey. What's happened to you here? You've gone all soft on me. What's the matter with — ?

"Hey, where're you goin'? We were just starting to have some fun...Hey, don't leave...Hey, Bob, what'd I do wrong?...What'd I say?...*Bob!* Come back and—

"I swear...I just don't understand men."

Splatter Me an Angel

James Kisner

Very little of Jim Kisner's writing is categorizable. None is remotely standard fare. If a publisher offered him enough to write a novel combining the countless icons of horror, he'd accept it, none too happily — then reoriginate the vampire, the manmade monster, the werewolf, and the child-in-peril and end-of-the-world themes (plus a few more) in such fresh ways that readers new to horror would forever after remain convinced that James Kisner created them all. His "voice" in the novels *Earthblood, Zombie House, Strands, Poison Pen, Night Glow,* and the upcoming *The Quagmire* is also fresh — the sassiest in-your-face style this genre has heard in years.

Dark Harvest has recognized the unmistakable talents of this droll Elvira and Linnea Quigley admirer and contracted to make Kisnerfiction a third of *Night Visions 9.*

An early *Masques* tale of Kisner, "The Litter," has been reprinted so often and in so many forms that Jim needed something really different — strong — to top it. After furiously writing four stories in a week, he let me read them for *M IV.* Half jumped out at me snarling, going for the throat, simultaneously turning playful as a puppy.

This one, with the unforgettable title, was my favorite of all four.

The angels came that morning for Ed.

He was lying face-down on the sidewalk in a pool of his own blood and vomit, waiting for them.

Before he walked down the tunnel towards the light, he asked the angels for a little time to think things over. The angels told him time was meaningless now. He could have as much as he wanted.

Ed thanked the angels.

He began to think.

Why am I here? was his primary thought. Then he remembered:

* * *

It was summer, perhaps a couple of years ago. Years were mere blips in his consciousness as he considered time past. Micro-blips. He could view a year in a microsecond. A nanosecond. Whatever increments smaller than that he could not comprehend.

But it wasn't much more than a couple of years; he was sure of that.

He saw a woman getting down from the bus, as he sat on a bench watching. Her legs were clad in dark nylon, her knees covered by a swaying dress which the wind threatened to whip up around her thighs. That didn't happen, no matter how hard Ed wished for it.

He was between women at the time. Actually, he had not been between any woman for a long time. His luck with the ladies was never too great. He had two failed marriages to confirm that, plus a less than exciting dating life. He spent a great deal of time in the bar on 32nd Street, a semi-respectable joint called Lou's Diamond Bar, where women came in frequently.

Mostly, the women patrons ignored Ed, though he was not unattractive. He had dark hair, a strong, square chin and dressed neatly, and he was only thirty-five. Maybe he was just too ordinary. Perhaps he lacked charisma. Or maybe it was because he wanted a woman so much that his desperation kept them away. Or maybe he just didn't know the right moves; he often observed other men who seemed to have a different woman every night. Some of these guys were butt-ugly and had foul habits. Ed couldn't figure out their secret.

There *had* to be a secret.

Being in a womanless state, as could be expected, honed Ed's desire for women to a fine edge, to the brink of a vast despair which seemed more awesome with each passing day. He wasn't sure how much longer he could endure.

So he watched them.

As the woman now in his sights finished her descent from the bus and walked, high-heeled, down the boulevard, prim and precious, Ed suddenly was filled with a revelation:

Women are disposable.

His mind almost caved in on itself as the underlying meaning of that concept rushed in to fill the spaces between his beleaguered brain cells. It was a concept, Ed quickly grasped, that could change the face of the world, and Ed had thought of it on his own, right there in the middle of the afternoon, while watching women get on and off the busses.

It was a concept destined to jerk him up out of the funk in which he languished.

Women being disposable, he didn't need to consider them human beings any longer. He didn't need to consider them at all.

With this revelation simmering in his mind, Ed's life changed entirely.

So many women walked the streets, just going from one place to another, probably not contemplating sex.

Ed would sit in the bar, waiting for them to approach him. And as soon as he had realized they were disposable, he found that many more women came to him, as if they *wanted* to be used like tissues. As if they were content to be mere depositories for Ed's teeming sperm.

Ed treated them like dirt. He made them do nasty things. He made them squeal like pigs. He cursed them for whores. He pissed on them. He refused to wear condoms.

They loved it.

For once in his life, Ed had all the women he needed; more than enough. It was like—when he was sitting in a bar, just smoking a cigarette and drinking a beer—like they sensed his disdain for them. His indifference was like a magnet.

After a while, Ed even grew tired of women, eventually developing a mild distaste for the opposite sex. He swore off women for a couple of weeks.

They still flocked to him, offering to buy him drinks, offering to give him blow jobs right there in the bar, offering to do threesomes with other women, giving him autographed pornographic pictures of themselves.

Ed fended them off. He blew smoke rings of disgust in their direction. He quaffed beer and belched loudly to ward them off. He stopped bathing and shaving.

Nothing kept them away. But Ed refused to participate.

The magical purpose of the universe which Ed had absorbed in that single instant on the bench kept asserting itself, however:

Women are disposable; *use* them.

Ed stayed away from Lou's for a few days and returned to sitting on the bench at the end of the day, watching women getting on and off the bus.

He was not even mildly aroused by the sight of a tightly-clad thigh in nylon, the thrust of a pair of aerodynamically superb breasts, the perfectly pert embouchure of pouting crimson lips, or the glitter in the eyes of the most sparkling blonde.

Life had become dull.

Repetitive.

Redundant.

With knowledge had come the responsibility of knowing. Some things, once learned, could not be pushed aside; they festered forever in the mind, like the multiplication tables, or one's Social Security number, or like an embarrassing moment from childhood.

With responsibility also came duty. Duty demanded that a man who had knowledge make use of it.

But, Ed reasoned with himself, he was not content. That women were disposable had been the most staggering revelation of his life so far, but, like anything of a revelatory nature, its novelty had worn off. You could only get saved once; you could only lose your virginity once; you could only grasp a particular staggering concept once.

Ed realized the underlying problem. There were too many things that you could do only one time. The second time was always different; so was the third, the fourth, and, so on, until the end.

Never, Ed thought, do anything for the first time.

Days passed. A discontented Ed spent most of his spare time feeling sorry for himself, sitting on the bench. Sometimes he sat there late into the evening, until the busses stopped running. People in the street would pass by him, regard him with scorn or pity, as if he were a vagrant, then go on.

Ed ignored them.

He was in stasis. He was, in fact, ignoring the universe.

Then one night, an angel appeared, floating just a few feet above the ground.

Ed yawned.

"I have come," the angel said, "to show you The Way."

Ed barely moved his eyes. He could see the angel well enough. It had an epicene, fey look about it. Its wings were so obviously for effect and not function. Its long white robe was so obviously part of the stereotype, as was the musical voice.

"I have no religion," Ed said.

"Even as I manifest before you?"

"An angel? Give me a break. If I'm going to go crazy, I think a bug-eyed monster would be more in order. Don't you?"

"I don't know what a bug-eyed monster is," the angel said in its lyrical, all-too-soothing voice.

"I get a *dumb* angel on top of it all. Why don't you go away? Send me a devil instead."

"You don't mean that."

"Goodness is boring. You should know that. That's why people don't believe in angels any more. They'd rather believe in bad things. Bad things you can understand. Good things are just plain unnoteworthy. Try to sell newspapers with good news and you'll go broke."

"May I tell you, Ed, that you are quite eloquent?" The angel's tone was mellifluous, genuinely admiring.

"Thank you."

"Your eloquence is born of despair, I realize — the despair that comes from contemplating the nature of the universe — but, still, I have to commend you for it."

"Now that you've admired my eloquence, would you please go away and let me suffer in peace?"

"I can't. I have to show you The Way." The angel pronounced the last two words with inspired emphasis.

"The way to what?"

"I hesitate to say 'salvation,' because that doesn't interest you."

"Too true, bud, or, sister."

The angel didn't flinch; nor did it reveal its sex as Ed hoped it might. Instead, it shook its head. "You're a hard case."

"Don't I know it."

"You need another revelation, perhaps?"

"What would *you* offer? Some kind of namby-pamby, goody-two-shoes philosophy? Is that what you're peddling?"

"No. Of course not. I wouldn't insult your intelligence."

"Well, I guess I can take another revelation. Why not?"

"You're a troubled man. You need something to live by."

"Well, shoot!"

"What do you mean?"

"Give me the revelation."

The angel fluttered a few inches higher, so it could look down upon Ed with its painfully obvious beatitude. It seemed to be thinking.

Ed couldn't help but cast his gaze upward now. He was merely trying to look up the angel's gown. But, strain as he might, he could see nothing; not even pubic hair. He tried to hide his disappointment by making his face receptive-looking to the angel. After all, the angel did promise to give him a revelation.

Finally, the angel waved its hands, causing a shaft of golden light to fall on Ed from out of the night sky.

"Women," the angel said, "are *prey.*"

As the angel floated away, Ed's brain had intercourse with itself. The right half humped the left half and vice-versa. The two hemispheres did a sixty-nine, throbbing in Ed's skull with cerebral lust. Had he heard the angel right?

Women are prey?

What kind of revelation was that? He compared it to his former revelation.

It made sense.

If women were disposable, then they were not only prey, but the *perfect* prey. Indeed, the first revelation was almost the same as this one; Ed had merely misinterpreted it.

He arose from the bench and walked home, his brain still engaging in lewd acts, while he mulled over the phantasmagorical scope of the revelation.

It gave life a new meaning.

It gave death a new meaning.

It gave Ed a new purpose.

The next day, he returned to Lou's bar.

Less than five minutes after Ed sat down, he was approached by a tall black woman with a bustline that resembled the twin turbines of a science fiction vehicle. She looked like she might be diesel-powered. Her hair was streaked with purple and orange and she had *eight* earrings in each ear.

"Hi," she said, taking the cigarette from between Ed's fingers and inserting it between her thickly-rouged full lips. Her lips were like two disparate beasts, like animated, imaginary things that could perform feats no real lips could. They wrapped around the end of Ed's cigarette so lusciously and with such accompanying movement that Ed was reminded of a tornado.

She opened her mouth briefly, curled her tongue around the cigarette, flicked it, and, leaning forward, put it in Ed's mouth.

Not many women could do that trick with their *tongues.*

He tasted lipstick on the cigarette. Not a bad taste. A womany taste. From a tasty woman.

"Hi," he said as the woman leaned even closer to him, almost falling into his lap. She wore a tight tube top through which he could see engorged thumb-sized nipples. She had on tight, shiny black leather slacks with a zipper that went from her navel down through her crotch and came out on the other side at the apex of her butt cheeks.

Despite his disdain for women, Ed found himself interested. The new revelation must be working, though he still doubted any of the old magic could still be there.

Ed sucked on the cigarette, highly aware of her saliva on its end, blew smoke sideways, and said, "I'm Ed."

"Wanda," she replied. "It all right if I sit with you, White Boy?"

"I'm not a boy."

"You like *hot* chocolate?"

"Any marshmallows come with it?

Wanda laughed. "That's the first time anyone ever had a good comeback for that line, mister." She draped her right arm over his shoulder. He ordered her a drink.

"Never do anything for the first time," he told Wanda.

They went back to his apartment. Perhaps in anticipation, Ed had cleaned it thoroughly before going to the bar. The place sparkled like the sheen on Wanda's ass. Even the bed was made.

Ed gave Wanda another drink — she liked gimlets — and sat on the edge of the bed with her and sipped a beer.

"You're not a working girl, are you?"

"Me? Hell, no. Do I *look* like a whore?"

"Well, to be honest, yes."

Wanda laughed. "Okay. Maybe I do dress up too much."

"It's okay with me. I like your outfit."

"Even the pants?"

"Yep. I never saw that kind of zipper before."

"It's made for action, honey. One zip and both sides fall down at once." She stood up. "Wanna see?"

"Sure."

Wanda reached behind her, tugged the zipper down the back of her ass, reached between her legs and pulled it up to her navel. She popped a snap and peeled down one leg of the slacks, revealing a thigh that made Ed think of polished ebony.

She quickly peeled the other leg. She stood there a few seconds, a broad grin on her face. She still had the tank top on, and it seemed to be even sexier with her lower regions on display.

Ed undressed slowly, deliberately. He focused on the black triangle he knew was twitching between Wanda's legs.

He twitched a little himself.

It was pretty good sex. Back before he'd had his first revelation, he would have considered it great sex. But his new awareness had taken the edge off total enjoyment.

Of course, now he had his new revelation to stimulate him, but he was saving it for later.

With a little effort, some imaginative placement of pieces, and a lot of sweat, Ed managed to get all of Wanda into two trash bags.

He took the bags downstairs, one at a time, and deposited them in the dumpster across the street, behind the hardware store. Ed returned to his apartment and cleaned up. The bed was a particular mess. He made a mental note to himself that he would have to buy new sheets.

Cleaning up the kitchen cutlery wasn't that bad, and the blood came up from the kitchen floor with a lot of paper towels. When he was finished, he had another trash bag to carry outside. This one he just left on the curb for the morning pick-up.

As he ascended the stairs the last time that night, he silently thanked the angel for the new revelation.

Life was good.

For the next year or so, Ed experienced the joy of sex again. Women flocked to him. He screwed them. He killed them. He stuffed them in trash bags. He left them in the dumpster across the street.

He experimented with ways of putting the women in the bags until he found the perfect arrangement for two bags, including the soiled paper towels and sheets. The only real problem with the whole thing was buying so many sheets and trash bags.

No one seemed to notice that women that went away with Ed never came back.

Women were disposable, after all.

Women were prey.

It was a big city. He'd have to dispose of many, many women before their disappearances would be noted. And who would suspect good old Ed, anyhow? He was just an average guy who happened to like having different women two or three times a week. Lots of guys who hung out in bars were like him.

The angel had saved not his life, but the *quality* of his life, which was much more important.

Ed was happy. His brain no longer contorted itself in multiple sexual positions while trying to understand things. He could appreciate the absolute ecstasy of sex again, because he always climaxed twice every time he was with a woman.

The second time was in his head, of course. His testicles couldn't manufacture two wads in an evening. Not any more—not when the second climax—the cerebral one—was so exquisite.

Life was fantastic. The women came to him with little or no effort on his part. They allowed him to do anything. He sometimes thought they even *knew* how the evening would end, but that they didn't care.

Yes, life was good, fantastic, wonderful, exciting.

But it was becoming boring.

Ed was sitting on the bench as he had before, awaiting a revelation. Had his angel forgotten him? He really needed its help now. What was there beyond the last revelation? How could he ascend to the next rung of enlightenment and spiritual pleasure?

The angel did not come.

Ed was about ready to leave, which meant he was about to give up on life, embrace its boredom and swear off women again.

Then *she* came along.

A woman who even in the dim light cast by the street lamp a half block away was stunning. Her movements were a study in fluid locomotion and the dynamics of kinetic science. Her breasts were two living, separate animals, hunching against the fabric of her white blouse like horny rabbits. Her stomach seemed to undulate in the throes of orgasm even as she walked. Her thighs smacked together like giant lips slurping up every last ounce of a man's seed like a hungry two-dollar whore. She wore black checked slacks. No panty lines. The puff of her bush protruded beneath the fabric. She had five-inch black heels on. She carried a large pocketbook under one arm.

Under the other arm was a whip.

She was like one of those cartoons in the back pages of men's magazines. Her hair was auburn, her eyes impossibly green, her lips magenta.

She sat down next to him.

"Hello," she said, her voice a rasp of lust cutting Ed to the core.

For once, Ed was not glib. He merely nodded.

"You want it here, baby?"

"What?" he asked hoarsely.

"Me, of course."

Ed shivered. Of all the women he had possessed the last couple of years he had never encountered anything like her. *She,* he realized, was the revelation.

In the flesh.

It was a quick walk back to Ed's apartment, during which his pants almost exploded. He held her hand all the way there, and it was like holding electricity.

They fucked like quicksilver minks. They twisted in and out of each other. They turned each other inside-out, ass-backwards, willy-nilly, cat-a-corner, upside-down, over and under, inventing new positions to accommodate their lust. Ed's brain was impressed.

Sweat, saliva, the mucilage of love, the fluids of conjunction, the spurts of jetstream jism — all flowed copiously, as if they originated in a bountiful, overflowing fountain that would never empty.

After it was over — or were they merely taking a break? — Ed was hungry for yet more.

He was, he realized in fact and not in fantasy — in love. And he didn't even know her name.

He gasped as she stood up from the bed and used a damp towel to sponge her glistening body.

"That was fantastic," he said weakly, hanging over the side of the bed. He had been drained dry, wrung out by a woman whose body was so different from any he'd ever seen before she could have been an alien. It was so goddamn, fucking, sonofabitching absodamnlutely *perfect*.

"Of course," she said, her voice a rasp that dragged across his spine and made his testicles draw up in anticipation. Her chest was not heaving as Ed's was. She didn't seem a bit tired. "Ready to go again?"

"I don't think I can immediately." He gulped air. "Not right this minute."

"Oh, well," she said. "It doesn't matter."

"It doesn't? You mean you're leaving?"

"No." She rolled him over on his back. "*I* still have to come."

"But, didn't you. . . ?"

"That was orgasm, not coming."

Before Ed could react, she had tied his arms and legs to the four posts of the bed. He didn't put up much of a struggle.

"Kinky stuff," he said lamely. "Maybe that'll work."

"It always works for me," she said. "And *I'm* all that matters."

Ed frowned with curiosity. Then he grimaced with pain. He'd forgotten the whip she had been carrying.

* * *

That next morning, Ed awoke through a cloud of agony. The woman was gone. So were Ed's private parts. The whip had snapped them off.

As she left, he had barely heard her say the words that now reverberated in his mind:

"Men are prey."

Ed realized the angel was toying with him. Or maybe the angel was playing mind-fuck games with everybody.

He hadn't lost much blood yet. He pulled his pants on, stuffed a towel down the front to staunch the flow, and put on a shirt and shoes.

He stumbled down the stairs to the street. The blood seeped through the front of his pants and, when he saw it, he vomited. Then he fell forward into vomit and blood ran from his mouth. He felt his life float out of him, taking the pain away, and he saw the angels come—

They were the angels of death and sex and taxes and things that go zip in the night and things that lie and fester, and things that just lie, and things that make the hapless brain do flip-flops like a badly adjusted television set.

They had been waiting for him. Now they beckoned to him. They said his time for thinking things over was up.

He started to protest that they had told him he could have all the time he wanted and they said they had lied.

He recognized the angels now. One was the angel of revelation. The other angel had a whip. The third, the last, strongly resembled the woman he had seen step down from the bus that day he received his first self-induced (or so he thought) revelation.

Ed started down the tunnel towards the light, just like in the pages of the *National Enquirer,* he imagined—but he didn't expect Jesus to be at the end.

The angels fluttered before him, beatific, holiest of all the holies there ever were.

Ed was muttering.

"What did you say?" the angel with the whip asked.

"I said I'm so damn pissed."

He threw himself at the middle angel, the angel of revelation, and tore open its back with his hands. He reached in and jerked out angel guts. Before the angel could scream—or make the sound dying angels made—Ed turned and snatched the whip from the second angel. He snapped the whip and lopped off the third angel's head. Angel blood spurted from the stump of its neck. Then he turned on the last angel, the one who had, in her earthly guise, rendered him unearthly, and expertly split her asunder with her own weapon. The two halves of the angel fell aside, and angel stuff oozed and spurted out of them.

That's funny, Ed mused. Angels are destructible. We never learned that in Sunday school.

The remains of the three angels hovered briefly, as if there was life left in them, and exploded. Blood gushed all over Ed and looped around the circumference of the tunnel, transforming it into a crimson corridor. Ed grimly sloshed through the blood, going beyond it, closer to the light.

Before he reached the light, he found his old bench sitting there off to one side, in its own alcove within the tunnel, just waiting for him.

Ed didn't care where the light led now. Where was it written he *had* to go to the light?

Fuck it.

He smiled, settled down comfortably on the familiar bench, and crossed his arms. The blood-drenched whip was clutched in his right hand, prepared for any heavenly bodies that might intrude.

Ed was sure there would be more revelations, and he wanted to be ready for them. In the meantime, he would warn any unwary travelers who came along:

Never — ever — do anything for the first time.

Untitled Still Life
with Infinity Perspective

Rex Miller

After successful careers as a radio personality, parodist, and record producer, and while operating a mail order business specializing in character collectibles and nostalgia, Rex Miller decided (in 1986) to begin writing fiction.

What he's produced since then includes two novels (*Slob* and *Stone Shadow*) nominated for awards from Horror Writers of America (and at least five others) and some two dozen much-discussed short stories. The latter have appeared in *Stalkers,* the *Hot Blood* series, *Midnight Graffiti, Cold Blood, Dick Tracy: The Secret Files, Masques III,* and elsewhere. *Rex Miller's Chaingang* is slated for Simon & Schuster's Pocket Books in 1992. Some used his detective hero, Jack Eichord, or his anti-hero, Chaingang Bunkowski. But "Dead Standstill" *(Alfred Hitchcock's Mystery Magazine)* gave us a different, gentler Miller and made the H.W.A. preliminary ballot for a Bram Stoker in the process.

One-third through my first reading of this story—blinking my eyes so I might go on thinking reasonably straight—it became clear to me that what happens to the writer protagonist in it is the very definition of horror, psychological and otherwise. Straddling genres boldly, it addresses the unspoken fear of every author who has found it necessary to become a human word machine. For any kind of reader, it probes both madness and the nature(s) of reality. Be warned, then—go with the flow. (But don't get too close to the *thoudiola.*)

He was a moderately successful, midlist genre writer, and he was dying. Humorously enough, his metier was bloody suspense books, horror, crime and violence, and a weird sub-genre called dark fantasy/cyberpunk/speculative science fiction, a category so strange that not even those who wrote it were altogether certain what it was.

The point being that for a man whose every waking hour was spent immersed in the topic of sudden death, his own sudden death, imminent or otherwise, was an event that found him singularly unprepared.

The curious biochemical anomaly that had been slowly killing him for the last few years produced several interesting side effects, one of them being that some corner of his brain had been unlocked. In a stream-of-consciousness flood he had written nearly forty novels in four years. His publishers would be cranking out his books forever. He would not be around to see it, alas.

In all fairness it had hardly been a sudden death, his impending demise-to-be, since he'd had a good four years to prepare for it. And every morning, like clockwork, he'd been at the keyboard of his word processor pounding out the purple prose. Seven to noon. Break for lunch. One to three. Year in, year out. His agent and his editors were amazed.

Truthfully, he wasn't a writer so much as he was a typist or a clerk. He simply typed onto the screen those dreams that came to him in the night. He always told interviewers who seemed awed by his prolificness, "I'd have written a lot more if I could've typed faster." He'd tried dictating to a speed-typist but that hadn't panned out. And what was the big deal? It would take them years to publish his oeuvre, as it was. Now his illness had progressed to the point where all he wanted to do was quit work and head for a warm, sunny clime. Drink tequila; sit on the beach. But it wasn't going to work that way.

Something was prodding him to write more. To write faster. To write and keep writing and write and never stop until the thing came and smashed him down once and for all. The dreams that had been a godsend for the last four years were now becoming nightmares. He dreamed all night long. Active, turbulent, strange dreams of bizarre characters acting out the weirdest death fantasies.

And in the morning, if he didn't start writing it all down, he'd begin daydreaming—and the daydreams were a thousand times worse than the others—horrible, seamless things that caught him up and imprisoned him inside their crazed storylines. With each successive daydream it was harder and harder for him to escape, to think his way out, to plot his way out of his own scenarios of paranoia and murder.

He'd come to Dr. Kervale to see if there wasn't some new medication he could try that would numb his brain, sedate him to the point where the stories might stop coming, where his ideas would leave him alone. It had become unbearable. It was like being inside one of those infinity drawings where you see a picture of someone looking at a picture of someone looking at a picture of someone looking at a picture of. . .and about the seventh or eighth level of hell, you began to go a little mad. What if there were an infinity picture that never ended, with a subject so mesmerizing it locked the viewer deep inside? That's what the dreams had become.

Kervale was apparently with a patient and presumably had let his receptionist go to lunch. There was no one at the telephone and he didn't see any nurses in sight. He was scarcely in any hurry so he sat in one of the chairs and skimmed through the magazines in the doctor's waiting room.

The thing tugged at him. There was no denying the ideas when they attacked, he'd tried again and again. This time he tried to force his mind to other things, to think about business: he wondered what sort of a cover mechanical they'd produced on *Lured,* the book they were doing as a lead the following month. Without knowing why, he got up, put his magazine down and went over behind the receptionist's desk.

This is absurd, he thought as he removed the cover from the woman's typewriter. His mind fought to regain control but his hands searched for paper in the unlocked desk drawer. It took him only a few moments to insert a sheet into the strange machine and begin looking for the power switch. Within a minute or so he was typing words and phrases on the unfamiliar typewriter in all caps:

NIGHT MAYOR. RAINSTREAKER. DURRELL. HEAD-RIPPER. THOUGHTGAME. OILSLICK. VENUSIAN BLIND. SEE VENUS AND DIE. MATA MUA. TIME SLIDES DOWN. DURRELL. MUTILATED CLOWN. Without warning he was slipping into the dark folds of the chilling plot, typing "Durrell, the neutered by-product of three confused bondings and eight bewildering cohabitations, is asexual/heterosexual. A burn-out with diagonal burn streaks on the right side of his face, a dead eye—which his triangular one-ways conceal—and no nose. Having only a left nostril and half a nose is not a serious handicap for a tactile audile." He was typing so furiously he didn't hear the doctor come out of the office behind him.

"You all right?"

"Mmm." He didn't bother to shut off the typewriter though he knew he was sliding down.

"Are you *doing all right?*" The doctor was a pleasant man, hair covered, face masked, gloved; plas-net to the breathing mask. So really all you could see were the eyes, slightly myopic through the thick eyeshield, a triangular pair of framed lenses that meshed tightly against the hood, everything in institutional charcoal.

"Fine." Half-five Alpha Durrell-Human, known as Durrell, felt nothing. He waited for the tingling sensation of the probe and the sound of his dreamkey. Knowing now the *real* reason he was there.

"Atta boy," the man said with his jovial workaday smile in place, preparing to look at Durrell's brain.

The probe hit tentatively, professionally centered. He opened the front section of his thoughtshield as he heard the first three words of The Fleetwoods' "Mr. Blue" sound familiarly in his ears.

On the word "STAR" he let the probe track and breathed deeply, smiling reflexively when he heard the doctor's surprised intake of air.

"Holy GOD!" he heard, almost laughing, as "All Along the Watchtower" blew across the eighth pair of cranial nerves, transmitting Jimi Hendrix to the part of his brain not sheathed in thoughtshield.

In the flash of a microtick he dreamthemed an icy moonlet near the blue edge of Triton's shadow, an ancient cornfield and the rusting tin sign "Funk's Hybrid," the whoreband of the same name, and a sidewalk mug joint on the Rue des Jasperjohns, a double-clenched shallop tethered to the balustrades and yawing gently in the petrotide. These were just "kneecaps," involuntary jerks to the non-hostile probe, so he forgot them instantly.

"Nobody told me you were—"

"A braincop?" Durrell chuckled softly, his head in the padded, vise-like maw of a NECAP. He couldn't recall just that moment what the acronym represented; the fanciest new neuro-something, something-probe. The operating theatre was one of the finest and there was nothing to fear but the unknown. Nobody kills a galactic-class champion gamer, except maybe another gamer, so he was relaxed and totally at ease.

You die of a killer virus, a spontaneous act of random violence in isolated instances—and old age. Nothing can sneak up on you. No plan to injure you will succeed—because when the perp or perps reach that instant of crystallized thought, you *share* it with them. If a doctor was going to play games with your thoughtshield, the second he even contemplated a hostile mood you'd know it, too, and you could gangslam him braindead before his heart could beat again!

Mindscans were part of the deal, like the dental plan, the annual physical checkup. It paid to take advantage of Uni's resources, the ultimate state of the art in dreamtech sciences; better safe than sorry.

The cartel used them like truth serum. And what the doctor had read off his screen in that flashing microtick when the cop relaxed his brainshield was something that he would have to pass up the chain of command. It fell under the primary dictum, "Report any unusual discrepancies."

In the lightning bolt of electro-scan the machine had photographed a negative fault line cracking down through the braincop's quadruple-thick mindset as he dreamed the probe in for a peek. It wasn't anything major; just a jagged line that would end up on some controller's desk back at Threat Directorate, probably in the Department of Sensorium Analysis—a misnomer if ever there was one.

The doctor did nothing to pass the report up the line. The NECAP unit was programmed to report any unusual discrepancies, and the small, jagged line instantly became spoonfeed.

Deep inside the labyrinth of Uni Central a woman sat watching a bank of consoles. One of them glowed blue. She watched the tiny, negative fault in Half-five Alpha Durrell-Human become hard downlink.

The tech keyed Durrell-Human, ½5 Alpha, hit the Data Transfer, and got DENIED.

Hit a query and got DENIED.

Hit an explain-query denial and got DENIED. Turned it over to her supervisor who contacted *her* supervisor who asked for the same information in a different way and was told—

ACCESS DENIED.

Explain query denial to supervisor?

ACCESS DENIED.

It went on like this until they reached an Assistant Controller in TD-5 who had supersecret security clearance and his screen advised him—

ACCESS DENIED. SUBJECT/PROJECT/PROGRAM UMBRA/ PENUMBRA SENSITIVE.

An umbra/penumbra-cleared executive, who was at home with her family and not at all pleased by being disturbed for something so routine, had to call *her* boss and get him to open his supersecret document vault and trot out the codeword, which in machinespeak was §§§§§§§§§§§ stroked-ampersand 10 ¶¶¶¶¶¶¶¶¶¶, followed by the unit or cipher numbers and designations 1191-Y/E-4-91284-Y, and the crypto-brackets which were 7-place KER-prefix nymics, KERATIN/KERZEAL. The program in which Half-five Alpha

Durrell-Human worked was locked tightly under the classification crypto KERVALE.

Armed with all of this, the long-suffering executrix accessed the interlink again and saw the following exchange:

CRYPTO	UNIT NUMBER
KERATIN	1191-Y
KERBATE	399910-E
KERBIZA	33880-EE
KERCINE	861515-Y
KERCHOY	91-E-4485
KERDART	81831-7Y-3
KERELAN	UTILITY-1Y7
KERFBAT	63518-E-7Y
KERGONE	FEED 7Y-E
KERJURA	66120E-Y
KERKIMO	718518-Y
KERLECH	442-E
KERMESS	101072-Y
KERMOTH	5123E-Y-9
KERNELS	UTILITY-LOCK-Y-2E77
KERNITE	99-99Y-5-3
KEROGEN	E-8245-Y
KERPLOP	E-FEED-1Y8154-E
KERSHAM	Y8117234-E
KERSTOP	6570-E-26
KERTREL	7E-1Y-399-0
KERVONA	588E-2222-Y
KERWAKE	2003-E
KERYGMA	7-E-7-Y-LOCK
KERZEAL	E-4-91284-Y

PROGRAM LOCATE: KERVALE
CLASSIFIED ULTRA MOST SENSITIVE TOP SECRET
UMBRA/PENUMBRA EYES ONLY MAXGRADE
UMBRA/PENUMBRA EYES ONLY MAXGRADE SEC/CLR
PROGRAM LOCATE: KERVALE
Entry?
(A) CODE STAR / 661-33 EDICT COMMCENT/ CLEAR/
PRIORITY 1 PLUS/ ACCESS
Access:KERVALE

MAXGRADE SEC/CLR EMPLOYEE HISTORY

Employee Name:	½5 Alpha Durrell-Human
A/K/A:	Durrell
ER:	Access: PAYROLL [COALITION]
CODE:	Star/661-33
AUTH:	Edict CommCent
RANK:	Access: UNIWORLD CONTROL
OS:	Enforcement
SI:	491-38-408-689-UNI-A-(OP)
ASSND:	Freelance (GAMER)
DESK:	SSB/Action
PROJECT:	Access: CONTROLLER [COALITION]
CRYPTO:	KERVALE
Status:	Audit
N/C:	A1-30
ASMT:	4410, 5111, 5190-K, 6827, 9901, 9992 10725, 11186, 14833, 14994, 17665, 18322
Uniworld Credits:	Access: BANKING [COALITION]
Emergency Access:	VASTAR SYSTEM
Dreamtheme Keys:	Mr. Blue/All Along the Watchtower
Response Type:	Audile
Termination:	Audit
Languages:	English, Franco, Vorse, Mata, Seblenese

The executrix keyed TRANSFER AND CLEAR and washed her hands of it. Far away, on Santa Satana Breton, a senior controller examined the display and said, "Easy way to fix that. Put him to work." He tapped the photo on his desk.

"You sure?" his colleague asked.

"I *run* Durrell. These two are perfect for each other." He looked into the cold eyes of a beautiful killer mutant.

Back on the home base of Uni Central, the umbra/penumbra-cleared executrix killed power on the interlink unit and left the console, moving down the hallway to her privacy cubicle. She plugged into a thoudiola and instantly relaxed as the opening chords of "Salo-tenwjopra," the Hotsteel rocker, slammed across the synapses. The second she crossfaded "Since I Fell for You" she heard:

You have accessed a Thought-HOlovid Uniworld Dreamtheme Disseminator. Alter reality at will.

And she was blissfully happy once again in the land of the midnight suns, where umbra and penumbra had far different meanings.

*   *   *

Renée was multilingual but she tended to think in Matamuan, so she appreciated the triple-entendre of stovepipe motif on yet another level. They were in front of some of her favorite mug joints along the oil canal and she told the gondolier to stop so she could admire the facades. She knew he would assume she was building a mindset, but Renée was merely admiring the witty facades of Hi Hat, Topper, and Nite Mayor, their three famous 'pipe hats soaring into the Venetian* sky.

The sky itself was a beautiful thought-xparency, which she knew was one-sided; but the Ub Iwerks Dreamtheme — stylized cartoon stars and ringed planets — was the perfect Olden Times backdrop for the clubs and fake painting operations along the canal. An anthropomorphic moon grinned down at her from what she knew to be the floor of the Oysla grav-wheel chamber.

Renée had fled here to the outlaw world of "Venice," deep inside the anti-grav popularly called Oilslick. She could blend in and take her pleasures.

The pipes of Hi Hat and the others were as different as up and down: Hi Hat's name only appeared across the very top of the stovepipe so you could identify it from a skyrocker or metro, but the facade was unmarked, a gently blinking figural of dyracolor thoughtwindows. Inside the fake painting operation it was all endless cake-out-in-the-rain graphics, after the wonderfully funny work of the rocker Ah-Ha. Topper, on the second level, sat above the face of a four-handed counter-clock, and the Mickey hand shot its middle digit in welcome. She pointed toward Nite Mayor and the gondola began to move quietly through the plastic pads.

They stopped against the formex and flexcal steps and she got out gracefully, entering the letter "O" on her eight-inch stiletto fetish heels. The "O" of Mayor was a fanged monster's mouth, the monster's stovepipe rising three levels above the mug-joint, and she walked seductively across the red carpeted tongue as "Schemer for Souls of Glass" roared from the dim recesses.

The sharp edge of Renée's mind pulsated with excitement as she felt herself moistening to the provocative notion of being surrounded by easy, vulnerable targets.

Inside Renée the voice of Linda Logs screeched "Shit Pile Shuttle" and she wet her perfect lips and stepped into the wall of sound.

*Venetian is spelled Venusian but henceforward all turvywords will be spelled phonetically. *[He dreamed that he crossed this out. His editors hated footnotes.]*

*THIS FACILITY IS FOR ZETA-CLASS ONLY. UNIWORLD
PROVIDES ADVANCED THOUGHTGAMERS WITH Z-CLONE
THOUDD THOUGHTFONES. BRAINALONES PROMOTE
SOCIAL SAFETY.*

Renée laughed in hot anticipation.

On an alien star that was home base for the intelligence and
enforcement directorates of the vast coalition owned by Uniworld
Petro, a tall, harlequin-masked man in a moderate stovepipe waited
to be cleared to Public Information, the huge monolith that housed
his employer's headquarters.

Fewer than two day cycles ago he'd been on V-41, in a drugged-out
jungle lab near New Orchid City. Now he was cooling his heels in
a Pro Dex THT outside the PI building on Santa Satana Breton. It
really was a small world.

"Here you are, sir," the young security man said politely, and Durrell
thanked him and clipped his breathprint I.D. on.

The pathway to the entrance was marked with the thought-balloon
arrows that were the ubiquitous trademarks of a Uni operation. Durrell
walked slowly towards the monolith, a tall man in black, face half
red-lined in the manner of a half-rainstreaker mutant, black eye
triangles over a rough-hewn countenance. He was early as usual.

All the way in he'd played Kenton and his wives: June Christy, Ann
Richards, interpolated with backgrounds of Intermission Riff. Dyna-
flow. Blues in Burlesque. Hallowed sounds from ancient purple discs
called 78s, found and restructured for thoudiola. Olden goodes.

Now the ever-present thoudd blasted C-Slash Gamma Utrillo at
him, and Durrell hummed along with their big hit, "000-111," in a
better mood now and glad to be back on his feet again. His metal-
shod cop shoes rang out on the hard surface of the formex as he entered
the massive structure. A thoudd lecture to other-worlder children
pulled at him as he walked past INDOCTRINATION, and he smiled
and thought, why not? — then stepped in to take an alcove and kill
some time.

The famous voice of the announcer Free Bird crackled resonantly
as Durrell took a comfort recliner and plugged in to the lecture.

" — time had elapsed since the fourth war, and in the parallel Milky
Way galaxy, it was discovered that time ran both forward and
backward, and spatial relationships varied from system to system and
from star to star.

"Following the breakthroughs in neural communication and

thought transmission, mankind learned to alter certain physical realities with a type of instantly-induced self-hypnosis or *dreamtheme*. Technological research and development provided industrial, medical, and military applications for these new abilities.

"After the Big War the top thoughtgamers were hired by Uniworld Petro, a multi-planet coalition for restratification, and by employing braincop tradecraft, the law enforcement and intelligence agency set out to restore order.

"Today freelance gamers are engaged to seek out and neutralize criminals and sociopaths who endanger social safety and subvert law and order.

"The most hazardous braincop jobs are those missions to the various satellites of Mata Mua, which means 'In Olden Tymes,' where the worst outlaw mutants gravitate. El-Ones, homicidal brainiacs, Brainfreak tax bandits, severely retarded 'Muans known as walking breadbrains, and other societal rejects populate the dark core-inverts, making such environments ideal camouflage for galactic-class thoughtgamers on the run." *You can say* that *again, Free Bird,* Durrell thought to himself.

"Post-War societies are called straights and anti-gravs. The latter are those stars with artificial gravities. These systems allow repopulated worlds to double in size, one class on the surface or within, and one 'gravitating' — up or down — to the reversed polarity. Core-inverts allow racial purification and promote social safety. Typically these environs utilize a petrochemical barrier that both divides the classes and houses the gravity brainwheels. The giant wheels maintain magnetic polarity, axis rotation, inworld ecospherics, and surveillance mechanisms."

Durrell tried to dream *THE END*, a trick he'd attempted before, but it only made the Free Bird narration louder.

"Matamuans and others often appear today in olden tyme regalia. Extremely tall stovepipe hats and rainstreak-motif bow-style ties are considered quite fashionable. Female role-players wear ancient ball gowns, or go nude and half-nude. Male and female roles are mentally, not physically, adaptive. And all three sexes wear triangular one-ways and foot-fetish shoes." The audience laughed as, on screen, a player in high-heeled stilts towered over her dancing partner.

"Languages include English, Franco, Vorse, Mata, and Seblenese. Many coreworlds are thought-xparent, dimensional and real from the outlaw side, but with the dreamthemes transvisible to the obverse. This feature allows such stars to be converted into tourist attractions, and flourishing resorts enable straightworlders to view mutated or outlaw societies in safety and comfort.

"An example of these is the fugitive star Oysla, where such a colony is gravwheeled. Mutants known as 'rainstreakers,' because of their distinctive facial radiation burns, live in a classical Italian-style city of old world architecture and contemporary metroblock, the town built on a spherical plan of interlocking oil canals, and structured inside Oysla's dreamtheme apparatus. The local nickname for the star is 'Oilslick.'

"Rainstreakers work and play in a culture of thoughtgaming, relaxing in mug joint holotechs and turvyworlds constructed to dreamtheme great paintings or famous classical dioramas.

"When the Thought-HOlovid Uniworld Dreamtheme Dissemina-tors, THOUDDs—called 'thoudiolas' popularly—were invented, music was used to key the neural transmission states. Uniworld's Museum of Popular Culture supplied all the two-step masters. Every gamer has his own dreamtheme key, unique to him in all the worlds—a combination of registered melodies recorded between the early 1900s and the Trimillenery. Mine are 'Time Slides Down' by Calico Jack, and Lenny Skinny's four-cycle version of 'Free Bird!'" The audience applauded as the screen displayed the announcer's baroque and audioscopic dreamtheme.

"Uniworld controls every step of thought-holovid gaming from first generation production to management seminars, offering safe appli-cations of the latest dreamtech to major manufacturers such as Visa-Rama, Universal Control Systems, Imaginex, DreamCorp, and others. The Diorama Mark IV, Uni-9000 Dreamscanners, DreamCorp Inter-world's Xparenlator, and NeuroPathic Viewscape machines are just a few examples."

Durrell unplugged and got out of the recliner as Free Bird's dream-theme dissolved from the screen, and he heard the special track telling other audiles like himself that

THOUGHT-HOLOVID UNI-9000s ARE COMPATIBLE WITH VORSE, MATA, OR SEBLENESE BRAINSHIELD APPARATUS AND CAN BE EXPANDED TO STORE UP TO A VEZILLION ANTI-GRAVS.

Durrell had more time to think on the long walk to the Coalition Controller's office, a small room in an out-of-the-way alcove marked only with an unobtrusively-rendered black infinity sign. He could have ridden the moving walkways, but he preferred to walk and peer into the huge, open rooms. It was immense, the Public Information monolith.

He stopped in front of a room that appeared to have no walls — a room anyone would be afraid to step into — and Carmel Pucker hammered from the thoudiola inside. Durrell examined it for a moment until he assimilated the data: the room's walls were like matte paintings, but you could see through them infinitely and he heard, *YOU HAVE ACCESSED A THOUGHT-XPARENCY. UNI-WORLD DREAMTHEMES ARE MAINTAINED FOR YOUR PLEASURE. PLEASE REPORT ANY UNUSUAL DISCREP-ANCIES.* He glanced at the sign on the doorway. "Journey to the Heart of the Brain." He hurried down the hall, thinking that was the last place he wanted to go.

He saw again the small black infinity sign that always brought a slight pain to his chest, then he walked through the outer alcove. *YOU HAVE ENTERED A UNIWORLD PETRO UNAUTHOR-IZED AREA. DO NOT MOVE. REMAIN IN YOUR PRESENT POSITION AND YOU WILL BE REPROGRAMMED. FOR YOUR SAFETY DO NOT MOVE.* He flashed I.D. and kept moving past the thoudiola.

Inside the Controller's office it was blazing high noon on the Western Matamuan desert.

"Nice," Durrell gestured admiringly.

"You like that?"

"I like."

"Thanks. Sit."

"Sure." He took a seat and adjusted the position for his height.

"You look fit," the Controller said.

"Feeling fine." Durrell knew the man across from him had scanned his field meticulously. There were few secrets left unprobed. "So far as I know."

"Mindset-wise, I mean."

"Yeah?"

"I'm just asking if you want to do a piece of work."

"You mean will I be *enthused* about it?" Durrell laughed as the man in the bow tie and one-ways glowered at him. "Listen, what I want and what I *have* to have are two different things."

"At least two," the Controller said wryly; "maybe three."

"Right. Sure, boss." They were speaking conversationally, which Durrell found tedious in the extreme; but this man was not one to forego the polite social amenities. Durrell realized he'd scanned a grav-sign as he looked into the reflection of the man's mirrored eye triangles. He flashed on it and his boss caught the take.

"You're seeing those signs because of the target. Might as well get you started thinking top-side up right away." He reached for reprogramming and the western desert dimensional dissolved into a full scale cutaway of an anti-grav. "This is Oysla; Oilslick, remember?"

"From the first time." Durrell didn't mention his refresher course taken on the way down the long hall. The realistic cutaway was POV-specific, moving eastward through the oil pole to the gravity brainwheels. It stopped at the Sector Zeta delineation and began to refocus on the oil canal ring and its Venice Rainstreak Colony coreworld.

"I thought you might. You pulled one of the 5100 numbers in there—right? Well, this ain't no tame duck, kid." A beautiful, flawless face supered over the legend VENUS. "This is a Matamuan calling itself Renée MeXXico. Wanted for Lobotocide One. Alive and well inside the rainstreak colony."

"Nice mouth," Durrell grunted.

"That's an ARIZONA CLASS 12, sonny boy! It's hiding in there with a bunch of the Zeta clones and if you go in after her, you better keep your shit screwed down tight or that mean Matamuan will have you braindead and floating under the plastic lily pads in the fucking oil canal!"

"Nice. Pasadena, eh? I'll give this one a wave."

"Up to you, Durrell. There's a trey on it."

"Please?"

"30,000 urt-keys, ace—30,000 Uniworld Tax Credits. Lordy, Durrell! Let's see. . .that's roughly 90,000 in tax-free *UP* scrip! You say you'll pass, huh?"

"Did *I* say that?"

"I guess not," and they both laughed. "So. You want this whore?"

"She know a braincop is coming?"

"Count on it."

Durrell looked at the screen full of history below the mug shot. *Nationality:* Matamuan. *SI:* R140 something. A 12-rated Arizona Class killer android! *Man,* he must love money even more than he thought. "Infiltration?"

"Thought-resistant Corvallis Galileo. Nighttime insertion. You could go right through the East Pole oil lock like you did before."

"Why me? Not that I'm looking a trey in the mouth, but—"

"You're part rainstreaker. You were there and you came out alive, didn't you?"

"Barely."

"Okay." The Controller shrugged, leveled. "You're also the craziest brainman we've got. If that won't make you 101% thoughtproof against a galactic-class freak like little Renée, I don't know what the hell will."

Durrell said no more.

At 02503050 they stood on the blastpad, the Controller's briefing at its end.

"Remember, you want to start retraining your senses for Venice." He didn't mean it in the literal sense. He was an audile like Durrell. "When you go into reversal-inversion your bloodflow will regulate the autonomics, but orbitlag becomes a factor. Now, you only have twenty hours in the day cycle, and at least five of them go dark as you rotate. Oysla itself is on a twelve-day cycle week, Aurelius system — and remember, when you're in Venice, time moves *counter-clockwise*."

"What are the surveillance parameters?"

"The usual shit, turrets and gondolas." Durrell headed toward the metro but the Controller added, "Renée likes to play lame duck, then gangslam you braindead before you can think a shield, so keep a strong thoughtjacket up."

"Yeah. So long."

"If you drop your field you've got *serious pain.*"

"Just deposit the trey," Durrell called back over his shoulder.

The metroliner was an old type, one of the dependable Lindbergh shooters, the U.S.S. George Méliès.

But the in-flight braincop loopner was some silly garbage about dreamtheme brainmanuals. Durrell wiped it in disgust and played Dyna Borzoi all the way to Osyla.

The Méliès landed on a tri-D blastpad with a hologram of the weeping eye moon logo. "Q Phone Suicide Rennaissance" by Botz blasted from the thoudiola and he plugged in, heard: *PREPARE TO BRAINTRAIN INWORLD. CORE-INVERTS PROTECT ECOSPHERICS AND PROMOTE SOCIAL SAFETY.*

Durrell nodded, passed through a security thought-field, and instantly felt the old memories of Oilslick wash over him. It was one of the only counterpops within metro shot that still displayed all the old "down is up" stuff. Uniworld Petro, UP on the interstar xchange, owned the satellite which had gone fugitive right at the end of the war. But afterward they kept it for tourist rights and concessions, allowing the renegade in-core to self-regulate. At one time the corporate slogan had been "On Oysla down is up — and if UP ever goes *down,* down goes *under!"*

Oilslick's surface was a beehive of industry. Here the huge cogs that powered the master gravity wheels intermeshed in perpetual motion. Uni's C.O.N.T.R.O.L. offices were here.

The COalition of Nationalities and Technocracies for Repopulation of the Outer Locales, originally responsible for restructuring the satellites of Mata Mua with cogwheel races, was headquartered on the surface, and used the rainstreak colony as a kind of lab and working model.

Venice specialized in exploded heads, walking breadbrains, brain-dead, longneckers, and Flemish runners. Rainstreaked outlaws could blend in to this multi-faceted mutant community and leave no trace.

Rainstreakers hated other-worlders and would have loathed them all the more had they realized they were a tourist zoo regularly surveilled from the surface of Oilslick itself. "Recherche" was one of the olden tyme words you heard a lot now, here. Outlaw viewing was chic again.

Durrell was bemused by the stream of skyrockers and streetrockers zooming hither and yon, and the intrepid holo-happy tourists everywhere one turned, tripping out to endless dreamthemes of "Un Viage a la Luna" and "Timeslide." The constant din of the cogwheels and the oiling mechanisms was an incessant background hum against the back beat of Antique Hard Rocque, also. Everywhere on Oysla the petrochemical stench was overpowering. Durrell's half-nose wrinkled in disgust; he thanked the stars he was an audile.

As soon as he'd obtained clearances he climbed into the Corvallis Galileo, a nifty sub-mariner model, and spent the rest of the day cycle brain-flying and practicing converting the craft to air bathtub.

At precisely 2000:00:00:00 Hawkins Mean he was standing in the industrial oil lock chamber, the large egress area between Tourist Surveillance and Population, looking down through the "sky" xparency. When the timer hit, Durrell climbed into the sleek CG and plugged in.

POLARITY REVERSAL IS IN EFFECT. TIME MOVES COUNTER-CLOCKWISE. ADJUST YOUR MINDSET TO THE 20-HOUR DAY CYCLE AND REVERSAL-INVERSION. PROTECT YOURSELF AT ALL TIMES.

Durrell took her straight in, figuring the egress lock would be under the canals like before; but it was an old "breakfront" type, and when the CG hit something solid he knew he was in a spot of trouble.

By the time the next sun cycle broke, Durrell found himself in somebody's scum tree and a good five to ten el-exes from the oil canal. He waited a few hours, then came up properly, his scope between two plastic lily pads.

Now to find Renée. *Don't walk away, Renée,* he hummed as he began his search.

For nearly a week Durrell worked to penetrate the rainstreaker night scene. He managed to befriend maybe a tenth of the Zeta bandit crowd; Ozz, Zebra, Azure, Insane Zane, Zulu. But nobody had seen anyone who looked even remotely like Renée MeXXico. And you didn't blunder around showing somebody's picture in renegade mug joints or mutant mumbo-jumbos unless you were a braincop or somebody very stupid, or both. Durrell knew word would get around.

He paid special attention to the mug joints playing PXL 5Rem stuff. "Mutilated Clown" was Renée's dream-trigger. The words laid an icy finger on him every time he heard—

> ROLLER COAST KILLER DWARF,
> > CARNY THRILLER MESOMORPH,
> GHOULIE-RAMA, ULTRA-SLIME,
> > HEAVY DUTY COUNTERTIME.
> DON'T BE SHY NOW STEP RIGHT DOWN,
> AND SEE THE MUTILATED CLOWN.

One night cycle he heard about "this girl who's trying to pass." A Z-clone sneered, "The bitch is Matamuan, I'd bet my six on it." And that night Durrell dreamed of a dark gondola archway, number 1872, and an air tub capsized by a mighty oilcruiser, the U.S.S. 1872; and he was in the tub, going down, his lungs bursting; and he screamed "help!" but the thought transposed itself so that the letters became numerals: 1-8-7-2; and then he woke up drenched in the heat of a waking dreamtheme, his mind wrenching itself free of the impending slam.

He found her in a fake-painting operation called 1872—no surprise—after Claude Monet's stolen *Impression: Sunrise,* the most famous holo on Oilslick. It was a murky, single-sun operation, painted in shades of tan, pinkish gray, dark blue-green, and sleitch. Female gondoliers and a nude brainwhore band shook the immense room with noise while Zep's Stairway blasted.

They did a slow touch and took a break, a thoudd booming an invitation to "See El Mirador & Punkster Funkster starting next week at Snotto's, Brighton Canal at 28th!" And Acillatem's Heavy Water Band smashed out of the thoudiola, rocking "Half Red," the half-rainstreaker anthem.

Durrell sauntered across the floor, scanning, singing along with the band. A nude gondolier asked him if he wanted to order but he ignored it, focusing his concentration into the chilly depths of a galactic class thoughtfreak:

Renée MeXXico, wearing cosmetic streaks across half her beautiful kisser, a nipple-clinging silver sweater — and nothing but Last-tan from the plexus down.

Durrell was forming the first thought when her automatic probe hit. He'd forgotten what it was like to get broadbrained like that. It hit like an involuntary dreamtheme, and she almost slipped inside before he could block. It was *clever.* The sort of brain gangslam that swallows you like a thousand vezillion simultaneous migraines and he thought himself going —

"Faut-il croire a une evolution of mankind *presentaient des temps?"*

"Mais, suivant des Malakei Elyon Mitteilugen fuer juedischevarno sakra d'aujourd'hui — (funny you don't LOOK Jewish!) *— qui faveur chez nous des le oder das schaedliche welches ces lointaines cette diffusion des suffisent a expliquer?"* Much as you might ask "Pardon me, but would you happen to — ?" but so clever and quick you think you're listening to a thought; reacting; assimilating; preparing normal response; but you're only dreamtheming gibberish camouflage over a probe.

(1/50th of a microtick, the thing hits; 2/50th, she tries to turn him into a chess piece she can PLAY; 3/50th nearly brainsplits Durrell's halves; and in the DOWN quarter of 3/50th she braingames him with a fucking joke of a half-masked Zorro icon and a snake's head.

(At the instant of 4/50th, going for an inverted thought balloon, she tries to think his arms flexcal, and he reaches toward her and smashes it with his *own* thought, ballooning her back into the snake twist as hard and fast as he can. Everything he has is in it — flat out, foot to the floorboard, *plunging* into the darkness at Mach 100, afraid of nothing — *try or die!*)

Renée was the fastest galactic-class Matamuan still surviving, certainly the most formidable Arizona Class 12 he'd *ever* come down against. His counter made her so ferocious she almost penetrated his thoughtshield.

For the *full mini-micro* of 5/50th Durrell felt himself ballooning as she tried her damndest to gangslam him into a pig. It was all he could do to force-feed her a column of scan digits from the 'droid's own central compu-rig. He was too *old* for this work; the trey waiting for him back on Breton suddenly looked like urtkeys he'd *never* spend.

And she was fighting with *everything* she had! She made him see heads on spikes, disembodied organs, balloon brains baking in bloodbroth. She crucified his image with the window, and hung his shadow upside down in his head; attacked him with a windmill razorman and tried to make his hands and feet decoagulate the way a mutant kid will when it's backed into a corner.

"Sorry, Renée," he thought to her — "I'm a headripper!"

And the full power of his mind rainstreaked her for real right before he carried her twitching body past the Z-clones.

She might have weighed 85 pounds tops.

Durrell buried the remains under the brown mountains of chocolate Sierra Merde, leaving the killer mutant braindead, streaked, and cooling in a cheap thoughtcoffin with the black infinity sign. By the time he'd worked his way back to the little Corvallis Galileo he'd dreamthemed away the trey maybe eight times and he was drag-ass, dead dog *tired.*

The gangslam hit Durrell when he was going through the oil lock — hit him so hard he was braindead before the CG popped through the surface. Oddly, he'd never dreamthemed himself as a liability and the moment he felt it coming, and he understood, it just laid him right out . . .

There was only one way to slam a thoughtgamer the likes of ½5 Alpha Durell-Human. You let him wear himself down and hit him when he completely dropped his thoughtjacket. When he knew he was out of danger.

Durrell just had time to see himself reversing his mindset to Aurelius System, moving away from the little Corvallis Galileo and heading for the brown mounds of Sierra Merde, when he went out altogether. The Coalition stopped him at the thoughtcoffin, naturally. They buried him in the same box with Renée MeXXico, both of them braindead, dreamless, and six feet over.

One of his most painful deaths.

With a sigh of relief he typed, *THIS DREAMTHEME IS TER-MINATED, so* thankful that, at last, he had pulled out of another one. He'd been typing so furiously he had not even heard the doctor come out of the office behind him.

"You all right?" he heard the doctor say. He recalled the name "Kervale" from the dream. His forthcoming novel, *Lured,* an easy to decode transposition of the name Durel(l). His preoccupation with death, an obvious dream trigger.

"Mmm," he said, noticing his fingers on a typewriter keyboard. The keys felt oddly-placed; unfamiliar. On the paper inserted into the machine someone had typed in caps:

UNTITLED STILL LIFE WITH INFINITY PERSPECTIVE.

The thing tugged at him again, mercilessly. His mind fought to regain control but his hands hovered over the keyboard and his fingers began pecking out the words.

NIGHT MAYOR. RAINSTREAKER. Without warning, he was slipping back down into the dark folds of the same plot.

"Are you *doing all right?*" The doctor was a pleasant man, hair covered, face masked, gloved; plas-net to the breathing mask. So really all you could see were the eyes, slightly myopic through the thick eyeshield, a triangular pair of framed lenses that meshed tightly against the hood, everything in institutional charcoal.

"Fine," he said, waiting for the tingling sensation of the probe and the sound of his dreamkey.

"Atta boy," the man said with his jovial workaday smile in place, preparing to look at Durrell's brain. . . .

Pratfall

John Maclay

One of the begetters of this anthology series, the publisher of the first two volumes (not to mention the popularly admired *Nukes* and books written by William F. Nolan and Ray Russell), refused to permit his own fiction writing to appear in *Masques* until he'd earned his spurs elsewhere.

With two novels, his story collection (*Other Engagements,* Dream House, 1987), and all-on-his-own short fiction or poetry in publications ranging from *Twilight Zone* and *Night Cry* to *Pillow Talk* and *True Love* — from *Footsteps, 14 Vicious Valentines, Grue,* and Nolan's *The Bradbury Chronicles* to *Crosscurrents, Amazing Experiences, The Horror Show,* and *Anti-War Poems* — from *Hardboiled Detective, Human Digest, Cemetery Dance,* and *Horizons West* to *Borderlands, Pulphouse* (#5), *Scare Care, Whispers, Stalkers* and *Urban Horrors*... there simply was no reason not to accept the editor's invitations to the third *Masques,* and the fourth.

Award-winning Bruce Boston wrote elsewhere that John Maclay is "a master of that most difficult of literary forms, the short-short story." He means "story," not vignette, and Bruce was right in both assertions. Recall Maclay's "Death Flight," "The Sisters," "Safe," "Black Stockings," "Models," "New York Night" — and meet Josef, the "clown."

My name is Josef Stern. I am seventy-five now, but with my full head of dark hair and my small, wiry body, I could pass for years less. Born in Vienna, I have lived through two world wars, two world peaces, and everything in between. I take things in stride. You see, I am a clown.

It used to bother me some, seeing people laugh as I tramped around the sawdust rings of the great circuses of the world. Berlin, Paris, London, I played them all. Moscow and Washington. I knew that I thought more deeply about things than did the crowds who watched me from above, even the leaders and crowned heads. One has to feel, to be a clown. To create laughter, one also has to cry. I foresaw what havoc Hitler would bring, even before he came to power. I knew that the Cold War would follow. Therefore it seemed ironic that my audience was so secure, while I carried on in such a trivial manner.

But then I came to know that this was exactly my defense, and my victory. My white makeup, my painted smile hid attitudes that might have put me in trouble with the vast, unthinking majority. My polka-dotted suit inspired smiles, instead of the vengeance which always follows the prophet. Nobody kills a clown.

So I was able to do good, in my own small way. I saved Jews, hiding them in a circus wagon on the road to Berne. Evenhandedly, I later smuggled Germans through the Wall. There was even a young man fleeing the F.B.I. after the events of 1968; America or no, it was all the same.

Yet there was another part of my job which caused me concern. That was the violence, the continual slapping around. Reflecting upon it, I feared it would inspire real anger, real bloodshed, real war.

However, an older clown told me that it served a useful purpose, it was merely relief. By acting out their primitive urges through me, he said, people rendered them harmless. So I went on.

And then, scarcely a year ago, the barriers came down. It did my old, good European's heart proud to see the end of that same Wall, the people surging happily through the streets of the capitals I knew and loved, even the Russians speaking freely in a way I had never known. The American leader had also called for a kinder, gentler time, and I believed that he had the peaceful strength to bring it. In Berlin, I danced, now, for joy.

Such was my feeling, when the circus finished its engagement in Tel Aviv. Such it was, when I set out alone to visit Baghdad.

The war began, as all wars do, with a spark. There was the rape of the tiny country. But then, through intransigence, through the visceral rush of blood, it flared. I have never seen anything to war, no glory or honor. Even the "noble" emotions it inspires are, to me, bogus, given their origin in animal slaughter. War is, in a word, stupid.

Yet I was caught in it, as I had been caught in worse ones. My rented car was diverted from the Amman-Baghdad road, to carry some Iraqi troops to the front. And there I was, invited to share a hole near the Kuwaiti border, in the middle of the desert.

Spirits were high at first, food and water was in good supply, and I spent some of my time entertaining the soldiers. I pulled my age-faded, polka-dotted suit from my trunk, painted my face, and made them laugh heartily at my antics. None of them really wanted to be there, except for a few of the pathological sorts that one finds in any army.

Then the bombing began, the metal death loosed by the swooping eagles and the lumbering cranes that had long since removed war from the hands of man, made it impersonal. The effect, however, was very real, as my ears were deafened and huge geysers of sand rose into the mockingly blue sky. Very real, as a man who had laughed at me a moment ago was surreally torn into four pieces, his mouth now an obscenity, gushing blood. Yes, the sand was red that day, as if from a child's drink spilled on a playground.

There were rumors of peace, and rumors again. But the food stopped, the men grew gaunt, and even the water became nothing but dew collected from spread canvas. I could no longer perform my pratfalls, I could merely survive.

One night, as I lay looking at the stars, I began to think again. Had I been wrong; had the violence in my act truly inspired the portrayal of more, as in the films exported in such quantity from the land of peace? Had these, indeed, become a self-fulfilling prophecy, along with the fervor of those who called upon the Islam God?

But no, I decided. It was unsmiling men who made war, those who followed concepts instead of life, those who could not find humane answers before further evil ensued. Those who were still in thrall to the weapons which had become their masters. Those who had stayed serious during my antics in the ring. Those who, well, had never been clowns.

Still the bombs came. Yet one day, there was silence. I awoke to find my companions gone. And when I poked my head above the sand, I saw two lines of tanks a thousand yards on either side, facing each other, facing me.

I did not know what to do, when the muzzle flashes began. Some rounds fell short, exploding merely a stone's throw away, so I had to decide. I considered running toward one of the lines, waving a flag of peace, but shells were falling even there. I thought to remain in my hole, but it provided little shelter. I did pray to my God.

But then, slowly growing in my old mind, behind the eyes that had seen so much, came the thought. Throwing my wiry body erect, I donned once more my faded suit, bounded up and out into the light.

And I danced there, danced on the desert floor! As the mechanical lines drew closer, as the explosions shook the land, I danced for love and joy! I was giving the performance, perhaps the last, of my long life. I danced against war. I danced!

Do as I do, I seemed to be saying to the men in the machines. Come out now, and dance with each other, dance with Josef Stern. The violence was never meant to be real. This is insane. Paint a smile on, slap yourselves around a bit, but dance! Then go home and tell your leaders, your nations, what you have done.

That was when, as if I had been given preternatural sight, I saw the two projectiles, one from either side. Both headed, unerringly, for me.

What sort of people? I marveled, as my body left the earth.

What sort of people would kill a clown?

The Heart of Helen Day

Graham Masterton

Even after he's edited the fine anthology *Scare Care* — proceeds from which go for the care of abused and needy kids in America and England — Graham Masterton is a tough man to sum up. With his black, curly hair, his smiling way of leaning forward to be sure he hears every word, he looks the part of a sophisticated former editor of the British *Penthouse* and *Mayfair.* But there's this beautiful and witty lady named Wiescka, his wife and agent, and their sons Roland, Daniel, and Luke. (Roland was eleven when he penned the book-closing "In the West Wing" for his dad's *Scare Care.*)

Then there's the Masterton who wrote historical and mainstream novels such as *Solitaire, Rich,* and *Railroad,* and the literarily inquiring *Mirror,* "based very much" on Lewis Carroll's *Through the Looking Glass.* And any bio of this Scot must make it clear he's the last thing from the *Masterpiece Theatre* vision of an English stuffed shirt, because he's the kind who leaves playful messages on your phone machine — and still earns enjoyable royalties from early sex manuals such as the best-selling *How to Drive Your Man Wild in Bed!*

Now, settle your attention on the Graham Masterton whom Stanley Wiater featured as one of the 27 "Masters of Horror" in *Dark Dreamers* — the author of *Charnel House, Feast, The Manitou, Night Warriors,* and *Night Plague* — the versatile author and anthologist* who told Wiater, "I *have* to be frightened by what I'm doing. . . (to have) a true feeling of fear in me." And add what Graham said on the phone from Surrey, describing this new story to me: "I think I may be writing this one over and over as the years pass." It fascinated him; it contains the "true feeling" he had discussed. You'll have it, too, in the Sweet Gum Motor Court of Henry County, Alabama.

A huge electric storm brewed up as Martin drove out of Tumbleton, in Henry County, Alabama, and fat warm raindrops began to patter

*Scare Care, TOR Books, $19.95, ISBN 0-312-93156-5.

onto the windshield of his rented Pontiac. Over to the east, above the Chattahoochee valley, the sky was so dark that it was purple, and snakes'-tongues of lightning licked the distant hills.

Behind him, to the west, the sky was still clear and serene, and Martin was tempted to U-turn and drive back. But he was expected in Eufaula this evening at six, and he still had a hell of a haul; and he doubted in any case if he could outrun the approaching rainclouds. The wind was rising, and already the bright green sunlit trees were beginning to thrash and dip like panicky women.

He switched on the Pontiac's radio, and pressed "seek." Maybe he could find a local weather forecast. But all he could hear was fuzzy voices. One of them sounded just like his ex-wife nagging. Over and over, *"you bastard, you predictable bastard."* He pressed "seek" again and picked up *"—vorce becomes final today..."*

"Divorce" — shit! That was all he wanted to hear. If he hadn't gone to that sales seminar in Atlanta last April...if he hadn't picked up that ridiculous ass-wiggling girl in the hotel bar...if Marnie hadn't flown to Atlanta to surprise him...if life wasn't always so damned grisly and so damned absurdly *un*surprising.

Marnie had always told him that it would only take one act of infidelity to destroy her trust in him; and it had.

She and her lawyers had systematically dismantled his life. She had taken the house, the cars, the paintings, the silver, the savings. She hadn't taken Ruff, his retriever, but the day after the divorce became final, Ruff had slipped the dog-sitter's leash and been fatally injured under the wheels of a van.

Martin was now reduced to old-style town-to-town traveling, the Alabama and Louisiana representative of Confederate Insurance, selling packages of cut-price business cover to one fat, sweaty redneck after another. He could sum up the majority of his customers in just a few words: bald, bigoted, with appalling taste in neckties. But he wasn't complaining. It had been his own choice to travel. He had the experience and the references to find himself a much better job, but (for a while, anyway) he felt like letting the days go by without name or number, and he felt like exploring the South. Days of steamy heat and sassafras; days of rain and bayous and girder bridges; days of small towns melting under dust-beige skies; and deputy sheriffs with mirror-blind eyes.

The rain lashed harder and harder. Martin flicked the windshield wipers to HI, but even when the wipers were flinging themselves from side to side at top speed, they were scarcely able to cope. The evening grew suddenly so dark that Martin felt as if the highway had been overshadowed by the wing of a giant crow. *Just then flew down a monstrous crow, as black as a tar barrel...*

He kept driving, hoping that the storm would ease. But after nearly an hour the rain was just as furious, and lightning was crackling all around him like a plantation of tall electrified trees. He had to drive slower and slower, down to 20 mph, simply because he couldn't see where he was going. The ditches at the sides of the highway were gorged with sewage-brown water and the water suddenly began to flood across the blacktop. The Pontiac's air conditioning worked only intermittently and he had to keep wiping the inside of the windshield with his crumpled-up handkerchief. He was terrified that a truck was going to come cannonballing out of the rain and collide with him head-on. Or—almost as bad—that another truck would rear-end him. He had seen that happen only two days ago, on Highway 331 just a few miles north of Opp. A whole family had been sent careening in their Chevy Blazer right off a bridge and down a steep embankment, where they had lain in individual depressions in the lush green weeds, bleeding, broken, screaming for help.

He had woken up in his motel room the same night and he could still hear them screaming.

Lightning crackled again, followed almost at once by a catastrophic rumble of thunder, real heaven-splitting stuff. If it were possible, the rain cascaded down harder and the floodwaters spurted and bellowed against the Pontiac's floorpan. Martin smeared the windshield with his handkerchief and strained his eyes and prayed for some kind of a turn-off where he could wait for the storm to pass.

Then, through the rain and spray and the misted-up glass of his windshield, he saw a pale illuminated blur. A light. *No*—a sign, of some kind. A green neon sign that (as he slowed and approached it) read "Sweet Gum Motor Court." And, underneath, flickering dully, the word "acancies."

O Lord I thank Thee for all Thy many favors, and in particular for the Sweet Gum Motor Court in Henry County, Alabama, with its acancies.

Martin turned off the highway and down a sloping driveway that, in this weather, was almost a waterfall. Then ahead of him he saw an L-shaped arrangement of cabins with wooden verandahs and corrugated-iron roofing, and (on one side) an oddly-proportioned clapboard house which at first appeared to be gray but, in the sweeping light of his headlights, turned out to be pale green. There were lights inside the house, and he could see a white-haired man in a red plaid shirt and suspenders, and (O Lord I really *do* thank Thee) the smell of hamburgs in the air.

He parked as close to the house as he could, then wrenched open the Pontiac's door and hurried with his coat tugged in a peak over his head to the brightly-lit front verandah. Even though the highway had been flooded and his wipers had struggled to keep his windshield clear, he hadn't realized fully how torrential this rainstorm was. In the few seconds it took him to cross from his car to the house he was soaked through, and the new light tan Oxfords that he had bought in Dothan were reduced to the consistency of blackened cardboard.

He opened the screen door but the main door was locked, and he jarred his wrist trying to pull it open. He rattled the doorhandle, then knocked with his wedding band on the glass. Yes, he still wore his wedding band. It gave him a ready-made excuse when pink-lipsticked strumpets slid up onto barstools next to him and asked him in those cheap husky accents if he needed a little friendship, sugar.

He didn't need friendship. He needed hot timeless days, and miniscule communities where it was interesting to watch flies walking up a window, and electric storms like this; the catharsis of being unimportant, and adrift.

The white-haired man in the red plaid shirt came to the door and somehow he was uglier and less welcoming than he had appeared through the rain. He had a face that would have looked better the other way, chinside up, like Old Man Muffaroo. Dull-brown suspicious eyes that reminded Martin of olives left on a lunch counter too long.

"What do you want?" he shouted through the glass.

"What do you think I want?" Martin shouted back. "Look at me! I'm soaked! I need a room!"

The white-haired man stared at him without answering, as if Martin had spoken a foreign language. Then a big henna-haired woman in a green dress appeared behind him, and Martin could hear her say, "What the hell's going on here, Vernon?"

"Fellow wants a room."

"A room?"

"That's what he said."

"Well, for God's sake, Vernon, if the fellow wants a room, then for God's sake open up that door and give him a room. You don't get any damned better, do you? You really don't."

She unlocked the door and held it wide so that Martin could step inside. As he passed her he smelled frying hamburgs, sour armpit and Avon scent.

"Hell of a storm," she said, closing and locking the door behind him. "Come through to the office, I'll fix you up."

Martin followed her along a red-lino corridor flanked with damp-stained posters for Martz Airlines' "Safe Scenic Swift Service" and vacations in Bermuda. In the office there was an untidy desk, a whirring electric fan, and a pegboard with rows of keys hanging on it. There were no keys missing so Martin assumed that he was the only guest. Not surprising, the reception that would-be customers were given by old upside-down-face Vernon.

A ragged-looking brown dog was slumbering on the floor. "Just for the night?" asked the woman, stepping over it.

"That's right," Martin told her. "I was supposed to meet somebody in Eufaula at six, but there's no hope of my getting there now." As if to reassure him that he had made the right decision by stopping here, the rain rattled noisily against the window, and the dog stirred in its sleep. Dreaming of quail, maybe; or hamburgs.

Vernon was standing just outside the office, scratching the eczema on his elbow. "You'll find plenty of peace here, mister. You won't be disturbed."

Martin signed his name in the register. The pages were deckled with damp. "Anyplace I can get something to eat?"

The woman peered at his signature. Then she said, "Used to be a diner down the road about a half-mile did good ribs but that closed. Owner blew his head off with a shotgun. Business being so bad and all."

She looked up at him, aware that she hadn't yet answered his question. "But I can rustle you some eggs 'n' bacon or cornbeef hash or something of that nature."

"Maybe some eggs and bacon," said Martin. "Now. . .maybe I can get myself dried off and use the telephone."

The woman unhooked one of the keys, handed it to Vernon. "Number Two'll do best. It's closer to the office and the bed's new."

She unlocked the front door and Vernon led him out into the rain again. The concrete parking lot was awash with floodwater and bright brown silt. Martin heaved his overnight case out of the trunk of the Pontiac and then followed Vernon across to the first row of cabins. Vernon stood hunched in front of the door with his white hair dripping, trying to find the right way to turn the key. At last he managed to open up and switch on the light.

Number Two was a drab room with a sculptured red carpet and a mustard-colored bedspread. There were two dimly-shaded lamps beside the bed and another on the cheap varnished desk. Martin put down his case and offered Vernon a dollar bill, but Vernon waved it away. "That's not necessary, mister; not here, on a night like this. So long as you pay before you go." It occurred to Martin that — almost uniquely for these days — the woman hadn't taken an impression of his credit card.

"Food won't be long," said Vernon. "You want any drinks or anything? Beer maybe?"

"A couple of lites would go down well."

Vernon frowned around the room. "These lights ain't sufficient?"

"No, no. I mean 'lites' like in 'lite beer.'"

"Lite beer," Vernon repeated, as if Martin had said something totally mysterious, but he was too polite to ask what it meant.

"Miller Lite, Coors Lite; anything."

"Coors Lite," Vernon repeated, in the same baffled way.

He left, closing the door firmly behind him. It had swollen slightly in the downpour and needed to be tugged. With a loud, elaborate, extended sigh, Martin raked back his wet hair with his fingers, lifted off his dark-shouldered coat, and loosened his wet necktie with a squeak that set his teeth on edge almost as much as fingernails on slate.

He pushed open the door to the bathroom and found dismal green-painted walls and a shower curtain decorated with faded tropical fish. But there were four large towels folded up on the shelf, three of them marked "Holiday Inn" and the fourth marked "Tropicana Hotel, Key Largo." He stripped and dried himself, and then dressed in clean pajamas and blue silk bathrobe, and combed his hair. He wished that Vernon would hurry up with that beer: his throat was dry and he felt that he might be catching a cold.

He looked around for the tv. Maybe there was a cable movie he could watch tonight. But to his surprise there was no tv. He couldn't believe it. What kind of a motel had rooms with no tv? The only entertainment available was a pack of sexy playing cards and an old Zenith radio. *Shit.*

He pulled open the cabin door and looked outside. The rain was still thundering down. A rain barrel under the next row of cabins was noisily overflowing and somewhere a broken gutter was splattering. No sign of Vernon. No sign of anything but this shabby huddle of cabins and the dim green light that said acancies.

He wedged the door shut. He thought of all the times that he had cursed Howard Johnson's for their sameness and their lack of luxury. But a Howard Johnson's would have been paradise compared with the Sweet Gum Motor Court. All it was doing was keeping him safely off the highway and the rain off his head.

He sat down at the desk and picked up the telephone. After a long, crackling pause, the voice of the henna-haired woman said, "You want something, mister?"

"Yes, I do. I want to place a call to a number in Eufaula — Chattahoochee Moldings, Inc. Person-to-person to Mr. Dick Bogdanovich."

"I'm frying your eggs 'n' bacon. What do you want first, your call or your eggs 'n' bacon?"

"Well. . . I really need to make this call. He usually leaves the office at seven-thirty."

"Eggs'll spoil, if they haven't already."

"Can't I dial the number myself?"

"'Fraid not, not from the cabins. Otherwise we'd have guests calling their long-lost sweethearts in Athens, Georgia, and chewing the fat for an hour at a time with their folks back in Wolf Point, Montana, wouldn't we, and the profit in this business is too tight for that."

"Ma'am, all I want to do is make a single fifteen-second telephone call to Eufaula, to inform my client that I shan't be able to make our meeting this evening. That's a little different from an hour-long call to — Wolf Point, Montana." *Thinking:* what on earth had inspired her to say "Wolf Point, Montana?"

"I'm sorry, you can't dial direct from the cabins; and I can smell eggwhite burning."

The phone clicked and then he heard nothing but a sizzling sound. It could have been static, it could have been frying. It didn't much matter. Frying and static were equally useless to him.

His eggs and bacon eventually arrived at a quarter after eight. Vernon brought them across from the office building under a rain-beaded aluminum dish-cover. Vernon himself was covered by an Army surplus parka, dark khaki with wet.

"Rain, rain, goddamned rain," said Vernon. He set the plate down on the desk.

"No knife and fork," said Martin. "No beer."

"Oh, I got it all here," Vernon told him, and fumbled in the pockets of his parka. He produced knife, fork, paper napkins, salt, pepper, catsup, and three chilled bottles of Big 6 Beer.

"Denise fried the eggs over, on account of them being burned."

Martin raised the aluminum cover. The eggs and bacon looked remarkably good: heaps of thin crisp rashers, three big farm eggs, sunnyside up; toast, fried tomatoes, and hash browns; and lots of crispy bits. "Tell her thanks."

"She'll charge you for them, the extra eggs."

"That's okay. Tell her thanks."

After Vernon had gone, wedging the door shut again, Martin propped himself up in bed with his supper balanced in his lap, and switched on the radio. It took a few moments for it to warm up: then the dial began to glow, and he smelled that extraordinary nostalgic smell of hot dust that his grandmother's Zenith had always given off whenever it heated up.

He twisted the brown bakelite tuning knob but most of the dial produced nothing but weird alien whistlings and whoopings, or a fierce sizzling noise, or voices that were so blippy and blotchy that it was impossible to understand what they were saying. As he prodded his fork into his second egg, however, he suddenly picked up a voice that was comparatively crisp.

"*...Eight-thirty, Eastern Time...and this is the Song O' The South Soda Hour...coming to you from the Dauphin Street Studios in Mobile, Alabama...continuing our dramatization of...'The Heart of Helen Day'...with Randy Pressburger...John McLaren...Susan Medici...and starring, as Helen Day...Andrea Lawrence...*"

Martin turned the dial further but all he could find were more fizzes, more pops, and a very faint jazz rendition of the old Negro ballad *Will the Circle Be Unbroken*.

"*...in the same old window, on a cold and cloudy day...I seen them hearse wheels rolling...they was taking Chief Jolly away...*"

He decided that he could do without a funeral dirge, so he turned back to *The Heart of Helen Day*. This turned out to be a chatty romantic radio-soap about a busybody girl who worked for a tough-talking private detective and kept losing her heart to his clients, even though the tough-talking private detective really loved her more than anybody else.

Martin finished his supper and drank two bottles of beer and listened to the serial in amusement. It sounded incredibly 1930s, with all the actors talking in brisk, clipped voices like *One Man's Family* or the *Chase & Sanborn Hour*.

"*But he's not guilty, I tell you. I just know he's not guilty.*"

"*How can you know? You don't have any proof.*"

"*I searched his eyes, that's all.*"

"You searched his eyes but I searched his hotel room."
"Oh, Mickey. I looked in his face and all I saw was innocence."
"You looked in his face? That's unusual. I never knew you looked any higher than a man's wallet."
This week's episode concerned a famous bandleader who had been accused of throwing a beautiful but faithless singer out of the seventh floor window of a downtown hotel. The bandleader's alibi was that he had been conducting a recording session at the time. But Helen Day suspected he had used a stand-in.

Martin got up off the bed and went to the door, opened it. The room was becoming stuffy and smelled of food. He put his plate out on the boardwalk, where it rapidly filled with rain and circles of grease.

"It couldn't have been Philip, Philip always taps the rostrum three times with his baton before he starts to conduct...and in this recording the conductor doesn't tap the rostrum at all."

Martin stayed by the door, leaning against the jamb, watching the rain barrel overflow and the silty mud forming a Mississippi delta in the parking lot, and the distant dancing of the lightning. Behind him the radio chattered, with occasional melodramatic bursts of music, and interruptions for commercials.

"'The Heart of Helen Day' is brought to you by Song O' The South Soda...the fruitier, more refreshing soda that makes the whole South sing..."

Then it was back to Helen Day. She was talking at a cocktail party about her success in solving the case of Philip the rostrum-tapping bandleader. Martin drank his third and last beer out of the bottle and wondered why the radio station had even considered broadcasting such a stilted, outdated radio soap, when there was *Get a Life* and *The Simpsons* on tv and wall-to-wall FM. Everyplace except here, of course; the Sweet Gum Motor Court, in Henry County, Alabama, in the rain.

"He was so handsome. Yet I knew that he was wicked, underneath."

Suddenly, there was the sound of a door banging in the background. Then the clatter of something falling over. A muffled voice said, "Get out of here, you can't come in here, we're recording!" Then another shout and a blurt of thick static as if somebody had knocked the microphone.

At first, Martin thought this must be part of the plot. But the shouting and struggling were so indistinct that he realized quickly there must be an intruder in the radio studio, a *real* intruder, and that the actors and technicians were trying to subdue him. There was another jumble of sound and then an extraordinarily long-drawn-out scream, rising higher and higher, increasingly hysterical.

Then the most terrible thing Martin had ever heard in his life. He turned away from the open door to stare at the radio with his eyes wide and his scalp prickling with horror.

"Oh God! Oh God! John! John! Oh God help me! He's cut me open! Oh God! My stomach's falling out!"

A noise like somebody dropping a sodden bath towel. Then more shouts, and more thumps. A nasal, panicky voice shouting, "Ambulance! For Christ's sake, Jeff! Get an ambulance!" Then a sharp blip — and the program was cut off.

Martin sat on the bed beside the radio waiting for the program to come back on the air, or some kind of announcement by the radio station. But there was nothing but white noise which went on and on and on, like a bus journey along an endless and unfamiliar highway through thick fog.

He tried retuning the radio but all he got were the same old crackles as before, or those distant foggy Negroes singing. *"I saw the...hearse wheels rolling...they were taking my...mother away..."* Did they always sing the same dirge?

Sometime after eleven o'clock he switched off the radio, washed his teeth, and climbed into bed. But all night he lay listening to the rain and thinking of *The Heart of Helen Day.* He guessed if an actress had really been attacked in a radio studio he'd hear about it on tomorrow's news. Maybe it had all been part of the soap. But — up until that moment — it had sounded so normal and correct, even if it had been ridiculously dated. Maybe it had been one of those *War of the Worlds*-type gimmicks, to frighten the listeners.

Or maybe it had actually happened, and Helen Day had really had her heart cut out.

He was awakened at seven o'clock by Vernon tapping at the door. Outside it was lighter but still raining, although not so heavily. Vernon brought pancakes and syrup and hot coffee. He set them down on the desk and sniffed.

"Thanks," said Martin, sleepily smearing his face with his hands.

"Don't mention it."

"Hey...before you go...did you watch the news this morning?"

"The news?"

"The tv news...you know, like what's happening in the world?"

Vernon shook his head, suspiciously.

"Well...did you hear about any radio actress being murdered?"

Vernon said, "No...I didn't hear anything like that. But what I did hear, the highway's all washed out between here and Eufaula, and 54 between Lawrenceville and Edwin's washed out, too. So you'll have to double back to Graball and take 51 through Clio. That's if you're still inclined to go to Eufaula, can't stick the place myself."

"No," said Martin, sipping coffee. "I don't think I can, either."

When he had finished his breakfast Martin packed his traveling bag and looked around the room to make sure he hadn't left anything behind. He stood by the open door listening to the rain clattering from the gutters and stared at the radio. Had he dreamed it? Maybe he would never know.

He put down his bag, walked across to the radio and switched it on. After it had warmed up, he heard a stream of static; but then— so abruptly that it made him jump—an announcer's voice said, "'—of Helen Day,' brought to you by Song O' The South Soda..."

He listened raptly, standing in the middle of the room with the door open. It was the same episode as last night, the story of the bandleader who didn't tap the rostrum. Then, the same words: *"He was so handsome. Yet I knew that he was wicked, underneath."*

Then again, the door opening. The shouts. The microphone knocked. Scuffles, screams. And that terrible, terrible cry of agony, *"Oh God! Oh God! John! John! Oh God help me! He's cut me open! Oh God! My stomach's falling out!"*

Then, nothing. Only crackling and shushing and occasional spits of static.

Martin swallowed dryly. Was that a repeat? Was it the news? If it was the news, how come there was no commentary? He stood with his hand over his mouth wondering what to do.

He drove into Mobile late that evening. The sky was purple and there was still a strong feeling of electricity in the air. That day, he had driven on Highway 10 all the way across north Florida, and as he made the final crossing of Polecat Bay toward the glittering water-distorted lights of the docks, he felt stiff and cramped and ready for nothing but a stiff drink and a night of undisturbed sleep. But first of all, he was determined to find the Dauphin Street radio studios.

It took him over an hour. The Dauphin Street Studios weren't in the phone book. Two cops he stopped hadn't heard of it, either, although they asked in a tight, suspicious drawl to look at his driver's license and registration. Eventually, however, he stopped at a bar called the Cat's Pajamas, a noisy, crowded place close to the intersection with Florida Street, and asked the bartender, whose bald head shone oddly blue in the light from the shelves, as if he were an alien.

"Dauphin Street Studios closed down before the war. Nineteen forty-one, maybe nineteen forty-two. But ask Harry. He used to work there when he was younger, studio technician or something. There he is; second booth along."

Harry turned out to be a neat, retired character with cropped white hair, a sallow face, and a whispery way of talking. Martin sat down opposite him. "Understand you worked at the Dauphin Street Studios?"

Harry looked at him oddly. "What kind of a question is that?"

"I'm interested in something that might have happened there."

"Well. . .the last broadcast that went out from the Dauphin Street Studios was March 7, 1941; that was when WMOB went bust. That was a lifetime ago."

"Do you want a drink?" Martin asked him.

"For sure. Wild Turkey, on the rocks."

"Do you remember a soap called *The Heart of Helen Day?*"

There was a long silence. Then Harry said, "Sure I do. Everybody remembers *The Heart of Helen Day*. That program was part of the reason that WMOB had to close down.

"Tell me."

Harry shrugged. "Not much to tell. The girl who played Helen Day was real pretty. I never saw a girl so pretty, before or since. Andrea Lawrence. Blonde, bright. I was in love with her; but then, so was everybody else. She used to get all kinds of weird mail and phone calls. In those days you could still be a radio star, and of course you got all the crank stuff that went with being a star. One day, Andrea started getting death threats. Very sick phone calls that said things like, 'I'm going to gut you, you harlot.' Stuff like that."

Martin said, "It really happened, then? She really was murdered in the studio?"

"Most horrible thing I ever saw in my life. I was only a kid. . .well, nineteen. I had nightmares about it for years afterward. A guy burst into the studio. I never even saw the knife, although the cops said it was huge, a real hog-butchering knife. He stuck it in her lower abdomen and whipped it upwards — so quick that I thought he was punching her. Then her entire insides came out, all over the studio floor. Just like that. I had nightmares about it for years."

Martin licked his lips. He didn't seem to have any saliva at all. "Did they catch him? The guy who killed her?"

Harry shook his head. "There was too much confusion. Everybody was too shocked. Before we knew what had happened, he was gone. The cops went through the city with a fine-tooth comb, but they never found him. *The Heart of Helen Day* was canceled, of course; and after that, WMOB gradually fell apart and went out of business. Not that television wasn't slowly killing it already."

"Was there a recording of that broadcast?" Martin asked.

Harry said, "Sure. We recorded everything."

"Do you think somebody could be transmitting it again?"

"What?"

"I've heard it. I've heard the episode where she gets murdered. I've heard the whole thing. . .even when she says 'Oh God, he's cut my stomach open.'"

"That's impossible."

"I *heard* it. Not just once, but twice."

Harry stared at Martin as if he were mad. "That's totally impossible. For one thing, there was only one recording, and that was my master tape; and my master tape was destroyed in a fire along with all of WMOB's other tapes, in January, 1942. Insurance arson, if you ask me. But I saw the burned spool myself.

"For another thing, I jumped up as soon as the guy came into the studio and accidentally switched off the tape recorder. The actual killing was never recorded. If you heard it, my friend—you were hearing ghosts."

"Ghosts? I don't think so. I heard it clear as a bell."

"Well. . .you're not the only one who's heard stuff from the past. I was reading the other day some guy in Montana picked up his dead mother arguing with his dead father on his car radio whenever it thundered."

Martin had been ready to leave, but now he leaned forward and said to Harry, "Whenever it *thundered*? How?"

"I don't know. It sounds far-fetched. But the theory is that the human brain records things it hears as electrical impulses, right? Normally, it *keeps* them stored. But in certain atmospheric conditions, it *discharges* those impulses. . .so strongly that they can get picked up by a radio receiver. In this case, the guy's car radio. But apparently they have to be real close. Seventy or eighty feet away, not much more."

Seventy or eighty feet away. Who had been seventy or eighty feet away from that old Zenith radio when it thundered? Who had been old enough and unhinged enough to have attacked Andrea Lawrence all those years ago in the Dauphin Street Studios? Who wouldn't have been found in the city because, maybe, he didn't actually live *in the city?*

There was no proof. No proof at all. But apart from the actors and the radio technicians, only the killer would have heard Andrea Lawrence's last words. . .only the killer would have remembered them. So that one thundery night, nearly forty years later, they would have come crackling out on an old-fashioned radio set. Not a program at all, but a *memory*.

It was late in the afternoon and unbearably steamy when Martin drove his mud-splattered Pontiac back to the Sweet Gum Motor Court. There was a strong smell of drying mud and chicken feed in the air. He parked and wearily climbed out.

He knocked at the screen door. He had to wait a long time before anybody answered. The ragged tan dog sat not far away, and watched him, and panted. Eventually Vernon appeared and unlocked the door.

"You again," he said.

"Is Denise around?"

"What do you want her for?"

"To tell you the truth, it's *you* I wanted."

"Oh yeah?"

"I just wanted to ask you a couple of questions about Andrea Lawrence. You ever heard of Andrea Lawrence? She played Helen Day, in *The Heart of Helen Day*."

Long silence. Eyes dull as olives behind the reflective glass. Then the key, turning in the lock. "You'd best come on in. Go in the office. I won't keep you more'n a couple of minutes."

The tired-looking redhead took the barrettes out of her hair and shook it loose. On the desk, the remains of her evening meal had attracted the attention of two persistent flies. She picked up the whisky glass and swallowed, and coughed.

She couldn't believe there was no tv here. If it hadn't been such a stormy night, she would have driven further, to someplace decent. But half the roads were flooded out and she was frightened of lightning.

She switched on the radio. Fuzzy jazz, dance music, some kind of black funeral song. Then two voices in what sounded like a radio play. She lay back on the bed and closed her eyes and listened. If only her husband could see her now.

"You again."

"Is Denise around?"

"What do you want her for?"

"To tell you the truth, it's you I wanted."

The woman sipped more whisky. Outside, the thunder banged grumpily, and the rain started to gush down more heavily.

"I heard something pretty curious on my radio last night."

"Oh yeah?"

"I heard—hey, what are you doing? What the hell do you think you're doing? Get away from—aahh! Jesus Christ! Aaaaggggh! Jesus Christ! You've cut me! Oh Jesus Christ you've cut me open!"

Muffled knocks. A sound like a chair falling over. An indescribable splattering. Then an awful gasping. *"Help me, for Christ's sake. Help me!"*

"Help you what? Help you get me and Denise put away for murder? Or a nuthouse or something?"

"Help me, Jesus, it hurts so much!"

"And didn't it hurt Denise, to listen to that Helen Day every single week, and how Helen Day got men just by winking her eye, and Denise's only fiancé left her high and dry for a girl just like that? Same given name, too—Andrea! Don't you think that hurt?"

"Help me, Vernon."

"Help you nothing. You're all the same. Leaving Denise for your fancy-women."

There was a cry like an owl being dismembered alive by a coyote. Then nothing but white noise, on and on and on.

The woman was already asleep. The white noise continued through the night, like an endless bus journey along an unfamiliar highway, through thick fog.

Nothing But the Best

Brian McNaughton

With lucid, needle-sharp stories in the 1990 centenary anthology, *Lovecraft's Legacy,* as well as that year's World Fantasy Convention souvenir book ("The Vendren Worm"), Brian McNaughton has begun to realize his potential as a special craftsman of memorable yarns — just as people expected him to do several years back when he was regularly selling to the major men's magazines. Be on the alert for still more fiction by Brian in upcoming issues of the always-coveted *Weirdbook.*

With stops in Maine and Neptune, New Jersey, McNaughton is a devotee of the poet Swinburne, "a wild and roaring boy who suddenly switched off like a lightbulb at the age of about thirty." He believes that there are "explicit photographs" of Algernon's affair with a bareback rider "under lock and key in the British Museum."

Be that as it may, McNaughton's bulb shines brightly, emanating something of Ray Russell's sleek inventiveness and apt choice of words. Yet the wit is all his own.

"You're ugly, you're creepy, you're the filthiest man I ever knew!" Jessica Sexton cried.

"Yes." Ahab Wakefield's head was meekly bowed to hide the fury in his eyes. "But I'm rich."

"And that's the filthiest thing you ever said!"

She flung back his gifts. The emerald necklace bit his cheek. The tiger-skin coat she hurled shrouded him momentarily in the ghost of its original owner's clutch.

"No, please keep them," he said, "they're — "

"Impossible to explain to my husband."

He learned that her laugh could be splendidly scornful. He had possessed only her body, and she had so much more to offer — but it was hopeless.

"Impossible to explain. . . like so much else." Having admitted the futility of his love, he allowed his lips to relax into their most comfortable sneer. "How do you propose to explain why you left him? And what you've been doing all this while?"

"Bruce will forgive me. And even if he doesn't, I can go to any hospital for the criminally insane and find a hundred better men than you'll ever be. You don't know. . .*anything.* Did you really think you could impress me with this?" Her toe, perfect to its pallid lunula, nudged the coat with disdain.

"You deserve nothing but the best."

"Do you know how few of these magnificent creatures are left in the world? To kill one of them for a lousy coat — that disgusts me even more than you do."

Ahab sighed, admitting his miscalculation. The greatest burden of his long life, he often thought, was trying to keep up with current fads.

"But there is only one Jessica." The pain of that truth drove him to his knees.

"Very bad." She spoke with critical detachment. "Sometimes I think you learned how people behave from watching silent movies. What I ever could have seen in you, why I should have left the husband I love so much. . ." She paused, as if realizing that these questions had no sane answers. "This hogwash" — her gesture included ancient volumes on swaybacked shelves, dried herbs and fungi hanging from the ceiling-beams, the uniquely malformed skull on his desk — "it doesn't really *work,* does it?"

He rose deliberately to his commanding height and gazed down on her with less warmth than a corpse from a gibbet. "You will see."

Fright was another emotion Jessica had not shown him, and she expressed it fetchingly. As she fled, Ahab vowed to see more.

He had indulged this folly before, and with the same result. To win a love freely given, he had released Chastity Hopkins, of Portsmouth, N.H., from a similar enchantment in 1652. She had called him a pig-swyving pissabed and scurried off to lodge a complaint of witchcraft. Jessica Sexton had no such recourse. In some small ways, the world had changed for the better.

"When will I learn?"

Thester, the malapert creature that nested in the skull, croaked: "Nevermore."

Ignoring his familiar, Ahab took a knife from his desk and cut a strip of tiger-skin long enough to bind his cadaverous waist. He had no qualms about ruining the fabulously expensive coat. Cheating fools was his hobby, and he had paid the furrier with illusory cash. That he had not given Jessica an illusory coat proved the depth of his sincerity. It was fitting that the rejected love-token should be his instrument of vengeance.

"Master!" Thester's agitated claws rattled the skull. "Master, give her the pox, give her the flux, afflict her with some cagastrical distemper beyond the skill of the most learned surgeons—"

"Death by dismemberment and ingestion," Ahab said as he assembled further materials, "is beyond their skill."

"Remember what happened in Avignon in 1329?"

"Avignon? My memory. . ."

"That time you turned into a wolf to assassinate Pope John XXII. And the gamekeeper who sold you the wolfhide belt neglected to inform you that the animal had died after chewing off its trapped leg. Whereupon you learned—"

"Yes, yes, yes!" Ahab snapped, having remembered.

"—whereupon you learned that a three-legged wolf is no match for a pack of hounds. You had to spend the Renaissance in bed."

It was true that Ahab would assume the form of the particular beast whose pelt he used. He gave the strip of fur a covert inspection, but it told him nothing. He would have to translate himself to Malaysia to trace the provenance of the hide, and that might take hours. He dismissed Thester's quibbles.

"My dear abomination, a three-legged tiger—even one that's blind and toothless to boot—will be all that's needed for our loving young couple."

"And their dog?"

He winced. Shape-changing was a young man's game, and Ahab was no longer the sprightly bicentenarian who had disported himself as a crocodile among the wading courtlings of Nitokris. He had feared dogs ever since the Avignon fiasco, but he had forgotten the Sextons' pet, a Doberman pinscher who had in its last life commanded— with notably more audacity than brains—an SS panzer division. Unaware of this background, Jessica had christened it Muffin.

Climbing over the doomed couple's back fence, Ahab was thankful for Thester's reminder. Forewarned, he had rendered himself not just invisible, but inaudible and inodorous. Even so the dog sprang from its doze on the patio and paced the backyard, tunelessly growling the dimly recalled Curse-motif from Wagner's *Ring*. Ahab would never admit to Thester that he'd spared him an embarrassment, but he resolved to find the little horror an especially roly-poly child soon.

He stripped to the furry belt, opened a vein unseen, and made the appropriate symbols in blood on the flagstones of the patio. The dog sprinted and snarled at random shadows as Ahab crouched on all fours and spoke the required words.

Instantly the vigor of a healthy young beast surged through him. The formerly still night echoed with racketing bats and clamorous moths. The neutral smell of the yard was submerged under a canine stench so vivid and frightening that it hurt. It was the memory of Avignon that pained him, of course, potentiated by even the biggest cat's hatred for its old enemy.

As the other enchantments were canceled and Ahab stood revealed in all his fearful symmetry, the stupid dog charged. Ahab's sharper eyes, no doubt, made the puny creature seem like a black and tan locomotive bearing down on him, but he stood his ground and drew back his paw to blast Muffin's bones to gravel.

"What in hell was that?" Bruce Sexton gasped.

"Does it matter?" Jessica tried to draw him down again.

"I guess—" A second piteous cry froze him in the act of being drawn. He tumbled from bed and ran to switch on the patio lights.

"My God! Look—no, *don't* look, Jess. Muffin's got hold of something, a..."

"A what?"

Not believing his eyes, he forced them again toward the patio. "It must've been somebody's pet," he said. "But what kind of a nut would dye a rabbit with orange and black stripes?"

Somewhere

Denise Dumars

The editor and publisher of her own review journal *(Dumars Reviews)*, Denise Dumars is the author of a published book of poetry, *Sheet Lightning* (Terata, 1987), a frequent contributor to respected "smaller" publications such as *Grue, Eldritch Tales* and *Space & Time,* a library professional in the city of El Segundo, and "an Aquarius, near the cusp of Pisces."

Dumars holds A.A., B.A., and M.A. degrees in English, teaches an advanced poetry workshop in her "spare time," and resides in Hawthorne, California, with her author husband Todd Mecklem.

And as it is always the case with the very good ones, all her work speaks — eloquently — for itself.

The grope and blink of sun versus night
is all one, really.
Somewhere it is always midnight
somewhere it is always dawn
somewhere there is always someone
pleading with the gods,
throwing the bone,
scourging the back.

Dogs boil out of the kennel
lights refuse to stop blinking.
So much for the Tarot,
so much for the future,
so much for the reason to raze
the hate from each breast.

*　　*　　*

Over a field of daisies
an aeroplane falls down.
Heads splat amongst the foliage
in a dewy afternoon,
and sunflowers turn their heads
to the momentary streak of silver
lighting up the sky before the bird descends.

Local women burn the field days later,
and the children who have eaten
of the sunflowers, unbeknownst
to their mothers, begin
to grow extra limbs.

Sitting in the shade
with black glasses on, I drop
my withered hand into the hat.
I draw out two cards, six dice,
and a bundle of dried wheatstraw.
I throw the straw and the wind takes it
and it grows like morning light
and all over the town great shocks of wheat
erupt through gardens and garages,
break the soil and stun like ball lightning.

Everyone who knows me
dons black glasses
and pretends not to see.

Milestone's Face

Gary Brandner

Another horror-hand from the midwest — Kisner, Gorman, Tilton, Rex Miller, Castle and the editor are some others — Gary Brandner is one of the 26 writers Stanley Wiater interviewed for *Dark Dreamers,* the subtitle for which is this: "Conversations with the Masters of Horror." That says a lot; so does the way Gary's first horror novel, *The Howling,* became the Academy of Science Fiction, Fantasy, and Horror Films' Best Horror Movie of 1981.

But instead of focussing on the film and its sequels, then dismissing Martine's husband the same way Filmdom does most horror novelists, consider: Werewolves have been a staple of horror for eons. Who but this pleasant guy had the imagination to use them so effectively that, King-like, he built a cottage industry out of fangs and hair?

And what of 30 other books, including *Walkers — West Coast Review*'s Best Original Paperback of 1980? And his first pro sale in 1970 to *EQMM*? Brandner told Wiater he's a "*book* writer" first, and he clearly meant it. Read *Floater,* for evidence, or the novella "Damntown."

Or Gary Brandner's seventieth or so short story, up next. *Then* read *Floater*!

Georgie the makeup man applied sooty smudges under the blazing blue eyes of Stuart Milestone. He thumbed ghost-gray under the cheekbones to impart a hollow look to Milestone's firm, ruddy cheeks. He carefully pencilled lines from the flare of the nostrils to the corners of the determined mouth. Finally Georgie stood back, cocked his head, and studied his work.

"It's a real challenge to make you look like a bum, Mr. Milestone."

"Homeless person, Georgie. We don't have bums any more."

"Oh, right. It's still a chore. I mean, even your stubble looks healthy."

Milestone flashed the grin that kept The Big Six News at the top of the local ratings among female viewers. "This will be the last time," he said. "We wrap the series today. A week from Monday it goes on the air in time for sweeps month."

"We all think you've got a winner," Georgie said.

"I'd love to see their reaction over at Eyewitness News when we hit them with social consciousness. They're still doing T and A. Times have changed. People want *real.* They want to feel the grit, smell the dirt. That's what we're going to give them."

A short knock at the door of the makeup cubicle, and a tall young man with a long, serious face entered.

"Stuart, I've made a couple of changes in your close for tonight. Want to look it over?"

"What for? Just make sure the cue cards are legible."

The younger man started to leave.

"Oh, say, Alan, I meant to tell you you've been doing a fine job filling for me this week."

"Thanks."

"But don't get too good. I figure I've got a few more seasons before you take over as anchor." Milestone laughed to show he was joking.

Alan Baird laughed because he knew Milestone was serious.

The last day of shooting on Skid Row went without a hitch. The Channel 6 camera van, its logo painted over with a grubby brown, went undetected parked in a loading zone. During the week only one local, a wheezy derelict called Walter, had recognized Stuart Milestone. Fred Keneally, the producer, gave him ten dollars to shut up and go away.

In the cramped interior of the van Keneally and Alan Baird watched Stuart Milestone on the monitor. Camera and Sound concentrated on their equipment while a young production assistant waited for orders.

For this segment Milestone was pretending to be a panhandler. He was not doing well. Real panhandlers knew better than to work a street where there was no money.

"He makes a convincing bum, wouldn't you say?" Alan observed.

Keneally looked at him. "Do I detect a note of jealousy?"

"Not me. We know who the star is. My time will come."

On the monitor screen Milestone turned to face the camera and gave the finger-across-the-throat sign.

"That's it," Keneally said. "Let's go outside and set up for the closing speech. Dexter, got the cue cards?"

The production assistant jumped to attention. "Got 'em, Mr. Keneally."

"Wait a minute, what's he doing?"

Out on the street Milestone saw a woman approaching him. She was a perfect bag lady specimen — eroded face, bent-over walk, stringy hair hanging from a motheaten fedora. She wore several baggy sweaters, a black skirt that hung to her swollen ankles, grubby sneakers. Milestone flashed the sign to the camera van to keep rolling.

The woman walked up close and gave him a blast of winebreath. "You're new on the street, aren't you, honey?" Her voice rattled with phlegm.

Milestone nodded, sinking back into the homeless character he had played over the past few days.

"I'm Jessie. I know about everybody on the street, and I knowed you was new. What's your name?"

"They call me Whitey. I been in town most of a week."

"Where you from?"

"Lots of places. Minneapolis last," Milestone said, using the bio Alan Baird had worked up for his character.

"Cold back there, I'll bet."

"Yeah, cold." Milestone shifted his position so the camera could get an open shot at the women while picking up his best profile. "Tell me about yourself, Bessie."

"That's Jessie." She looked away and back in an oddly girlish gesture. Milestone found her eyes disturbing. Black and lustrous as ripe olives, they did not belong in that wreck of a face. "Ain't much to tell. I been around here most of my life. I do what I can to get along."

"What about your family?"

She gave him a gap-toothed laugh. "Hell, I got no family. The people here on the street are my family. How about you?"

"Nobody," Milestone said, spreading it on. "All alone."

"You don't look like a bad guy, Whitey. You got a place to flop?"

He shrugged. "Just, you know, doorways. The alley. Like that."

"You want to come up to my place? I got a nice room. Stove and sink and everything. You could stay until you get yourself set up."

Milestone bit down on a knuckle, trying to look thoughtful as he fought to keep from laughing. "That's nice of you, Jessie, but I couldn't — "

"Hey, don't worry about it. I got food up there. I'll bet you'd like a hot meal. And I got a bottle of wine. Nearly full."

"That sure sounds good." He pointed at a sputtering neon sign across the street. "How about if I meet you over there at the Horseshoe Bar at, say, eight o'clock?"

The woman's grimy face split in a grin. "Like a date, huh, Whitey? Okeydoke. I'll go on home and get fixed up." She shuffled off down the street, looking back once to flutter her gnarled fingers at him.

Once she had rounded the corner Milestone sat down on the curb and yanked off the stocking cap that had concealed his thick blond hair. He smacked his knee and laughed until tears blurred the dark makeup under his eyes.

Keneally and Alan Baird came across from the van accompanied by young Dexter with the cue cards.

"What was that for?" the producer said.

"It was too good to pass up," Milestone said, getting to his feet, still laughing. "Did you catch that old bat coming on to me? It will make a great scene."

Alan cleared his throat. "Don't you think that's a little cruel? She was just trying to do something nice for you."

"Nice? Bullshit. She wanted my body. *'I got a bottle of wine. Nearly full.'* Can you believe that?"

"I don't like it," Alan said.

"Hey, Mr. Sensitivity, if it will make you feel better I'll slip the old bat a few bucks tonight, okay?"

"Tonight? You're going to keep the date?"

"Oh, hell yes. It will make the party. Picture the look on the crone's face when she sees me without the tramp getup and realizes she made a date with Stuart Milestone. Beautiful! Fred, tell everybody the crew party will be over there at the Horseshoe Bar. This is going to be priceless."

Alan turned and walked back to the van. Fred Keneally looked after him with a worried expression.

"He'll be all right," Milestone said. "His nose is out of joint because I ad libbed the bit with Jessie. He doesn't think I can talk unless he puts the words in my mouth." He ran a comb through his hair. "Let's shoot the final speech. I want to get cleaned up."

Someone clutched at his jacked and wheezed, "Mr. Milestone?"

He turned to see Walter, the bum who had recognized him the first day.

"What do you want? Didn't you get paid off?"

"Oh, yes sir, no problem. I just wanted to tell you that you ought to be, well, careful about fooling with old Jessie."

"Careful? What are you talking about?"

"I heard what you were saying just now, couldn't help it. And you oughtn't to play a joke like that on Jessie. She wouldn't like it."

"So what?"

"She's a witch."

"Hell, I could see that."

"No, I mean she's a *witch*. A real one."

"A witch," Milestone repeated slowly.

"That's right. She doesn't make any trouble for us down here, but I've heard stories. If you go ahead and do her like you were sayin', well. . ." Walter let his voice trail off.

"Gee, thanks a lot for the warning, fella. I'll sure be on my guard." Milestone rolled his eyes and brushed Walter aside to join the others at the van.

The Big Six News took over one end of the Horseshoe Bar for Stuart Milestone's wrap party. They had just watched a tape of Milestone's encounter with Jessie. They looked to the boss for his reaction before venturing their own.

Stuart Milestone, freshly bathed and barbered, laughed. The others, with a couple of exceptions, laughed with him.

"Isn't she marvelous?" he said. "Wait till you see her in person." He shot a cuff to consult his Rolex. "Hey, it's after eight. You don't suppose I've been stood up? Stuart Milestone left waiting at the bar by the ugliest thing ever to put on a skirt. How embarrassing!"

The party people were laughing so hard, again with a couple of exceptions, that nobody saw her when she first stood up from the high-backed booth where she had been sitting. One by one they looked over there, and as they did the laughter died.

Her drab hair was washed and combed straight down. She wore a dress that was thirty years out of date, but clean. There was a dab of rouge on each withered cheek. The black lustrous eyes, the eyes that did not belong in the old face, reached into the soul of each and every one present, settling at last on Stuart Milestone. The silence was deep as a grave. After a long, long minute she turned and walked away from the party and out the door.

For a dozen heartbeats nobody moved. Then Alan Baird stood suddenly.

"Excuse me," he said, and followed Jessie out the door.

"Hey!" Milestone called after him. "Hey, Alan, where do you think you're going?"

The younger man went out into the night without responding.

"Aah, who needs a skeleton at the feast, anyway? Drink up, guys, the boss has deep pockets tonight."

But the fun was gone. The joke was stillborn. After ten minutes even Stuart Milestone heard the false note of his crew's laughter. "Let's call it a night," he said. "This place is depressing."

The Big Six News party straggled out of the bar, paying no attention to the lone figure standing in the shadows. When Milestone came out she stepped into the light to block his path. The thin old lips with their pitiful dabbed-on color drew back to expose stained and crooked teeth. The black, ageless eyes blazed. In one hand she held a small jar of dark red liquid.

"You didn't want my wine," she said in a dead level voice. "Try *this!*" She splashed the contents of the glass into Milestone's face and vanished into the night.

He staggered back against the building. Half a dozen handkerchiefs were whipped out to wipe away the fluid.

"What is it?"

"Wine?"

"Blood?"

"Get away from me," Milestone ordered. The others backed off and he scrubbed at his face with his own monogrammed kerchief.

"Are you all right, Stuart?" Keneally asked.

Milestone touched his face gingerly, first on one side then the other. "Yeah, I'm fine. For a minute there I thought the crazy old broad threw acid on me. Come on, let's get out of this sewer."

He slept poorly that night, troubled by dreams of ugly people pursuing him down an endless Skid Row. He awoke Saturday with a sour taste in his mouth and a slight but persistent headache. The symptoms were those of a light hangover, though Milestone had drunk nothing stronger than club soda.

He shuffled into the bathroom and began brushing his teeth. In mid-stroke he stopped and leaned close to the glass. Under his neon blue eyes were smudges of brown that definitely did not belong. Left-over traces of makeup? He wiped at his face with a damp cloth. The smudges remained.

Too much time on Skid Row, he decided. He switched his thoughts to the future. Monday he'd be back at the anchor desk, and a week later they'd be showing the homeless special. Big ratings were assured, and possibly an Emmy. Then he could sit back and wait for offers from the networks.

Milestone went back to bed, slept most of the day away, and felt better when he awoke at dusk. A good dinner with attractive company, and he'd be 100 percent again. He flipped through his Rolodex and chose Chelsea Porter, a bosomy swimsuit model whose dark beauty complemented his blond good looks. Chelsea aspired to a television career and believed Milestone could help her. He did nothing to discourage the idea.

She was ready when he arrived at her apartment. She was stunning, as usual, in a form-fitting blue-black dress. Her smile slipped a notch as she opened the door.

"Something wrong?" he said.

"No, honey, it's just...are you okay?"

"Of course I'm okay. What are you talking about?"

"You look kind of peaked, that's all."

He pushed past her to the mirror over the mantel. The bimbo was right. The smudges under his eyes were darker, and the flesh had a puffy look. His overall color was not good despite the thrice-weekly sessions at the tanning parlor. And had the spark dimmed in his eyes?

Chelsea moved up beside him. Comparing her vital young beauty to his new pallor depressed him.

"You've been working too hard," Chelsea suggested.

"Yes, that's it. I had a hard week on Skid Row. What I need is rest. I'll call you next week."

He left Chelsea standing in her doorway wearing the blue-black dress and a puzzled frown. He wanted only to spend the rest of the weekend alone and undisturbed so he would look good for his return to the anchor desk Monday.

"Jesus, Stuart, what *have* you been doing to yourself?" Georgie flitted from one side to the other as Milestone sat rigidly in the makeup chair.

"You got a problem?" The anchor man was in no mood to discuss it.

"Well, *one* of us has. Take a look."

He held the magnifying hand mirror up in front of Milestone's face. In the unfiltered light of the makeup cubicle the flaws were apparent. His eyes were watery with a light crust on the lids. Crow's feet radiated from the outer corners. His jawline was less well defined as the flesh seemed to have loosened. His color was worse than ever.

"Now you tell me if there's a problem," Georgie said.

"Never mind. Just fix me up for the camera."

It took until five minutes before air time for Georgie to restore Milestone to his handsome self. His reading of the news that night was perfunctory, his byplay with Sports and Weather more forced than usual. Not even the promo for next week's homeless series brightened him. After the show he walked off the set and out of the studio without a word to anyone.

He awoke Tuesday from another night of unpleasant dreams. For a long time he lay in his king-size bed, staring up at the beamed ceiling of his bedroom, trying not to think about his face. When finally he could stand it no longer he got up and walked into the bathroom.

After a frozen ten-second look at his image, Milestone brought up a groan. All the imperfections of the day before were there, only deeper, darker, worse. And there was more. Pinches of loose skin drooped over his eyelids. His firm cheeks were sallow and sagging. There were deep wrinkles across his forehead and an angry cleft between his eyebrows. The creases Georgie had last week penciled from nostril to mouth were there now for real.

That night George made no comment as Milestone presented himself in the makeup chair. His frown and his tight little mouth said it all. He worked feverishly on the anchorman right up until air time.

Milestone ignored the startled looks of Sports, Weather, and the crew as he took his place at the anchor desk. He raced through the reading of the news so fast that Sports and Weather had to pad out the close with more inane chatter than usual.

On Wednesday Milestone showed up early in Makeup. All day he had avoided mirrors, but he could feel the scaly patches of skin on his face. He saw in his comb the wads of hair that came away from his crusted scalp without a struggle. The sagging jowls weighed like saddlebags. And on his upper lip something like a cold sore had broken open to discharge a viscous fluid.

Georgie dealt swiftly with him this time. He blow-dried the thinning hair into a semblance of fullness. He spread Tahitian Bronze pancake like frosting, shaded the loose flesh at the jaw, sealed the open sore, and dusted the surface with talc. Without comment he yanked the towel from Milestone's collar and scurried off on some unspecified errand.

The show was a disaster. Milestone's voice cracked. He misread cue cards. The heavy makeup lay on his face like a death mask. No one on the set would meet his eye.

Afterwards, as he was heading for the door, a hand fell on his shoulder. Milestone flinched as though expecting an axe between the shoulder blades.

Fred Kineally said, "Stuart, before you go Mr. Lichty wants to see you."

"I'll call him tomorrow," Milestone said without turning around.

"Now, Stuart." The producer's tone was gentle, but there was an icy core to his voice.

A week ago Stuart Milestone would have told the station manager where and when a meeting would take place. Not tonight.

"Have a seat, Stuart." Norman Lichty—overweight, balding, pock-marked—sat unsmiling behind his power desk. A station executive did not have to look good.

"Can you guess why I asked you up here?"

"I'm in no mood for games, Norman."

"Well, neither am I, so I'll be direct. The Big Six News this week has been deplorable. Tonight's was the worst yet. Your mind isn't on your work, and you look terrible."

"I've been hitting it pretty hard, what with the panhandler series and all—"

"I didn't say tired, Stuart, I said *terrible.*" He adjusted the desk lamp so the light shone full on Milestone's face. "Have you taken a good look at yourself? The switchboard is jammed with calls asking what's wrong with you. What *is* wrong with you?"

Milestone opened his mouth for an indignant reply, but it died in his throat. All he could manage was a shrug.

Lichty turned the light away. "I want you to take some time off, starting tomorrow. Rest up. See a doctor. Do whatever you have to do."

"But the show. . .the homeless special. . ."

"The special is in the can. Alan can handle the anchor desk until you're ready to come back. Believe me, Stuart, this is the best for everybody."

"Oh, sure," Milestone mumbled. "For everybody." He left the building the back way and hailed a taxi.

The next day he sat alone in his apartment with the lights out and the blinds closed. He avoided the mirrors. He knew what he had to do, but not until it was dark. He would not go out on the street looking like something from *Night of the Living Dead.*

When at last the sun was down he pulled a hat low on his head, where the hair now grew only in sparse patches from the liver-spotted scalp. He put on his largest pair of Foster Grants, pulled a coat collar up to his ears, and ventured out.

The bartender in the Horseshoe eyed him coldly. "Jessie? I ain't sure I know the name. Who's asking?"

Milestone pulled a crumpled wad of bills from his pocket and threw them on the bar without looking at the denomination. "Just tell me where she lives. I haven't got time to waste."

The bartender smoothed out the bills one by one and folded them neatly. "Go two blocks to your left, turn right half a block, and you'll see a boarded up store. Jessie lives upstairs in the back."

Milestone covered the distance in a swift walk, holding himself back to keep from breaking into a run. He took the stairs two at a time, raced down a dim hallway and pulled up short before a door at the far end. He drew a deep breath and knocked on the peeling wooden panel. For a heart-stopping moment he thought Jessie might not be home, then he heard her voice from inside.

"It's not locked."

He pushed open the door and entered. The room was what he expected — threadbare carpet, mismatched furniture, peeling flowered wallpaper. A huge new television set looked out of place on a backless wooden chair at the foot of the bed. Jessie stepped from behind a stained green curtain that closed off the kitchen alcove. She wore a faded orange blouse and black skirt with many folds.

She looked at him, saying nothing.

Deliberately Milestone removed the hat and the dark glasses. He turned down the coat collar. "Do you know who I am?"

"I know you, Whitey. What do you want here?"

The words gushed out of him like vomit. "I want my face back. You made me ugly and old. I don't know how, and it doesn't matter. Maybe I had it coming. God knows I'm sorry if I hurt you. I'll make it up to you. Just put my face back the way it was. Please, Jessie!"

She rolled her head slowly from side to side. "Can't be done."

"Don't say that! I'll pay. Anything you say. I've got money. Just tell me how much. Whatever you want to fix my face."

"I don't need your money, Whitey. All I wanted from you was friendship. Now I don't need that either. I've got a friend."

Jessie turned and pushed the curtain to one side. Seated at a rickety wooden table was Alan Baird.

He looked at his watch. "Hi, Stuart. Love to stay and chat, but I've got a show to do. See you later, Jessie."

The new anchor man kissed her withered cheek and walked out the door. The old anchor man felt his face crumble.

Julia's Touch

David T. Connolly

An equally praised and criticized custom of *Masques* anthologies is the inclusion — in each book — of work by writers who are either "underestablished" or new. The idea was borrowed from Frederic Dannay, co-editor of *Ellery Queen's,* who was the first to buy one of J. N. Williamson's early yarns. Fred called it his "First Story" department. I loved him, it, the magazine.

I met David Connolly at a combined SPWAO/NECON gathering where his easy warmth of personality and love of writing and writers were obvious. He was too modest to ask me to read what he'd written — rare enough feat — but the big guy with the sort of unaggressively earnest manners my mother always hoped I'd develop made me *want* to read his stuff.

Born December 1, 1957, married to a "wonderfully supportive" Paula Jean, Connolly didn't want his work plugged. "My horn's still too small to go blowing it in public." He asked me to say he's a member of Small Press Writers and Artists Organization, which has had a "positive effect on me." Okay. Still. . .think how few writers of horror attempt to craft it *movingly.* In this series, I remember Ray Bradbury, Castle, Gary Braunbeck, Stanley Wiater, Maclay, Diane Taylor, Tem, and Ardath Mayhar doing so to rare effect. And Ray Russell's non-*Masques* "Xong of Xuxan" made your mean old editor cry.

David T. Connolly is in excellent company with his debut.

Julia spent most of the afternoon decorating the small apartment for her husband's birthday party. She braided crepe streamers and blew up so many brightly-colored balloons that it left her dizzy. She was in the middle of preparing the cheese and cracker plate when she realized she hadn't picked up Robert's cake. This being his thirtieth birthday, she wanted everything to be perfect. Then maybe at least for one night Robert would call a halt to the critical self-examination his approaching birthday had triggered.

Glancing at the clock, Julia saw she had just enough time to get to the bakery and still make it back before Robert arrived. Hurrying, she popped the cheese plate into the refrigerator, wiped her hands and prepared to leave.

She went to the hall closet for a coat and chose the one with the genuine fake-fur collar. The walk would be short but cold. Though Robert worked hard at his job, he earned little and drove their car to work. Because most of the places Julia shopped were close by, she never really felt inconvenienced.

On her way out of the apartment Julia couldn't resist another look over her shoulder at the decorations. Then she checked the deadbolt, walked quietly down the stairway and out onto the crowded sidewalk.

Julia smiled privately, imagining how surprised Robert was going to be! She knew he'd laugh at her for having gone to all this trouble just for the two of them. But she also knew, deep inside, that Robert would be thrilled. And she was happy to be surprising him; after all, Robert had never forgotten *her!*

Of course, this was a lot of trouble to go to just to see a surprised and delighted smile on his face. Nonetheless, Julia knew for a fact her man was worth it.

Wrapped in thought, she never saw the car. It jumped the curb, its drunken driver passed out at the wheel. Striking Julia from behind, the car shoved her through the thick plate-glass window of the florist's shop. The clerk called the ambulance. Julia was pronounced dead at the scene.

Feeling a light tap on his shoulder, Robert turned, surprised to see his shift-foreman standing behind him. Following the man back into the office, Robert was told that he had best sit down. At first the news of Julia's death had no effect. After all, how could it be true? Julia, the only bright spot in his life — *dead?* No, it just wasn't possible. He got back onto his feet and walked out of the office without a word.

Blindly following routine, stared at by his fellow workers, Robert was shutting down the lathe when the police arrived. They asked him to get into his car and follow theirs. It wasn't until he was staring down at Julia's corpse that he truly understood she was gone.

"Is this your wife?" It was a man in a long white coat.

"Yes," Robert answered. The word barely cleared his lips. He felt the word on them, felt it fade away, wanted to take it back. Instead, the tightlipped officers walked Robert back to his car. Slowly then, alone, he drove home.

Entering the quiet darkness of the apartment, his hand went to the light switch. A choked sob pierced the small apartment's silence. He was in the middle of a party for one, prepared by the only woman he had ever loved. Prepared by a woman who lay cold on a slab.

His tear-filled eyes grew redder at the sight of the lovingly draped decorations. Looking from the artfully wound crepe-paper that hung from a bouquet of balloons to the sparkling handmade, "Happy Birthday, Honey" banner, he wiped at the tears with his calloused hand, stopping when he realized the corners of his mouth had pulled back up into a smile — a smile he knew Julia had felt would be worth all her trouble.

Then he felt the smile shatter like a mishandled champagne glass.

He crossed into the kitchen and opened a drawer, withdrew a roll of electrical tape, then a small box of single-edged razor blades. In the living room Robert pulled the album of wedding photos out from underneath the coffee table. Then he took the balloons down from the wall.

He carried his belongings into the bathroom, closed the door behind him.

Quietly, Robert eased down the lid on the toilet and sat, arranging his personal items around him. Tearing off several short lengths of the black plastic tape, he pressed one onto the skin of each balloon. Finished, he set them aside and opened the photo album at his feet.

Squinting down through his shifting curtain of tears, Robert inspected the pictures one by one. In the first photo he was kissing Julia, outside the church where they'd married. The picture had been snapped moments after they went outside; you could just make out the small drifts of rice in the creases of his jacket.

Robert took a blade from the small, red box, peeled off its wrapper.

His tears fell freely, the heavy drops pattering like soft rain on the close-up of the misty-eyed newlyweds. Robert brushed them away; they were quickly replaced.

He reached down to choose a balloon, his damp fingers slipping ever so slightly. He made a tiny incision in the short length of tape. When he'd done that, Julia's captured breath drifted toward his face. Her warm, moist breath slowed his flow of tears, drying them for him as if Julia had never died at all. Very slowly, with infinite care, Robert bled the breath from each bright party balloon — all but one.

Before opening the last, he opened himself. At the wrists.

The rain of tears dropping down onto the newlywed faces was overtaken by a crimson flood.

There was time for the final cut and Julia's breath playing softly on Robert's wet and trembling eyelids.

Savages

Darrell Schweitzer

There are tales written for the moment, what's hot or trendy, and there are tales that have a dream-like quality that makes it seem they have always been with us. One kind of story is not superior to the other, I think; few of us set out to write either kind.

But certain writers are nearly always primarily intrigued by whatever is newest or appears most currently relevant in their lives, others tend to craft their fiction as if having attained a hovering-above-this-world state which mysteriously detours around the significances of time, and Darrell Schweitzer seems to me to dwell in the latter category as (possibly) an unconscious preference.

A reviewer who always lets readers know whether he recommends a work or not (and in either instance, why), an editor of the revived *Weird Tales,* the Pennsylvania writer is the kind of man who confides hilarious anecdotes about the disorderly political shenanigans he perceives in his community and somehow makes it sound a fascinating place to visit. A contributor to the British *Fear* and to *Amazing* (most recently March '91), Darrell also had fine fiction in Tom Monteleone's *Borderlands* and Gary Raisor's *Obsessions.* Even he believes that this story is something special, so here it is: One that will seem as if you've remembered reading it for years, perhaps a classic-in-the-making... "Savages."

To Oliver, he was always Billy, never Bill or William, much less Mr. Porter, even after the two of them grew up. To Oliver, Billy was perpetually nine years old, crawling down the embankment behind the old Drake house, under the thick tangle of honeysuckle and briar, completely at his ease under the vaulted arches of the forsythias like something used to all-fours.

"Come on," Billy would say. "I'll show you something *neat.*" And the ritual would begin. Oliver followed him always, breathless with expectation, and sometimes he let his three-years-younger brother Daniel tag along, and maybe Howard Gilmore who lived across the street and down two.

Billy led the way. He was a natural bush-rat, a burrower, able to slip with ease through the tightest hedges, the one who always found the way for the others through the thorn bushes. Down the embankment they went, where their parents had so often forbidden them to go, along the railroad tracks that ran behind the whole neighborhood, then down again, where the hill was so steep they had to take to the trees and lower themselves into a cool, secret place where a stream emerged from a tunnel beneath the tracks.

They had to do it just right, touching all these special places, never revealing themselves to the eyes of others, creeping like Wild Indians through the undergrowth along the edge of the St. David's Golf Course when it would be so much easier just to walk across the grass. If they did it right, if they all ran like startled deer across Lancaster Pike when there were no cars coming and quickly regained the safety of the shrubbery on the other side; if they made their way from there deep into Cabbage Creek Woods with its soapy-smelling skunk cabbages, braving the mud and mosquitoes and stinging nettles that grew by the edge of the stream there; if they did all these things as Billy directed, they would come to a path where the land rose into a gravel heap near the abandoned trackbed of the P&W line and come to Billy's fort: a kind of cave supported by logs, dug deep under the old rail ties.

You could never get there without him. No one else could find the way. And, if by chance you did, there would be Billy's anger to contend with, and he was just too strange, too wild. Even from the beginning, everyone was just a little bit afraid of Billy.

Oliver would always remember Billy that way, his incongruously tubby form able to squeeze through the tightest opening with natural ease, almost always barefoot and shirtless, smeared with dirt, his hands and feet almost black from the dirt and cinders along the railroad embankment.

Billy would take the others into his confidence and show them something "really neat," which might really *be* neat: a Nazi dagger somebody's father had brought home from the war, an amazing collection of firecrackers, baseball cards, a golf ball he'd sawed in half with no apparent ill effects, monster magazines, what seemed to be a real revolver, several pet snakes he swore were poisonous and only Billy would touch —

For long afternoons every summer they'd sit there around a smoldering fire — there always had to be a fire inside the fort; it was part of the magic — and as shadows lengthened and evening came on, Billy would tell them the stories of the Blood Goblin who had been a medicine man, centuries ago, with the disconcerting habit of lifting his head from his shoulders till his spine and his guts dangled in the air. Then he would fly through the night, shrieking, his eyes burning red, his teeth distended into enormous fangs with which to rip out the throats and drink the blood of passers-by.

He was still here, too, Billy said. His body had been stolen and burned while he was away, so he couldn't leave. Once in a great while a kid disappeared. You'd hear he'd been kidnapped. The police would search and search but never find him, because the Blood Goblin had found him first.

Only Billy had seen him and lived to tell about it, because Billy was magic. He was at home there in those woods, clad only in a ragged pair of shorts, so dirty he looked more like an animal than a human. Everyone's parents went on about how poor Billy was, how neglected, but that was precisely why Oliver, Daniel, and the rest envied, all but worshipped him. Billy didn't have to wash up or dress right or go home when his mother said he had to. He was free. He lived in the woods like a savage, something all of them aspired to become but knew, deep inside, that they never would.

Sometimes Billy's idea of what was "really neat" could be distressing, like the dead cat he insisted on cutting into fine pieces with a long, incredibly sharp knife while Oliver and the others looked on in disgust and fascination — both at the insides of the cat and at the spectacle of Billy flaying it with such obvious relish, muttering all the while as if carrying on some obscure argument with himself. One hand would seize the other and force the knife away, and the blade would weave back and forth in the air in front of all their wide-eyed faces. Then, suddenly it jerked down and Billy stabbed himself in his round stomach. Daniel screamed. Oliver forced Billy's arms aside and had a look, but it was just a scratch. Blood trickled through the grime.

But Billy remained oblivious to them all and completed his operation, meticulously saving the cat's heart, lungs, liver, intestines, and even its penis in plastic jars.

Oliver watched with a terrible, breathless expectancy he couldn't even put into words.

Then Billy yanked the remaining hide off the carcass and held the bare skull up, his hands slimy with blood.

"Isn't that *neat?*" he said.

"No!" Oliver said. "It's *horrible. . .*"

"Maybe you're lying," Billy said softly. "Just maybe you *like* it."

"No!"

"Maybe it's not enough for you. I think you want more. Wouldn't it be neat to do this to *people?* Wouldn't that *really* be something?"

What frightened Oliver more than anything else was the realization that deep inside a part of him thought doing it to people *would* be neat. Somehow, the way Billy said it, or just the fact *that* Billy and not, say, Howard Gilmore had made such a suggestion overwhelmed all objections, enchanted him, and an inner voice said, *Yes, that would be neat,* and for just the barest instant he agreed with all his heart and soul — before his sanity returned and he recoiled from what he was thinking. But the thought remained, like a stain.

Nobody said anything more. Daniel went home crying that day. Oliver was silent for a long time.

Billy was the first one to figure out how to masturbate. He showed the others. He set up a bull's-eye target on the wall of the fort and he was the only one who could hit it. But he never got any further than that. He never developed any interest in girls.

The boys were older by then; but that was the odd thing: they were changing, and Billy was not. Oliver read more and more books. He wanted to talk about rocketships and explorers and outer space. Billy preferred dead animals he could take apart. By now the inside of his fort stank like a garbage bin, and skulls and skins and wings decorated the walls.

"Come and see something *neat,*" he still said, but the others didn't always come. When they were with girls they pretended they didn't know him. The girls held their noses with exaggerated gestures and whined, "Eeew! Gross!" And Billy would scream at them and vanish back into his woods and everyone would laugh.

Nobody saw Billy pass from grade to grade like the rest. He went to some other school somewhere. Rumor had it it was a place for retarded kids. That brought more laughter.

Only Oliver knew that couldn't be true, that Billy had chosen some secret, magical path which kept him apart, which changed him and wouldn't let him change again. Oliver *didn't* laugh.

But certainly Billy was losing whatever charm he had. What was fascinating at nine is okay at eleven and a bit boring at thirteen, and when the human body stays that dirty and gets older, it starts to stink. After puberty you learn about B.O. Billy had it in epic proportions.

"Come on!" he pleaded. "I know something *neat!* What's the matter? Are you afraid?"

Not even Daniel visited the fort much anymore.

Oliver went one last time when he was fourteen. It was one of those growing-up things, like the last time you play with your electric trains. He somehow knew it would be the last.

He had been a freshman at Cardinal O'Hara for two months. It was October, but almost as warm as summer. In the evening, after he'd finished delivering his newspapers, Oliver stood among the fallen leaves behind the Drake house at the top of the embankment, waiting, remembering; and suddenly Billy was there, as he had always been, clad in dirt and a pair of cut-offs that were ripped up both sides almost to the waist so that he looked like a jungle cannibal in a loin-cloth. He wore a necklace like one, too, of dried snakeskins and animal bones.

"Hello, Billy."

The other said nothing and Oliver followed him down the embankment under the thorn-bushes and vines, trying very hard not to soil or tear the new jacket he'd gotten for his birthday a week before.

The golf course was being torn up to build a Sears but the construction area was deserted, and skulking among the huge piles of earth and among the idle machines was an acceptable substitute for the bushes that were no longer there.

He sat with Billy on the threshold of the fort for what must have been an hour. The woods grew dark. The first stars appeared and the rising full moon shone fleetingly among the tree trunks. Oliver zipped up his jacket, but Billy didn't seem cold.

Billy talked about bats, his latest fascination.

"I like bats too," Oliver said. "Did you see *The Kiss of the Vampire* where they killed the vampires at the end — ?"

But, no, Billy meant real bats, soft, warm, sharp-clawed things like mice with wings. Sometimes he would lie in his fort at night listening to the distant howling of the Blood Goblin still angrily searching for its stolen body, and the bats came to cover him up like a chirping blanket. He *really* liked that. It was neat. The bats told him all their secrets. He had learned their language.

He made a chittering, whistling sound.

Oliver shivered, laughed nervously. "You're making this up. . ."

"No!" Billy leapt to his feet, towering over Oliver, his fists bunched up, his belly wriggling. "Don't be a asshole!"

That was how he said it, Oliver would always remember. Not *an asshole* but *a asshole.*

"Hey, I'm sorry, Billy. I mean it."

Billy spat and sat down, his chin on his grubby fists.

"If you're really sorry, you'll look at the neat thing I got to show you."

"Okay, Billy. . ." Oliver was more than uneasy then, definitely afraid. He could sense the magic in Billy, the power which wanted to anchor him here, to drag him back from fourteen to nine again and keep him that way forever.

"It's something the bats showed me," Billy said. "They can do it with their wings. I always wanted to see the insides of things. They showed me how."

"Huh?"

"Just watch. You promised."

"Yeah. I promised."

Oliver had no idea what was to follow. He sat there watching as Billy sat very still, his hands folded, eyes closed, head down. That was the strangest thing of all. Oliver had to control his impulse to laugh. It was impossible to imagine Billy *praying.*

Then Billy lowered his folded hands until the edges touched the dirt floor of the fort; and he parted them, brushing a little dirt aside. Suddenly there was an *opening.* Not a hole. No. He hadn't scooped out that much dirt. It was as if the earth were scum on the surface of a pond, and Billy's hands had broken it. The blackness suggested an infinite depth.

"Jesus!"

"Now look down there," Billy said. "You promised. Just look and see what the insides of the world are filled up with."

Oliver looked, and suddenly felt Billy's hands grab him by the shoulders of his jacket, yanking his head down; and then Billy was on top of him, heavy and fat and hot, breathing hard, his stench almost unbearable. He forced Oliver's head down into the hole and held it there.

"*Look!* Dead people! The world is full of dead people! Look! There's your grandmother! Isn't that *neat?*" He laughed, squealed, grunted like a pig, shaking Oliver, pressing him down, down—

Oliver opened his eyes in the darkness, flinching from the expected dirt, but there was none. He seemed to be hanging in a dark space . . . and then he saw the dead people, like pale bubbles suspended in the black fluid of the night, the array of them extending into infinite distance, their faces and naked skulls glowing like stars, like dim moons. They were all somehow aware of him, angry that he had intruded upon them. They froze him with their terrible gaze, those shrivelled corpses, those skeletons, those heaps of scraps and darkened bones. Nearby, an ancient lady in an old-fashioned dress, lying with her hands folded over rosary beads, glared up at him.

She opened her mouth as if to speak. He shouted, "No! Go away!" But she was *not* going away and there was no sound. Her voice, he knew, would be the most horrible thing of all, and he would never stop hearing it.

But she said nothing. There were only wriggling worms.

"Isn't that *neat?*" Billy whispered.

He let go and Oliver broke free, running through the darkened woods, tripping over vines, tearing his precious jacket among the thorns. Once he fell and landed face-down in a stream.

At last he came to the edge of the woods, where two holes remained of the old golf course. Alice, his girlfriend, lived nearby. He had planned to visit her tonight. He was late and a mess but he didn't think he would make it all the way back to his own house. He would be safe with her.

"What happened to *you?*" she said, giggling when she saw him.

"I fell," was all he could say.

Afterward, Oliver glimpsed Billy only at a distance once or twice, crouched under a bush, watching. He was almost able to deny him, to convince himself that he had never been fascinated with the things Billy considered neat. Almost.

Alice was succeeded by Marlene, who was succeeded by Janice, then Jeanne, then Dora, and that took him to the end of high school. College was more a matter of books, then computers. All that talk about spaceships was rapidly turning him into an astro-physicist.

But he dreamed of Billy Porter at the oddest times. Once he seemed to doze off in a lecture hall, and someone nudged him on the shoulder; and there was Billy beside him, naked and dirty, garlanded with dead leaves. He followed Billy out of the hall while the professor droned on and no one seemed to notice he was going. Outside was not the corridor that should have been there, but the deep woods where the wind rattled branches and heaved vines, and the trees were alive with presences which welcomed Billy and rejected Oliver. They came to the fort and Billy squatted down before the fire, then lifted his head off until his spine and entrails dripped in the air. Oliver let out a cry and awoke back in his seat in the lecture hall. The students around him turned to look, and a couple snickered, but the professor didn't seem to have noticed.

At twenty-three, he began graduate work at the University of Pennsylvania, and, after that was done, moved to Princeton. There he met and married Eileen. For several years, that looked like the best idea he'd ever had, and for several more after that, the worst.

He couldn't begin to say precisely when the marriage went bad, but it did, with the glacial inevitability of a mansion built on an unsound foundation, tottering to a fall. The petty bickerings started, continued, became almost constant, over just anything — who was right in El Salvador, whether or not flying saucers exist — *anything*. It didn't matter. They weren't really fighting over the ostensible topics, Oliver wearily concluded, any more than the people of the Middle Ages *really* fought wars over which way you make the sign of the cross or whether the spirit flows from the Father and the Son, or from the Father alone. It was all ego, authority-turf, conquest and humiliation, territorial squabbles in that most personal of personal spaces, the mind.

At the end, he suspected Eileen had a lover. He didn't care. Fine and good-riddance, he told himself.

But she wouldn't let him off so easily. She was going to make it messy. At the very end they found themselves screaming at one another, and before he knew it he'd raised a silver candlestick like a club.

"Go on, you stupid fuck," she said, her voice even, contemptuous and not at all afraid. "Go on and kill me. That'll solve everything."

He walked out of the house, got in his car, just started driving. He had no idea where he was going. Just *going*. He joked to himself that he'd always thought that driving your emotions away with a car was a California trait, but no, they do it in New Jersey too. Driving, on and on like a record that's come to the end but the needle won't lift, so there's nothing left but an empty rasping noise.

An hour passed, more. His mind was on autopilot. Autopilot took him across the Ben Franklin Bridge into Pennsylvania. Autopilot turned west on the Schuykill Expressway and exited at Gulph Mills. His motions were as mindless as the orbits of asteroids —

"My God," he said aloud. "St. David's PA."

His mind cleared somewhat as he recognized the old neighborhood, or what was left of it. The Sears which had replaced the golf course was itself gone, turned into a corporate center. Across the street a B.Altman's had come and gone, the building empty. He didn't turn left to see if the parking lot had obliterated Cabbage Creek Woods. Instead, he continued on, turned right into Cambria Court, his old street, parked, and got out to walk.

He wanted to proceed slowly. He wanted to touch and feel and hear, not just to glance from a moving car. More than that, he wanted to put off the time before he'd have to inevitably go back and face Eileen. He wanted this moment to last forever.

It was dusk on a long summer evening like so many he'd known here. He walked past the house with the arched gateway over the path where he'd come that Halloween when he was fourteen, the very last time he'd ever gone trick-or-treating, and the man had said, "You're getting a little tall for this, aren't you?" Not old, tall.

He knew these places, every tree, every stone, for a child can trespass into any number of back yards without being noticed or driven away. Now he could only stand in the street and look.

The upper court was hardly recognizable. An apartment building had wiped out his own family's old house and the empty lot behind where, when he was very small, a Victorian pile had burned to the ground amid screaming sirens, flashing lights, and thick smoke. It was his most vivid memory from the beginning of his life: the firemen dragging hoses across the lawn, the snapping as the sparks and cinders flew into the air. He remembered standing in the driveway holding his mother's hand while his father hurried to pile valuables into the car in case the fire spread and they had to leave.

Now he could only look for traces of that former place, what was his whole world then. Yes, there was one twisted dogwood tree at the edge of the street which had been in their yard, but that was all.

As he stood there, as the evening shadows deepened, he was able to imagine what it had been like. But the scale was all off. Things were smaller: that dogwood tree, even though it should have grown, was no longer the labyrinthine tower of wood and leaves it had been. It was just a tree. And across the street, behind him, was a walnut atop the rising ground at the edge of the Drake property. He remembered crawling up that little hill on his hands and knees, resting beneath the tree. Now it was no more than a foot above the road surface. He could take the journey in a single step.

He leaned down and picked up a walnut, its green and black shell peeling to reveal the nut inside. Nobody ever ate them, but he remembered the strong, almost sweet smell which got on your hands and stayed for hours.

"Hello."

He turned, still holding the walnut. "I used to live here," he said quickly.

"I know."

He took the other for a handyman of some sort, a stocky fellow dressed in a dirty, dark uniform of the sort filling-station attendants sometimes wear. But there was something about the way the man moved, some unforgotten tone in his voice that made him hesitate. For just an instant, he felt a touch of the old fear again. *That* he recognized unquestionably.

Then he saw the face clearly. A face as it ages is like a waxen mask slowly melting, stretching. The basic pattern remains for a long time.

"Bil-ly?"

"Hey old pal, wanna see something *neat?*"

It was so easy, so utterly effortless to follow Billy through the hedge and into the Drakes' yard, even as some voice in the back of his mind said, *Wait a minute. We're grown men, we're trespassing on these people's property.* He crawled down the embankment, under the arching forsythias, through the thorns, and it was much easier than he thought it would be. He followed, even as he thought again, *How could you possibly know I would be here this particular night?* and Billy seemed to answer in his mind: *You thought of me and I waited. You were the very last one to come to my fort, and I waited.*

Billy took him by the arm, led him along the tracks. He cringed at that, because everyone knew that trainmen went by and took pictures of people who walked along the tracks.

He noticed that Billy was barefoot and his clothes were rags.

He climbed down the second embankment to the stream, clumsily, sliding amid a shower of sticks and gravel. Billy was ahead of him somewhere, in the trees perhaps, moving swiftly, easily; then waiting for him by the stream.

They walked out onto the deserted St. David's Golf Course in the deep twilight, and fireflies rose from the green earth; and a part of his mind said, *There's been no golf course here since JFK was president.* And a part of him thought it odd that he marked time that way, since JFK, *not* since he was in the sixth grade; and he reflected how each of us matters so little against the larger pattern of events. But the whole of his mind did not listen to those voices and they receded to a nonsensical whisper.

It was so easy. A downhill slide away from pain, where Eileen could not follow.

They came to the clump of trees behind the clubhouse, where some kid or other supposedly found a Spanish-American War sword once. Oliver wondered if Billy had that sword now, among his collection of neat things.

In Cabbage Creek Woods, among the skunk cabbages, the soft mud was almost frigid between their toes.

And, finally, the two of them crouched in Billy's fort before a smoldering fire, dirty, almost naked, clutching stone-tipped spears, hooting and howling into the night.

(Like the kids in *Lord of the Flies,* that other voice said. But he didn't understand. *No, this is all wrong. You're thirty-five. For Christ's sake what happened to your clothes?*)

"Isn't this *neat?*" Billy said.

Shaking, sobbing at some memory he could no longer quite define, Oliver said, "Yes. Neat."

"Here. Let me show you something."

Billy folded his hands, then brushed his own bare, mud-streaked chest, splashing away the skin like scum on pondwater, and Oliver could see Billy's ribs clearly, his lungs inflating like bags, his heart beating deep inside.

"My God—"

For an instant Oliver remembered. He struggled back into himself like a drowning man reaching for the surface. He remembered that he was a full professor at Princeton, that he'd parked his car over in Cambria Court. But he looked down at his slender, hairless legs, at his muddy knees and feet, and he wept and thought, *This can't be real. What is* happening *to me?*

"Neat, huh?" Billy laughed, like a kid who's just chewed up some food but not swallowed it, and opens his mouth in order to be deliberately disgusting.

It was so easy to stop weeping, to sit with Billy, to try to be just like him, to listen to his stories of the Blood Goblin and of the wild Indians who lived in these woods once, and what terrible tortures they performed on their enemies. If he listened very hard, if he stared intently out into the darkening woods, he could hear the tom-toms and the screams, far away.

Something moved furtively among the nettles by the stream, ruffling them.

"Billy," he said slowly. "I want to stay here. I want to learn to see everything you see. I want you to teach me."

(*No!* his adult self screamed within, like a prisoner in a cage being wheeled to execution. He tried to remember science, equations, the names of stars.)

Billy stood up. He opened his arms wide and the whole forest was transformed. It was utterly dark now. The bird-calls were exotic screeches. Something huge, like a giant on stilts, stalked among the trees, its bestial head glaring. Below the fort, by the stream, a huge serpent coiled, its scales gleaming with their own light. Its face was that of a bare human skull. Its tongue flickered between the rotting teeth like a thin knife.

"Just like me," Billy said, putting his hand on Oliver's shoulder in what had to be a gesture of acceptance at last, of genuine friendship. The master of the forest had accepted an apprentice.

(*No!* the buried, adult Oliver screamed from within his head. *I don't want to be like you. I'm not like you. I grew up! You never did!*)

"You're *exactly* like me," Billy said aloud.

And the two of them crouched inside the fort. Oliver, looking up for Billy's approval first, leaned down, placing his folded hands in the dust.

It was so easy. He didn't have to be forced. He looked down into the hole as if peering through a ceiling from the floor above, and he saw Eileen there, lying on the kitchen floor in their house back in Princeton, blood pooling around her throat. She gasped softly. Her fingers opened, closed, opened, were still.

He screamed, turned away. For an instant he crouched low beneath the cramped roof of the fort, his back pressing into dirt and roots, naked, a savage, yes, but in his adult body, and he saw the wild boy before him and was filled with horror and disgust. He shoved Billy aside, crawled to the doorway of the fort —

(*What do you really want? Be honest. Really.*)

(And all he could think of was that time when they were children, when Billy held up the bloody animal skull and said, *"Wouldn't you like to do this to people?"* and for an instant he'd known he *did*. Then the idea was like a horrible jack-in-the-box he had to shove back inside with enormous effort, but he had done it, and closed the lid. Now the lid had burst right off its hinges, useless, gone.)

The Blood Goblin rose out of the nettles by the stream, eyes glaring, its spine dangling below.

Billy spoke. His voice was deep and harsh. "You will slay her. You will resume your former guise long enough to execute the appointed task, then return and dwell here forever."

That wasn't Billy talking. Billy never used words like *former guise* and *execute the appointed task.* That was the Blood Goblin, grown eloquent in the long years of searching for rest.

Not Billy.

Billy was a dirty little boy. He didn't mean any harm.

"Something *neat,*" Billy said solemnly. He put a stone dagger into Oliver's hand, closing his reluctant fingers over it.

And Oliver began to chant, softly, hardly realizing he was doing it, "Slit her throat. Kill her dead. Drink her blood. Bash her head."

Billy smiled. He seemed to like that a lot.

"*No,*" Oliver said aloud, his voice rising in tone, sinking into youth, into childishness, cracking, even as his body changed, as the room was comfortably-sized again, as his bare, hairless legs gleamed in the firelight. "I don't want to hurt her. I don't hate her. If only she'd leave me alone." He was pleading now. "If only we could talk it out like civilized human beings."

(Civilized? We're savages, remember?)

Billy was pounding on the dirt with hands and feet. "Slit her throat! Kill her dead! Drink her blood! Bash her head!"

Oliver-within-Oliver, drowning, struggled one last time for the surface, reached up but didn't make it. So easy to let go. To sink down. It made things so simple.

(I won't let you do this to me. I won't.)

Oliver crouched down by the fire, chanting along, "Slit her throat! Kill her dead!"

(You will. You'll do it yourself, to yourself.)

He looked at Billy as if he'd seen him truly for the first time. It was so easy, like letting go, sinking down.

(What makes you think I want to be like you?)

(You already are.)

And the Blood Goblin hovered before the fort's single opening, and the huge thing among the trees leaned down and whispered terrifying things; and the wild Indians crouched with them in the darkness, describing whom they had tortured and how. The great, bone-faced serpent entered the fort and circled around the two boys, again and again.

Oliver looked into Billy's eyes and understood fully, and he thought that Billy understood him, and for the first time it was Billy who was afraid.

(*No. This isn't happening. You are a teacher, a scientist, a grown, decent man. No. Billy was a dirty little boy you knew years and years ago.* What was that voice? It was so easy to ignore it.)

Oliver looked into Billy's eyes, and he understood that there could be no two masters of the forest, that there could be no apprentice. It was not like that. The fort was built for one.

He knew what to do now. It was clear. Billy had shown him the way, had been showing him the way all these years, had ultimately seduced him, even as he allowed himself to be seduced.

"It'll be *neat*," Oliver said. "*Really, really neat.*"

Billy screamed and Oliver opened him up. He methodically peeled Billy apart, tearing out his ribs, his lungs, his heart, dropping them down the hole into the kitchen, on top of his wife's body (Whose wife?), while the forest birds screamed and the Blood Goblin chanted and the sound of the wind through the trees was a kind of song.

Very carefully, he placed Billy's skull among the trophies in the collection.

(*Try to remember.* Gone.)

He crawled out of the fort. The doorway was too small for him. His bare, broad shoulders brushed it on either side.

In the end he stood there above the stream, naked but for his loincloth, conversing with the Blood Goblin whose entrails dripped down over his shoulders and chest.

In the end, he smeared himself with blood like warpaint, and he held up his stone knife and Billy's stinking hide and shouted a great shout of triumph, of victory. The master of the fort and forest had come home.

(So easy to slide down. Into darkness. He'd always wanted to, ever since he was a child. Now he was just being honest with himself.)

He had to get back to Eileen. To explain. To resolve things once and for all.

He raised his knife and shouted a great shout.

The Collapse of Civilization

Ray Russell

For a recommended reading list at the back of *Horror: 100 Best Books,* after noting it wasn't "comprehensive," editors Stephen Jones and Kim Newman cited five books or stories for 1962 and applauded five more for 1967.

Ray Russell was singled out once in the former year, for *The Case Against Satan* — and *twice* in the latter. (For a still-splendid *Playboy* anthology he edited, and for *Unholy Trinity,* genuine Gothic horrors reprinted just a few years ago by Maclay & Associates in the comprehensive collection of dark tales, *Haunted Castles.*)

It's prideful to remark that the creator of *Sardonicus* and *Incubus* has had original stories, now, in all four *Masques.* It's also very pleasant, because readers of this series have seen at least a few sides of this cunningly versatile writer; Ray has the facets of a prized jewel. One such was the humor of satire in an hilarious 1988 gem, *Dirty Money* — a novel that might've been written by a vastly sophisticated member of Monty Python — and a slightly different facet was evident in his 1991 article called "Of Human Brundage," sold to *Playboy* for what its former editor — Ray — termed "a stunning sum."

Here you get withering wit centered on a possibly-fictive rock 'n' roll group that will surely break up, if they exist, after reading "The Collapse of Civilization." So will you, probably, but in a different way. (I hope.)

The Collapse of Civilization has always been an out-of-sight group — those four topless teeners yelling their guts out and sweating real sweat, mean as life and all for you in your very own digs on your very own holographic video cassette — but they didn't make it really *big*-big until last year, that runaway hit of theirs.

The popularity had very little to do with the music, or even with the lyric, which was not what you might call brilliant —

Honey baby sweetie when you hold me tight
When you grabba hold o' me and treat me right
When you give me all you got
Never mind the speed or pot
It's like
        RED! HOT! NEEDLES!
In my fingers and my toes!
Gloryosky, it's like
        RED! HOT! NEEDLES!
In my nipples and my nose!
Leapin' lizards, it's like
        RED! HOT! NEEDLES!
In my belly and my buns!
Hallelujah, Lord, it's
        RED! HOT! NEEDLES!
Like a flamin' pair o' guns!
Oh I'm tellin' you, it's
        RED! HOT! NEEDLES!
In my soul and in my brain!
Gotta have those crazy
        RED! HOT! NEEDLES!
Though they're drivin' me insane!

A long way from genius, but "Red Hot Needles" had been top-of-the-charts for a whole lot of weeks, and some of the smart freaks thought maybe the background sound effects had something to do with it.

The way the rumor had it, it was all Torquemada's idea.

She's the head-head of the group, Trish Torquemada, not her square name, of course. The brainblower was sort of a spin-off from their previous hit, a funky little number called "Ball," which had a background noise of a sister gasping and moaning and carrying on like she was making it. And it wasn't acting, they say. It was Trish herself, recorded later on a separate track, being balled by some dude she had around for a while. The record was a smash as a single. The guy, they say, had been Joanie's before Trish trashed him, but you know these show-biz rumors, there's probably nothing in it. Joanie is the junior member of the group.

Anyway, that's supposed to be how Trish flashed the idea for "Red Hot Needles." She wrote the song first, and they recorded it straight, without sound effects. Then, when they were rapping one day and smoking zilchsticks, she popped the wad to the other sisters in the group.

"It's *heavy*," said Joanie, "but how we gone find someone dumb enough to let us stick red hot needles into her?"

"Simple," said Trish. "There are four of us. We draw straws. Whoever loses..."

Joanie lost.

They made a deal with the recording boys, and late one night, they got it all together. Stripped Joanie down to the raw and spread-eagled her to the legs of an up-ended table right there in the studio. The other three—wearing motorman's gloves—heated big long darning needles in the flame of a blowtorch and started in on Joanie. She got those needles every place the song said and in a few places it didn't. They recorded for about half an hour, and later they picked out the best screams and laid them on the record, behind the song.

It was a real bummer for Joanie, but she's all right now, they say. Spent some time in a private hospital, being treated for burns and a bad case of nerves, but she rejoined the group. That's the story, anyhow.

"Simply Shocking" was their next big score—all those electronic effects and lots of *double entendre* with "hot seat" and "plug-in-socket" and so on. Then they did "Rack and Ruin." You must remember it—

> *Goin' to rack*
> *And ruin*
> *Breakin' my back*
> *With screwin'*
> *Makin' me black*
> *Makin' me blue*
> *Makin' me crack*
> *Splittin' in two*
> *Makin' me shriek*
> *Makin' me weak*
> *Makin' me feeeeeeeeeeeeel*
> *Your love*
> *Crankin' the wheeeeeeeeeel*
> *Of love*
> *Goin' to rip-rip-rack and ruin over you!*

There were all sorts of stories about that one. You don't have to believe them if you don't want to. I don't think I do. Anymore than I believe the one about their next song, "Crash." You know that background noise of screeching brakes and some guy yelling and then that enormous crunch and explosion when the car hits the wall on the last note? They say Trish engineered that one, too, and the stud in the car was the same one she used on the "Ball" record. People love to heap the hype.

Nobody's seen Trish Torquemada for a while. The rest of the sisters get all vague when you ask about her. Vacation, they say, resting up, and like that. Maybe so. But I wonder.

Collapse's next release, coming out next week, is called "Witch." I heard a demo. The group expects to get a Grammy and a Gold Record and ten million balloons for this one. The sound effects are something else, and the lyric isn't bad. Joanie wrote it—

> *Oh she stole my lovin' guy*
> *So that witch is gotta die*
> *And the way that witches die*
> *Is ablaze!*
> *She's a traitor and a liar,*
> *See the smoke a-climbin' higher,*
> *Hear her screamin' in the fire*
> *As she pays...*

Animal Husbandry

Bruce Boston

One of the versatile ones is the Californian who made his *Masques* debut (in *III*) with his and Robert Frazier's hauntingly knowing poem, "Return to the Mutant Rain Forest." Subsequently, it was selected by Ellen Datlow for 1990's *Year's Best Fantasy and Horror* (St. Martin's Press) and by Karl Wagner for *Year's Best Horror* (DAW). That probably wasn't a huge surprise to a man who has won the Rhysling and SPWAO awards in addition to the reader polls of both *Asimov's* and *Aboriginal SF,* had his short works collected for Ocean View Books, and enjoyed translations into German, Spanish, Polish and Japanese.

Here, the free-lance book designer from Berkeley returns to prose, as he has in *Skin Trades, After Magic,* and *Short Circuits.* Orson Scott Card said of the poet Boston, "the images flash" and the work is "piercingly intelligent."

The same may be said of his short fiction.

When Stuart Evers came home with a vasectomy, his wife Marilyn threw what he could only describe as a tantrum. She stood in the center of their spacious living room with its high Victorian ceiling. Her fists were balled, her face red, her body wracked with sobs. Tears seeped from the corners of her eyes and ran down her cheeks.

"I don't understand!" she screeched in a voice bordering on hysteria. "Why didn't you ask me first?"

Stuart, sprawled in the leather easy lounger, was glancing through a copy of *Forbes* and sipping a glass of white zinfandel. He was astonished at his wife's reaction, but not about to show it. In twelve years of marriage he had hardly heard her raise her voice.

"But we agreed years ago," he stated without looking up, "that we didn't *want* any children."

"That's just the point, it *was* years ago," Marilyn shouted. He could see from the corner of his eye that she was shaking her fist at him. At the same time she was trembling. "How do you know I haven't changed my mind?"

Stuart didn't care for this behavior from his wife. He dropped the magazine and met her accusing stare head on. "Children are dangerous at your age," he informed her.

"I'm only thirty-five! My mother had William when she was forty-two."

"And look how he turned out," Stuart smirked. "An unemployed steeplejack who makes illegal drugs in his bathtub. He hasn't been coming around here again, has he?"

"Willie's a writer and a damn good one at that. It's not his fault if society is too crass to appreciate his talent."

"Sure, just like you're a *brilliant* artist."

There! He'd said it at last.

Marilyn screamed, she actually screamed. Bending to the coffee table she picked up the cut glass ashtray, the one they'd bought last year in Bimini, and hurled it across the room. Stuart was too surprised to even duck. The ashtray rebounded from the wall, taking a large chunk out of the plaster, and thudded solidly to the carpet. If Marilyn's aim had been better, the chunk, Stuart realized, would have been out of his skull.

Over the next few days an uncomfortable silence settled upon their lives. Marilyn still performed the domestic duties that Stuart expected of her. The house remained clean. There were fresh shirts in his drawer. When he came home each night he found his dinner in the refrigerator, waiting to be warmed up. Other than that, she treated him like an unwanted boarder. She only spoke to him when it was absolutely necessary, and she spent most of the time locked in her studio.

By the third night of his wife's retreat, Stuart had to admit that their king-sized bed was beginning to feel other than spacious. His doctor had claimed that he'd be functional within a week, and when the time came, he didn't want any delays. Stuart put on his robe, went back downstairs, and knocked on the door of the studio. He had already tried pounding, at great length and to no avail.

"Marilee. . .honey. . .why don't you come out so we can talk?"

Silence.

"You were right, dear, I should have asked you first. But I did it for the both of us. I thought it would improve our sex life."

A muffled laugh.

Stuart had never thought of his wife as a bitch, but he was beginning to get the idea.

"Marilee, you know what I've been thinking?"

A loud thump.

"Maybe we should get ourselves a pet. I've always liked animals."

Silence.

Stuart had exhausted both humility and patience, so he made his way back upstairs. If he'd known what was to follow his suggestion, he would have bitten his tongue on the way.

Stuart arrived home later than usual to find Marilyn's brother waiting for him in the kitchen. William had helped himself to Stuart's imported pilsner. He was drinking directly from the bottle, his third. His boots were up on the kitchen table and he was stretched out and balanced, rocking back and forth, so that only two legs of his chair were on the floor. Stuart felt an urge to kick the chair from beneath him.

"You should have never done it, Stu," William growled at him. "This time you've gone too far. A marriage is a sacred trust and you've betrayed it. Your body is a temple and you've desecrated it."

The hairiness of the man appalled him. William's beard disappeared into the collar of his shirt with no visible sign of a neck between. The hair on his head was even longer than the last time Stuart had seen him and now trailed down his back. In truth, everything about William appalled him. His slothfulness, his disregard for accepted fashion or mores, his theatrical pronouncements. Yet most of all, Stuart suddenly realized, it was the way William smelled. Even from across the room, he was positively gamy. Naturally, Stuart thought; his bathtub was always full of some mind-bending and no doubt gene-mangling brew. He knew that before their marriage, Marilyn had sampled more than a few of these concoctions. Reason enough for them not to have children. There was no telling what sort of monstrosity the woman might produce.

"It's none of your damn business what I do!" Stuart shouted. "Particularly this. And don't call me Stu."

"It's just no way to treat my sister, Stu. Even if you don't care about her anymore, *I do.*" William swung his legs off the table and his chair clumped to the floor. His brow furrowed as he rose to his full six-three, half a head taller than Stuart, who suddenly found himself backing away. "You know I warned you even before you married her." The man was *threatening him* in his own home.

"If you don't get out of here," Stuart stated, "I'm calling the police."

William snorted and took another step forward. Stuart moved back, never taking his eyes off William, and reached behind him for the wall phone. "I'm not kidding!" The receiver came loose from its cradle, slipped from his grasp, and banged loudly against the counter. A plaintive howl sounded from the back yard.

William took another swallow of his beer. "We got that pet you wanted."

He was in the habit, Stuart remembered, of referring to himself and Marilyn in the first person plural, as if *they* were the couple. There was no doubt about it, the man was disturbed.

"We put his food under the sink," William added as he strolled out of the kitchen, "and he needs to be fed."

"Go get a haircut," Stuart called after him.

In the backyard he found a dog, a St. Bernard of all things. At first the animal growled at him when he tried to approach, but once he filled its dish it settled into dinner and ignored him. As he watched the dog eating, he sighed deeply. He supposed he could learn to live with it.

Back in the house there was no sign of William except for his third beer bottle, empty, on the arm of the living room sofa. Stuart made sure the front door was locked so he couldn't return. Then he went to Marilyn's studio. A thin crack of light showed under the door.

"Marilee," he called, "I like the dog."

Silence.

"Do you have a name for it yet? I had a dog when I was a kid. We named it 'Buck.' He was a collie. Remember, I told you about him." This was ridiculous, Stuart thought. Having a conversation with oak paneling. And veneer at that! "Well, any name's okay with me, as long as it isn't 'William,'" he added spitefully.

He was turning back to the kitchen to get something to eat, when he heard voices from the studio. Not a voice, but voices. Damn, Stuart thought.

"Is he in there, Marilee? I told you I don't want that man in the house. He's unstable. For all we know, there's a warrant out for him right now. It wouldn't be the first time. And I don't want you taking any of his drugs!"

Stuart considered pounding again, but the heel of his palm was still sore from the last time.

* * *

On Friday morning Stuart left for a management conference in Houston that would run through the weekend. The conference was a washout: a series of boring exhibits and tedious presentations. He hadn't expected much else. His frequent out-of-town trips weren't taken with the expectation of any professional development, but rather for the extramarital opportunities they provided.

On Sunday night, three hours before his return flight was to leave, he met an ethereal and glitzy blonde in the hotel bar. She was the perfect counterpoint, Stuart thought, to Marilyn's increasingly stocky domesticity. When he steered the conversation in the right direction and told her of his recent surgery and its as yet untried results, the inevitable followed. Back in his room, which he had reserved through Monday in the hopes of such an encounter, he confirmed his doctor's claim more than once.

When he finally reached home at four in the morning, an endearing Texas drawl still echoing in his ears, he heard the St. Bernard howling in the yard. Stuart found its empty dish on the kitchen floor. He opened a can of dog food, the foul gravy spurting out and staining the sleeve of his suit coat. When Stuart deposited the dish on the back porch, the animal was so ravenous it nearly took his thumb off.

After he bandaged the cut, his mind rife with thoughts of blood poisoning and rabies, all Stuart wanted to do was get to bed. In the upstairs hall he was stopped in his tracks once again.

An aquarium, twenty-five gallons if it were an ounce, now dominated their French provincial sideboard. As he edged past the loudly bubbling tank, edged quite literally in the narrow hall, he couldn't help but take a look. The water seemed overcrowded... and with one of the oddest assortments of tropicals he'd ever seen. A transparent worm-like creature, resembling a centipede more than a fish, scurried up and down one side of the glass. On the floor of the tank, which was covered with multicolored gravel, what he had at first taken for a large red rock suddenly darted behind a ceramic treasure chest from which bubbles spewed. Near the top of the water, a black angelfish, a species he *could* identify, listed badly to one side and swam in circles. Its delicate fins were slack and ragged. A school of smaller fish tracked its death dance and nipped at it unmercifully.

Stuart grimaced and stumbled into the bedroom where once more there was no sign of Marilyn. He slammed the door to block out the bubbling of the tank.

* * *

In the next few weeks additional pets continued to appear at the house with frightening regularity. Stuart would arrive home from work, usually late, increasingly intoxicated, never knowing what new animal he would have to confront or what catastrophe he would have to assimilate into his evening.

Tuesday. A plump calico cat was perched atop his easy lounger, its claw marks already visible upon the leather. Stuart chased it into the yard where it immediately tangled with the dog.

Friday. A pair of guinea pigs in a wire cage in one corner of the kitchen, arduously mating while he ate his warmed-over dinner.

The following Monday. A large green parrot, so tame it was cageless, perched by the bay windows in the living room, its droppings staining the hardwood floor Stuart had refinished himself. He spread newspapers under the perch and sent a prayer on high that whatever pet store Marilyn was frequenting didn't stock orangutans or asps.

Stuart decided that the animals must be Marilyn's way of punishing him. Then it occurred to him that it could be William who was responsible. He swore his imported beer was disappearing faster than he was drinking it. At least once he thought he detected his brother-in-law's distinctive odor, though he couldn't be sure since the downstairs reeked from the cat box and the upstairs from the aquarium, which had quickly transformed itself from crystal clarity to a disgustingly cloudy morass.

Stuart had always thought of himself as someone who liked animals. On the other hand, he now realized that he didn't like taking care of them. He remembered that was how he had lost Buck. His father had taken the dog to the pound because he always forgot to feed it. And besides the time and trouble, there was the expense. Financial freedom was one of his reasons for not having children. Granted, the pets would never go to college or get married, but the food bills for this burgeoning menagerie were no pittance and the trips to the vet had already begun: the dog had developed an abscess in one eye where the cat had mauled it. Yet what annoyed Stuart most, beyond the time spent, beyond the money expended, was the parrot.

For the most part the bird remained as motionless on its perch as a piece of bric-a-brac. It was nothing the parrot did that upset him, but what it said. Only one phrase, repeated endlessly: "Tell them Willie-boy was here. Tell them Willie-boy was here." A coincidence, Stuart thought, or further evidence that William was involved?

Regardless of who was responsible for the pets, his wife, her brother, or the pair of them in conspiracy, the presence of the animals had done nothing to soften Marilyn's behavior toward him. If anything, she was even more remote than upon first hearing about his operation. Every time Stuart entered the house, she retreated to her studio and locked the door. No amount of pounding — the veneer was beginning to splinter — or pleading could elicit a response. Their sex life, which he had sincerely hoped the vasectomy would help, was nonexistent. And their once-active social life had followed suit.

At first he tried to go to the usual round of parties, to see their usual friends and maintain appearances. Stuart quickly grew tired of making excuses for his wife, excuses that were met increasingly with knowing nods. His so-called friends, most of them divorced or already on their second or third marriage, seemed to be taking a perverse pleasure in the fact that his marriage was on the ropes. Stuart had never dreamt that his life could disintegrate so rapidly, or that so many would take so much satisfaction in its collapse.

Returning home early from one of these parties, Stuart sank into a morose reverie. His worst fears took flight in a nightmare scenario of exaggerated proportions. He saw his house transformed by William into a zoo both animal and human, inhabited by a hippie cult, with black-light posters on the walls, cat shit on the floors, dog fights in the hall, heavy metal on his turntable, his demented and ursine brother-in-law presiding over an unwashed assemblage of freaks and burn-outs, dispensing unknown drugs in indiscriminate quantities and preaching on the demise of civilization. It was just such an environment he had rescued Marilyn from in the early days of their relationship, and as his imagination continued to play, he saw her returning to her old ways, glassy-eyed, heavily adorned with costume jewelry, lighting incense and wearing beaded shawls. But no, he assured himself, even William couldn't pull that off. People just didn't live that way anymore.

He was very drunk. He was balanced on one foot on the gas meter at the back of the house. The tips of his fingers, in an uncertain purchase on the window ledge, were holding him in place. He was trying to peer into Marilyn's studio while beneath him the St. Bernard crouched, growling softly yet from deep within its throat. Unless he was actually feeding the animal, it remained hostile.

Through the thinly cracked slats of the wooden blinds he saw only part of the room, and no sign of Marilyn. What he could see were her paintings, a half dozen new canvases mounted about the walls. At first he thought they were abstracts, like the rest of her work, but as he looked more closely he noticed that these pieces were representational. And they were all depicting the same thing. Embryos. Dozens of embryos in every shape, size and stage of development. Incipient embryos with their cargo still boneless and gilled. Final trimester embryos with full-fledged infants already sucking their thumbs. All of them a mottled and sickly green.

At that moment the St. Bernard began tugging at his pant leg and Stuart toppled from his perch into the damp hydrangeas.

His temples were pounding timpani. His mouth was stuffed with spackle and rancid cotton. Stuart cracked one eyelid. . .peered at the clock on the bedside table. . .and felt the rush of panic.

He was two hours late for work!

Struggling with his robe as the room performed several cartwheels, he tottered to the hall. Before he could reach the bathroom, Stuart pitched head first onto the carpet. He groaned mournfully as he rolled over into a sitting position and leaned back against the wall. Something had tripped him. . .and that something was. . .a turtle!

Stuart couldn't believe his eyes. It was in the middle of the hall, drawn back into its shell, and the damn thing must have been two feet long. As to when it had arrived at the house he had no idea and he suddenly didn't care. Despite his hangover, despite the fact that his toe was bleeding, despite the fact that he liked animals, yes, he really did, a blinding rage seized him. A wave of blood red washed across his vision as he grabbed the turtle and standing with difficulty beneath its weight, hurled it at the aquarium with all the force he could manage.

The glass exploded in an earsplitting crunch. Slimy water cascaded, flooding the floor with writhing fish and a shower of multicolored gravel. Stuart hopped back awkwardly to avoid the deluge and nearly fell again.

As he watched the turtle slowly poke its head from its shell and begin to lumber into the bedroom, he realized it was Saturday. He didn't have to go to work.

The day had been well spent, Stuart thought.

He savored the silence as he cracked his second bottle of cabernet. He suspected he should cut down on his drinking, but the now animalless house seemed cause for celebration. Now only one problem remained.

It had been days since Stuart had seen anything of Marilyn except her back as she scurried into her studio. Their relationship had become more of a cold war than a marriage. He would give her one more chance, he decided, then it was over.

He marched down the hall and pounded on the studio door, being careful to avoid the splinters.

"In case you haven't noticed," he shouted, "I've gotten rid of your animals. Every damn one of them!"

Silence.

"This is your last chance, Marilyn, either come out of there right now and come to bed...or I'm leaving you!"

Silence.

"To hell with you, then!"

Upstairs, Stuart quickly packed a suitcase and zippered a few suits into carrying bags. First thing in the morning he would take a hotel room in the city, something close to work, while he looked for an apartment. Of course that would be temporary. He knew a good divorce lawyer, and one way or another he would make sure the house remained in his name. As for women, he'd never had trouble finding one in the past, and he didn't expect to have trouble finding another one now.

Stuart awoke in the middle of the night to hear footsteps on the stairs. For a moment he was startled, but then he saw his wife's familiar silhouette, framed by the hall light, as she paused in the bedroom doorway.

At last, his waking mind thought with satisfaction, she'd come to her senses.

Yet as Marilyn moved across the room, Stuart sensed that something was wrong...terribly wrong. For although it was his wife who lowered herself onto the bed beside him, she now seemed to smell exactly like William.

"Marilee...?" he whispered hesitantly.

In the dark, Stuart reached out to touch his wife's arm...and suddenly realized how hairy it had become. He heard a fierce growl rising from deep within her throat. He felt the claws of her nails, impossibly long, as she ripped the pajama top from his chest.

Sounds

Kathryn Ptacek

The author of *Ghost Dance* and *In Silence Sealed* (writes reviewer T. Liam McDonald in *From the Time Tunnel*) crafts "powerful" horror and is "probably one of the most underrated writers of dark fantasy," the author of subject being Kathryn Ptacek. Not "K. Ptacek" or some such maiden name madness as "K. Collinsworth Ptacek." Kathryn, as in "Kathy."

And yes, her writing *is* "potent," "forceful," and one I like from my thesaurus: "equal to." As in, "equal to other respected writers of horror." In fact, her anthologies *Women of Darkness* and *Women of Darkness II*— the latter published last winter by Tor — powerfully advanced the careers of other people who agree with what she argued in *The Blood Review* (January '90): "Stop saying men write one kind of horror, and women another." Kathy also edits *The Gila Queen's Guide to Markets,* an excellent addition to Janet Fox's *Scavenger's Newsletter.* I recommend each with enthusiasm.

Darkness came into being because, as Ed Bryant has also observed, few horror anthologies were being published with more than one female contributor, many with none. In hope that Ms. Ptacek will soon have reason to edit books with room for writers who have first names like "Gerald," let me note that four *Masques* books have contained 14 works by an even dozen women, the number per volume increasing with my growing awareness of the deficit. For sheer boasting, I'll mention that my *How to Write Tales of Horror, Fantasy and Science Fiction* featured seven females. Where do I find them? Check out the quintet in this anthology, and go *read* writing by Katherine Ramsland, Ardath Mayhar, Sharon Baker, Diane Taylor, Marion Zimmer Bradley, Anne Rice, Melanie Tem, Kathleen Jurgens, Yvonne Navarro, Jeannette Hopper, and...Ptacek. I heard somewhere that the author of *Frankenstein* was a woman!

In *Gauntlet,* Nancy Collins *(Sunglasses After Dark)* was asked by editor Barry Hoffman if "female representation in anthologies" is presently an example of censorship. Like Hopper in my how-to, Ms. Collins wound up with this kind of thought: "There are only two kinds of writers in the world; Good Writers and Bad Writers."

Exactly. Here's a good one.

Hammer, hammer, hammer.

Faye Goodwin pursed her lips, sighed and pulled the pillow over her head. Damned roofers.

Hammer, hammer.

Even through the thickness of feathers, she could still hear the whacking of the workmen's hammers on the slate roof next door.

She opened an eye. Read the clock. 7:07. In the morning, for God's sake, on her one day off this month — a Friday to make a long and very welcome weekend — and she had to be awakened by that damned whacking.

Someone started a buzzsaw. She winced. She glanced over at her husband, Tommy, lying serenely on his back, one arm flung over his face. He was soundly asleep, would remain soundly asleep no matter what noise followed.

She envied him. She sighed, punched up her pillow, closed her eyes. She would fall asleep again and sleep until nine, maybe even ten, and then —

A drill whined.

She sat up in bed.

"W-What?" her husband mumbled, only disturbed a little from her abrupt motion. Then he was asleep again, snoring mildly.

Snoring.

There'd be no more sleep for her today.

She shook her head, pushed the covers back and got out of bed. She went to the window in the hallway and stared out at the workmen. They went on their ways blithely, completely unaware of her baleful glare.

She knew the workmen had to get an early start or they'd be working too many hours in the 90-plus temperatures under a burning sun. But still. Couldn't they go about these improvements a little more silently? She grinned at the thought. She went into the bathroom, washed her face, and even over the running water she could hear the rapping.

Ignore it, she told herself, not for the first time. She tried to blot out the alien sound, tried to concentrate on the rushing water, a much more serene sound. A gentle, soothing frequency, hypnotic almost, peaceful and —

Tap, tap, tap.

No good.

She stepped into the shower, turned on the water full blast, and only then under the stinging stream did the other noise fade away.

She dressed, swallowed an aspirin. It was going to be one of those days.

Downstairs she retrieved the newspaper off the porch steps, sat down at the table to enjoy her first cup of hot tea for the day. The dining room windows faced onto the house under renovation, and she could see the crew crawling like immense ants over the grey roof.

Before she could get irritated, she got up and pulled the windows down. The noise dimmed a little, but didn't go away.

A few minutes later Tommy came downstairs. "Mornin'," he said, as he bent over to kiss her. He smelled of some lemony aftershave, and she smiled.

"Sleep well?" she asked.

"As always," he said, going into the kitchen. "You?"

She shrugged.

"Woke up again, huh?"

"Yeah."

"Maybe you need some sort of sleeping pill, something over the counter."

She sloshed her tea around in the mug. "I think I've tried just about every one out there. They work for the first night or two, you know, and then after that I keep waking up. In fact, I think they keep me awake."

"Well," Tommy said, sliding into the chair opposite her and dipping his spoon into his bowl of cereal, "maybe you should go to see a—"

"A therapist?" Faye asked, her voice a slightly sarcastic.

"Let me finish, okay? I was going to say a hypnotist."

"Oh. I hadn't thought of that."

"A guy at the office went to one—I could probably get the name, if you want—and he quit smoking. He used to smoke two-three packs a day."

She nodded thoughtfully. "Get the name, if it's no bother. I think that might be good. Sure is worth a try, I guess."

"Maybe you can take a nap today."

"Not with that going on," she pointed with her chin toward the windows.

"Isn't it kind of warm? Do you really want the windows closed, Faye?"

"It cuts down on the racket."

He gave her That Look—the expression she always hated, and always felt held more than a little condescension. "Hon, you've really got to do something about that. Face it, we live in a noisy world, and it's not going to get any quieter." He took his bowl out to the kitchen and ran water in it.

She made a face at his back, then looked down at her mug. She didn't know why she did that, except that she always suspected that he really didn't understand how horrible it was for her. How bad the level of noise could get.

"It would be much more quiet if we lived in the country," she said.

"Hon, don't start on that again. I told you that with the cost of property, we just can't afford it. At least right now. If one of us gets a raise, maybe we can sock the extra dough away. Until then you'll just have to put up with a boisterous town. At least it's not the city."

She said nothing.

"See you." He kissed her again, picked up his jacket and a few minutes later she heard him chatting with the workmen. A few minutes later the car started up. It popped and sputtered; the engine needed tuning.

Faye gritted her teeth.

With mug in hand, she wandered into the living room and draped herself across the easy chair and turned on the tv. She didn't normally watch television in the daytime, but she was curious to see what was on at this hour. An earnest-looking host talking about incest, and some quiz show with lots of buzzers and flashing lights, a nature show about koalas, a couple of music stations, the weather channel, CNN, others. She flipped through the stations, then again as if expecting to find something else, then finally turned the tv off. Too much noise.

From one of the houses across the street she heard the faint beat of rock music. Something by some heavy metal group.

Swell.

A car went by, the windows rolled down, a Bach concerto blasting out.

Not even the classics were sacred, she thought with a faint smile.

Enough of this. Faye stood, looked around the room. So, what was she going to do? Well, she could go to the mall, but that meant a thirty-minute drive, crowds and that maddening piped-in music that followed her everywhere. Couldn't people survive without having to listen to something every minute?

The mall was definitely out. The grocery store was not. Once there, she claimed a cart and started up and down the aisles.

The p.a. system played songs from the late '60s, all homogenized into bland music. The system crackled and a man's voice announced a special today on lean ground beef. He droned on about the different uses for ground beef. Finally, the ad ended, and the music—the Beatles' "I Want to Hold Your Hand," one of her favorites—came on in mid-tune.

That irritated her even more, but she wasn't sure which was more offensive—the lackluster renditions of the music or just the plain fact that there was music. She didn't know why she hated noise so much; from her early childhood on she had been particularly noise-sensitive, at least that's what her mother had called it. Faye had always disliked loud voices and sounds, and had always crawled into her parents' large walk-in closet when thunder boomed outside. She could hear the whine of air conditioning as she walked into department stores when no one else could. Once she had begun crying as a small airplane circled over their house. Her father had sworn it was simply a stage that she would outgrow; only she hadn't.

It hadn't gotten better with age; it had grown worse, much worse.

Most of the time she had an uneasy truce with her sensitivity. Then there were the other times. . .days like today.

Somewhere, maybe a few rows over, a young child began crying. Faye waited for the child to stop, but it didn't; it was building to an enthusiastic crescendo. It was a wonder those small lungs didn't give out. Her hands clenched on the cart handle. She braked before the paper products and tossed in paper towels.

The wailing grew louder. The high-pitched voice rose and fell in a pathetic undulation. The mother's voice was shrill and she was telling her child that the child really shouldn't cry.

Faye shook her head in disgust. The mother ought to just say no, and then bop the kid on the butt once or twice. That would stop the whining. God knows, it had happened enough to her. Of course, she hadn't been prone to pitching temper tantrums, either. That wasn't allowed in her family.

A gentle throbbing began in her temple; her headache was returning.

Faye pushed her cart toward the end of the aisle, trying to get away from the noise. But it followed her wherever she went.

She hurried through the produce section, lobbed lettuce and radishes and spinach into the basket. She would surprise Tommy with a really big salad. Somewhere else in the store another child began crying, picking up the refrain of the first. Then a third started whimpering.

When she got to the check-out stand, Faye flung her items onto the belt as quickly as possible and watched the checker ring them up one by one.

"How can you stand to work with all this noise? These kids must drive you crazy."

The checker, a woman with a big black mole on her chin, shook her head. "Don't hear it after a while. It just sort of blends together pretty soon."

"You're lucky."

"Yeah, I guess so. That's twenty-three fifty. You should have been here when they were remodeling the store. All that hammering and drilling day in, day out—it was terrible."

Faye shuddered, drove home. The workers were still next door; she had entertained some vague hope that they might have called it quits. Right.

After she had taken several more aspirin, she wandered into the living room. She was going to read. She should do a little housework, but she knew she couldn't take the howling of the vacuum cleaner. She read for a while and only gradually became aware of another noise, a clanging and banging. She glanced out the window and saw the garbage men. Why, she wondered, when the garbage cans were plastic now, did these guys have to make all this noise? The truck moved slowly down the street, the noise finally receding.

It was noisy at the office, too, where she worked as staff writer. Her job was to translate computer talk into people talk, and the constant clatter of printers and phones and people talking, chairs squeaking, doors being slammed grated. Some days she wondered how anyone—how she—could take it. But no one complained about the noise, and she figured she was just being sensitive.

Too damned sensitive for her own good—wasn't that what Dad always said?

At lunch she fixed a simple cheese sandwich and had a soda, and while she was sitting at the dining room table still reading, she heard a high-pitched whining. Like a buzzsaw, only she knew that sound very well. Even over the sound of hammering and the shouts of the workmen, she could hear that grating noise, though.

She stepped out onto the front porch; the sound grew louder.

Something bright flashed along the street. The whining came from it.

It turned out to be one of those remote control cars, and she watched as a man with his young son played with the toy. Around it went, then up and down in front of her house. It was nice that he was with his son, she thought, but why couldn't they have found something silent, like a kite, to play with?

She found herself gritting her teeth, forced herself to relax, went back in and closed the front door and windows facing that direction.

Not good enough, but the best she could do.

She read until the kids came home from school, then, her finger marking her place in the book, she looked out the window and watched as the junior high kids cut across her lawn. They were yelling to one another, and one of them held a large silver radio that blasted out some loud song with a fast beat. They cursed at each other and pushed each other around, and shouted, even though they were standing only a few feet away from each other.

Didn't kids speak in civil tones any more? In *hushed* tones? she wondered.

It had always been hard to deal with, this noise sensitivity. She'd tried ear plugs years before, but they really hadn't helped. She tried ignoring the sounds, but couldn't concentrate fully.

Maybe the hypnotist Tommy had mentioned that morning would help, though; she hoped so. All these noises were driving her crazy.

It didn't help that Tommy snored so loudly sometimes at night that she woke up and was unable to go back to sleep until she came downstairs and camped out on the sofa. Even then, she'd be able to hear the snoring faintly, but at least it no longer kept her awake.

And he always kept the television volume much too high, just like her father had. Her father had been slightly deaf, though; Tommy was young yet. Maybe she would suggest that he have his hearing checked out.

She knew hers didn't need it.

At least, she thought, the boy and his father and the awful toy had gone off. Maybe the thing was broken; that would be good news.

Her mother had been the type to slam drawers and doors. If she was mad, slam went a dresser drawer. Or the door to the oven. Or the backdoor. With each jar, Faye had jumped. She was always glad that she came from a family of three rather than thirteen.

After a while she heard the ticking of the clock in the hallway. Tommy had bought that for their anniversary. With each swing of the brass pendulum there was a resonant echo, like the striking of a padded hammer on wood. Almost a muffled sound. Not muffled enough.

The refrigerator went on. The appliance needed work, and for years it had made cooing noises, like a dove. Sometimes at night as she lay in bed, trying to sleep, she could hear that persistent cooing.

Water dripped from the kitchen faucet. Drop by drop. She would have to remind Tommy again this weekend to get a new washer for the faucet. They were wasting too much water.

Her headache was back, and growing worse. It was centered over one eye and throbbed. She bet if she put her fingers on that spot she'd feel it pulsating. She got up and took some more aspirin, took a deep breath, and told herself to relax.

Somewhere, on the other side of the street, a phone rang and a loud voice answered it, and she listened to a conversation she didn't want to hear.

Kids squealed as they played in their front yards.

Bluejays squawked at each other in the mulberry tree outside her window. A lawn mower growled two houses down.

Tommy really was pretty good about all of this, she told herself. She tried not to complain about the noise, because he didn't understand. No one — not even her closest friends — did, because none of them could hear as well as she could. They all complained about varying hearing loss, and she always thought that they were the lucky ones, that she was the cursed one.

A jet shrieked overhead.

You're too sensitive, her father always grumbled, as if it were really something she could control.

The neighbor next door began working on the sports car he never drove. She heard the racing engine, a grinding of gears, the beeping of the horn.

Another phone shrilled.

It was just that she never could seem to get away from the noise. It was always badgering her, assaulting her. She hated it.

A television blared.

Too sensitive.

A piano — someone playing "Heart and Soul" over and over and over.

The pulsating pain returned.

An ambulance, or perhaps it was a police car, raced down the next block out, the wailing siren rising and falling, rising and falling.

Another lawn mower roared into life, while the kid and his father returned with the remote control car.

Too damned sensitive. . .

The refrigerator hummed again, while the furnace rumbled on.

Her phone rang. And rang, and rang, and rang, and still she sat on the couch, and listened to all the noises of the house and her neighborhood.

* * *

Tommy parked the car in the driveway, waved to old Mr. Miller who was just finishing clipping his hedges two doors down. He went into the house.

"Faye, hi, I'm home." He heard nothing but the ticking of the grandfather clock in the hallway. He listened for running water, thinking she might be taking a bath, but he didn't hear it. Maybe she was out back.

"Faye?" This time louder.

Still no answer.

He heard something in the kitchen then, and he realized she was out there, probably making dinner.

He stopped on the threshold of the kitchen. "Hi, hon, how are you?"

She stood at the counter with her back to him. She was cutting up vegetables for a salad.

"Hon?" Was this a game, he thought with a sly smile? Then: was she mad at him for some reason and ignoring him?

He stepped closer.

On the counter, not far from the salad bowl, he saw an icepick, and a smear of something red on the countertop.

"Honey, I got the name of the hypnotist; it's some guy who just—" he began, then stopped when Faye turned around and he saw the blood trickling from her ears.

Whispers of the Unrepentant

t. Winter-Damon

The bad news is, I don't know either what the lower-case "t." stands for.

What I know is that he's a "he," his gracious and attractive wife is named Diane, they reside in Tucson, Arizona, he's affable and has a mustache, and his work has appeared in over 200 magazines or anthologies in seven countries. I also know the other six are England, Canada, Australia, N. Wales, France, and West Germany.

And that he is a poet, reviewer, novelist, short-fiction writer and artist whose time under limelight is due. (We're into the good news now.) The assertion is given substance by work in *The Year's Best Horror* (twice; in *XVI* and *XVII*), *Fantasy Tales, Fear, Deathrealm, Midnight Graffiti, Eldritch Tales, Grue,* and something intriguing entitled *Semiotext E SF Anthology.* Winter-Damon was pleased to say it contained "nearly the entire cast of the Cyberpunk movement," citing J. G. Ballard, Robert Sheckley, William Burroughs, Philip Jose Farmer, and William Gibson.

The rest of the good news about this Rhysling and Bram Stoker nominee and Small Press Writers and Artists Organization Poet of the Year is that his new work is up next.

I.

I am bored with this grey, untextured tapestry —
    These chafing shackles of restrained banality,
        Unleavened wafers,
           Tepid water,
              Saltless meat . . .
Your perfumes no longer seem so sweet,
    Fire without warmth,
        Frost without chill . . .

Your laughter is silent, the strains of your music still.
                    I AM THE HELLRAKE...
                              I am the footsteps in the darkness

I crave—
        To shed the fabric and stain it red;
                These moral chains to smash and rend;
                        To glutton the blue and mouldy bread;
                                To swill the Dark Gods' crimson wine;
                                        To gorge on savory, dripping flesh.

My pulse throbs—
        To the coffin's wild, necrotic scent,
                To the warm and fragrant musk of blood;
                        Hell's fires fill me with their molten flame;
                                Arctic ecstasy the stolen corpse cold kiss.
Demons' laughter echoes in the wind.
        The dirge rapture sets my head awhirl.
                The choirs of The Damned: quicksilver bliss...
                    I AM THE HELLRAKE...
                              I am the footsteps in the darkness

                            II.

Sister Drusilla, dearest of the three—
        Shall we wash our hands in blood while you sit upon my
        knee?
                    I AM THE HELLRAKE...

My name the epithet for lust-inflicted pain—
        That fixation of disgust soon waxes pleasurable as cherished
        vices wane...
                              I am the footsteps in the darkness

Whitechapel five? or seven? harlots wedded to my blade—
        Lawyer? surgeon? jew? or prince? What a novel masquerade!
                    I AM THE HELLRAKE...

                        *   *   *

Death to pigs! Acid family, blind carnage yet to wreak —
    Apocalypse in black and white the vision that I seek...
                    I am the footsteps in the darkness

This is my cold and sweating hand that holds the .44 —
    You know it is the mongrel's voice that leads me to *your*
        door!
            I AM THE HELLRAKE...

My wife's head turns backwards in mock disbelief —
    I have a freezer full of secrets and some most suspicious
        beef...
                    I am the footsteps in the darkness

III.

Cloying Virtue's sugared promise, bile upon my lips,
    Dark Angel rising through The Well of Time.
Your cretin philosophies term each crimson masterpiece
    Yet another violent crime...
            I AM THE HELLRAKE...
                    I am the footsteps in the darkness.

Obscene Phone Calls

John Coyne

John Coyne tells stories. Whether in novel or short story form, he tells stories. About real people. About things people do—to themselves, to others—and he tells them plainly. Stephen King said it in a cover blurb: "Coyne plays rough." He does, because—so often—that's what people do.

His novel writing includes *The Legacy* and *The Searing* and heart-stopping numbers such as *Fury, The Hunting Season,* and *Child of Shadows.* None of them contains hit-or-miss experimentation; all of them are invariable in a way that's important to readers: When you want to read a new book by John Coyne, that's what you get. Not an imitation of another author.

Until Ed Gorman and Martin H. Greenberg edited their first *Stalkers,* John hadn't written a great many short stories for publication. "Flight" changed that and led to Coyne-of-the-realm appearances in *Cemetery Dance, 2AM*...and *Masques IV.* Here's one of those tales written so plainly that it penetrates, seems to have been around always. It's about things that are done, not done, undone. It's about people.

"You're a sonovabitch!" It was a woman's voice, strong and wide awake.

"Hello?" Steve yawned and glanced at his SONY Digimatic glowing in the dark. It was already past midnight.

"You're a bastard!" She spoke again with authority. "I've been up half the night and you're not going to sleep at my expense."

"Hey, what's this?" Steve whispered back. Beside him, the woman stirred.

"Why are you whispering? Got some woman with you?" Her voice was quick and sharp.

"Say, listen, sweetheart, you've got the wrong guy..."

"You really are something else!"

"It's the middle of the goddamn night, and you've got the wrong number, sister."

"Your name is Steve Mirachi and you live in an apartment on Hillyer Place above Dupont Circle and this evening at Discount Records you spent ten minutes eyeballing me and I just wanted you to know I think you're a goddamn sonovabitch!" She slammed the receiver in his ear.

"Bitch!" Steve swore and then, shaking his head, replaced the headpiece.

"What's that?" the woman mumbled.

"I have no idea. A wrong number, I guess." He slid down next to the sleeping woman.

He remembered watching several women in the record store, but he always watched girls, and now no face or body came to mind. Whoever it was must have followed him home, seen where he lived. Weird! The thought made him nervous.

He had gone out again later in the evening, around the corner to Childe Harold and there he had met Wendy. He glanced at the girl burrowed in bed beside him. Or was her name Tiby? He couldn't remember and he fell asleep trying to recall her first name.

The next morning he was up early and out of the apartment before the girl woke. He disliked awkward morning goodbyes and he only left her a note next to the Taster's Choice.

> I'm off; Saturday shopping day!
> Leave a phone number, okay?
> We'll get together...
>   Love ya,
>   Steve

Steve had been transferred by his company to Washington only that spring and when he wasn't on the road selling his line of leather goods, he'd spend his Saturday mornings in Georgetown, wandering from shop to shop, watching the women. Then he'd go to Clyde's for a Bloody Mary and omelet and stand by the bar so he could see the door.

He had never seen so many women: tall and thin and braless. Breathtakingly beautiful women! They'd come through the door, toss their long hair into place with a flip of their heads while scanning the room with wide dark eyes. They never missed a thing, or a man. He could see their eyes register when they spotted him.

On Saturday mornings he always dressed well. The clothes alone attracted their attention this Saturday. He was wearing a bold flower design shirt and had left the four top buttons open to show his chest and, in his patch of thick black chest hair, an imitation Roman coin dangled on a gold chain.

Steve was built like an offensive lineman, with short legs, a thickly trunk and no neck whatsoever. His square head appeared as if it was driven down between his shoulders with a sledge.

It was a head with surprisingly small features. The nose, lips, and ears were tiny and delicate, almost feminine. His eyes were gray, the color of soot, and set too close together. He had lots of hair and that he let grow, but it was fine hair and wouldn't hold its shape, even with conditioner.

Steve spent at least two hours every Saturday at Clyde's, watching and meeting women. It was an odd Saturday when he didn't come home with a new name and telephone number. Steve was on a first name basis with all the bartenders at Clyde's. He was also known at Mr. Smith and up Wisconsin at the Third Edition, and at most of the bars on M Street. For a newcomer in town, he thought with some pride, he had gotten around, become known.

"You've been a pig with a friend of mine." She phoned again a week later, and again it was after midnight.

"Who are you?" Steve whispered. The girl beside him began to stir.

"Don't you respect women?"

He strained to recognize the voice.

"You only make a woman once or twice, is that the average?

"Go screw yourself!" Steve slammed down the phone, and it rang again immediately.

"Who's it?" the woman in the bed mumbled.

"Some goddamn nut case. . ." The phone kept ringing. Steve swore again and, climbing out of bed, took the receiver off the hook. He wrapped a towel around the headpiece, as if he were smothering a small animal, and put the telephone in a dresser drawer. The next morning, he told himself, he would have his number changed and left unlisted.

Nevertheless, for several weeks afterwards whenever he brought a woman home with him, he'd take the phone off the receiver and place it in a drawer, out of sight and sound. He also found himself searching for the caller. He listened carefully to all the women he met on the job and after work in the Washington bars. He made lists of the women he had slept with since moving to the District and eliminated those he knew wouldn't call.

Still, he wasn't certain. He became less sure of himself around women. At Bixby's where he always stopped after work, he found himself drinking alone, like some married guy from out of town. And for awhile, he even stopped hustling in the bars.

"You're doing lots better, Stevie," she said, telephoning two weeks later.

"How did you get this number?" he demanded.

"Friends. Women stick together, Stevie, haven't you heard? I just called to congratulate you." She sounded friendly.

"Thanks."

"I passed you at the bar in Bixby's and you even kept your hands to yourself, didn't make one smartass remark."

"I probably didn't see you."

"You saw me."

"Are you going to tell me your name? Let me take you out on a date." He was nervous, asking her.

"Oh, Stevie, com' on!"

"Why not? We're probably neighbors." He pressed like a teenager.

"You're not my type."

"Bitch!"

She slammed the phone in his ear.

Steve sneaked about town on dates the next few weeks like he had done as a kid, looking for a place to park. He rented motel rooms in Virginia when he had to, or stayed overnight at the woman's place. He was convinced the caller lived on Hillyer and he spent hours watching through closed blinds the houses across the street. He checked all the names on the mailboxes and then telephoned each one. He listened to the way they said hello. Nothing turned up.

A month later, the first time he did bring someone home, she called as he came into his apartment.

"I'm having this call traced," he told her.

"Let me speak to the woman."

"You're crazy, did you know that?"

"And you're a pig. Let me talk to her!"

"I'm alone."

"She's blond with shoulder length, five-six, wearing a knit blue shirt, carrying a sling purse with a gold chain strap. And she's about eighteen, I'd guess. When did you start hanging around sock-hops, Stevie?"

"You live across the street, right? One of those brownstones." He stretched the cord and peered through the front window. She was there, he knew. Somewhere in the dark houses across the quiet street, she was watching him. It gave him the creeps.

"Quit staring out the window. I'm not outside. I don't live across the street."

"How do you know I'm looking?"

"You're the type. You don't have much imagination. Now, come on, Stevie, let me talk to the woman, or are you afraid?"

Steve muffled the receiver with his palm and explained to his date. "It's some crazy chick that keeps calling me. She wants to talk to you."

"Oh, no!" The teenager backed away.

"It's okay. I'm here." He smiled his little boy smile to show she had nothing to fear and coaxed her towards the phone.

She took the receiver cautiously and, keeping it at bay, whispered hello. She was a cute peaches 'n' cream high school graduate from Virginia that Steve had met that night at The Greenery. Steve wasn't sure, but he thought her name was Shirley.

Shirley listened attentively to his caller and Steve had a moment's panic. He had an urge to pull the telephone from her, but he didn't want to seem nervous. Instead, he went into the kitchen to mix drinks, and when he returned, the girl was replacing the phone as if she had just heard bad news.

"I'd like to leave," she whispered.

"For Chrissake. . .what did that dyke say?"

"She's not. . .that way."

"Like hell! That's the reason she's after me. I know about that stuff." He kept talking rapidly, afraid to let the girl talk.

"Would you please call a taxi?" she finally managed to say.

"You can't pull that crap on me! I have a right to know what she said."

"It doesn't concern you."

"It's my damn telephone!" He began to stride about the apartment, pacing to its walls, then spinning around and striking off for the other side of the room. "Goddamn dyke!" he mumbled and finished off his drink. To the girl, he said, "If you want to leave, leave, but find your own taxi!"

She left without a word and when Steve heard the door close behind him, he spun around and gave the finger to the empty room.

*   *   *

He now couldn't find a date in Washington. The word, he knew, had spread about him. That woman had done it to him. At night when he wandered up and down M Street, women looked away. It was done subtly. Their eyes swept across his face when he walked into a bar. The eyes registered him, then moved off. No one seemed to even see him. It was as if he wasn't there any longer.

He went home early after work, turned on the tube or worked with his weights. Then before ten o'clock, he took a cold shower and dropped into bed. He let the radio play all night to keep him company.

At work when he made his calls none of the saleswomen noticed him. And there were women in those stores that he had taken home, who had cried for him in the night, and whimpered against his chest. Now they let him pass. His swaggering attitude crumbled. He no longer winked at strangers, checked out women's legs. He began to hedge with work, phone for orders, and never left his desk. He took days off to sit by the window of his apartment and watch the street like an abandoned pet, left home alone.

"Are you sorry?" She telephoned again, early one evening.

"I haven't done anything. I'm no worse than the next guy. You're being unfair."

"Have you been fair to us? The women you've taken home?" Her voice had a curl to it.

"They came of their own free will. I'm the one being punished. No one in Washington will date me. You started this!"

"It's not my fault you can't date. Washington's a small town. Word gets around."

"You owe me at least one meeting, you know, after all of this." Steve began to pace. "I'm not giving you a line. How 'bout a drink some night? I'll meet you at Bixby's. . .you like that place."

She was silent and Steve let her take her time deciding. With women like this, he knew he had to be cool.

"I'm not sure."

"One drink. A half hour. I'd like to ask you a few questions. I have to hear your rap, okay? Maybe you've got a point."

"No drinks."

"Okay. Lunch?"

"No. I'll meet you at five o'clock in Dupont Circle."

"Fine! How will I know you?"

"Don't worry. I'll find you." And she hung up.

*   *   *

Steve would have rather met her at the Dupont Circle Hotel. A nice, cool and dark afternoon lounge where there were private booths, well-dressed people, the feeling of leather under his fingers. He appreciated quality and operated best in such places. But Dupont Circle! The park was full of young people and the homeless. They cluttered the grass like litter.

He sat away from the center fountain, picked a spot in the shade away from the crowd. He had come ten minutes early to give himself time to be settled and positioned. Steve had taken time dressing. He wanted to look good for this woman.

He had dressed conservatively and wore a navy blazer, a striped tie, white shirt, and summer linen slacks. It would impress her, he knew. Also he had a couple days of early summer tan and his weight was down. Just thinking about the fine impression he'd make made him feel great.

He'd be boyish with her, he decided. He'd keep the conversation general, and not push her for a date. Only a name and a phone number. She was going to be someone special. Anyway, he thought, it was about time he dropped all those salesgirls and secretaries. A guy with his position, the whole District as his territory; he could do a lot better, he knew.

"Hi!" A woman spoke to him.

Steve glanced along the bench at the young girl that had been sitting there. He looked over at her defensively, expecting trouble. She smiled. She was wearing a short dress, sandals. Her blond hair was long and loose. She wasn't bad looking, with big brown eyes and a bright smile. She looked, however, about sixteen.

"Your questions?" She tossed her hair away from her face and stared regally at him. Her brown eyes tightened and her wide mouth sealed up like a long white envelope.

"You?" He began to perspire.

She nodded.

"Well...ah...I was...I guess I was expecting someone else." He shifted around, clapped his hands together as if gripping a football, and thought: she made the whole story up. She was some kind of sex freak. He had never in his life tried to pick up a kid. "Okay, sister, you're not what I had in mind. Forget I arranged this, okay? We don't have anything to say to each other."

"You poor bastard."

"Why don't you stay with your gang?" He waved toward the grass.

"What's the matter? You don't hustle young girls?"

"I wouldn't touch you with rubber gloves. No street traffic for me."
He wiped his face with a handkerchief, looked away.

"I bet you're something in bed." She kept a smile on her face like an insult.

"Better than anything you've had, sister." He sat up straight.

"I'm not going to call you again," she said calmly. "I had this notion I might be able to reach you, but you're such a pathetic person. Oh, you'll get women to date you, Steve. Silly women who don't know better. But you have nothing to offer a real woman."

"Hey, bitch, you don't know me."

"Stevie, you boys are all alike." And with that she left him alone on the bench.

He retreated to the cool, dark bar of Dupont Circle where he bought the only other guy at the bar — a furniture salesman from North Carolina — a round of drinks. Steve told him about the girl, about his phone calls and meeting her in the park, but the salesman didn't see the joke. Well, Steve summed up, you had to have been there.

He stood back from the bar, shook his head and grinned, "Goddamn bitch!"

He'd get another apartment, he decided. He'd move out of the District. He'd live somewhere over in Virginia or Maryland, maybe Vienna. He'd live out where normal people lived, and get away from the crazies in the city.

Several months later, just before he did move out of the District, not to Vienna but instead to Gaithersburg, he saw her again. Steve's boss was in town and he had taken him to the Hay-Adams for lunch. It was the kind of restaurant Steve liked to be seen in. People in position and with money, he knew, ate there, and sitting among them made him feel special.

He saw her when she was leaving the restaurant. She was passing tables and causing a stir. All around the room businessmen looked up and smiled at her. She moved gracefully and quickly through the tables, her long blond hair styled and swept away from her face. She was wearing makeup, but not enough to draw attention away from her brilliant bright eyes, her perfect white skin.

She was wearing a pinstripe trouser skirt, long-sleeve shirt, weskit and blazer. In one hand she carried a thin leather attaché case. Steve realized as he watched her that she was the most beautiful woman in the city.

She saw him. Her large brown eyes held him briefly in focus and then she looked away and continued past him. He didn't exist at all.

The Children Never Lie

Cameron Nolan

Her first job, though she was very young for it at age 13, was as a baby-sitter—for Richard and Ruth Matheson!

If that doesn't surprise you, you're probably new to the fantasy/horror field and need to be reminded that Matheson wrote *I Am Legend, What Dreams May Come, The Shrinking Man,* and some of the best stories and scripts ever produced for "The Twilight Zone." And perhaps you need to know that one of the Matheson children was a little boy called Richard Christian...

Cam Nolan did many interesting things as a native Angeleno. By the time high school was over, she had over three dozen professional credits in Southern California newspapers (including the *Examiner*). She "folded (Dodger pitcher) Don Drysdale's socks in a laundry," assembled electronic inertial guidance systems for the Air Force, and became, in her mid-twenties, a purchasing clerk for Capitol Records. From that there was a stint of completing an article a day for *Tiger Beat,* a teenage mag. She wrote and published five non-fiction books—

And married the multi-talented consummate pro, William F. Nolan.

At a time when we're still reeling from reports of widespread child abuse and yet more terrible instances are discussed almost regularly on tv talk shows, Cameron needed courage to explore the subject in this, her first short story. "The Children Never Lie" is an understated examination of the volatile subject which, it's safe to say, simply takes one of the most startling turns you will ever read.

"I tellya, Addie, it's our chance. Almost as good as winning the Lottery. Hell, maybe better." He picked up his coffee mug, the one with his Valencia County Sheriff's shield on the side, a personalized (and cheap) gift from the Chamber of Commerce. Twenty-five years of service. He shook his head at the thought. Too long. As he took a swig from the cup he looked out the kitchen window at the flat brown fields which rolled toward the purple mountains in the distance.

Cotton and sugar beets, not what usually came to mind when people thought of California. Five thousand square miles of farms, just like back home in Libertyville, Nebraska, only there it had been corn and sorghum. He'd come 1,500 miles to trade corn and sorghum for cotton and sugar beets, and a county sheriff's pissy salary.

But things were due to change.

He thought about the beautiful Spanish colonial sign outside the La Palma Mobile Home Estates in San Diego. He already had the lot for a trailer picked out: Number 15-A. It overlooked the ocean, had palm trees front and back, a sweet little side yard, and a clear view of San Diego twenty miles to the south. Blue sky and blue ocean and white sea gulls. . .It was all going to be theirs, he really believed it now. For the first time, he really *believed* it.

He took a long drag on his Marlboro and fingered the collar of his uniform shirt where it rubbed against the wrinkled flesh of his neck. He knew he looked older than his sixty years. Too damn much sun, he thought. It was hard to avoid in farming country.

He looked over to where his wife was flouring the meat for chicken fried steak. "Dr. Martin says these kids were 'probably' molested. *'Probably,'* he says! Shit!"

He sighed and took another drag on his cigarette. "I called Ben in Sacramento — at the Attorney General's office — and he told me to phone the Sarazan Center in San Francisco and have their psychologists come down to examine all the children. So when I call them, they tell me they'd be *happy* to do it — for their regular fee. Gonna run over a thousand per kid before this thing is over, maybe a whole lot more than that. Last election the good voters of this county decide they can't raise my salary a lousy two thousand a year, and suddenly they're pleased as punch to pay maybe fifty thousand to some head doctors from Frisco. It isn't fair, Addie. It just isn't."

She looked up from the boiled potatoes she was mashing. "Millie at the grocery store told me people want to pay whatever's necessary. She says it's all anybody talks about these days. Clint, do *you* think it's true? You know more than anybody else right now. Do *you* believe it?"

He looked at her quickly, then shifted his eyes back out the window again, looking deep into the horizon. He shook his head. "I don't know, Addie. I just don't. It seems unbelievable that something like this could happen out here in the sticks. But it's my responsibility as an officer of the law to investigate this to the fullest extent. That's what I'm gonna do."

He drank from his mug. "Whatever happens, I give the big city papers two days — maybe three — before they pick up on it. And once it's in the headlines up and down the state, *everybody* is going to know who Clinton Lansdale, Sheriff of Valencia County, California, is.

"And then two things are gonna happen. First, we're going to get a lot of calls from movie and TV producers who want to buy the story. Just like that teacher up in Placerville a few months ago who got two dozen calls from producers after his story hit the big city papers. So that guy's set for life — all 'cause he got fired for doing too good a job! One way or another, I tellya, we're going to be seeing some real money real fast."

He looked at her, his eyes intense.

"The second thing that's gonna happen is the people of this county are going to see me in a whole new light. I'm going to be Big Time, Addie, a real celebrity. And when elections come up next year, they'll be *proud* to vote me a salary increase. So no matter what happens now, we're gonna be okay. Honest to God, honey, we're gonna be okay."

"The children *have* been molested, Sheriff Lansdale. Every one of them. We have proof." The smartly-dressed woman searched through her expensive leather briefcase for some papers.

"Here we have a preliminary summary of the results of our examinations. The completed examinations are all on videotape, of course, for use in court, and we still have several weeks of investigation ahead of us. More detailed information from each child is needed; obtaining that data is our next task. But the preliminary results are quite important. Just look at these."

Melissa Hamilton handed over several sheets of expensive paper with the Sarazan Center logo engraved at the top of each one.

Class, Clint thought. He didn't have much use for psychologists but Melissa Hamilton and this Sarazan Center were class all the way.

"As you'll see, we have documented a variety of criminal charges for you to choose from when you and the District Attorney prepare your indictments. We at the Sarazan Center pride ourselves on the professionalism we bring to our legal services. We offer depth *and* breadth, in order that local law officials can create airtight cases that are virtually guaranteed to result in guilty verdicts."

He looked over the summary sheets, blinked. What he was reading was bizarre, beyond belief. "It says here that some of the children were taken to Nevada and used in child prostitution!" he exclaimed incredulously.

"Oh, yes, we found that quite interesting. We have established scenarios in both Reno and Las Vegas."

"What's all this devil worship stuff?" He looked at Melissa Hamilton skeptically. "We sure don't have any devil worshippers here in Valencia County."

She smiled with the syrupy condescension of the sophisticated city professional towards the country bumpkin.

"Of course, this is a shock to you, Sheriff Lansdale. We run into such disbelief all the time. What you must realize is that the sexual abuse of children is the most well-hidden of crimes. Usually, no one other than the abuser and the victim knows what is occurring. We're lucky in this case because we have more than two dozen children involved, and the abusers appear to number at least ten. We're not sure yet just how many people are involved or exactly who those particular people are, because our established investigation format focuses first on breaking down each child's personal privacy boundaries. *Then* we detail specific acts which have occurred. That's where we are now. After we get the children to trust us – tell us the things they thought they couldn't tell anyone – we then go into the specifics of exactly who did what to them, how many times, under what conditions, and so on. It's a multi-step procedure which has been developed in order to maximally utilize the memory potentials of the children we are examining."

He put the papers down on the desk. "How do you know the children are telling the truth?"

"We have scientifically-approved ways of establishing data," she said. "Initially, we use anatomically correct dolls in which the genitals are greatly enlarged. When a child manipulates two or more dolls in such a manner as to indicate oral sex, for example, we know that such an act has occurred in the life of that child."

"Couldn't they just be playing with the dolls and however they put them, it's still just a child playing?"

"Oh, no. When a child manipulates an anatomically correct doll, each action has specific meaning. That's been well established in scientific literature."

"And how do you know who supposedly did this to them? Do you ask the child for names?"

"We do, of course. But we seldom get a direct answer. Instead, the children answer *indirectly;* all children do. We give them crayons and paper and they draw pictures. Whenever they draw monsters, we ask them who the monsters are, what the monsters are named. *That* they tell us — *then* we know who the 'monsters' in their real lives are. Once a child identifies an abuser, we ask the other children about that particular person. They are relieved the secret is out and usually admit quite readily that that person also abused them."

"You mean, you take a child and give it naked dolls with big genitals — some crayons and paper — and whatever the child seems to indicate, you depend on that being the *truth?*"

"Oh, absolutely. It's well established medical procedure used by virtually all child abuse investigators throughout the United States."

Clint shook his head in disbelief. The county was paying thousands of dollars for just this information, and he couldn't accept any of it. Well, maybe sometimes it worked, some of it. But *all* the time? These people might be doctors and have initials after their names out the ass, but he'd developed a lot of common sense over the years and his gut told him this was, mostly, totally nuts. But he held a tiger by the tail now and he knew it. One way or another all this had to be seen through. Besides, these Sarazan Center people were *professionals.* Surely they knew what they were doing.

One way or another, his future and Addie's depended on him doing his job and doing it right.

If only it didn't seem so crazy.

"What do you do now?" he asked her.

"At the moment, we don't have any idea who did these things to the children. The next step is determining who is involved. We must quantify data: names, dates, times of day, locations."

"How long do you expect everything to take?'

"Another two weeks, perhaps three. I have five experienced interviewers working on the children now. We ought to begin getting specific data within the next day or so. My interviewers know what they're doing, Sheriff," she added. "We've obtained data on some of the most resistant cases imaginable. Compared to some, this is a piece of cake."

"And you're *certain* this is *real?* This is the *truth?*"

"Just remember the first rule of child sexual abuse, Sheriff: The children *never* lie."

There was a hoot owl outside and he always felt good when he heard a hoot owl greeting the moon. Comforted. You knew that wise bird (all owls *were* wise, he'd been convinced of it since he was a child) was somehow watching over you. Which made life a bit easier to take when everything seemed so all-fired crazy. Clint looked out into the lonely moonlit fields from the living room. He'd stubbed out three Marlboros since he sat down, unable to sleep, and now he sat in the dark without even the friendly red glow of a cigarette to keep him company.

The last of the arrests was over, he hoped. Twelve people — people he'd thought were among the good people of Valencia County — were now in the county jail. Which meant, of course, that the jail was three hundred percent over maximum legal capacity. Nobody'd ever figured on a series of crimes like this in Valencia County when the jail was built. God, he still couldn't believe it.

Duane MacAllister, who owned the feed and supply store, the principal sponsor of the Valencia County 4-H Club. Agnes Hobson, the music teacher for all the Valencia County public schools. Pete Dubrevick, who carried the mail for half the county. And Dr. Martin, the one who'd said the kids had "probably" been molested. He was one too. It was like the whole world had suddenly gone nuts. These people he'd known intimately all these years.

It was sick and awful, his soul hurt, and there wasn't a damn thing he could do to make sense out of it. If all these people were guilty, then Sheriff Clinton Lansdale didn't know a damn thing about human nature.

It was time, he realized suddenly, for him to retire.

The realization had been coming a long time. Hell, he probably would have done it five years ago if he'd had the money. But he didn't then, and now he did. Well, almost. The producers had been calling, just like he'd promised Addie. It was the biggest news story of the month and not just in California, either. It was all over national television — even around the world — and Clinton Lansdale was now an honest-to-God celebrity. A week ago he'd even gone to San Francisco to appear on "Nightline" with Ted Koppel. The network had sent their own plane, flown him to San Francisco, put him up in a suite at the St. Francis, and then flown him home again.

He'd never been so scared in his life, not even the time years ago when that murderer had escaped from San Quentin and was ready to kill him in Mike Cahill's barn. But he'd looked fine on TV — everybody said so — and it was a shoo-in for him to get a fat raise in the next election.

But he didn't have to depend on that now. No, he was going to sell his story to the TV movies for a quarter of a million dollars. That was the price and the contracts were being drawn up. Two hundred and fifty thousand dollars. Enough for the rest of their lives in San Diego.

Another six months, and Number 15-A at the La Palma Mobile Home Estates would be Home, Sweet Home.

Outside the living room window he saw the glint of shiny metal moving in the night. Someone was in the front yard. His cop's senses aroused, he suddenly realized there was more than one person. He could see dark motion by the eucalyptus tree, more over by the wooden fence. Quietly, Clint stood and went for his weapon.

He couldn't figure out why, but the house was under siege. Terrorists? Drug-crazed motorcycle freaks? He didn't know, but he *did* know that it would take at least ten minutes for backup to arrive from town. By that time, if he wasn't careful, he and Addie could both be dead.

Adrenalin pumping, his mind clearer than it had been in years, Clint walked softly towards the bedroom to wake her. Every second counted.

The door exploded open with light and sound. A spotlight, his mind registered — the type used by city SWAT teams. He was pinned in its beam, unable to move. He noticed that he could see the weave on his cotton pajamas, each hair on the back of his hands. Those lights were damn good, some part of his mind registered. I wish Valencia County could afford one.

"Freeze!" an authoritative voice ordered. "This is the FBI. Turn around and face the wall, hands in plain sight. Spread your legs apart."

Incredulously, automatically, he did what he had ordered so many others to do over the years. The hands that patted him down were professional. It didn't make any sense, but these were no terrorists or hippies. They *were* the law.

The man in charge, keeping him covered, came nearer. "You are under arrest. You have the right to remain silent. If you give up the right to remain silent, anything you say can and will. . ."

Addie was suddenly there. Nobody could have slept through the last five minutes. When had she appeared in the doorway? Clint didn't know. She was looking at him oddly, which he found strange. Then the other FBI man, dressed in camouflage, was talking quietly to her. Her eyes were getting big and round like she couldn't understand what the man was saying, except she did.

He'd never seen that expression before on Addie's face, but he'd seen it on lots of others. First was years ago when he'd had to go over to Emma Dunham's place and tell her Frank had been killed in a tractor accident near the bridge. That was the first time he'd seen that expression — just a couple of months after he became a deputy sheriff — but he'd seen it plenty of times since. Total disbelief mixed with total belief, all at the same time.

It was the horrible look of a human being stretched to the limits of endurance, and now it was on his own wife's face.

The trial was a nightmare. At first, in the months before the trial began, Addie came to visit him every week. Then gradually, as his bail was denied and the press and television went to work, she came less and less. She was in court the day the verdict came in — he saw her sitting next to the back door — but she acted as if she'd never seen him before. Her face didn't have any expression on it. She was just going through the motions, living each day as it came until God called her home, just like she'd been taught at the First Baptist Church back in Nebraska when she was a little girl.

His last thought before the verdict was read was that he wasn't married anymore. His wife had died, though her body continued to function. It was a sobering thought: it hit him more deeply than the guilty verdict which he had already come to expect.

It didn't matter that he'd never done any of the things he was accused of. He was innocent, but he knew that his innocence was irrelevant in this age of scientific knowledge and expert witnesses. The children had identified him. They'd told immensely detailed stories of how he had done ghastly perverted things to them, and to chickens and rabbits and geese and sheep and cows and horses and dogs and cats.

They told of things he'd never heard of in all his career as a law officer.

It had happened — was *supposed* to have happened — Wednesday nights. Those interminable Wednesdays when he had all night patrol duty. But the children said those were the nights he did things to them and to the animals. He had no alibi — why would a sheriff, doing his job as he was supposed to do, need an alibi? — and the children were so sincere, so detailed, so...*right.*

Except none of it ever happened.

After a while, as the trial dragged on (one of the longest trials in California history), he gave up. He didn't know how to answer the child abuse experts with their degrees and their graphs and their scientific studies and their videotapes of children identifying him as the ringleader of the "cult."

That's what the newspapers and the experts called it, a "cult."

It seemed so weak just to say that it never happened.

But the children never lie. "The children never lie." Over and over and over again the numerous official experts agreed: the children *never* lie.

The verdict was guilty on all counts.

The prison sentence didn't matter to him. He was past feeling. What *did* matter was that the producers of the TV movie about him and Valencia County didn't pay Addie a dime for the rights to the story. They didn't have to. He was a convicted child molester, and the facts were on record. So the dream was over. Addie was going to live the rest of her life in Valencia County. Eventually she would die there, a broken woman with a broken soul.

Somewhere inside, Clint knew that he was crying for her and for him and for their destroyed lives. But the tears were so deep that his eyes were never moistened. He doubted he would shed a tear again.

James Hutchings, twenty-seven year old accountant, was undergoing hypnosis in the office of therapist Jon Sherman, trying to determine the actual source of his post-traumatic stress syndrome disorder. Not that the source was ever in great question: as a child, Hutchings had been one of the many victims of the Valencia County child sexual abuse ring. Not only had his initial molestation experiences been traumatic, but the subsequent trial of the defendants, which lasted for more than two years — with him testifying before the world via television cameras and in open court — had further traumatized him greatly.

Afterward, he'd gone on to a seemingly "normal" high school and university life, become licensed as a top flight C.P.A., and earned, at a very early age, respect for his professional accomplishments.

But the post-traumatic syndrome had surfaced three years ago: nightmares, impotence, hallucinations, eating disorders, addictive behavior, suddenly stressed interpersonal relationships. His marriage failed, his two children were being raised three thousand miles away, and Hutchings couldn't seem to get it together in any phase of his life other than work.

Nine-to-five he was "normal" — brilliant, actually — and every other hour Hutchings was a walking disaster case. He'd tried psychotherapy; it hadn't helped. He'd tried all the different groups which had helped so many, but they had resulted in only cosmetic improvements.

He was strongly considering suicide and his turn to hypnotherapy was the very last try Hutchings would make to regain his mental health. If this failed, he had already decided to kill himself.

"And now that you are completely relaxed, more relaxed than you have ever been before, I want you to breathe slowly and deeply. Take a deep, deep, slow breath and then hold it, hold it...now exhale slowly...slowly...slowly. Exhale completely. Inhale deeply again.

"I want you to go back into your existence, Jim, back through your entire history. I want you find the source of your present troubles. Be there, but realize that you are actually here with me, right now. It is safe for you to be there mentally, at the source of your problems, and tell me what you are experiencing.

"Where are you, Jim?"

"In a...a barn, I think. There's hay, and there are cows and chickens...yes, it has to be a barn."

"Good. That's very good. Now tell me what's happening."

"It's night. It's dark outside, it's cold. I'm cold. I'm so cold."

"Why are you cold, Jim?"

"Because I don't have any clothes on. Oh, I'm scaredl I'm *so* scared! It's the night of the ritual, and I'm supposed to be in it."

"What ritual, Jim?"

"The wedding of the devil. The devil is going to get married tonight, and I'm to be a gift for him on his wedding night. They're going to do...things!...to me. I'm so cold and I'm so scared."

"That's okay, Jim. You aren't really there. You're here, in Los Angeles, and you're safe. It's okay to relive what went on back then, but realize that you're safe *now* and no one is going to do anything to you. Do you know you're safe?"

"Yeah. Um...uh, nobody *looks* right. Everybody looks different. Sheriff Lansdale is here but he doesn't look like he does now. He's wearing a cape and his hair is different. And he's got a big scar on the side of his cheek. He never had a scar when I knew him, but he has a scar, a real big, ugly scar. Why didn't he have one when I was a kid? But he *had* to have a scar, because that's when I knew him..."

"That's okay, Jim. Don't worry about the scar. Let's go to something else. I want to get you out of that barn. Let's go to your house. What do you see in your house?"

"Uh...it's my house, I know that. But it's just one room! It's made of stones, and there's straw on the floor where we sleep, and a fire in one corner, and the walls are all black where the smoke goes. I don't understand! I *know* this is my house, but it *isn't* the house I grew up in!"

"That's okay, Jim. Don't worry about the discrepancies. Let's just go with what you're getting. Is your mother in the house?"

"Yes, she's coming in the door. She's got roots in her hands — she's all dirty. She's been out digging roots for us to eat. She looks like she's never taken a bath in her life! And she's got scars all over her face — the pox, I think. And she's dressed funny. She's got on a long skirt and her hair is all wrapped up in a cloth and she smells bad — oh, my God, does that woman stink!"

"Jim, how old are you?"

"Fourteen. I know 'cause it's time for me to get married. My pa's arranged for me to marry the girl from the next estate. We're going to get married on Whitsun, and then I won't have to be in the rituals anymore."

There was a long moment of silence, which only the hypnotist noticed. When Jim Hutchings was fourteen, Sheriff Lansdale had already been in police custody for over five years. And the boy certainly had never been part of an arranged marriage at that age. A thought . . .

"Jim, can you tell me what year it is?"

"It's the tenth year of the reign of our king, Edward of Caernarvon. We had the celebration last month."

"Jim — what country are you in?"

"England, of course. What country do you *think* King Edward rules? Are you French? Are you an enemy of our king?" Hutchings was moving about on the couch, obviously disturbed, completely involved in his hypnotic experience.

"No, Jim, I'm definitely not an enemy. I'm your friend. I'm going to check on something and, while I'm checking, you just see whatever it is you want to see. I'll be right back."

He went over to his bookcase to pull out a pocket encyclopedia. The list of English monarchs was, Sherman was grateful to see, complete. King Edward II (Edward of Caernarvon) had ruled from 1307 to 1327.

Over six hundred years ago.

The standing room only crowd in the packed hotel auditorium was silent, totally involved in the words Jon Sherman, Ph.D., was speaking. It was the best attended lecture in the history of the conventions of the American Association of Child Abuse Professionals. Reporters and news crews clustered in the aisles and in front of the dais and only the insistent clicking of Nikons punctuated the hypnotist's amplified voice.

"And so what I'm saying to you, fellow professionals, is that our knowledge of the human potential is so limited even today, that often we don't know what we *assume* we have already scientifically established.

"I have now regressed all twenty-six of the people who, as children, were involved with the Valencia County child sexual abuse ring. Every one of these adults relived a lifetime in the target year 1317, near Lancaster, England — where they were, indeed, victims of such a ring. According to historical documents which I have carefully researched, a severe famine existed in England during this period. Worship of the devil was considered by many to be a way to bring about the end of the famine. These victims all agree that the person you know as ex-Sheriff Clinton Lansdale — as well as the storekeeper, the music teacher, the mail carrier, the doctor and all the others — were also involved in this ancient ring of devil worshippers.

"It may well be true that 'the children never lie.' But I put the question to you: Are we, as a modern society, prepared to punish people for what they did hundreds or even thousands of years ago? Is that our responsibility? Because, while I have no doubt that these people did molest these children, I also have no doubt that this mass molestation took place across the Atlantic Ocean over six hundred years ago.

"And I strongly suggest that when we, as professionals, use advanced psychiatric techniques — some of which border dangerously close to the methods used to brainwash political prisoners — to access the memory banks of children or adults, we may be obtaining far more information than we are capable of dealing with. We may be dooming people who are innocent in the present, but whose guilty pasts have not been forgotten by their victims."

Clinton Lansdale, California penitentiary prisoner number 344187, read the cover stories in *Time* and *Newsweek* with great interest. Now, at last, he knew for sure he wasn't crazy. He wasn't angry at the system because he knew, as a lifelong law officer, that guilty people must pay for their crimes. After six hundred years, he was paying the price for his.

He got out a piece of prison stationery to begin a letter to Jon Sherman. He knew the prison authorities would allow him to be hypnotized by a qualified hypnotherapist, especially one as famous as Sherman was now. It might gain him a new trial, and a new verdict. Hollywood was sure to be interested. There would be a lot of money after all — and at last, Addie could buy the trailer in San Diego. *She* could live in it even if he couldn't.

His lips curved upward into a smile as he envisioned the ocean as it looked from the yard of Number 15-A. He could see the gulls swooping across the sky, hear their cries as they searched the beach for food.

It was going to be one hell of a story.

The Other Woman

Lois Tilton

Few things can be more satisfying to an anthologist than discovering a writer who clearly possesses a slightly off-center imagination, the talent to get a really unusual premise on paper, and the intelligence to respond professionally to the editor who expresses genuine interest in his or her work.

With a novel already in print (*Vampire Winter,* 1990) and horror/dark fantasy fiction in *Weird Tales* and *Women of Darkness II,* Lois Tilton may not qualify fully as *my* discovery but I'd be proud to make the claim stand up. Certainly "her work" is the term since I met Lois at World Fantasy Convention in '90, not far from her home in Glen Ellyn, Illinois. She requested a try at getting into this book, I asked her to submit "a different sort of story, 2,500 words or fewer in length," and that's what she did —

And more. Because "The Other Woman" is about the kind of person implied by the title and it's so inventive, poignant, surprising, and so...well, *different*...that I asked permission to hold it for a fifth *Masques*. Within three weeks, though, the subtle force of the tale was haunting me so much I realized it belonged in *this* book, *now*. Wild horses won't make me say more about it except to add that you may want to glance back at Lois Tilton's title when you've read it and consider all the ramifications.

I lie naked on the bed, wet hair covering my face. I can't see, and I panic for a second until I discover I can lift my hand to brush it away. It's time, again.

I can hear my mother's cold silence in the hallway: the disapproving footsteps that stop just outside my door, then move on. "Why do you keep doing this to yourself?" she always asks. "He's a married man, almost twice your age. Don't you have any shame?"

The warm glow from the shower is fading, my skin prickles with the chill, and I get up, wrap my robe around me and switch on the hair dryer, filling the silence with the rush of heated air. I can't argue about it with her. I know she's only thinking of me, but she just can't understand how it is, what we have to go through just to be together. Even this way.

I shake out my hair, halfway dry already. My face is a little flushed from the hair dryer's heat, and I turn it off for a second to look into the mirror, lightly brushing a finger across my cheek, the smoothness of the skin. With makeup, the faded scars are almost invisible.

"I'm pretty," I tell myself, still not quite believing in the miracle. His gift, the money to pay for the treatments. So much I owe him, I think, finishing my hair and shaking it out so it flows down my back the way he likes it. I dress slowly, for him, as if he were here watching me. The panties, real silk, so sheer they reveal more than they hide — I feel shameless and love how I feel. I won't wear a bra or slip tonight; the fabric of the dress caresses my bare skin, glides sensuously across the silk.

Earrings, the diamond pendant — I never asked for such things, but he likes to see me wearing them. I look at my watch. 6:45. Two more minutes until the car will pull up.

My mother sees me coming down the stairs. *You look like a whore,* says the set of her head, averted. Then her eyes, more merciful, turn back. *Don't you know he'll never marry you? Never be able to give up his wife?*

But I do, I do know. What I can't explain is that it doesn't matter, that nothing else matters except being with him. Our few hours together are worth all the pain.

I see the headlights of the car turning into the drive, and I open the door to leave without looking back.

He already has the car door open, and I slide down into the smooth leather of the seat. He's just shaved, I can catch the faint mint scent of his shaving cream, and I lean close against him, fingertips lightly tracing the lean smooth line of his jaw. Oh, how I want him!

Suddenly his whole body stiffens. My breath catches in my throat. I see it in the mirror, the car driving past in the darkness, its headlights off . . .

She's seen us!

But the car turns the corner without slowing and we both exhale in shaken relief. He turns to kiss me, cupping my chin in his palms, and I open my mouth to his desperate intensity, forgetting about the car, about everything. We only have time for each other now — so little time. Finally we break apart, and I can see his hands are trembling as he puts the car into reverse, backs down the driveway. It's harder for him, I know it is, having to live with her.

In less than half an hour we're outside the city limits, heading down the highway into the night. I don't ask where we're going. I know we can't risk being seen together. She's suspicious already.

I remember the first time I saw her, only a few weeks after I was hired—my very first job, right out of high school. She was coming out of his office, I was crossing the hallway on the way to the copier room. I remember how her look stopped me, and I pressed my lips together to try to hide my overbite while her eyes took in every detail of my face, my body, my clothes. I'd never felt so ugly, so ashamed.

Later, looking around the office, I realized that there wasn't a woman working in the place who could even be considered marginally attractive. Naturally, naturally, they had hired *me*.

"Who was that woman?" I asked Beverly at lunch. Beverly was his secretary then, swarthy, with a mustache on her upper lip. She weighed close to three hundred pounds. "This morning, with the full-length fur coat, the heavy perfume?"

Her thick eyebrows lifted. "You don't know? Listen, this whole company belongs to her, every share of stock. *He* just runs it, and you'd better believe she don't let him forget it, either." She shook her head emphatically, added, "She's in and out of here all the time. And let me tell you something else: you want to keep your job, you stay away from *him*."

So I learned to keep my face down whenever she came into the office, which was three or four times a week. Maybe it helped me keep my mind on my job, knowing that at any time I might look up to find her narrow, suspicious eyes watching, her lips pressed thin with distrust. When Beverly quit, when she couldn't stand it any more, she warned me not to take her job, but I needed the money; my mother had hospital bills and she couldn't even work part time any more. And the benefits were good. The company's dental plan paid for the braces I'd needed since I was twelve.

It wasn't long before I learned to be alert for the heavy scent of musk perfume wafting across my desk. "Is he in?" she'd demand, then push through the door of his office before I could get out an answer—as if she could catch him that way, unprepared. It made me sick to have to listen to the screaming from behind the closed door, the insane accusations, the threats. I came into the room once with some papers, five minutes or so after she'd gone. I saw him there with his face buried in his hands, his shoulders shaking. I backed out, saying, "I'm sorry, sir, I thought you were alone." Pretending like he did that there was nothing wrong, as if I didn't know, as if the whole office didn't know.

Then one day he called me in. He had a folder on his desk and he looked slightly uncomfortable as he opened it and looked up at me. He cleared his throat.

"I hope this isn't something too personal, but I see here that the company's medical insurance has turned you down for a procedure — cosmetic surgery?"

My face went hot and I knew how I must look with the acne scars all flaring red. I shook my head, keeping my head as low as I could. "It was for dermabrasion treatments. But, no, they said the insurance wouldn't pay, not for — something like that."

His voice was so soft, careful not to embarrass me. "If a loan would help, I could arrange it. Not through the company, I mean. You could repay the money out of your salary, a little bit each month. I can understand. . .what it might mean to you."

Oh, I know, Mother said he was only doing it to take advantage of me. But she was wrong, they were all wrong. There was nothing else, we never even touched each other. Not until that day. . .

The scent of her perfume warned me to look up just as she brushed past my desk, ready to push open his door. Then, suddenly, she froze, staring at me. My face flushed. My braces had just come off a week before and the raw look from the dermabrasion was starting to fade. Now, the way she looked at me, the way her face went — all brittle with hate. Malicious, jealous hate. Her fingers curved into claws, and I flinched away involuntarily.

She stormed into his office. I had never heard such screaming: *bitch. . .whore. . .* I couldn't stand it. I ran into the ladies room and hid in one of the stalls, in case she might come in after me.

When I got back, he was waiting by my desk. His face was pale, as if he were in shock. "I'm sorry. I'm afraid I'll have to ask you — "

I spared him, saying quickly, "I understand. I don't want to cause you more trouble."

He nodded but then, suddenly, he caught my hand in his, so tightly it hurt. But I would never have pulled away, not if he'd held me for a thousand years. Our eyes met and the hurt I saw in his made me burst out. "I'm sorry, I'm so sorry."

"Will you meet me?" It was a whisper so low I almost doubted what I had heard. But I already knew my answer. "Yes."

Yes. It would always be yes, no matter what we had to go through to be together. It always will.

I sigh as his hand strokes up the length of my thigh. I move closer to him while he drives, fitting my body against his. He turns his head slightly to catch a glimpse of my breasts visible beneath the sheer fabric of my dress. I can hear the intake of his breath, his wanting me.

We stop at a bed-and-breakfast place in the country. A car behind us slows slightly, accelerates. I glance at him to see if he noticed, but his face shows nothing.

Our reservations are under an assumed name. The room is pleasant, decorated in Williamsburg style with landscape prints on the walls, but we ignore the amenities, we ignore everything else to press ourselves against each other. His hands slide up the backs of my thighs, across the silk panties. He pulls them down. His mouth is on mine, it moves to my throat, my breasts. I can feel his hardness against my belly.

We can't wait. My dress is on the floor, I'm lying on the bed, lifting my hips. He fills me with himself.

It's over too quickly. I bend over him. My tongue teases his nipples, moves lower. He reaches up to pull me down on top of him. I can hear the sound of a car outside in the driveway. So little time left. I close my eyes, closing out everything else but the sensation of him. With my body I worship. I cry out, shuddering with pleasure almost too much to endure. His hands clutch my hips. He gasps. We look into each other's eyes with awe.

I fall onto the bed next to him. We lie next to each other, my head on his shoulder. I breathe in the scent of him. I wonder for an instant that I have never found her scent on him, the musk she always wears; he feels my shudder. He pulls me closer to him and we cling to each other. Our eyes are closed. This is the moment when I always think: let it stop here. Let time stop here and leave us together like this forever.

I hear a noise—the creak of the door hinges—then a sound like wood splitting. His body jerks violently in my arms, and warmth hits my face, fragments of him splashing me.

"Bitch!" The voice spits venom. I turn away from the bloody ruin on the pillow next to me to see her standing in the doorway with the gun still in her hand. It has a silencer on the barrel. I want to scream but terror is choking my throat. The insane, hateful satisfaction on her face tells me everything. She's *glad.* I realize now that she had driven him to this all along, tormented him with her jealousy until he was desperate enough to risk both of us. But I—I'm the one she really hates. Younger than she is, prettier than she is.

The gun had been for him. Now she closes the door and takes the razor from her purse, the old-fashioned straight razor. *This* is what she means to use on me.

I panic, I try to rush past her to the door, but the razor is a bright flash slicing open my breast. I try to fend it off but the razor lays open my palms, my forearms. My blood is spattered on her face. It smears the polished surface of the razor like a crimson oil. I'm screaming now, but her laughter is more shrill. Her face is alive with insane hate, her eyes burn with it. She's been wanting this for a very long time.

I fall back onto the bed, and hot pain slashes across my belly. I scream again, but she pulls my arms away and the razor slices across my throat. Silenced, I still struggle, gasping for breath, inhaling my own blood through my gaping windpipe. It starts to fill my lungs.

She's still laughing as she starts to cut my face. My face, my breasts. Angry slashes between my legs. A great rip across my scalp, pulling it away, blinding me with my own hair. The scent of her perfume is suffocating. The pain is fading, sensation ebbs with my blood. It will be over soon.

More noise now, a banging on the door, shouts from outside. Too late, too late. Her laughter is breaking down into sobs. Through the bloody veil of my hair I see her put the gun to her own head. Suddenly she falls across the bed, across his legs.

We are all together now. Again.

I'm fading, the cold is spreading through me, but I still can't let go. Never to see him again. *It was worth it. I would go through it again. For him. To be with him one more time.*

I lie naked on the bed and brush the wet hair out of my face. I shiver a little and reach for my robe. The warmth from the shower is fading.

My mother's footsteps pause in the hallway outside my door. *Why do you keep doing this to yourself?*

I stand up, pulling on my robe. I don't want to argue with her. She can't understand.

But to myself, I whisper the answer. "Because I love him."

Love, Hate, and the Beautiful Junkyard Sea

Mort Castle

Mort Castle isn't just one of the meager few writers to appear in all four *Masques* anthologies plus the editor's non-fiction book, *How to Write Tales of Horror, Fantasy and Science Fiction.* He thought up the idea for said how-to — and he wrote a story for a Williamson anthology that was paid for but never published!

And this, by the author of the widely admired novels *Cursed Be the Child* and *The Strangers,* is it. At last.

Since writing it, Castle crafted exquisite tales for *Twilight Zone* (which wanted "Love, Hate" but folded before they could publish it), *Nukes* ("And of Gideon"), *Masques III, Lovecraft's Legacy* and other excellent publications, one of the newest of which was *Still Dead.* His novella there, "Old Man and The Dead," is Hemingwayesque and enviably outstanding. He found time to create "Buzz Mason, The Original Intergalactic Hero" for Northstar Productions, to edit *Fear,* write a column for *Afraid,* and to option *Strangers* to O'Gore Productions. Awarding *Cursed Be . . .* five stars, *Rave Reviews* cited Mort as "an emergent master" and said the novel "deserves to be acclaimed a classic of its kind." So did this editor when he put it on his favorites list in his how-to, back when the working title was "Diakka."

Castle never forgot this story. Neither did I. Neither, I believe, will you.

It wasn't until the third grade I learned I could love. It was in third grade I met Caralynn Pitts.

Before that, seems to me all I did was hate. I had reason. As everyone in Harlinville knew and let me know, I was trash. The Deweys were so low-down you couldn't get lower if you dug straight to China and kept on going. My daddy was skinny, slit-eyed, and silent except in his drunken, grunt-shouting, crazy fits that set him to beating on my mother or me. Maybe it was the dark and dust of the coal mine—he worked Old Ben Number Three—that got inside him, poisoned him to turn him mean like that.

My mother might have tried to be a good momma, I don't know, but by the time I was able to think anything about it, she must have just given up. In a day she never said more than ten words to me. Sometimes in a week, maybe she didn't say ten words to me. At night, she cried an awful lot. I think that's what I mostly remember about my momma, her crying that way.

So trash, no-account trash, bad as any and worse than most you find in southern Illinois, that's what I was; and if you're trash, you start out hating yourself and your folks and hating the God Who made you trash and plans to keep you that way, but soon you get so hate filled, you have to let it out or just bust, and so you get to hating other people. I hated kids who came to school in nice clothes, with a different shirt everyday, the kids who had Bugs Bunny lunchboxes with two sandwiches on bread so white it made me think of hospitals, the kids who lost teeth and got quarters from a tooth fairy, the kids whose daddies never got drunk and always took them on vacations to Starved Rock State Park or 'way faraway, like Disneyland or the Grand Canyon. I hated all the mommas up at the pay laundry every Monday morning, washing the clothes so clean for their families. I hated Mr. Mueller at the Texaco, who always told me, "Take a hike, Bradford Dewey," or "Boy, jump in a hole and pull it in after you," when I wanted to watch cars go up on the grease rack, and I hated Mr. Eikenberry, the postmaster. Mr. Eikenberry had that breeze-tingly smell of Old Spice on him. What my daddy smelled like was whiskey and wickedness.

If you hate somebody, you want to hurt them, and I thought of hateful, hurting things happening to all the people I hated. There wasn't a one in Harlinville I didn't set my mind on a wish picture for, a hate-hurt picture that left them busted up, bleeding and dead. I imagined a monster big as an Oldsmobile grabbing up Rodney Carlisle—his father owned the hardware store on the square—and ripping off his arms and legs, a snake as long as the Mississippi River swallowing Claire Bobbit, Patty Marsel, Edith Hebb, *all* the girls who used to tease me, and an invisible vampire ripping the throats out of all the teachers at McKinley School.

You might think maybe that I really did try to hurt people, I mean, use my hands, punch them in the nose or fling stones at them, or hit them on the head with a ball bat or something like that, but that is not so. Never in my whole life have I done that kind of hurt to anyone.

What I did was to find another way to get people. What I did was, I started lying. It's this way: You tell someone the truth, it means you trust them. It's like you got something you like them enough to *share* with them. Doesn't have to be an important piece of truth, either, it can be a little nothing: "I went to the show last night and that was one fine picture they had," or "It's really a pretty day," or "My cat had kittens," or anything at all. You tell someone the truth, it's just about the same as liking them.

So when you *lie* to a person, it's because you got no use for them, you hate their guts—and what makes it really so fine is you're doing it without ever having to flat-out say what you *feel*.

So I lied, lied my head off. I told little lies, like my Uncle Everett sent me five dollars because I was his favorite nephew and I did so have a wonderful birthday gift for Rodney Carlisle but I wasn't giving it to him because he didn't ask me to his party; and I told monster whopper lies, some of them super-crazy, like I was just adopted by the Deweys but my real parents were Hollywood movie stars, or once I saw a ghost who had this big red butt like a baboon, or I had to kill this three-hundred-pound wolf with just my bare hands when it attacked me out at the junkyard.

I didn't really fool anyone with my lies, you know. That wasn't what I was trying to do. All in all, I'd say Miss Krydell, the third grade teacher, was right when she used to say, "Bradford, you are a hateful little liar."

But all that changed when Caralynn Pitts came and showed me the beautiful junkyard sea.

You've probably had to do it yourself, I bet—stand in front of the whole class and tell who you are and all because you're the new kid—and you're supposed to be making friends right off. It was the first week in May, already too hot and too damp, an oily spring like you get in southern Illinois. The new girl up by Miss Krydell's desk was Caralynn. She had this peepy voice about one squeak lower than Minnie Mouse. Her eyes and hair were the same shade of black, and she was wearing this blue and dark green plaid dress.

Caralynn Pitts didn't say much except her name and that she lived on Elmscourt Lane, but in a town the size of Harlinville, everyone knew most everything about her a week before she'd even moved in. Her daddy was a doctor and he was going to work at the county hospital and her momma was dead.

Well, Caralynn Pitts wasn't anything to me, not yet. I went back to drilling a hole in my desktop with my yellow pencil. Some kids do that sort of a thing without even thinking about it, just something to do, but with me, well, I could feel hate running down my arm into the grinding pencil and all the time I was doing that, I was mashing my back teeth together, if you know what I mean.

It was a week later I talked to Caralynn Pitts for the first time.

It was ten o'clock, the big Regulator clock up near the flag ticking off the long, hot and miserable seconds, and that was "arithmetic period," so, like always, Miss Krydell asked who didn't do the homework, and then she started right in on me, first off, of course: "Bradford Dewey, do you have the fractions?"

"No, ma'am."

"Please stand, Bradford, and stop the mumbling. It would help, too, if you were to take the surly look off your face."

"Yes, ma'am."

"Didn't you *do* the homework?"

I actually had tried to do it but, when I was working at the kitchen table, my daddy came up and popped me alongside the head for no reason except he felt like it, so I lit out of the house.

Not that I was going to tell Miss Krydell any such thing. "Ma'am, I did *so* do the homework. I don't *have* it, is all."

"Why is that?" said Miss Krydell.

I felt this good one, a real twisty lie getting bigger, working its way out of me. "What it was, see, I was on the way to school and I had my fractions, and next thing I knew, the scurlets come up all around me. And that's how I lost my homework."

"The scurlets," said Miss Krydell. You just know the kind of face she was making when she said that. "Please tell us about 'the scurlets.'"

There was a laugh from the first row and someone echoing it a row over, but Miss Krydell gave the classroom her special poison radiation eyes and it got dead quiet real quick.

I said, "Well, the scurlets aren't all that big. No bigger than puppies. But they are plenty mean. There's a lot of them around every time it gets to be spring."

"Oh, is that so?" Miss Krydell said.

"Yes, ma'am. It was running away from the scurlets so they wouldn't get me that I dropped my homework, and I couldn't go on back for it, could I? See, the scurlets have pointy tails with a stinger on them, and if they sting you, you swell up and turn blue and you *die.* And when you're dead, the scurlets eat you up. . ." I was really running with it now. "They start on your face and they bite out your eyes, first thing. . ."

"That will be enough, Bradford."

". . . I guess for a scurlet, your eye is kind of like a real tasty grape. It goes 'pop' when they bite down on it —"

"Enough."

I stop right there. Miss Krydell says, "You are a liar, Bradford, and I am sick and tired of your lies. You'll stay after school and write 'I promise to tell the truth' five hundred times."

I sat down, thinking how much five hundred was, how much I hated Miss Krydell, and how bad my hand was going to feel when I finished writing all that rubbish.

The day went on, and, it was strange, but every time I happened to look around the room, there was Caralynn Pitts looking at me with those black eyes big as the wolf's in "Little Red Riding Hood." I didn't quite know what to make of that. I did not know if I liked it or not or what.

After school, I wrote and wrote and wrote, each "I promise to tell the truth" sloppier than the one before it. Miss Krydell didn't take her eyes off me, either, so I couldn't do it in columns, which is a lot easier way. With my hand feeling like someone had taken a sledge-hammer to it, Miss Krydell finally let me go.

I cut back of the school through the playground to take the long way home. I heard this *shh-click* like someone running on the gravel, and then she was calling my name — somehow I knew it was her, right off — so I stopped and turned around.

She ran up to me and, before I could say anything, she said, "You can see things, can't you?"

Not knowing what to make of that, I said, "Huh?"

"*See* things," she says.

I figured Caralynn Pitts had hung around school just to tease me and pick at me the way Claire Bobbit, Patty Marsel, and Edith Hebb always did, and so I answered kind of nasty, "Sure can." I pointed over at the monkey bars. "You go hang by your knees over there and I can see your underpants. What do you think about that?"

Caralynn said, "You can see things other people don't, can't you, Bradford? Like the scurlets."

Then Caralynn started talking real quiet, like she was in church or something. "Bradford, *I* can see things, all kinds of things, too. I can see tiny people living under sunflowers and I can see giants jumping from cloud to cloud and bugs that fly in moonlight and spell out your name on their wings and once I saw a stone in the sunshine and it was trying to turn itself into apple jelly!"

I said, "What are you talking about?"

"Both of us, we can *see things,* so that means we ought to be friends."

I said, "No sense to what you're talking, Caralynn. I can't see anything much, nothing like what you're saying, and if *you* can, then you sound crazy."

Caralynn said, "I can't tell my daddy about what I see because he says it's only pretend and I'm too old to pretend that way. I used to tell Momma, before she died. She said I had imagination and some-times, when there was nothing worth seeing in the whole world, all you had was your imagination. When Momma was so sick, dying, I guess, it seems like it rained every day. I used to sit with her, and we'd look out the window; and every day, Bradford, *every day* I could see a rainbow. It had twelve colors, that rainbow, colors like you don't ever see in a plain old rainbow. I used to tell Momma how the sun made the colors change from second to second. Momma said that was our rainbow. That was the rainbow over the graveyard the day we buried her. It wasn't even raining, but I looked up and there it was, and where it bent and disappeared on the other side of the world, I saw Momma, and she was waving to me."

"I don't know," I said. "I don't know anything about that or rainbows."

"Bradford," Caralynn said, "there's something I want to show you. Something beautiful. Can I?"

"I guess," I said.

I'm not a bit sorry about saying that, and I haven't been since the words slid off my lips. But in all these years gone by, I sure have asked myself why I didn't tell Caralynn to just go on and get lost. Maybe the reason is, I was small and dirty, my whole life was small and dirty, but packed inside me was this big hate — and hate is such an ugly thing — so I guess I was tired of all that ugly and there was something inside me, too, that was ready to be shown something... *beautiful.*

Oh, not that I believed Caralynn had a thing to show me. To tell the truth, I thought she was off some — and we're talking more than a little. But I did go with her, all the way past the edge of town, through Neidmeyer's Meadow, and then along the railroad tracks until we came to the curve; and there, by this rusted steel building that I guess the railroad must have once had a use for but didn't anymore, there was the old junkyard.

It wasn't the kind of business junkyard where you go to sell your falling apart car. It was an acre or so where everybody dumped the trash that wouldn't burn and was too big for the garbage men to haul off. It was all useless, twisted garbage, a three-legged wringer washer with the wires sticking out the bottom, and a refrigerator with the basket coil on top, and an old trunk without a lid like maybe a sailor once had, and a steam radiator, and a bathtub, and hundreds of pipes, and a couple of shells of cars, and thousands of tin cans. Everywhere you looked were hills and mountains of steel and glass and plastic, all kinds of trash that came from you didn't know *what* stuff. Flies swarmed in bunches like black cyclones, and over it all, hanging so stink-heavy you could see it, was the terrible smell.

And that was what Caralynn Pitts had to show me.

Not more than a spit away, a rat peeked from under a torn square of pink linoleum, its nasty whiskers quivering. I chucked a stone at it. I told Caralynn Pitts maybe she thought she was funny but *I* didn't think she was funny — and I started to run off.

I didn't get a step before she had my elbow. "Bradford — can't you see it?"

"It's the junkyard. That's all."

"It's the *sea*, Bradford, it's the beautiful junkyard sea. You have to look at it the right way. You have to want to see it to see how beautiful it is. *Please* look, Bradford."

Then Caralynn Pitts started talking to me in this whispery voice that seemed to crawl from my ear right into my brain. "Look at the water. Can't you see how blue and green it is? See the waves..."

...the water goes on forever and sends the waves to us from beyond nowhere, the waves gentle as night breeze, the rippling tiny hills rolling in to wash against the diamond dotted golden sands where we stand...

"...and a sea gull..."

...its wings are white fire cutting through layered-blue sky, its eyes magic black...

"...and way out there..."

...there, at the horizon line where water and sky are one...

"...a whale..."

...whales, placid giants, their strange squeaking pips and rumbles unearthly and eternal...

"Bradford," Caralynn said. "Can you see it, the beautiful junk-yard sea?"

"No," I said, and that was the truth. But in the moment before I said it, I think I *almost* saw it. It was like someone had painted a picture of the junkyard on an old bedsheet and the wind catching that sheet as it hung on a line was making everything ripple and change before my eyes.

It was because I almost saw it — and because, I know now, there was a fierce *want* in me to see it — I came back to the junkyard day after day with Caralynn Pitts.

And on a Wednesday, in the afternoon — a week after school let out — it happened.

I saw the beautiful junkyard sea.

The forever waters, sun light slanting, cutting through foam and fathom upon fathom, then diminishing, vanishing into the ever night depths. The sea gulls, winged arrows cutting random arcs over the rippling waves. A dolphin bursts from the sea, bejeweled droplets and glory, another dolphin, another and another, an explosion of dolphins . . . explosions of joy . . .

Far off, a beckoning atoll, a palm-treed island. Far off, a coral reef, living land. Far off, the promise of magic, the assurance that a lie is only a dream and that dreams are true.

Good thing you do not have to learn or practice love, that it just happens.

In the fine sea spray
in the clean mist of air and salt water
in the best moment of my life
I kissed Caralynn Pitts on the lips.
I told her I loved her.
And I loved the beautiful junkyard sea.

Every day that summer, Caralynn and I visited the beautiful junk-yard sea. It was always there for us.

Then late in August, she told me she was moving. Her daddy was joining the staff of a hospital in Seattle. She told me she cried when her daddy told her about it.

I said I would always love her. She said she would always love me.

"But what about the beautiful junkyard sea?" I asked her.

"It will always be ours," she said. "It will always be here for us."

She promised to write to give me her address once they were settled in Seattle. We would keep on loving each other and, when we grew up, we'd get married and be together forever.

The next week, she moved. Months and then years went by and there was no letter.

But I had the beautiful junkyard sea.

And this is the truth: I never stopped loving Caralynn Pitts or believing she would return.

She did.

I was 22 years old. When I was 12, my daddy got drunk and drove the car into a tree and killed himself. My momma did not cry when he was buried. She said she had already used up all the tears my daddy was entitled to.

What with my father's miner's benefits and insurance, and no money going out on whiskey, Momma and I got by. I scraped through high school, pretty bad grades, but I learned in shop class that I did have a way with engines. Pop the hood and hand me a wrench, chances were good to better yet that I could fix any problem there was, and so I was working at Mueller's Texaco.

On a sunny day in late April, Caralynn Pitts drove her white LTD up to the regular pump and asked me to fill it up, check the oil, battery, and transmission fluid.

Stooped over, I just kind of stood there by the open car window, jaw hanging like a moron. There was a question in Caralynn Pitt's big eyes for a second—and then she knew.

"It is Bradford, right?"

"Yes," I said.

"You've changed so much."

"I guess you have too," I said. That was probably the right thing to say but to tell the truth, she hadn't done that much changing. It was like she was still the kid she had been, only bigger.

"Growing up's a strange thing," Caralynn said.

"You came back, Caralynn," I said.

She gave me another funny look, then she laughed. "I guess I have. I work out of Chicago—I'm in advertising—and I was on my way to St. Louis and, well, I needed gas, so I didn't even think about it...just pulled off I-57 and here I am."

"You came back for the beautiful junkyard sea," I said.

"Huh?" Caralynn Pitts said. "Huh?" is something most women just can't say right and it bothered me to hear her say it.

She laughed again. "Oh, I get it. I remember. 'The beautiful junkyard sea,' that was some game we had. I guess both of us had pretty wild imaginations."

"It was no game, Caralynn," I said. "It isn't."

"Well, I don't know. . ." She tapped her fingers on the steering wheel, looked through the windshield. "Could you fill it up, please? And do you have a restroom?"

I told her, "Inside." I filled the tank. Everything checked out under the hood. When she came back a minute or two later, I said, "Maybe we could talk just a little, Caralynn? It's been a long time and all and we used to be good friends. We used to be special friends."

She took a quick look at her wristwatch. Then in her eyes I saw something like what used to be there so many years ago. "We were, weren't we?" she said. "Maybe a quick cup of coffee or something. Is there someplace we could go?"

"Sure," I said, "I know the place. Just let me tell Mueller I'll be gone awhile."

I drove her LTD. She told me she had gone to college, Washington State, majored in business. She told me she and a guy—I forget his name—were getting serious about one another, thinking about getting engaged. She told me she hoped to be moving up in advertising, to become an account executive in another year or so.

When we got out past the town limits, she said. "Bradford, where are you taking us?"

"You know," I said.

"Bradford. . .I don't know what's going on. What are you doing? You're acting, well, you're acting strange." I heard it in her voice. She was frightened. She didn't have to be frightened, is what I thought then. She'd understand as soon as she saw it.

"There's something I want to show you," I told her, and I drove to the junkyard.

She didn't want to get out of the car. She was scared. She said, "Bradford, don't. . .don't hurt me."

"I could never hurt you, Caralynn," I said.

I took her arm. I could feel how stiff she was holding herself, like her spine was steel.

"Here it is," I said. "Here we are."

We stood on the sun-washed shore of the beautiful junkyard sea.

She jerked like she wanted to pull away from me but I held her arm even tighter. "I don't know what you want, Bradford. What am I supposed to say? What am I supposed to do?"

"What do you see, Caralynn?" I asked.

"I. . .I don't see. . .anything, Bradford."

"Don't say that, Caralynn. I love you." What I was thinking then was, *Don't make me hate you. Please, please don't . . .*

"Bradford, I . . . I can't see what isn't there. This is a junkyard. That's all it is. It's ugly. And it stinks. It's a junkyard! *Please . . .*"

They never found Caralynn Pitts. I left her car there, walked back to town. The police did have questions, of course, since I was the last person to see her, but like I said, I know how to lie, and so I made up a few little lies and one or two big ones and that took care of the police.

All these years, I haven't gone back to the beautiful junkyard sea. Maybe I never will.

But I cannot forget, won't ever forget, and I think I don't want to forget how Caralynn looked

when the waters turned black and churning and the lightning shattered the sky and the sea gulls shrieked and the fins of sharks circled and circled and the first tentacle whipped out of the foam and hooked her leg, and another shot out, circled her waist, and then one more, across her face, choking off her screams, as she was dragged toward that thing rising in the angry water, that great, gray-green, puffy bag that was its head, yellow eyes shining hungrily, the corn-colored, curved beak clattering, as it dragged her deeper, deeper, and then she disappeared and there was blood on the water and that was all until, at last

the sun shone
and all was quiet in
        the beautiful junkyard sea

The Sources of the Nile

Rick Hautala

"I have a pretty good idea for a short-short," said the author of the novel that had just made the Horror Writers of America Preliminary Ballot, "if you want to hear it."

I did, and I found it — just listening to this super-pleasant Maine writer relate the details over the phone — pretty strong, nearly repulsive stuff. I was interested! There was also a new twist on one of our stalwart pet legends, and when Rick Hautala's final product arrived, it was everything I hoped it would be.

The novel I mentioned above is *Dead Voices*, which followed *Moondeath, Moonbog, Nightstone, Moonwalker,* and *Little Brothers* and preceded his '91 spellbinder, *Cold Whispers* (presumably available now).

But what this good-looking family man hoped I'd mention was his short fiction scheduled to appear in *Night Visions 9* (with that of Tom Tessier and James Kisner), "Untcigahunk," and this sinewy yarn, "The Sources of the Nile." That river is navigable the year round, from Aswan. We hope you don't drown crossing Rick's first short-short story.

"Why are you tormenting me like this?" Marianne Wilcox said. I looked at her, cringing beside me in the soft darkness of my car, her blue eyes illuminated by the faint glow of a distant streetlight. I couldn't have denied the overpowering swell of emotion I felt for her at that moment. I wanted to take her right then — that instant! I knew that, but I couldn't — not yet...no, not quite yet...

"Look, I don't *like* having to be the one to break it to you this way," I replied. "Honest! I mean — Christ, I just met you for the first time ...when? Last week, at the Hendersons' party. You hardly even know me, and I'd understand if you didn't trust me; but you would have learned the truth sooner or later."

"Maybe I...maybe I didn't *want* to learn the truth. Not really," she said. Her chest hitched; her eyes glistened as tears formed, threatening to spill. "Maybe I just *wanted* a...wanted a...Oh, *Christ!* I don't know what I wanted!"

She beat her small fists on the padded dashboard once, then heaved a deep sigh. Blinking her eyes rapidly, she turned away and looked out the side window. We were parked at the far end of the parking lot at the Holiday Inn in Portland, back where it was dark so we wouldn't be noticed. Minutes ago, we had watched Ronald Wilcox, her husband, walk into the motel arm in arm with another woman. This wasn't the first time—nor was it the first "other" woman.

"Look, I'm just telling you this because—well, I've known your husband for quite some time—through mutual friends, you know. And frankly, I like you," I said, struggling hard to keep my voice as soft and sympathetic as possible. Women fall apart when you talk to them like that. "Something like this hurts me too, you know? But after meeting you, I felt a—I don't know, an obligation, I guess, to let you know that your husband was having an affair." I nodded toward the motel entrance. "Now you've seen that for yourself. As painful as it might be, you asked me to bring you here. I...I didn't want to do this to you."

"I know that," she said, glancing back at me for a moment. My heart started beating faster when I saw the tears filling her eyes. They would spill any second now. A cold, tight tingling filled my belly and I can't deny that my erection hardened as I shifted closer to her and placed one hand gently on her shoulder.

"I don't *like* seeing you upset like this," I said. "I'm not *enjoying* this, but you have to remember that *I'm* not the one who has hurt you. It's *him.*" I jerked my thumb toward the motel. After a moment of silence, I leaned forward and withdrew a manila envelope from underneath the car seat. "If you'd like, I could show you these photographs I—"

"*No!*"

Her lower lip trembled as she looked at me. Her eyes were two luminous, watery globes. Just seeing the wash of tears building up there twisted my heart. I tried to push aside, to resist the powerful urge to take her in my arms and caress her, but I couldn't deny that there was an element of spite in what I was doing. I wanted her to see *everything.* I wanted her to *imagine* it all; and if she couldn't imagine it, I was ready to *show* it to her—every instance, every second of her husband's infidelity. I wanted—I *needed*—to push her until she broke because after she broke — ahh, sweetness! — *after* she broke, she would be mine!

"No, I don't. . .don't need to see your — your photographs." Her voice was tight, constricted. "I don't *want* them!"

"Of course not," I whispered, tossing the envelope onto the dashboard and inching closer to her. "I understand."

My heart throbbed in my throat when I saw a single, crystal tear spill from the corner of her eye and run down her cheek. It slid in a slow, sinuous, glimmering line that paused a moment on the edge of her chin and then, pushed by the gathering flood of more tears, ran down her neck and inside her coat collar. Gone. . .lost. . .!

"Please — don't cry," I whispered, knowing it was a lie. I brought my face close to hers, feeling the heat of my breath rebound from her smooth, white skin. My gaze was fastened on the flow of tears as they coursed from her eyes, streaking in silvery lines down both sides of her face. Her shoulders hunched inward as if she wanted to disappear inside herself.

"But I — I — "

She couldn't say anything more as she stared at me, her glazed eyes wide — two lustrous, blue orbs swimming in the pristine, salty wash of tears. My hand trembled as I traced the tracks of her tears from her chin to her cheek. Heated rushes of emotion filled me when I raised my moist finger up to the light and studied the teardrop suspended from the tip. It shimmered like a diamond in the darkness. Slowly, savoring every delicious instant, I brought it to my lips. The taste was sweet, salty. The instant I swallowed it, I knew I loved her as deeply as I have ever loved any woman.

"I — I wish I could have spared you all of this pain," I whispered as I lowered my face and kissed her lightly on the cheek. The briny taste of her tears exploded in my mouth. The effect was overpowering; I could no longer hold myself back. Like a snake, my tongue darted between my lips and, flickering, trembling, caressed her skin. I grew dizzy, intoxicated by the hot, sweet taste of her.

She moaned softly, barely at the edge of hearing. My arm went around her, pulling her closer — comforting, reassuring, like a good friend.

"Go on," I whispered. "If you have to cry, let it out. Let it *all* out."

I could barely hear my own voice above the roaring rush in my ears as my face brushed against hers. Ever so lightly, my tongue worked its way up from her chin, over the soft contours of her cheek until — at last — I reached her eyes. My hand grasped the back of her head, turned her gently to face me, and pulled her tightly against my greedy, eager mouth. Moving my head from side to side, I kissed and lapped her lower eyelids, savoring the salty explosion of taste on my tongue. With slow, sensuous flicks, I licked the bulging circles of her closed eyes.

"No — please!" she whispered, squirming on the seat. "Not now. . . not here!" But I knew she didn't mean it. Her body was molded against me like a tight-fitting glove. The passion consuming me filled her, too. I could feel it thrumming through her body like an electric current. Her hands worked around behind my back, clutching, clinging desperately to my coat. She shook with repressed sobs as I moved back and forth, kissing the corners of each eye. While I was busy drinking the flood of tears from one eye, my hand wiped the other until it was slick with moisture. Then I slipped my fingers into my mouth and sucked them clean, not wanting to miss a single delicious drop.

"Please. . ." she moaned, and I knew what she was asking for. This wasn't denial; it was passion, raw and desperate. Puckering my lips, I feverishly kissed first one eye, then the other. She gasped for breath, the tears streamed down her face, but my lips were there — eager to savor every pearly drop. Oceans of passions raged in my head, my heart pounded heavily in my chest as I pressed myself against her, crushing her back against the seat of my car. The world outside disappeared in swirling passion. For a flashing instant, I knew she sensed danger, but it was already too late. I possessed the source of her tears, the twin rivers that fed the raging of my desire.

"White Nile" — I said before kissing her left eye, " — and Blue Nile," before I kissed the other. Then I clamped my mouth over her right eye and, pressing my tongue hard against her eyelid, began to suck — at first gently, then more insistently. I'm sure she thought I was lost in sexual desire but I knew she would never truly understand. None of them ever did. I applied more pressure, suctioning hard until her eyeball bulged against her closed lid.

She began to struggle, making soft, whimpering sounds; but here in the shadowed corner of the parking lot, I knew no one was going to notice us. As my sucking grew stronger, more insistent, she screamed, sharp and shrill. I covered her mouth with one hand, pulled back, and stared at her eyes, glistening and round with fear.

"Please — *don't,*" she said, her voice a wet rasp. Her throat was raw with tortured emotions and the tears she had already shed. Her fists beat helplessly against my back as I leaned forward and sucked all the harder. Her resistance was futile. She was mine now. I *had* her!

Her low, bubbling scream continued to rise, stifled by my hand. I was afraid I'd have to kill her before I could finish. It usually happens that way no matter how hard I try to keep them quiet. Marianne thrashed with frantic resistance, but I wouldn't stop, I *couldn't* stop. I had to have her — I had to lay claim to the source of my passion! I was only dimly aware of her long, agonized screech as my cheeks, working like strong bellows, sucked harder and harder until — *at last* — something warm, round, and jellied popped into my mouth. I nibbled on it until I felt the resilient tube of her optic nerve between my teeth, then bit down hard, severing it. A warm, salty gush of tears and blood — an exquisite combination — flooded my throat. I was dizzy with ecstasy as I reached down to the car floor, found the jar I kept under the seat for nights such as this, spun open the top — and spat her eyeball into it.

Then I went back to draining the empty socket dry of tears and blood. Precious drops dribbled from the corners of my mouth, but I eagerly wiped them up with my fingertips.

"I...love...you," I gasped. With one hand still covering her mouth, I sat back to wipe my chin with the back of my wrist. Then, moaning softly, I shifted over to her left eye and clamped the suction of my mouth over it. She struggled again, harder now, writhing and screaming in pain and terror; but my weight held her fast while I dragged the tip of my tongue hard against her eye, lapping up more tears. Then, unable to hold back any longer, I sucked her other eyeball out of its socket and spat it, too, into the jar.

For long, dizzying minutes, I pressed her down against the seat while my tongue tenderly probed both empty holes for the last traces of tears. After a while, her body shivered; then she lay still as her heart quietly slowed and stopped. My rapid-fire pulse eventually lessened as well — but all of this happened nearly four weeks ago, and I feel it coming on me again. I have to go out tonight. That urge, that demanding, thirsty need is strong inside me... like the irresistible pull of the ocean's salty tide.

Collaborationists

J. N. Williamson

Highlights in the professional life of this writer include coaxing four of these anthologies into existence, plus the non-fictional *How to Write Tales of Horror, Fantasy and Science Fiction,* and working with the contributors to them. . .writing the novels *The Ritual* (my first, in '79), *Playmates, Ghost, Wards of Armageddon* (with John Maclay), *The Black School* and its Jacob Wier continuation, *Hell Storm*. . . following Bob Knight's I.U. basketball and Bob's coaching techniques. . . realizing that Robert Bloch's and Rick McCammon's story acceptances for (respectively) the two *Psycho Paths* anthos and Horror Writers of America's first, *Under the Fang,* put my published story total safely over 100. . . and writing my most mature novels, *The Night Seasons* and *Monastery,* for upcoming publications. (So what if following basketball isn't a professional endeavor; in Indiana, it amounts to that!) My work in progress is a psychological horror novel. It's also approximately 70% autobiographical.

Here's one of my rare humorous horror stories. Even if the qualifier places me at risk, "humorous" was certainly my intention. Its influences aren't my usual ones; they're authors such as P. G. Wodehouse, Dotty Parker, Ray Russell, and the lighter-than-air Jim Thurber. It probably won't scare you, unless you're a male writer too!

As if it had been ordained by Someone on High, Mel always came to the convention with Valerie, his wife. I'm certain he knew we would expect to see that old horror writer's most supportive fan but there was no decent opportunity to ask Mel why she *wasn't* present this year until the final day of the convention, Sunday, and he hadn't uttered a word about her absence. I was, frankly, mildly hurt.

Until this convention, Valerie and Mel, Carol and I had made it a matter of course to attend the awards banquet and for the four of us to sit together. But Carol and I had suffered a bad year financially, hadn't bought banquet tickets, and our plane for home would leave in a couple of hours. Carol left the hotel to look around town and, I supposed, to avoid any risk of embarrassment. I waited in the lobby and was startled when Mel dropped heavily into the leather chair beside me.

I said, "Aren't you going to the banquet either?"

"No," he said. "It won't really be any fun without Valerie." He crossed his long legs, busied himself lighting a cigarette. That surprised me too because Mel had quit smoking two years back. "Go ahead and ask," he told me. "I won't like it, but you might as well get the question off your chest."

I took that for one of his customary sardonic replies. "All right." Casually, I sipped at a coke — this was Sunday, remember — I'd brought out to the lobby with me. "Why isn't Valerie with you at this convention?"

Mel swiveled his oblong head around to peer directly at me and I was reminded of some aging horse that had learned even his stud services were no longer required. He took a moment. "On Thursday, a week ago," he said, "Valerie woke up and found that she was an entirely happy woman."

"Why," I breathed, "that's wonderful." Now came Mel's famous punch line.

"No. It is not." He took his time about getting a long drag into his lungs and tried not to cough when it came back out. "I'm afraid you aren't understanding me."

"I'm sorry."

"My fault. I'm not getting it right."

"Why don't you try again?"

"All right," Mel said. His eyes burned into mine. "Val said she was in a condition of absolute ecstasy."

"Good Lord."

"Had been, she said, for at least twenty-four hours."

"My God," I said. "How? Not to be overly inquisitive, but why?"

"That's what I asked her. I mean...I'm a *writer.*"

I said, "My point exactly." I shifted nervously in my leather chair. "How could a thing like that happen to a writer's wife?" I found the concept wholly confounding. "Was she drinking?"

"Not a drop. Remember; she never cared for the stuff." Mel gazed thoughtfully at the burning end of his Winston but it had no answers for him. "Well, I tried not to make too much of it; played it down. Not time yet for hysterics, I thought. Then I poked around in her things." A deepening frown. "I was looking for it, you know. Dope."

"Why, certainly." I tried to be as reassuring as humanly possible. Drugs was as good a guess at explaining Valerie's condition as anything, I thought. I added to Mel, manfully, "You had no other choice."

"But there was nothing narcotic anywhere I looked," he said. "Except for a fantasy novel — leprechauns and unicorns, you know — and one of those exquisitely subtle horror anthologies." His shoulders moved. "Nothing, however, she could possibly put into her nose or arm or could conceivably swallow."

Wonderingly, I slowly shook my head. I yearned to help, but I could not bear imagining what I might do if Carol was ever —

"My Val has been a genuinely decent woman, a devoted wife, always," Mel choked. I tried not to see his eyes at that instant. "Truly devoted. Understand, I don't want to make Valerie out to be some kind of angel —"

"But she was," I said. I changed it hastily. "*Is.* Listened to every word you got down on paper, I know. Typed your manuscripts. Put off having more children, even held down the basest, most menial jobs just so you could —"

"It was *together,*" Mel interposed a trifle sharply. "For *both* of us. The long climb up, grubbing for a dollar, an agent; prostituting oneself. You know how it goes."

"How true," I said and chuckled. Mel and I had often laughed together about the deceit, the lies, the royalty departments, computer downtime, though I didn't know why. "Mel, I know. I remember when —"

"You *can't* know," my friend argued. "You *can not know* what passes through one's mind when your wife, out of the blue, announces that she is one hundred percent content."

"You're right," I nodded, "I can't."

"Well, *try,*" he urged me.

"I cannot. I wouldn't know where to start," I admitted. "Mel, surely she didn't mean what she said. Not literally."

"One hundred percent," he answered with a stricken, stately nod. "I sought immediate clarification, suggested eighty-nine, proposed ninety-four. She swore that she meant every percentage point. Just sat there, grinning. Smirking like a devil."

"No one has ever heard of such a thing." Then the idea hit me. "A possibility comes to mind, one only — a single, nebulous, wholly absurd, exceedingly remote possibility."

"Thought of it in the wee hours." He had stopped with his cigarette an inch or two from his lips. "You're wondering if she's having an affair. Has taken a lover."

"No!" I shouted. One of the people moving around behind the check-in desk almost lifted his head to look at me. "Well, *yes.*" I felt my cheeks color. "But only because it can happen to the best of us. Remember Allen? And Wally?"

Mel looked me in the eye. "I demanded the truth of Valerie and she swore that there has never been a man in her life since we married."

I used the occasion of my friend's growing ash drawing within inches of my nose to raise a hand and conceal my errant smile. Mel, meanwhile, tapped hell out of the cigarette in a tray.

And then — to my astonishment — he was beaming the broadest of smiles at me. "Put two and two together and you can imagine what I did next." He made his face go blank, glanced carefully around and then back at me. "I took advantage of the situation."

"You mean, you and Valerie. . .?"

Light reflected off his high forehead as his head bobbed. "Took Val straight to bed. We had at it. We had at it." He went on nodding.

"And?"

"It was as good for me as ever." His expression remained blank.

"But?" I prodded.

His chin lowered. "She said it was fine."

"Lord," I sighed, "that bad?"

He spoke into the collarless neck of his sweater but I heard him. "It was as good as it had ever been for her, too — and she was *still* perfectly happy. 'Ecstatic' remained her exact term." The mumbling got worse. "She said she had no complaints about either that particular sex or our sex life in general. Absolutely none."

"Sweet Jesus," I remarked. "She's in even worse shape than I'd thought."

He didn't hear me. "She strongly implied that that aspect of our marriage should in no way be held responsible either for how awful she used to feel *or* how ecstatic she felt after we'd just had 'our little romp.' It was. . .*fiiiiine.*"

This was intolerable! "My poor, old friend. What happened next?"

"What else could I do but accept it? I was neither responsible for making my wife miserable nor for making her content." Mel's face was a mask of horror. "A husband can occasionally strike out; we all know that. But I was no longer even a member of our marital team! It wasn't as if I couldn't get the bat on the ball, it was as if—"

"I understand," I told him, and edged slightly away.

"Well, the kids came over. Not because I phoned them; they'd already been invited to dinner."

In mind's eye I saw my friend's grown children and their mates. Mel, Junior, had a wife I'd had to use — on paper, that is. The daughter was as lacking in talent as Junior. "How awful was it?"

"Awful enough." His shudder started out life as a sigh. Perhaps everything did, I thought, and tried to remember the insight till I got to make note of it. "Before they were through the door, I had to tell them about Valerie. 'Your mother is happy,' I said. 'She has just informed me that she's never before felt so fulfilled.'"

"That was her choice of words, 'fulfilled?'" I stammered. *"That?"* Nothing had prepared me for such a disclosure. I doubt anything could.

"Do you know what Junior asked me?" His baseball mitt of a hand squeezed my knee. "Do you *know?*" His face was red so I winked back tears of pain and he continued. "He asked if his mother — *my* wife — had asked for a divorce!"

"He wasn't expecting such news, Mel," I reasoned. "He's a man, too."

Mel's fingertips dug in. "That little son of a bitch!"

"Easy, buddy." Prying his fingers out of my knee was like extracting steel pins. Mel has written several million words. "It's a dreadful thing to ask his father, but he's your own flesh and blood. You must try to forgive him." We were sitting side by side and I began to wonder what was detaining Carol, my wife. Into my friend's sudden, growing silence, I whispered: *"Did* Valerie go to an attorney?"

Mel snatched the can of coke from my hand. For a moment, I swear, I think he wanted to dash it into my face. Then, emitting a moan unlike any I'd heard from an unfettered man, he crushed the can between his typewriter-trained fingers and paid no heed to the drops raining on our knees. "She did not. *I* thought about it, but the only one I know is a man who was always out of town when I wanted him to read a multi-book contract. Besides, if I *did* seek a divorce, I'm reasonably sure. . ."

I was staring at him when his words began to trail away. "Go on," I said.

Mel turned to peer at the check-in desk. The people behind it were obviously trying not to look at us. "I'm sure that if I got a divorce, it would mean no more to Valerie than if I *didn't.* It's — all the *same* to her, now. She's *happy!"*

I let seconds tick away, to think. What I needed to say to Mel then was hard, very hard, and Mel's face looked as if a powerful storm was building, broodingly, behind it. "Mel...old friend...there's a possibility"—I broke off in order to furnish suspense—"that Val has...gone."

"Gone?" he repeated. "How do you mean, 'gone'?" One eyebrow lifted. "Do you mean her soul may have been replaced by that of some demonic entity—that sort of 'gone'?"

I considered the idea for an instant, then shook my head. Valerie wasn't Catholic. "No, I meant that writers' wives are often under great pressure. Since they lack the creative outlets we possess, at least when the child-bearing years have passed, a few of them have been known to—become neurotic. Flip out, as it were."

"Not Valerie." Rather wearisomely, Mel again shook his head. "Carrie, our daughter, ruled that out. She had a little heart-to-heart with Val and said she's perfectly sound mentally. Or did I tell you Carrie graduated from that psych course she took? 'Everything You Needed to Know about Your Woman's Mind but He Wouldn't Let You.' My girl is *Doctor* Carrie now."

"Then I'm at a complete loss to understand Val's problem," I confessed. A surreptitious glance at my watch told me the plane home would leave in an hour and Carol was still window-shopping in town. Several ideas played torturously at the fringes of my mind, one of them worth writing down, but I remembered my friend still had not said why his wife had not come to the convention. I approached the matter with delicacy.

"Did you ever sit Valerie down and demand to know what was making her imagine she is contented; fulfilled? Did you confront her?"

"In a way," he replied vaguely. "I asked if I was the last to know of her damnable ecstasy. It seems Val admitted it to two friends. One of them got quite angry, I understand. The second believed Valerie was just making it up."

"That's not like Val," I mused. "I doubt she's ever imagined a thing."

"Well, I counted on that, of course." Something in Mel's tone informed me that he hadn't said it all, that he was getting to it at last. "Before telling me, she went to a doctor. I gather he gave her a complete examination, asked many of the questions we've asked, but he confessed it was beyond his expertise and sent her home. I spoke to him on the phone. Good health is over his head, that's the size of it."

"He's a doctor," I murmured, relieved to hear Valerie's condition did not appear to be contagious. "Of course it is."

Laughter from the ballroom where the convention awards were being presented trickled to my ears when the door opened briefly and one of the losers fled to the rest room. When I next looked at Mel, he summoned his courage and finally started to explain the reason for his wife Valerie's singular condition of happiness.

"I did not say," he began, "that Val did not accompany me to this city. You just assumed it. She's here."

"Where?" I turned my gaze in every direction. "In the hotel?"

"No, in this metropolis of commercial sin," he said. "In its suburbs, to be more precise. At another, newer, more sumptuous hotel."

A gleam of insight became an icicle at the back of my head. Dimly, I recalled hearing that another writers convention was going on here at the same time.

Seized by panic, I leapt to my feet. "Where in heaven's name is Carol?" I checked my watch once more. "Mel, I'm sorry. But if we don't get to the airport by 3:40 — "

"I know," said my fellow writer with a meaningful nod. "Yet if you catch that plane, you will be flying home...alone."

"What do you mean?" I asked it while my heart thundered in my chest.

"You've been deep in your next novel or you might have seen it for yourself." Mel spoke with infinite gentleness, and clear regret. "Your wife, too, is supremely happy." He blinked his eyes shut, snapped them open. "She is with Valerie this minute. In a way, she has been with Valerie for weeks now."

I could no longer stand. I toppled back into my lobby chair, gaping at him.

"Carol and Valerie are collaborators," Mel continued remorselessly, getting it all said. "No; don't think of *Casablanca* or other theaters of war. Think of the frilly, very feminine dress Carol was wearing when you arose this morning."

I nodded, but my mind was a blank. It contained no memory of my wife's apparel. For the fraction of an instant, it contained no recollection of Carol's face. "Collaborators?" I said feebly.

"Both of us should have seen the signs," Mel admitted. "The sudden preference for large quantities of time alone. Few complaints when we were late for meals. Happiness predicated upon absolutely nothing real. Their eyes raised, fixed upon sights and scenes only they could see."

"They are *writers*?" I cried, and I suppose my mouth fell open. *"Our wives?"*

"Unreasoning tolerance of one's surroundings, that's the first clue. Smirking. Joy which surpasseth understanding when nothing whatever has improved." Mel was relentless. He gripped my biceps as if to prevent me from hurting myself. "No poorly-concealed anxiety when the mortgage goes unpaid. No threat to leave unless *we* abandon our plans to attend the convention — instead, *real interest* in being here. . .where each woman keeps her little secret and mysteriously melts, seemingly alone, into the big city."

"They've *sold* their *book?*"

"Far worse," Mel hissed, bracing my arms to keep me from falling from the chair — "they were nominated for a major award!"

"Oh, dear God," I gasped, weeping briefly against my friend's shoulder. Then I stared up at Mel. "But, *how?* They cannot have put much time into it. My meals, my clean clothes, have been done on time. Carol hasn't been a moment late typing my pages." An idea occurred to me. "Now I think of it, she has had a faraway look of late. She did have her hair done before we flew here. Rather girlishly, as I recall, but there were only going to be other writers of horror here, and I — "

Mel gave me a solemn nod and assisted me so that I could rest my head back against the chair. Quickly, he lit two cigarettes, and I took the second one between shaking fingers. He went on sadly nodding.

Valerie's condition of absolute ecstasy; the novel finished fast, and already nominated for an award. Carol's frilly costume, her girlish hair style. Valerie, untouched and unmoved by sex with her husband. Carol, leaving me alone in the lobby. . .keeping to herself. . .wandering off to another hotel with her collaborator to be feted in the most romantic of ways.

"It's a romance novel the two of them wrote," I gasped into my friend's persistent nodding. "They're — *romance writers!*"

Only Mel's already-tested, steady gaze kept me from going over the deep end.

"I've had time to get used to it," he said softly after gesturing at me to stop using such words at an audible level. "Not that I have; not that I ever can. I knew no other way to break the news to you than face to face. But I have thought of two ameliorative facts that might hearten you and ease the blow."

I mumbled, "Go ahead. But they'll do no good."

"My Valerie," Mel said in a whisper, "doesn't *mind* having intercourse now. She — doesn't notice it, as I remarked."

I looked hopefully at him from between half-hooded lids. "She did tell you it was 'fine'?"

"She did," he said. "Off in her own little world, it seems. And the other fact..."

"Yes?" I prodded him.

"The demand for those so-called romantic novels turns out to be virtually insatiable." Mel's eyes seemed to be in bold face. "Carol and Valerie can knock one out in less time that it takes a publisher to accept one of our contracted novels!" His lifted hand made certain no lip-readers detected what he was whispering. *"Our wives* can sell one of those babies every couple of months for up to ten grand each. *Ten grand."*

"Several books a year," I asked, "and they're splitting the take?"

"Val told me," Mel said, "fifty-fifty."

"Upfront, right?" I said, doublechecking. "On acceptance?"

Mel was nodding again. "They're something like dot-to-dot books, or fill-in-the-missing-word. It's Follow the Magic Formula time, said Valerie." Mel had a look to him then that was the first living demonstration of the clichéd "dancing eyes" that I had ever seen. "Fill in the words just so, and the check follows like day the night. The girls will have a feeling of accomplishment over this, of course."

"Of course," I said, and found I was smiling. Laughing, really. In waves that kept coming up to the moment I saw Carol and Valerie hurrying into the lobby.

"Why are you laughing?" Mel demanded under his breath. I noticed our wives were also trying to subdue a mood of hilarity.

"Because it just dawned on me that they've done a collaboration," I explained, holding it down.

"Go on," he said — "but hurry!" Carol and Val were drawing nearer.

"Well, the author's byline on romance novels is always sweetly feminine or borrows a man's name such as 'Alex' or something, and is so pretentious that no one in the real world could possibly believe that it was anything but a pseudonym."

The smile was restored to Mel's face. "So there's no chance in the world they they would take either of *our* names and ruin them!"

"Right," I hissed back at my friend, slapping his knee. "Kuntzedale and McWilton are safely preserved in horror!"

We were on our feet to make it a foursome again, our wives' wearing the most apologetic of expressions, and I saw clearly that my term "girlish" for Carol's new hair style might well have been far too hasty.

My Private Memoirs of the Hoffer Stigmata Pandemic

Dan Simmons

Just back from Transylvania — "I am not making this up," as Dave Barry might express it — Dan Simmons went rapidly to work on his story for *Masques IV* "because it stayed on my mind while I was out of the country." A lot of things have been on this thoughtful and original writer's mind since his prize-winning first story appeared in *Twilight Zone* in 1981. That was apparent when his first novel, *Song of Kali,* became one of the most popular choices for a World Fantasy Award ever. I heard about it from several of the genre's leading lights before I'd found a chance to read it and, for once, the seeming hype was absolutely well-earned praise; *Kali* made me a Dan Simmons fan when I'd read only half of it.

That happened a lot in 1985.

Hyperion (demonstrating the writer's versatility) reaped a Hugo for the graduate of Indiana's Wabash College and St. Louis' Washington University. In a return to horror, all Dan did was win the Bram Stoker Award from Horror Writers of America for *Carrion Comfort.* Along the line, his story in the third *Masques,* "Shave and a Haircut, Two Bites," was selected for the annual *Year's Best Fantasy and Horror* and then reprinted in Simmons' magnificent story collection, *Prayers to Broken Stones.* Right now I am halfway through reading his 1991 novel, *Summer of Night,* and, with Stephen King — who says so on the back of the dust jacket — "I am in awe. . ."

In Dan's newest short story, "My Private Memoirs of the Hoffer Stigmata Pandemic," we have before us a futuristic satire at once perspicacious and epigrammatic, comedic and cautionary and painfully sad. In its nearly bitter and sardonic mood, it reminds us that we are all contaminated by society's opportunities and temptations and, in the process, Dan quite probably creates a new language with which to examine ourselves with greater, cleaner conscientiousness.

. That's quite a lot for a short story to do, but it's not entirely unexpected. Dan Simmons wrote it.

My Dearest Son —

The fact that you will never read this does not matter. Peter, my son, I think it is time I explained the events of thirty years ago to you. I feel a great urge to do this, even though there is much I do not understand — much that no one understands — and the time before the Change has long since become vague and dream-like for most of us. Still, I think your mother and I owe you an explanation, and I shall do my best to provide one.

I was watching television when the Change came. I would guess that a majority of Americans were in front of their TVs that evening. As luck would have it, I was tuned to the *CBS Evening News with Dan Rather,* and because we lived in the Eastern time zone then, the news was live.

Now some think that because the Change began first in our hemisphere, that it was the result of the Earth passing through some belt of cosmic radiation. Other "experts" suggest that it was a microvirus that came filtering down through the atmosphere that day and just spread like algae in a stagnant pond. The religionists — back then when there were religionists — used to talk about God's judgment beginning with America because it was the Sodom and Gomorrah of its day. But the truth is, no one knew then where the hell the Change came from, or what caused it, or why it began in the Western Hemisphere first, and the truth is that no one knows now.

And we don't really give a damn, to tell you the truth, Peter.

It came, and I was watching the *CBS Evening News with Dan Rather* when it came. Your mother was cooking dinner. You were in the crib that we kept in the dining room. Dan Rather was on the screen talking about Palestinians when suddenly he got a startled expression on his face sort of like that time a few years earlier when protesters got in the studio and started screwing around while he was on the air, only this time he was alone.

What was happening was that Dan's face was melting. Well, not melting exactly, but *flowing,* shifting, sort of running downhill like it had been turned into wax and held over a hot stove.

For a minute I thought it was the TV or the damn cable company again and I was halfway to the phone to give the cable people a piece of my mind when I saw that Dan Rather had stopped talking and was grabbing his face as it flowed and shifted and reformed like silly putty, so I put the phone down and sat back in my chair and yelled "Myra, come in here!"

I had to shout again but finally your mother came in, wiping her hands on a dish towel and complaining that dinner would never be done if I kept yelling at her and...she stopped in mid-sentence. "What's happening to Dan?" she said then.

"I dunno," I said. "Some sort of joke, maybe."

It didn't look like a joke. It looked awful. Dan's aging-but-still-handsome face had quit running like melted wax but was twitching and reforming into something else. The muscles and bones under the skin of his face were moving around like rats under a tarp. His left eye seemed to be...well, *migrating*...moving across his face like a chunk of white chicken floating in a bowl of flesh-colored soup.

There were shouts from off-camera, the picture blurred and bounced, then cut away to the *CBS Evening News with Dan Rather* logo, but a few seconds later we were back live to the shot of Dan and the news desk, as if someone in the control room or whatever you call that place where the director works had decided that *this* is news and to hell with it.

Dan had gotten up and was stumbling around then, his hands still holding his face, obviously peering in monitors as if they were mirrors. Whatever had happened, I could see that the silly-putty part was over. Nothing was moving under those splayed fingers any more. Dan was making sort of choking sounds, although he'd ripped his microphone thingee out so the sounds were distant and echoey. Then Dan dropped his hands.

"Jesus Christ," said your mother. She never cursed, never took the Lord's name in vain. "Jesus H. Christ," she said a second time.

Dan Rather's face had turned into something out of one of those *Tales from the Crypt* shows we used to avoid on HBO. But not really like that, because no matter how good make-up is, you can always tell that it's make-up. Just like you could tell that this was *real*.

Dan Rather's face had Changed. His forehead had sort of collapsed so his combed mop of graying hair — we'd noticed he'd just gotten a haircut that week — was down about where the bridge of his nose had been two minutes before. He didn't have a nose any more, just an open-holed scoop of a snout — a sort of tapering, anteater-like proboscis that sloped down below his jaw and ended in a pulsing pink membrane that looked like you imagine your eardrum might look. If it was infected. And every time it pulsed, you could see right into Dan's face — I don't mean into his eyes or anything, I mean *inside his face* — all the green, mucusy things in there, and bones and flesh from the inside and other things, glistening things.

Dan's left eye had stopped migrating about where his left cheekbone used to be. That eye seemed much larger now and was bright yellow. His other eye was fine and looked familiar, but above it and below it, the red wattles began growing. These wattles hung down from what used to be his cheek and what had once been his brow and they seemed to congregate along that scaly, bony ridge that had grown out of his right cheek like the whatchamacallits on the back of a stegosaurus.

And Dan's teeth. Well, we soon knew what everything meant — the hypocrisy proboscis, the power-abuser scales on the cheek, the Ambition teeth curling in and out of the skin around the flesh-sutured mouth like that — but you have to realize that this was the first time that we'd seen the Change and we didn't have any idea that the stigmata had something to do with a person's IQ or temperament or character.

Dan Rather tried to scream then, the Ambition teeth cut through cheek muscle, and your mother and I screamed for him. Then the director *did* cut away — to a Preparation H commercial — and your mother said, "How about the other channels?"

"No," I managed to say, "I'm sure it's just Dan." But I clicked over to ABC and there was Peter Jennings pulling at what looked like a pink, half-eviscerated squid that had attached itself to his face. It took us almost a minute of slack-jawed staring to realize that this *was* his face.

Tom Brokaw had been the least affected, but he'd clapped his hands over the power-abuser scales erupting from his cheek, jaw, and neck and run from the set. We saw it later on tape. But right then, all we saw was the empty NBC set and all we heard was a sound like a coyote gargling rocks. We found out later that this was John Chancellor screaming when the mucus began erupting from his pores.

Finally I clicked off the TV, too shocked to keep watching. Besides, it was all commercials by then. So I turned to your mother to say something, but the Change had started on her by then.

I pointed and tried to say something, but my mouth was too dry and it felt like it was full of jagged potato chips or something. Your mother pointed at me and screamed, the sound seeming filtered coming as it did through the rows of baleen that had replaced her teeth and made her face look something like the grill of a '48 Buick. The rest of her face was still flowing and dripping and clumping.

I felt my own face twitch. My hands went up to my cheeks, but the cheeks were no longer there. Something else was: something that felt like a cluster of fleshy, pulsing grapes. Something had grown out of my forehead enough to block the vision in my left eye.

Your mother and I looked at each other again, pointed again, screamed in unison, and ran for the bathroom mirror.

I should say right up front, Peter, that you were fine. When we finally could think again, we went into the dining room and peered down into the crib with some trepidation, but you were the same healthy, handsome ten-month-old who had been there half an hour before.

When you looked up at us, you started crying.

I won't pull any punches, my dearest son. I had the fleshy blood-horns that only adulterers grew. We didn't know what it meant for a few weeks. It took a while — sorting everything out, I mean. But we had time. The Change was permanent. Not necessarily complete, we soon learned, but permanent. There was no going back.

The pulpy-looking masses of flesh-grapes on my cheek and neck were later called Barabbas papillomata by whoever the hell named all this stuff. The Surgeon General maybe. Anyway, the Barabbas papillomata only showed up if you'd played a little fast and loose with other people's money. With me it was just a few thousand bucks overlooked on some pissant IRS forms. But Christ, you should've seen the photos of Donald Trump in *The National Enquirer* that next month after the Change. He had papilloma so thick that he looked like an ambulatory grape arbor, only not as pretty since you could see through the skin and see the veins and yellow ichor and all that.

Your mother's baleen mouth, we found out later, was connected with malicious gossip. If she looked like a '48 Buick, you should have seen Barbara Walters, Liz Smith, and that bunch. When their pictures first leaked out, we thought we were looking at a *fleet* of Buicks.

Your mother's Quasimodo eye and mantis maxilla were the results of small cruelties, hidden racial prejudices, and self-imposed stupidities. I had the same symptoms. Almost everyone did. Within a month, I considered myself lucky to have only the adulterer's bloodhorns, a moderate cluster of Barabbas papillomata, mantis maxilla, a trace of Rathersnout, some apathy osseus turning my brow into Neanderthal ledges, and the usual case of Liar's leprosy that took my left ear and most of my remaining left nostril before I learned how to control it.

I need to say again that you were untouched, Peter. Most children under twelve were, and all infants. Your face looked up at us from its crib or cradle and you were perfect.

Perfect.

Those first few hours and days were wild. Some people committed suicide, some went nuts, but most of us stayed indoors and watched television.

It was more like radio, actually, since no one at the networks wanted to go in front of the camera. For a while they tried showing a pre-Change photograph of the reporter or anchorman or whatever while you heard his or her voice in the background — sort of like when we were getting telephone reports from Baghdad during the war a few years ago — but that made people angry, and after a few thousand phone calls they dumped the pictures and just showed the network logo while someone read the news.

They announced that the President would address the nation at 10 P.M. E.S.T. that night, but that was soon cancelled. They didn't explain why, but we all knew. He gave a radio address the next evening.

None of us were very surprised when pictures of the President finally leaked out, although the bloodhorns and treachery-tumors were a bit of a shock. It was his wife that took everyone by surprise. She'd had such good press that we half expected her to be unChanged. For several months we heard and saw nothing of her, but when she finally appeared in public we could see through her Elephant Man veil that she had not only multiple horns but the face-turned-inside-out look of the Ultimate Arrogance Syndrome.

Still and all, she fared better than Nancy Reagan. Word was that the former First Lady wasn't even recognizably human during the first minutes of the Change and was gunned down in disgust by her own Secret Service guards. Official word was that Mrs. Reagan died of shock at the sight of her husband after the Change. It's true that Ron's case of Liar's leprosy, apathy osseus, and stupidity sarcoma was impressive, but the old gentleman took it good-naturedly and probably would not even have curtailed his schedule of paid public appearances if Nancy's demise had not intervened.

As for the then-current Vice President. . .well, word is that one had to be there to believe it. The press and media had been unkind over the previous years, but we discovered that their unkind remarks about the VP's limited IQ had been dramatic understatement. The young man who had been only a heartbeat away from the presidency is said to have deliquesced like so much wet cardboard left out in the rain. Word was that the stupidity sarcoma was so widespread that there wasn't much left but a suit, shirt, and red-and-blue striped tie lying amidst a heap of twitching snot.

The Vice President's wife became a textbook case of Ambition dentitus. It's not true that there was nothing left of her but the four-foot-long teeth, but that's the impression we had at the time.

Before you get the wrong idea, Peter, you have to understand that I'm not picking on the Republicans. Neither did the stigmata. Both sides of the aisle suffered equally. Our elected officials were so hard hit by the Change that the verb "senatored" soon came into use to describe anyone who had lost almost all humanity to their stigmata. They were a resilient bunch though, and some — like Ted Kennedy, they say — were out hunting new sexual conquests before the papilloma, sarcoma, fibroid masses, supraorbital distortions, and longitudinal sulci had quit pulsing and oozing.

For a while the TV kept showing reruns and old commercials — obviously none of the actors or pitchmen were spared in the Change — but eventually they started filming new stuff. It was about a year before we could go out to the movies and see post-Change actors, and by then we were ready for them. By then I wasn't bothered by the sight of Dustin Hoffman's UA-syndrome inside-out visage, or Eddie Murphy's racist albino-pox mottling, or the absolute ego-dripping, sex-obsessed-tentacled mess for a face that Warren Beatty's personality had given him, but I could no longer stand to look at pre-Change images of people. They seemed as strange as aliens to me. Most people felt exactly the same by then.

But I'm getting ahead of myself. Sorry, Peter.

Those first few weeks were nuts, to put it mildly. Almost nobody went to work. Mirrors were smashed. Suicides and homicides and unprovoked attacks reached such a high rate that the whole country began to have casualty figures as high as New York City's. I'm not exaggerating.

Today, of course, New York's violence has all but disappeared now that racial differences go almost unnoticed and the gangs have disappeared after it was shown that lip and eyebrow pus-lesions were the inevitable result of belonging to a gang. (Although some still wear the lesions with pride. . . but these idiots are easy to avoid.) Also, the Barabbas papillomata discourage a lot of the theft and . . .

Sorry, I'm way ahead of myself again.

Those first few days and weeks were crazy. We stayed in our homes, listened to TV, waited for the twice-daily news conferences from the Centers for Disease Control, smashed our mirrors, avoided our spouses, and then spent a lot of time seeking out reflections in any shiny surface we hadn't destroyed: toasters, silver platters, butter knives.... It was crazy, Peter.

A lot of couples split up then, Peter, but your mother and I never considered it. The bloodhorns took some explaining, but there was so much else going on that it didn't seem all that important at the time.

Eventually people started going back to work. Some never really quit working—reporters (newspaper reporters stuck by their jobs more often than TV people), firefighters, a lot of lower level medical personnel (the rich doctors were busy dealing with their Usury gluteal malformations), pickpockets (who quickly donned hoods to hide their peculiar strain of Barabbas papillomata), and cops.

Cops were perhaps the least affected of all professions. As individuals, they'd known for years the scum and pus and malformed souls that hid behind the pre-Change blandness of skin and bone. Now they tended to look at their own distortions, shrug, and carry on with their jobs which—if anything—had been made much easier by people wearing their insides on their faces. It was the rest of us— the multitudes who had pretended that human nature was essentially benign—who had trouble adapting.

But eventually we adapted. First we ventured out on the streets under hoods and balaclavas and old hats dug out of the closet, found the others in the supermarkets and liquor stores hooded and hidden the same way, and found that the shame is not so bad when *everyone* is in the same condition.

I went back to work after a week. I wore my baseball cap with the mosquito-netting veil during the first few days in the office, but I had trouble seeing the VDT and soon began taking it off once I was in the office. MacGregor from accounting still wears his Banana Republic mask to this day, but we know the Barabbas paps are there— you can smell them. Our boss didn't show for almost a month, but when he did he had nothing on his head. That took courage with his stupidity sarcoma so rampant that new fibroid pustules would appear between lunch and quitting time.

Everyone was oozing and dripping and squeezing and popping and lancing their paps and pusts in the restrooms, and pretty soon there was a company policy that we had to do it in the privacy of the stalls, where mirrors and handywipes were installed. The only guy I know who got rich during those first post-Change months was Tommy Pechota from Mergers and Acquisitions who invested heavily in Kleenex stock.

But back to those first few days.

The Russians had about ten hours to laugh their asses off at us and talk about the Western Decadence Disease before the Change hit them. It hit them hard. There was even a stigmata peculiar to current and ex-KGB guys that turned their faces into the equivalent of roadkill that you can't quite identify but definitely don't want to get too near. Gorbachev and Yeltsin got their share of what one Moscow analyst called the Commie Zits, but Gorbie had more problems than a few cosmetic difficulties. The Change got the March Revolution going in earnest and before summer started, the new leaders were in power. They weren't much to look at either—several had Ambition teeth—but at least none were oozing from Commiepox.

The Japanese took it pretty much in stride and began to see how the Change would affect the international market. The Europeans went a little berserk: the French launched a nuclear missile at the moon for no particular reason—but it seemed to settle them down a bit—the British Parliament passed a law making it a criminal offense to comment on another's appearance and then adjourned forever, and the Germans remained calm for three months and then, almost as a reflex action since the world's attention was distracted, invaded Poland.

No one had anticipated the Aggressor-simplex malformation. You see, we'd thought the Change was more or less complete. We didn't know at the time that even passive participation in an evil *national* act could add new and dramatic wrinkles to the physiognomy.

We know now. We know that the human face can twist, bend, and fold itself so dramatically during the throes of Aggressor-simplex dynamic that a living, breathing human being can walk around with a face that is almost indistinguishable from an anus with eyes. It's very easy these days to pick out a German who supported the Polish incursion, or an Israeli or Palestinian since most of them suffered Agg-simplex during the Change itself, or anyone—and we're talking several million people here—too active in the American military-industrial complex.

Speaking personally, Peter, it made me glad to be carrying the stigmata I had.

Churches were filled during those first few weeks and months, although one glance at most ministers, pastors, and priests did quite a bit to empty the pews. In all fairness, a high percentage of the men and women of the cloth did no better or worse than the rest of us during the change. It's just that it's hard to concentrate on a sermon when Liar's leprosy is eating away someone's eyelids while you watch. It didn't prove that religion was a lie, only that the majority of those peddling religion *thought* that they were lying.

The TV ministers were the worst, of course. Worse than senators, worse than insurance salesmen (and we all remember *that* stigmata), and even worse than the tentacles-in-place-of-tongue, polyps-in-lieu-of-lips stigmata of car salesmen.

Your mother and I watched on cable that first night, Peter, when the TV ministers self-destructed on camera, one after the other. The Barabbas papillomata came first, of course, but these paps were infinitely worse than the mere blood-and-ichor tumors on my cheek and neck. Most of the TV evangelists became nothing *but* papilloma, tentacles, and polyps. Even their eyes grew bumps and bloodwarts. Then the Liar's leprosy began eating at them, their paps suppurated and exploded, the centers of their faces began to grow inward in a style similar to the Aggressor-simplex mode only to pustulate again into something very much resembling an inflamed hemorrhoid...and then the process started over. We watched Jimmy Swaggart go through this cycle three times before we were able to change channels and get into the bathroom to throw up.

Not a whole lot of these TV evangelists are still on the air.

I guess I've been off the subject, Peter. I promised you an explanation...or as close to one as I could get.

Well, it's not an explanation, but I'll get to the facts and they may suffice.

Children were the hardest to watch. They generally began their own Change around the age of eleven or twelve, sometimes at puberty but not always, although some kids Changed much younger and a few lasted until their late teens.

They all Changed.

And we could see the reason. It was us. The parents. The adults. The culture-givers and wisdom-sharers.

Only the culture-giving brought on the racism albino pox in the children, and the wisdom-sharing tended to increase their chance for stupidity sarcoma and a dozen other stigmata.

It was heart-wrenching to watch, not only for what it did to the young people but for what it said about ourselves. Then the first post-Change babies were born and the stigmata were smaller, unearned, but already in place and growing. Our genes now carried the stigmata information and our personalities had been impressed even upon fetuses during the Change.

But you were perfect, Peter. By that June, you were one year old, healthy, happy, and perfect.

I remember it was a pleasant evening in the city when your mother and I dressed you in your finest blue baby clothes, tied on a little cap because the nights were still cold, and carried you down to the city park. Actually, your mother carried you while I lugged along a big box with all of our pre-Change snapshots, photo albums, home movies, and videotapes. There had been no official announcement about that first Catharsis Gathering in the park, but word of mouth must have been rampant for days before, if not weeks.

I remember that there were no official speakers and no one from the crowd spoke either. We simply gathered around the huge heap of kerosene-impregnated wood and broken furniture there on the parking lot near the municipal pool. There was silence except for the nervous barking of a few dogs that had tagged along: silence except for the barking and the cries and quickly hushed shouts of a few of the hundreds of children who had been brought along.

Then someone—I have no idea who—stepped forward and lighted the bonfire. An elderly woman with a lifetime's share of stigmata stepped forward then and began emptying her box of photographs. For a moment she was a lone silhouette against the flames and then some of the others began shuffling forward, usually the men while their wives held the children, and with no dialogue and no sense of ceremony, we began ridding ourselves of our boxes of photographs. I remember how the videotape cassettes melted and wrinkled and popped—so much like our faces during the Change.

Then we'd all emptied our boxes and backpacks and we stepped back, one hand raised to shield our faces from the terrible heat of the oversized bonfire. We could see nothing of the city behind us now, only the flames and the sparks rising into the starless night above us and the stigmatatized and heat-reddened faces of our neighbors and friends and fellow citizens.

I remember how excited your blue eyes were, Peter. Your cheeks were red in the reflected firelight and your eyes were luminous and you tried to smile, but some scent of madness in the air made your one-year-old's smile somewhat tremulous.

I remember how calm I was.

Your mother and I had not discussed it and we did not discuss it now. I looked at her with my good eye and she looked back and already our new faces seemed normal and necessary.

Then she handed you to me.

Most of those approaching the bonfire now were the fathers, although there were some women—single mothers possibly—and even a smattering of grandparents. Some of the children began to cry as we moved closer to the circle of heat.

You did not cry, Peter. You turned your face into my shoulder, closed your eyes, and curled your fists as if you could make a bad dream go away by not looking.

There was no hesitation. The man next to me threw at the same second, with the same motion, as I did. His little boy screamed as he flew deep into the bonfire. I heard nothing from you as you rose over the outer periphery of flame, seemed to hover a second as if considering flying upward with the sparks, and then dropped into the heart of the roaring bonfire.

The whole thing took less than ten minutes.

Your mother and I walked back toward the house and when I glanced back once, everyone had left except for members of the fire department who were standing by with a pumper truck to make sure that the bonfire burned itself out safely. I remember that your mother and I did not talk during the walk home. I remember how fresh and wonderful the newly mowed lawns and recently watered gardens smelled that night.

It wasn't that night but perhaps a week later that I first saw the graffiti spray-painted on a wall near the train station:

What monstrosities would walk the streets were
some people's faces as unfinished as their minds.
—Eric Hoffer

I didn't know then who Eric Hoffer was and I admit that I haven't taken the time to find out. I don't know if he's still alive, but I hope that he is. I hope that he was around for the Change.

I saw that slogan scribbled several places after that, although it's been years since I've noticed it and I may have gotten the words wrong. I know that some of the CDC people refer to the change as the Hoffer Stigmata Pandemic, but I think they're referring to that German neurologist who was the first to come up with that active-RNA enhanced plasticity or whatever-you-call-it retrovirus theory.

Big deal. It doesn't matter anymore because even the experts admit that the Change is final and there's no going back.

We don't want to go back. The Change was painful; a Changeback would be too much to endure. Besides, it would be almost impossible to live in a world where one had to guess what paps and sulci and lesions lurked hidden under the smiling, pink-skinned surfaces of our mates and friends and co-workers.

That's about all, Peter. It's about time for the *CBS Evening News* so I have to close.

I feel better having written to you. I'll put the letter away here in the box in the attic with the baby clothes that your mother carefully folded away so many years ago.

I just wanted to explain.

To explain and to say that I remain...

Your Loving Father

The Secret

Steve Allen

When applied to most people the word "versatile" may call to mind a person who not only writes serious fiction (whatever that is) but humor, not only juggles but yodels, and not only keeps up with politics but can explain them while simultaneously chewing gum.

We might as well let Steve Allen take custody of the word since he can do all those things (I'm not sure about the yodeling, actually) and a great many more. Better, he's often done them during the *same periods of time* — not just sequentially — and exceptionally well. Check the record:

Author of mystery fiction *(Murder in Vegas; The Talk Show Murders);* of story collections *(The Girls on the Fourth Floor; Wry on the Rocks);* of political viewpoint *(Letter to a Conservative);* of commentary and appraisal *(The Funnymen; Funny People; More Funny People);* of personal experience and loss *(Not All Your Laughter, Not All Your Tears; Beloved Son: A Story of the Jesus Cults)* — and more than three thousand songs.

Steve also created a science-fiction classic everyone who read it remembers, "The Public Hating." Sixty-five thousand people are crammed into Yankee Stadium to use their collective mind power on a convicted political prisoner...and hate him to death. (See? I knew you'd remember.) It's an apt tale to mention now. The fictional execution is televised on all the networks.

As the original host of "The Tonight Show" ('54–'56), Allen employed his talents as quick-thinking ad libber, pianist, interviewer, and uncanny discoverer of comedians and singers to open up late-night t.v.; as host of the Sunday evening prime-time show bearing his name, his work reached thirty-five million people. His appearances on such staples as "I've Got a Secret" and "What's My Line?" enhanced Steve's renown as the tube's best-informed wit (while putting the description "bigger than a breadbox" into the public consciousness), and his PBS program "Meeting of the Minds," co-starring his actress wife Jayne Meadows, painlessly enhanced that consciousness.

While Allen is getting ready to remind the world he has never been on a box of staples in Bostich's life, a personal intrusion: After I got out of the army, my similarly silly pal Don O'Brien and I enjoyed taping our ad lib impersonations of Steve and his hopefully immortal "men on the street." We took turns being the shaky Don Knotts, Bill Dana's "José Jiminez," the "gosh-I-drew-a-blank" Tom Poston, and my favorite, Louis Nye's irrepressible "Gordon Hathaway," the "party doll." Then I learned that Lynn, my father, was just as crazy about "The Tonight Show" and I began staying up late with my dad. That was the first time we'd ever been really close. It remained that way the rest of his life, because of laughter.

So, "Hi ho, Steverino," even though "The Secret" is not a humorous yarn. Instead, it's the kind of thoughtful and surprising story that fits as easily into the woof and warp of a *Masques* anthology as its remarkable author has fitted into our lives. Here's the answer, Question Man: the meaning of life. The question?

I didn't know I was dead until I walked into the bathroom and looked in the mirror.

In fact I didn't even know it at that exact moment. The only thing I knew for sure then was that I couldn't see anything in the mirror except the wallpaper behind me and the small table with the hairbrushes on it low against the wall.

I think I just stood there for perhaps ten seconds. Then I reached out and tried to touch the mirror, because I thought I was still asleep on the couch in the den and I figured that if I moved around a bit, so to speak, in my dream I could sort of jar myself awake. I know it isn't a very logical way to think, but in moments of stress we all do unusual things.

The first moment I really knew I was dead was when I couldn't feel the mirror. I couldn't even see the hand I had stretched out to touch it. That's when I knew there was nothing physical about me. I had identity, I was conscious, but I was invisible. I knew then I had to be either dead or a raving maniac.

Just to be sure, I stepped back into the den. I felt better when I saw my body lying on the couch. I guess that sounds like a peculiar thing to say too, but what I mean is, I'd rather be dead than insane. Maybe *you* wouldn't but that's what makes horse races.

My next sensation (that's the only word I can think of to convey my meaning to you) was that there was something pressing on my mind, some nagging matter I had almost forgotten. It was very much like the feeling you sometimes have when you walk over to a bookshelf or a clothes closet, let's say, and then suddenly just stand there and say to yourself, "Now why did I come over here?" I felt a bit as if I had an imminent appointment.

I went over to the couch and looked down at myself. The magazine was open on the floor where it had slipped from my hand, and my right foot had fallen down as if I might have been making an effort to get up when I died.

It must have been the round of golf that did it. Larkin had warned me about exertion as long as three years ago, but after a fearful six months I had gotten steadily more overconfident. I was physically big, robust, muscular. I had played football at college. Inactivity annoyed the hell out of me. I remembered the headache that had plagued me over the last three holes, the feeling of utter weariness in the locker room after the game. But the cold shower had refreshed me a bit and a drink had relaxed me. I felt pretty good when I got home, except for an inner weariness and a lingering trace of the headache.

It had come while I was asleep, that's why I didn't recognize it. I mean if it comes in the form of a death-bed scene, with people standing around you shaking their heads, or if it comes in the form of a bullet from an angry gun, or in the form of drowning, well, it certainly comes as no surprise. But it came to me while I was lying there asleep in the den after reading a magazine. What with the sun and the exercise and the drink, I was a little groggy anyway and my dreams were sort of wild and confused. Naturally when I found myself standing in front of the mirror I thought it was all just another part of a dream.

It wasn't, of course. You know that. You do if you read the papers, anyway, because they played it up pretty big on page one. "Westchester Man 'Dead' for 16 Minutes." That was the headline in the *Herald Tribune.* In the Chicago *Daily News* the headline on the story was "New Yorker 'Dead,' Revived by Doctors." Notice those quotation marks around the word *dead.* That's always the way the papers handle it. I say always because it happens all the time. Last year alone there were nine of us around the country. Ask any of us about it and we'll just laugh good-naturedly and tell you that papers were right, we weren't dead. Of course we'll tell you that. What else could we tell you?

So there I was, beside the couch, staring down at myself. I remember looking around the room, but I was alone. They hadn't come yet. I felt a flicker of some kind that would be hard to describe—an urgency, an anxiety, a realization that I had left a few things undone. Then I tried a ridiculous thing. I tried to get back into myself. But it wouldn't work. I couldn't do it alone.

Jo would have to help, although we had just had a bitter argument. She had been in the kitchen when I had gone in to take a nap. I hurried to the kitchen. She was still there. Shelling peas, I think, and talking to the cook. "Jo," I said, but of course she couldn't hear me. I moved close to her and tried to tell her. I felt like a dog trying to interest a distracted master.

"Agnes," she said, "would you please close the window."

That's all she said. Then she stood up, wiped her hands, and walked out of the kitchen and down the hall to the den. I don't know how I did it, but in a vague way she had gotten the message.

She let out a tiny scream when she saw the color of my face. Then she shook me twice and then she said, "Oh, my God," and started to cry, quietly. She did not go to pieces. Thank God she didn't go to pieces or I wouldn't be able to tell the tale today.

Still crying, she ran to the hall phone and called Larkin. He ordered an ambulance and met it at the house inside of ten minutes. In all, only twelve minutes had elapsed since I had tried to look at myself in the mirror.

I remember Larkin came in on the run without talking. He ran past me as I stood at the door of the den and knelt down beside my body on the couch.

"When did you find him?" he said.

"Ten minutes ago," Jo said.

He took something out of his bag and injected the body with adrenalin, and then they bundled "me" off to the hospital. I followed. It was five minutes away.

I never would have believed a crew could work so fast. Oxygen. More adrenalin. And then one of the doctors pushed a button and the table my body was on began to lift slowly, first at one end and then at the other, like a slow teeter-totter.

"Watch for blood pressure," Larkin whispered to an assistant, who squeezed a rubber bulb.

I was so fascinated watching them I did not at first realize I had visitors.

"Interesting," a voice said.

"Yes," I answered, without consciously directing my attention away from the body on the tilting table. Then I felt at one and the same time a pang of fear and the release of the nagging anxiety that had troubled me earlier.

I must have been expecting them. There was one on each side of me.

The second one looked at the body, then at Larkin and the others. "Do you think they'll succeed?" he said.

"I don't know," I said. "I hope so."

The answer seemed significant. The two looked at each other.

"We must be very certain," he said. "Would it matter so much to you either way?"

"Why, yes," I said. "I suppose it would. I mean, there's work I've left unfinished."

"Work isn't important *now*, is it?" asked the first one.

"No," I agreed. "It isn't. But there are other things. Things I have to do for Jo. For the children."

Again the two seemed to confer, silently.

"What sort of things?"

"Oh," I said, "there are some business details I've left up in the air. There'll be legal trouble, I'm sure, about the distribution of the assets of my firm."

"Is that all?" the first one said, coming closer to me. Larkin began to shake his head slowly. He looked as if he were losing hope.

Then I thought of something else. "You'll laugh," I said, "but something silly just came into my mind."

"What is it?" asked the second one.

"I would like to apologize to Jo," I said, "because we had an argument this afternoon. I'd forgotten I'd promised to take her and the children out to dinner and a movie. We had an argument about it. I suppose it sounds ridiculous at a time like this to talk about something that may seem so trivial, but that's what I'd like to do. I'd like to apologize to her for the things I said, and I'd like to keep that date. I'd like to take the children to see that movie, even if it is some cowboys-and-Indians thing that'll bore the hell out of me."

That's when it all began to happen. I can't say that suddenly the two were gone. To say *I* was gone would be more to the point. They didn't leave me. I left them. I was still unconscious, but now I was on the table. I was back inside my head. I was dreaming and I was dizzy. I didn't know what was happening in the room then, of course. I didn't know anything till later that night when I woke up. I felt weak and shaky and for a few minutes I wasn't aware that Larkin and some other doctors and Jo were standing around my bed. There was some kind of an oxygen tent over my chest and head, and my mouth felt dry and stiff. My tongue was like a piece of wood but I was alive. And I could see Jo. She looked tired and wan but she looked mighty beautiful to me.

The next day the men from the papers came around and interviewed me. They wrote that I was in good spirits and was sitting up in bed swapping jokes with the nurses, which was something of an exaggeration.

It was almost a month before I could keep that date with Jo and the kids, and by that time the picture wasn't even playing in our neighborhood. We had to drive all the way over to Claremont to see it, but we stopped at a nice tearoom on the way and had a wonderful dinner.

People still ask me what I felt while I was "dead." They always say it just that way, getting quotation marks into their voices, treating it as something a little bit amusing, the way the newspapers did. And I go along with it, of course. You can't say to them, "Why, yes, I was dead." They'd lock you up.

Funny thing about it all was that I'd always been more or less afraid of the idea of death. But after dying, I wasn't. I always knew I'd eventually go again, but it never worried me. I did my best to make a go of my relationships with other people and that was about the size of it. One other thing I did was write this little story and give it to a friend of mine, to be published only after my death.

If you're reading it, that means I've gone again. But this time I won't be back.

Afterword

In the fall of 1983, a year after I met J. N. Williamson, he suggested that we start a horror magazine. I declined, but I suggested instead that we try a hardcover horror anthology. That became, in 1984, the first *Masques*. In the course of assembling it, and with the help of William F. Nolan, both Jerry and I expanded our horizons. (I'd known no one else in the horror field, and he'd known few, despite his many published novels.)

To our surprise, *Masques* enjoyed, among other things:

A poem by Ray Bradbury

A previously-unpublished Charles Beaumont piece

A Robert R. McCammon story, "Nightcrawlers," which was later dramatized on television's *Twilight Zone*

An F. Paul Wilson story, "Soft," which became the title story of his later collection

A Balrog Award

A World Fantasy Award nomination (and one for "Night-crawlers")

Preferred Choice Bookplan and British paperback editions

As part of *The Best of Masques,* U.S. and Japanese paperback editions.

So we tried it again, with *Masques II* (1987), which included a 300-copy limited edition. We had, among others:

An original story by Stephen King

An Alan Rodgers novella, "The Boy Who Came Back from the Dead," which later won a Bram Stoker Award

A World Fantasy Award nomination (and one for Rodgers's "Boy," and for Douglas E. Winter's "Splatter")

British, German, Italian, and Spanish paperback editions

As part of *The Best of Masques,* U.S. and Japanese paperback editions.

By mutual agreement, Williamson did *Masques III* (1989) with St. Martin's Press. But now we're together again. We hope that you've found *Masques IV* a worthy continuation of the series. We also hope that these fictional horrors have put you in mind of the all-too-real ones, such as war, crime, and injustice. So, on with the masques!

— John Maclay